SAVING
MYLES

ALSO BY CARL VONDERAU

Murderabilia

SAVING MYLES

CARL VONDERAU

OCEANVIEW (C PUBLISHING

SARASOTA, FLORIDA

ISBN 978-1-60809-558-2

Published in the United States of America by Oceanview Publishing

Sarasota, Florida

www.oceanviewpub.com

10 9 8 7 6 5 4 3 2 1

PRINTED IN THE UNITED STATES OF AMERICA

SAVING
MYLES

CHAPTER ONE

Wade Bosworth turned on the front lights of his house for the men who would take away his son. He'd never met them, but on the internet, they appeared in their twenties. The men were driving down from LA and had texted that they'd be on time.

He made his way to the dark kitchen and sat down. Through the screen of the window, he heard the chirr of crickets, then the neighbor's tree rustling and settling back into the dark. He breathed in the quiet enormity of what he was doing. It was four a.m. His son didn't know what was about to happen. In less than an hour his life would be ripped in two. Myles was sixteen years old.

Wade put the water on the stove to boil and crept up the groaning stairs to the bedroom. He and Fiona dressed in the dark, then padded down the hallway to listen outside Myles' room. No growls and screeching of heavy metal music. No tapping computer keys. Wade eased open the door. The lava lamp Myles had begged them to buy oozed red bubbles that cast a blush over their son in his bed. Asleep, his face looked like a child's. It was hard to square that face to the rants in magic marker on the window shades. "Fuck families." "I'm an alien trapped in La Jolla." "Does a zombie know he's a zombie?" Wade breathed in the musky odor of marijuana. He needed to center that smell in his thoughts. It was evidence that they were doing the right thing.

Fiona's slippers swished ahead of him through the hallway. They creaked down the stairs to the kitchen and the beat-up oak table they'd bought a month before Myles was born. Tonight, Wade had to block off those memories. For Myles' sake.

He poured the boiling water and set the French press on the table. Wade had ground the coffee the night before so the shriek wouldn't wake his son this morning. Fiona sat opposite, her long back hunched. She was two inches taller than him but tonight seemed smaller. Splotches shadowed her angular cheeks and lines had deepened around her eyes. Needles of grey had snuck into her brown hair. In only a few months, ten years of aging had telescoped into her body. He was doing this for her too.

"We're saving Myles' life," Wade said, his voice low. When had they started whispering in their own house?

Fiona shook her head. "We let him come to this."

"We did everything we could."

"Did we?"

"Please, Fiona. We can punish ourselves later."

"Don't tell me what to feel."

He blunted his anger. He had to wear his banker's calm now.

Wade poured coffee into the two mugs. He watched Fiona interlace and unravel her long fingers. Those hands used to fly up in excitement and joy. Not for months. Or was it years? He laid his palm on her arm, his fingers touching the yin and yang tattoo on her wrist.

"All the experts told us this is the right intervention," Wade said.

She pulled her arm away. "But Utah is so far."

They'd been through this so many times. But Wade would do it again if that was what she needed. "San Diego is too full of triggers."

Triggers. The psychiatrist, the psychologists, and the teachers had endlessly repeated and defined that word for them. Triggers were so many things—friends, Myles' room, the school, San Diego. And especially his parents. That was what the director of the treatment center had said.

She extended her arms toward him over their table. "His highchair used to be right next to where you're sitting," she said.

He refused to look, refused to weaken when they all depended on him to stay strong. "Let me go over it again. Skipping school, plummeting grades, sneaking out at night, continuous pot smoking."

She was silent. He knew she was waiting for him to drop the last, incontrovertible reason, and he didn't restrain himself. Not tonight when their son's life was in the balance.

"OxyContin," he said.

She stared out the back window into the dark backyard. On the wall, his father's clock counted out seconds like a warden's pocket watch ticking down to an execution. It was four-twenty a.m. The men would arrive in minutes.

Wade had been flummoxed about how to get Myles to Hidden Road Academy. The treatment center was in the middle of Utah, and Myles would never go willingly. But the center had a solution for moving recalcitrant children to their facilities. Teen Rescue was based in Georgia, but they could go anywhere. The chirpy woman on the phone had assured Wade that they'd transported teens to safety hundreds of times. Their people made the trip to Hidden Road almost every month and no child had ever been hurt.

There was a knock at the door. Across from him, Fiona sucked in a breath.

Wade went to the front and opened the door. The whole block was asleep but for the two young men standing in the lights of their house. Ricardo and Sam looked like college students or trainees at his bank. Hair neatly combed, unwrinkled slacks, and long-sleeved Oxford shirts. Sam, the taller and thinner one, had a small beard. Ricardo was big-shouldered and cleanly shaven.

Fiona's shoulders seemed to loosen when she saw them. Perhaps these young men, just a few years older than Myles, could assuage her doubts. The four of them sat at the kitchen table and Wade poured coffee.

"We're going to do this with respect," Sam, the one with the beard, said.

Ricardo nodded at his partner and then at each of them. "No blaming," he said.

"We do this with dignity," Sam said.

Wade looked at Fiona. She stared at the two men as if they were selling insurance. Wade asked the question before she could. "Suppose he doesn't cooperate?"

Sam gave Fiona a sympathetic smile. "I've only had to use restraints once," he said.

"Restraints?" Fiona said. "Did you just say *restraints*?"

Wade steeled his palm against the chair. Why the hell did he have to say "restraints"?

"We won't have to do that here," Sam said.

Ricardo set his arms on the table. Wade noted how they were thick and muscular, like he'd been lifting weights. "That's why this happens at four thirty in the morning," Ricardo said. "Your son will be disoriented, his defenses down. We talk to him like men so he can retain his pride."

"Jesus," Fiona said.

Sam met her gaze. He must have dealt before with hesitant mothers like Fiona. "You set it up with the reason why. Very short. We don't want any arguments. I'd suggest that Mr. Bosworth do that.

Just tell Myles that, because of the choices he's made, you're sending him to a place where he can get help. He'll be shocked—"

"Shocked?" Fiona said. "He'll be scared to death."

"No no," Sam said, raising his palms. "We're not like that. You leave and we talk to him. All calm. We lay out everything we're going to do and tell him it will happen whether he wants it or not. But he chooses whether he keeps his dignity."

"They always choose dignity," Ricardo said.

Wade didn't like how they kept repeating "dignity."

"I guess you don't tell him you're taking him to a lockup," Fiona said.

He couldn't stop the words from busting out. "Damnit, Fiona, you know it's not a lockup."

"It's in a fucking desert. It's in Utah. How the hell is that not a lockup?" Her fingers had curled into claws.

Sam studied Fiona and scratched the part of his beard over his chin. "A lot of mothers feel exactly the same way you do. But these kids never volunteer to go to a treatment center. It takes people like us to persuade them."

Sam was all soothing comfort—his voice, his eyes, the way he gently moved his hands. But Wade suspected that would make Fiona trust him less.

Sam pointed to stocky Ricardo. "We've each done this more than fifty times. The kids are always better when you get them somewhere safe. And Hidden Road is one of the best."

Fiona locked her arms in front of her. Wade knew that sign and braced himself. *Jesus, not now.*

"None of you has any idea what it's like to be a mother," Fiona said.

She was sabotaging it. He wanted to start shouting.

"We've seen kids just like Myles," Sam said. "We understand what they're going through."

Fiona's eyes glistened. She swallowed and her head dropped. She was relenting and Wade released a breath. The only sound was his father's clock striking the seconds.

"I know we have to do this," Fiona said.

"You're a good mother," Wade said. "That's why you're rescuing him."

"But he'll never forgive us. Don't you see that?"

Sam slid his hand closer to her on the table. "Later, he'll thank you."

Her shoulders shuddered and she cradled her face.

Wade thought of something to make it easier for her. "You can stay here in the kitchen. Sam, Ricardo, and I can go to his room and get him."

Her hands dropped. She took a big breath. "I'm his mother. Of course, I have to be there."

Wade looked at his watch. It was late. They had to stop talking and do this.

Fiona stood. "Let's get it over with."

CHAPTER TWO

FIONA
May 2018

Fiona had found the plastic bags in the crawl space above Myles' closet. *OxyContin*. It was a word that didn't admit other words like *maturation* or *experimentation* or *youthful mistakes*. The only words that fit with *OxyContin* were *street* and *jail* and *organ donor*. Wade had searched out the treatment center. He'd called the references. "When he's eighteen we can't legally force him to get help," he'd said. Wade had pushed and pushed until she was too tired to fight.

The last family dinner was a bridge between what was and what would be. Fiona cooked Myles' favorite chicken so he'd remember that meal as something good. Her child set the table, praised her cooking, and helped wash the dishes. She saw the sweetness so clearly in him then.

Wade sat at the table like a man hiding his exhaustion. He still wore his pinstripe, the tie loosened, but worry weighed down his face. The grey streaks in his thinning hair seemed to have turned white since the day before. This morning she'd heard him crying in the shower.

After dinner Myles fled to his room. The rest of the night, heavy metal thumped and screeched through the walls, and the smell of marijuana seemed to seep through the ceiling. Myles smoked openly now, didn't care what they thought. Wade regarded it as defiance, but Fiona knew better. Myles was escaping from failures at school and at home. He was running from himself.

At eleven o'clock she and Wade went to bed and pretended to sleep. The clock beside her burned out each minute in ghostly green. In the darkness, she let the tears wash over her cheeks. A terrible emptiness radiated through her stomach and deadened the air between them. She wondered when she and Wade had begun to drift so far apart on the enormous bed.

They got up at four in the morning. In the kitchen, he said, "We're saving Myles' life." In the last week those words had become his mantra. He went through his list of reasons and, once again, his relentless logic bent her back until she felt she'd break like a stick. By the time the two young men arrived, she was ready to scream. *This is our son! This is Myles!*

The young men were so well dressed. They didn't look hopped up on steroids or just back from the horrors of Afghanistan. Ricardo was shorter with broad shoulders, Sam tall and thin with a whole repertoire of reassuring phrases. They crowded her into the table while Sam stroked his beard and quietly laid out how they would take away Myles. It was like being slowly buried alive.

Then Wade looked at his expensive watch, the Shinola that was supposed to last for generations. It was time. Time to do the thing that was as irrevocable as a shot from a gun. Even as they walked to Myles' room, she thought about her part in bringing forth this terrible morning. If she'd been stricter about rules and consequences. If she'd been more perceptive about what Myles needed. If she'd forced Wade to be even half a father instead of spending every night at his damn bank. Maybe then she wouldn't have been forced to sign the ten-page indemnity that gave her son to these strangers.

But a mother's first duty was to save her child's life. On the phone the director at Hidden Road Academy had said, "There comes a time when your boy is beyond you, and you can't help him anymore."

Wade opened Myles' door. He was so resolute, didn't even hesitate. She hated him then, standing there in his clean, unwrinkled shirt. She hated him when he flinched at the smells of marijuana and unwashed socks and the crusted plates of food. He was ashamed to reveal his son to these well-dressed young men. Did he even think about what he was about to do to Myles?

Myles lay asleep, his hair a brown tangle on the pillow, his leg half off the bed. He was still just an awkward boy.

"Please forgive me," she whispered and turned on the light. The room lit up like an explosion. "Myles, honey," she said.

He sat up in bed, his thin chest naked. "Who . . . who are they?" His Adam's apple seemed to quake with his voice.

Wade said, "Myles, because of your behavior we've decided to send you to a place where you can get help. These men are going to take you there."

"What?" Myles said.

Wade repeated his cold words. Couldn't he see the wound spreading over Myles' face?

She took a step toward her son, and Ricardo shook his head. "It's a treatment center," she said. "Like a private school. They can help you."

Myles' eyes bulged. She knew then that for the rest of his life he would relive this moment. She repeated her own mantra.

OxyContin.

"No, Dad."

Myles jumped from the bed and grabbed Wade's arm. He was taller than his father, taller than she was, but in that moment he looked small and frail. "Please, Dad." His voice was high and scared.

Now Ricardo looked huge, Sam towering with the beginning of his Rasputin beard. Ricardo unlatched Myles' hand from Wade's wrist. He stood between Myles and Wade. Wade stared at the red finger marks on his forearm. Why hadn't she seen the brutishness in these two strangers?

"Leave," Ricardo said to Wade. He broadened his shoulders and turned back to Myles. "We'll talk after the door is shut."

"You had OxyContin," she said.

"I never used. I was only holding for someone."

Sam gripped her arm. "Now is not the time."

All these men were telling her what a mother should do. She flung off his hand.

"Please, Dad. Why?"

"Because your mom and dad are good parents," Ricardo said.

Myles' face grew fierce. Her boy fought hardest when he was afraid. "This is what you think a good parent is?" he yelled.

OxyContin.

Ricardo had maneuvered himself between Myles and her. He'd spread his feet and arms as if he were about to tackle Myles. She could imagine Ricardo shoving her boy against the wall.

Wade had his arm around her, pulling her toward the door. "Get your hands off me," she shouted.

"Mom, it's Dad. You wouldn't do this." His young face shriveled and he started to cry.

"We have to save your life," Wade yelled.

She couldn't stand it. She had to say something. "Hidden Road is really nice. The people there will help you."

"Get out of here!" Ricardo pointed at the door.

Wade's hand pulled her. She couldn't resist anymore. Then she was outside in the hallway.

Sam was there. "Go downstairs," he said. No calming patter now. Sam sounded as hard as a prison guard. When he hurried back inside, she noticed his boots. Why hadn't she seen those heavy boots?

The door slammed. She couldn't move.

OxyContin. OxyContin.

Myles wept on the other side of the door.

Next to her Wade was shaking. He pulled her toward the stairs. One foot dragged after the other. She half-stumbled down the steps, holding herself up, propping her hand against the wall. Then she was in a chair in their kitchen. Wade was saying something about Myles, that they had no choice.

"Please, Mom!" His voice sounded far away, like a wail in someone else's house.

The hard chair was tilting. She reached for the table. She looked toward the hallway. Wade had sealed the door tight.

Upstairs he was shouting something. Then, "You fucking Nazis. You're actually putting me in restraints?"

She wept into her hands.

A half hour later she recognized the squeak of his sneakers trudging down the stairs. Two pairs of clomping boots. No words. No crying.

"My parents don't even love each other. How could they love me?"

She squeezed her eyes shut.

The front door whined open. "I'll never forgive you!" he shouted. She heard tears in his voice.

"We did it *because* we love you!" Wade yelled.

Love? He thought this was love?

The front door banged shut. There was silence but for the ticking of the clock on the wall. Ticking that would go on and on. Ticking that would make her scream.

Wade wrapped his arms around her. She untangled him and pushed away. She covered her face with her hands.

After a time, she caught her breath. She looked down at their dented kitchen table. The table where she'd fed Myles, where he'd hidden broccoli in the crevices of its pedestal. She remembered the panic in her son's not-yet-man's face. She'd always hear his crying. And that last sentence that would follow her forever.

I'll never forgive you!

Her child.

Wade said, "Sometimes being a good parent means you have to do terrible things. We had no choice. We had to do it."

She stared at him. His face was pale as bone. "*You* had to do it."

"*I* had to do it?" He filled his chest and stood. He shoved the chair and it skidded across the tiles. "*I* had to?"

Here was the old anger she knew so well.

Wade said, "You resent me so much you can't even help save our son."

How dare he. After everything she'd done to keep this family together. *How dare he.*

"I want you out of this house," she said.

CHAPTER THREE

The bar they wanted was hidden in a corner section of other dollar-shot bars on the Mexican side of the border. A neon sign glowed with EL ALACRÁN and the figure of a wriggling scorpion. A little shrine of skeleton candles, skulls, and fake orange flowers stood on a table outside the entrance door.

Myles grinned at Melissa. "My dad would hang himself with his gold tie if he knew I was here."

"I told you you'd like it," Melissa said.

Tonight she wore a spiked leather collar and tight black T-shirt that showed off her curves. Myles liked that she was so extra. He liked her loud laugh and big hips and shoulders and breasts. He deserved Melissa after more than a year in the reeducation camp.

The place was absolute fire inside. The music of Ulcerate throbbed with death growls, pounding double bass drums, and wailing guitars. Goths and metalheads packed tightly together around the tables, everyone speaking Spanish. Myles couldn't believe this was Mexico, the place that had mariachi bands and big sombreros. He found a table next to a wall with photos of dried-out shrunken heads and movie stars. He drew in the smell of weed and beer.

Even the waiter was awesome—like an extraterrestrial. The holes from his piercings had stretched his earlobes down to the back of his jaw and his spider tattoo seemed to pulse on his neck. They ordered and he disappeared into the crowd.

A guitar revved up from the speakers, then a shouting death growl that turned into melodic singing. Vintage Slipknot. It made Myles feel like he was coming back to life. In the last few weeks, his mind had started to go full vegetable. Walk to school. Walk back to the house. Homework. He was turning into his dad. But tonight he was stepping up and looking over the edge. Tonight he could let his heart pound with the double bass drum.

The waiter set down the beer. Myles and Melissa clinked mugs.

"Fuck our parents," Melissa yelled.

"Fuck *all* parents," Myles yelled.

She reached into her jeans and found a joint. She lit it, inhaled a lungful, and yelled, "Here's to no more drug tests."

No more drug tests because his mom trusted him. That thought gave him a pang. He toked up anyway.

Melissa took another hit and sucked in her lip piercing. Her hair was purple tonight. Last week it had been green. Or was it orange? It changed all the time.

"A year locked up and now you're partying in Tijuana," Melissa yelled.

He hadn't told anyone at La Jolla High about Hidden Road, but everyone seemed to know. He liked that they all thought he'd been shut inside some dungeon or bunched up in a straitjacket.

"It was like San Quentin," he shouted.

She pumped out a cloud of smoke. "Worse. It was in the middle of fucking Utah. What were you gonna do, escape to the Mormons?"

He sipped beer. For a second he asked himself why he was here. This place had every trigger he could think of—alcohol, drugs, metal music . . . Melissa.

The thought passed.

At the bar some dude was gulping straight from a pitcher. Above him a stuffed moose head stared out, metal studs in its lips and a ring on its nose. A string of white lights was draped over its antlers. *Feliz navidad,* Myles thought. He remembered Christmas the year before. The few restaurants in the little Utah town were closed and he and his parents ate 7-Eleven food in a hotel room. He got a sweatshirt as a gift because that was all that Hidden Road would allow.

Melissa stood up and waved. A man in jeans and a black leather coat scanned the bar. He looked in his twenties and had to be Roberto, the guy Melissa had met the week before. The man nudged his way toward them like he was swimming through the crowd.

He sat down beside Melissa and yelled, "It's party time!"

Myles introduced himself.

Roberto caught Melissa's eyes. "So this is the partner you told me about," he shouted.

Did he really want to start dealing? It didn't mean he had to use. But what kind of person wouldn't touch the drugs he sold?

Roberto dug into his leather jacket and pulled out a plastic bag with blue pills inside. He gave one each to Myles and Melissa. "Produced by a big pharma in the City of Mexico."

Myles turned the pill in his hand and tried to appear as if he knew what to look for. The "M" inside a square looked as if it had been embedded there by a machine. Same with the "30" on the other side above a horizontal line. It felt solid. Not something made by a couple of kids with a pill press.

The music stopped and voices rose in Spanish around Myles. He and Melissa gave the Oxy back to Roberto, and he put the plastic bags into the pocket of his leather jacket. He rose. "Let's go," he said.

"Go where?" Myles asked.

Roberto curled up his mouth and stared at him. "The product never gets sold in the bars. Just in the parking lot."

Myles shook his head. He and Melissa weren't going into some sketchy parking lot with this dude.

"Then we're done here," Roberto said.

Melissa whirled to face Myles. "I don't know why you're being such a pussy. There are guards out there."

She stood. She was going whether he did or not. But if this went to shit, he could outrun Roberto better than she could.

"Wait." Myles stood.

Roberto seemed to hold back a laugh. "There is nothing to be scared of." He looked at him as if he was a complete simp.

"Give me the money," Myles said to Melissa. "You stay here."

Roberto shook his head. "She made the deal. She comes too."

"Don't get all manly on me," Melissa said. "We'll both go."

This didn't feel right. Myles didn't know this asshole, and Melissa had only met him once. If anything happened, he could handle this guy better without Melissa.

"I didn't ask you to come with me so you could mess it up," Melissa said.

"Just me," Myles said. "Not her."

Melissa boomed out a laugh. She pulled the money envelope from her back pocket and gave it to him. "My brave knight."

Myles walked outside with Roberto. Once on the slate walkway he wondered if he was going with this dude just to impress Melissa. That was exactly what Hidden Road had programmed him to resist. *Fuck Hidden Road.* Time to man up.

"Born in the USA" pounded out from somewhere. There had to be twenty other bars and restaurants in the complex, all of them playing different music, all jammed with people. Roberto led him out to the parking lot and Myles spotted the two guards. This was okay. He had this.

"Over here," Roberto said.

A pitted drive led down a ramp to an underground garage.

"There are guards there too," Roberto said. He broke into a taunting grin.

Words from Hidden Road slipped into his mind. *Inhale your fear and step through it.* He wished he could tell Staff that their brainwashing helped him do a drug buy.

He followed Roberto down the potholed drive and into the entrance of the underground parking garage. It smelled like a moldy basement. Dirty LED light bulbs glowed beside pipes on the chunked-out ceiling. Music thunked faintly through the cement walls. Where was the guard?

"You don't have to be scared," Roberto said in a mocking voice.

This was whacked. He had to get out of here. He'd verify the boxes of Oxy, pay the money, and skurt.

They turned, and the garage grew darker. Myles' feet crunched over bits of concrete on the floor. A staircase rose up on the left. The jagged edges of a broken light bulb stuck out from the ceiling.

CHAPTER FOUR

WADE

Wade thought Hidden Road Academy was worth every thousand dollars. Worth every weekly phone call, every visit to Utah with Fiona. Hidden Road was behavioral modification pumped up on Red Bull. And Myles had excelled. He'd risen from the lowest treatment level to the highest. By the time he left, he was advising new boys and even girls on how to resist the lures of peer acceptance. "Reach inside for your true selves," he'd told them. Of course there were setbacks, but those were only at the beginning: when Myles stole a phone and begged Fiona to bring him home, when he wrote in code in his journal about how he would punish his father. "Normal early rebellion," the Hidden Road director had told them.

Then Myles had returned and the miracle expanded. He was eighteen but seemed so much older—his brown mop buzzed down to a stubble, his face thinned to angles, and his shoulders and arms defined with muscle. That first night Myles served everyone his favorite Chinese before touching his own food. His son listened when others spoke. He even turned off his new cellphone.

It all changed three months later. Nothing good ever happened at three a.m. on a Saturday. Wade lived by himself in a condo apartment on the fifteenth floor of a building in Little Italy. That morning the buzzer went off like something detonating inside his head. He stumbled out of his bedroom and swung open the front door.

Jimmy, the night receptionist for the building, stood in the hallway. He took in Wade in his boxers and said, "You didn't answer your phone."

He'd left his cell in the kitchen.

A tall blond man stood next to Jimmy and rubbed the sleeve of his monogrammed shirt. "I'm not sure you remember me," he said. "I'm Peter Vanhoven."

Wade tried to resurrect the name. And couldn't. "What's going on?"

Jimmy said, "He told me it was an emergency."

"La Jolla High School?" Vanhoven said. "Parents' night?"

The memory patched together. The investment banker. His daughter was a schoolmate of Myles. Wade jolted and grabbed the doorjamb. "What's happened?"

Vanhoven pursed his mouth. "There's a problem . . . in Tijuana."

"But Myles is in La Jolla. With his mother."

Vanhoven cupped one hand with the other in front of him. He regarded him as if he wasn't sure that Wade was awake. "Melissa called me. She's still there."

Melissa, one of Myles' new group of friends. Fiona was supposed to have screened her. *Damnit, Fiona.*

Vanhoven said, "They took Myles' BMW and snuck over to Tijuana."

Fiona's car. "What happened?"

Vanhoven swallowed. "Myles has disappeared."

The whole hallway seemed to tilt.

"Are you all right, Mr. Bosworth?" Jimmy said.

Wade steadied himself on the wall.

"Maybe I should come in," Vanhoven said.

Wade could only nod. He motioned Vanhoven inside and Jimmy left. Vanhoven waited in the front foyer while Wade went to the bedroom and put on jeans and yesterday's shirt.

Tijuana. The name ricocheted in his head. Cheap liquor, drugs, sex, and crime. It was a teenager's playground and a parent's nightmare. He sucked in long breaths. There must be a mistake. He had to think this through.

When Wade returned to the living room, Vanhoven was staring at the bills and loan write-ups splayed out on his dining room table. A yoga mat hung over the couch next to his guitar.

"We'll talk in the kitchen," Wade said. He led Vanhoven down the little hallway. He found his phone beside the dead pinot bottle and under the takeout bag. As he dialed Myles' number, he said, "I like to clean up in the morning."

No answer on Myles' cell. The Life360 program was supposed to show his location. Nothing. He called Fiona. She must have turned off her phone. He left a message. "Myles has disappeared in Tijuana. Why the hell did you let him go there?"

But Myles wouldn't know how to get to Tijuana. It had to be Vanhoven's daughter who knew the way. Vanhoven had sat down and was shifting his legs under the table. "Is Myles dating Melissa?" Wade asked.

Vanhoven's eyes widened. "You didn't know?"

How many times had Hidden Road told them that girls were Myles' weakness? They'd recommended that Myles not date for a year, and Wade and Fiona had written it into the home contract. Fiona must have been aware Myles was seeing girls; he was living with her. Fiona, who never respected rules, who probably wanted the house alone so she and Jasper could . . . He shook that image out of his mind.

"He disappeared two hours ago," Vanhoven said.

So much could happen in Tijuana in two hours. Myles hit by a car and lying on the street; Myles stabbed. Wade wanted to jump in his car. He wanted to stamp on the accelerator and strangle the steering wheel. "I need to get there fast," he said.

Vanhoven rose and held up his key fob. "I'll drive."

Wade grabbed the spare key to Fiona's car from the kitchen cabinet. When they found Myles, he and his son would drive back together in Fiona's car. A drive during which Wade was going to get royally and deservedly furious.

CHAPTER FIVE

Wade thought the interior of Vanhoven's SUV looked like a tricked-out tour bus—leather seats, leather cup holders, separate temperature controls. It reeked of cherry pipe scent from some expensive car wash. Just breathing that smell pumped acid into Wade's stomach. Then there was Vanhoven. He constantly rolled his shoulders and jiggled a foot and stretched his neck.

The SUV snaked across the empty downtown streets. At this hour, the shadowed office buildings seemed to hulk beside the slivered trunks of palm trees. Even the hotels were closed up. A man loaded abandoned scooters into a van. Another lay, as if dead, below a wrought iron light pole. In the silence, Wade considered the scale of his son's betrayal. Myles wasn't supposed to drink alcohol at all, much less in Mexico with a forbidden girlfriend.

And Fiona let him do it.

Vanhoven turned and the streetlights spotlighted him. Honed cheeks, thick blond hair that, even at this hour, was perfectly parted and combed. He looked like some green-eyed TV news anchor. An anchor who couldn't stop fidgeting.

"I don't understand how Melissa and Myles got separated," Wade said.

"They were both in the bar, everything fine. Then Myles went to get more money from his BMW."

Fiona wouldn't let him drive her car to Tijuana. That didn't make sense. But something else clawed at him. "Why more money?"

Vanhoven moved his shoulders up and raised his hand. "Who knows?"

The police in San Diego would be no help. Wade looked up the number for the American consulate on his phone, dialed, and got a recording. Myles had only disappeared for two and a half hours. Wade didn't know what message to leave and hung up. He tried to phone Fiona and again was bumped to her voicemail. What the hell was wrong with her?

Jasper.

"Trying to reach your ex-wife?" Vanhoven asked.

"We're only separated," Wade said.

Vanhoven cricked his neck. "My ex-wife doesn't know about this yet. Believe me, it's better that way. Less hysteria."

"My wife turned off her phone. Otherwise, she'd be here."

Why was he defending Fiona? Hidden Road had warned them that kids would mess up once they were home. She knew that Myles always chose wild girls.

They stopped at a red light. Wade stared out the window at a woman pushing a shopping cart full of clothes and plastic bags. He couldn't hear anything from outside and imagined her rusty wheels creaking across the intersection. They were heading to Mexico in a soundproof space capsule.

Why were they standing still? "You know there's no one on the streets at this hour," Wade said.

Vanhoven accelerated through the light. When they reached Highway 5, he sped up to seventy-five and his shoulders seemed to settle back into the seat. "I'm in mergers and acquisitions," he said.

Two high-test dealmakers with marital problems and kids in trouble. Could anything be more predictable? Wade looked at his watch. Myles had been gone for about three hours.

Vanhoven ran his bony finger through his perfect hair. He was so tall his head nearly touched the roof of his SUV. "Is that a Shinola Rambler?" he said. "How much did that set you back?"

"I can't talk about watches right now."

Vanhoven pushed some buttons, and a violin concerto floated out from hidden speakers.

"Can you turn off the music?" Wade asked. "It sounds like a memorial."

Vanhoven did what he asked. The only sound was the SUV's tires swooshing over the highway. Wade couldn't escape the question then. How did this happen? The director at Hidden Road had been so positive about Myles' reformed attitudes. "He was never on opioids," she'd said. But she didn't mention marijuana. And what about ecstasy, crystal meth, and LSD? Not to mention cocaine and all the newly invented drugs Wade didn't know about. His stomach clenched. Maybe adrenaline, maybe lack of sleep. Most likely the bleakness he was walling off.

They passed Coronado Bridge, then the naval base, its cranes reaching like skeleton hands toward the moon. A fortune teller's sign lit up the side of the highway: a florescent red palm with green lifelines and a single eye that stared at them from another dimension. Then the dark saltwater marshes that stretched out empty and wild to Mexico.

He thought of the dinner the night Myles had arrived home from Hidden Road. After they'd eaten, Myles rose and made his announcement. Because of the triggers with his dad, he'd decided to live with Fiona rather than Wade. "Without me at your place, you'll have more time to work," Myles said. The smells of fried dough, vinegar, and ginger bit into Wade when Myles said that. A few minutes later he trudged to his car and laid his head on the hard edges of the steering wheel. It took him ten minutes to turn on the engine.

Now, sitting next to Vanhoven, Wade knew the real reason Myles had wanted to live with Fiona. Myles could more easily manipulate his mother to break all the rules of the home contract. The contract the three of them had spent weeks formulating as a condition for Myles' return.

He had to face up to a bad deal; he was a conservative businessman, for chrissake. Hidden Road was a fiasco. All that money—they'd even put a second mortgage on the house—and Myles had never really changed. The hard truth of it brought tears to Wade's eyes. His son was not recoverable.

CHAPTER SIX

It had been years since Wade ventured to Tijuana, and he didn't recognize anything. It was all concrete and sheetrock, the businesses shuttered and the signs in a language he didn't speak. The woman on the GPS ordered them to turn again and again down empty streets of closed-up factories, houses, and schools with barred windows. Small restaurants stood next to warehouses. A tuxedo store flanked a muffler shop. Above them, a spiderweb of power lines zigzagged between buildings. It all seemed mixed up in another world's logic.

The woman's voice said, "You have arrived."

A mall with a movie theater rose in shadows to their left. To the right, a parking lot. Beyond the lot, a crowd jammed into a passageway of bars. It was four thirty in the morning and the party thrummed.

Vanhoven parked and they headed past two guards to the clamor of the buildings. Clutches of people spilled out from restaurants and bars onto a cement slab walkway. They found a waiter and got directions for El Alacrán, then pushed past more bars with swirling colored lights. Rock, Mexican pop, hip-hop, reggae, and Spanish rap bled into a mash that billowed over them in waves. At a courtyard, a disco bass thumped from a reconfigured church.

Vanhoven found the sign depicting a scorpion. Half hidden by cement stairs, El Alacrán was more a cave than a bar. Inside, electric guitar screeched and stuttered over the heavy-metal growl of a singer. It smelled like beer and something unidentifiably dank. He didn't see any drugs, but drugs seemed to hide among the dimly lit tables, the fake spiderwebs, and the unlit crystal chandelier. Wade shuddered. When Myles had come home from Hidden Road, he didn't even drink coffee.

Only two customers huddled in the back corner—a purple-haired girl and a man dressed all in black. "Daddy!" the girl shouted.

She slipped off the bench and ran to hug Vanhoven. She was tall and buxom, an oval face with round, teenage cheeks. Her tight T-shirt beamed out a picture of Christ screaming in flames with the words "Jesus Saves." Something like a screw pierced her lower lip, and a tattoo of an angel with a pitchfork gleamed on her bicep. She was the kind of girl Hidden Road had warned them against.

The drums on the sound system pounded so loud Wade could barely connect his thoughts. "I'm Melissa," the girl yelled.

The man in black rose in the corner. Tattoos covered his neck and arms. As he walked toward them, Wade saw that miniature chains and glass rectangles impaled the tops of his ears. He was some kind of mutant.

"Where's the owner?" Wade shouted.

"I am the owner. My name is Alejandro Morales."

Wade managed to shake his hand. The man's long, perfectly shaped nails were painted silver and looked like talons. Vanhoven looked as disgusted as Wade felt.

They sat at a table under a bare light bulb, Vanhoven next to Wade and across from his daughter and Alejandro. The guitar cut off in mid-flight and the bass from another bar beat through the wall into Wade's chest.

"What happened?" Wade said. His voice seemed to shout and echo in the silence.

"We were chilling, everything cool," Melissa said. "After a while we needed cash."

"When shots are a dollar apiece?" Wade said.

"We didn't want to carry much money . . . so we left most of it in the car. In case we lost it."

Wade rubbed his face and whiskers pricked his fingers. They were teenagers. What they did never made sense.

"Myles went to the car with Roberto," she said.

Vanhoven shifted forward on the chair. "Who the hell is Roberto?"

"I met him last week. He seemed so nice."

"You were here last week?" Vanhoven yelled.

Her lip quivered. She gazed down toward the cement floor. "With Tommy."

Tommy with the wild eyes. Myles had befriended him at La Jolla High almost as soon as he returned from Utah. Wade had met Tommy once and thought the boy had banged his head on his surfboard too many times. Why couldn't Tommy have come to Tijuana?

The man at the bar brought them mugs, and they drank coffee laced with cinnamon and sugar. As she sipped, Wade thought Melissa looked ready to cry. She'd caked on dark eyeliner and her eye shadow had bled down her cheeks. Wade didn't feel sorry for her.

Alejandro cupped the mug of sweet coffee. Even the bottoms of his earlobes were impaled—silver cones like bullets. "Many people come here I do not know," Alejandro said. "This Roberto, he does not pay with a credit card. Only cash." He pointed to the dark wooden rafters above the unlit chandelier. Red lights framed a blue banner that shouted, *Feliz Cumpleaños.* "We have a big celebration. Many, many people."

Wade bent toward Melissa so she'd feel the full impact of his glare. "When you were here a week ago, did you say you were coming back for the party?"

She crimped her face.

Nice Roberto had a whole week to plan.

Alejandro handed him a card that looked official. A policeman's card. "He comes before and talks."

"He already left," Melissa said.

"Law enforcement doesn't want to talk to the parents?" Wade asked.

Melissa said, "I told him everything. He like wrote it down."

As if she were so responsible.

"How about witnesses?" Vanhoven said.

Alejandro slipped off his cap and scratched his buzzed head with his silver nails. "In Mexico, it is best to no look. If you look, something bad happens with you."

It couldn't be as dire as this. There had to be people here who would help.

"It is still possible that the police arrest him," Alejandro said. "Sometimes they do this when someone is drunk."

Or because he was high on pot or some other substance. Or because Myles yelled that he'd never pay a bribe when a policeman stuck out his hand.

Alejandro looked up an address on his phone. He produced a pen and wrote it down on roach paper. "The police station is only ten minutes distance," he said.

For the first time in his life, Wade hoped that his son had been arrested.

* * *

The police station stood behind an eight-foot fence. To one side of the grey and white building, a panel truck unloaded prisoners through a metal gate topped with swirls of barbed wire. Wade searched the people for a slim body with a teenager's slumped shoulders. The arrestees were all men.

Vanhoven and his daughter stayed in the car while Wade hurried inside the building. Long lines led to two uniformed women behind a counter protected by heavy glass. Wade waited, shifting from one shoe to the other. When he reached the counter, one of the policewomen regarded him, her face expressionless. Wade spoke slowly in English.

"Name?" she said.

He wrote out Myles' name and she typed into the computer. She flipped through screens while the local people in the line behind him stared. How many screens did she have to go through for one name?

"He is not here," she said. "He maybe is at another delegation. We have eleven. You go to each one."

"I have to go to eleven police stations? You can't be serious."

Her stare raked his face.

He leaned into the glass between them. "Look, I'm his father. I'm desperate. He's disappeared and doesn't speak Spanish."

Her face softened. Maybe she was a mother. "Go to the hospital first. Cruz Roja."

Myles could have been beaten by thieves, shot, clinging to life on a gurney. Myles crying for help.

"We both pray," the woman said. The pity in her eyes made Wade tremble.

He shambled back to the parking lot, each step more exhausted. He pulled himself into the SUV's front seat and pressed his knuckles against his eye sockets. As Vanhoven started the engine, Wade realized there was another possibility the policewoman hadn't mentioned. The morgue.

His cellphone jolted him forward. The number was unrecognizable.

Soft static. As if it were a robocall.

"Dad?" Myles' voice was high, afraid.

"Are you all right?"

"I've been—" His voice broke. "I've been kidnapped."

Wade pushed his hand against his mouth.

"I'm in Tijuana, Dad."

"I'm already here. With Melissa and her father." His own voice was so calm. Maybe because Myles needed him steady.

"You gotta do what they say. I'm sorry. I . . . I screwed up."

The phone scraped. "Mr. Bosworth," a deeper, accented voice said. "We do not hurt your son yet. You can stop that this happens." The man's tone was steady, businesslike.

"How much money do you want?" Wade said.

The man laughed. "Your house is very, very nice. But we want more than your house. You are a man who knows about loans. Borrow the money."

"How much?"

The man disconnected.

CHAPTER SEVEN

FIONA

Something was wrong. Fiona grabbed her phone and turned it on. It was six fifteen in the morning and there were three messages from Wade. It had to be about Myles. She pressed the screen and listened. She stopped breathing.

The sheets rustled. Jasper stirred beside her. He turned on his nightstand light and faced Fiona. "What's going on?" he said.

"Myles is missing."

"From a campground?"

"He's not camping!"

Jasper squeezed his eyes shut as if trying to take it in. He shook his head and his hair swayed around his face.

She said, "He lied to me. He snuck off to Tijuana last night with Melissa."

Jasper drew himself up and sat beside her in the bed. "Tijuana? Now he's missing?"

Her feet slammed against the hard wooden floor. They were both naked and she was shivering. He stood and folded his arms around her. For a moment she rested her head on his shoulder and huddled into his warmth.

"There must be some kind of mistake," he said.

Not with Wade. Wade didn't make those mistakes. She pushed away and wrapped her arms around herself. *Myles is missing in Mexico.*

"Let me help," he said. Even in the dim light she saw the concern in his eyes. She heard it in his voice. But Jasper had never raised a child.

She had to be alone. "I need to use the bathroom," she said.

Fiona hurried to the master bath and shut the door. The night-light dimly illuminated her robe on the hook. She draped it around her and sat on the lid of the toilet. Her shaking hand punched in the numbers and pushed the cellphone to her ear. In the second message, Wade said he was on the way to Tijuana. "Why the hell don't you pick up?" he said.

Because she and Jasper had shared an intimate night. Because they'd eaten tofu laced with cannabis. And while she'd been making love like a twenty-year-old, Myles had vanished.

She'd believed him when he said he was going camping. She'd wanted to show she trusted him after his year of hell in Utah. But the whole world knew that *camping* was a teenager's excuse when he planned something forbidden.

She jerked herself to her feet on the tiled floor. She wanted to heave the cellphone against the bathtub. She wanted to watch it break into pieces.

Jasper knocked softly. The door whispered open. He'd put on camo pants, his painter's pants. "Call Wade," he said.

Why hadn't she already done that? She looked at her phone, then at Jasper. It was hard enough talking to Wade without Jasper beside her. Wade would feel his presence. "I really need some of your tea," she said.

Without a word, he shifted away and disappeared in the space between the frame and the closing bathroom door. His bare feet slapped against the bedroom's wooden floor.

She stumbled out and found the bed. The green numbers of the old clock radio screamed at her from the nightstand. *6:30! 6:30! How could you not know your son was in Tijuana?*

Wade picked up after a single ring. "Have you found him?" she said.

All she heard was his breathing.

"What happened to him?" she shouted.

"He's been kidnapped."

A single sentence. A sentence that shoved her onto the bed.

"He's alive," Wade said. "I got a call from the men who took him. I heard his voice."

Alive. That was a tendril of hope, wasn't it? "Is he okay?"

"Scared."

"But he's okay?"

"I think so."

She walked over the floor and the cold wood snapped her into focus.

Wade said, "He was with Melissa Vanhoven. You know about her, right?"

He was talking about the home contract. Even now he accused her. "Come on, Wade, do you really think a teenage boy can stop dating? He was getting straight A's."

"Melissa was the one who took him there."

Melissa, the girl with the blue hair and the screw in her lip. Why hadn't she forbidden that relationship? Because Myles would have dated her anyway. Because he would have stopped talking to his mother.

"Do you have a plan?" she asked. Wade always had a plan.

"I've talked to the consulate and the FBI."

Leave it to Wade to take action. Always one foot forward. "Have you talked to the police in Tijuana?"

He released a long sigh, as if he were emptying the whole night from his lungs. "Yeah."

"Yeah, what?"

"The police referred me to a special kidnapping unit. They haven't called back yet."

Shit.

"I'm driving your car."

She knew what Wade thought. Here was Fiona at it again, Fiona who'd lent Myles her car after they'd agreed not to do that. She had to wipe those thoughts out of her head. Get beyond fighting. Not now.

"An FBI agent is coming to the house," he said. "I'm on my way there."

Wade had been up all night; he had to be exhausted. But he still managed to get the right people to help them. "Thank you," she said. "Are you okay?"

"I'm fine."

Even now he thought that an act of will would hold him together. When he disconnected she bent over and ordered her lurching stomach to settle. *Strength.* They both needed to wall off their fears today.

Jasper came back with a mug of organic tea and left. It tasted like something chopped out of the backyard. She drank it anyway. She pushed herself up. Her legs barely worked. Hugging herself, she paced to the other side of the bed.

My child betrayed me. My child is missing in Mexico.

Jasper's black boots stood on the floor. She kicked them away.

CHAPTER EIGHT

Her arms and legs shook. She had to get dressed. Conservative clothes were better for an FBI agent, she decided, and went to the closet. The hangers screamed as she shoved one then another piece of clothing across the rack. She settled on a pair of slacks and a sleeveless top that emphasized her height and long arms. She had to, at least, look strong. Maybe the clothes would hold her together.

She went downstairs. Jasper hugged her, but she barely felt his arms. He pulled away, his black hair hanging to his shoulders. "This isn't your fault," he said.

"He's been kidnapped," she said.

He drew back. "Kidnapped?"

"They called Wade." She saw the worry in his face. But how could he understand what a mother felt for her son? "I know you want to help," she said. "But I can only deal with myself right now." His eyes looked both hurt and offended. She couldn't worry about that.

He slumped off to his painting studio and shut the door. She felt as if she were sleepwalking to the front of her house. She peered through the maritime layer that had fogged over the street. A few cars materialized from the grey, passed by, and disappeared into more grey. Joggers and bikers slipped past. A surfboard seemed to ride the haze as it passed by on the top of a jeep. Today, she hated La Jolla.

An hour later her own BMW emerged from the mist. She imagined seeing Myles through the window. The car would pull into the drive and he'd push open the door and his gangly legs would scissor out. She'd yell and cry and run to him. But it was only Wade. He got out and passed their oleander tree. Whiskers shadowed his face and sleeplessness hooded his eyes. She stepped outside onto the wet walkway. Waited for him to say something. Anything.

"No word from the kidnappers," he said.

She broke down and he held her. As she wept, she felt Wade's chest shaking.

A plain grey Ford ground to a stop outside the next-door-neighbor's house, its windshield wipers making swipes at the morning sea mist. The car didn't look like the BMWs, Lexuses, and SUVs in their neighborhood. She felt Wade's chest and shoulders straighten.

"The FBI is amazing to send someone so fast," he said.

The last two years she'd grown to detest his tough, unyielding demeanor. But not today. Today, she wanted to lean on that part of him.

The driver of the Ford stepped out, a woman with short brown hair who looked to be in her early thirties. Fiona was glad the FBI had sent a female. A woman would understand what a mother felt. The agent trudged toward them over the slick sidewalk. She was muscular, a computer bag slung over her shoulder. As she got close, Fiona saw acne scars pocking her cheeks. But she was still pretty in a broad-shouldered, masculine way. The woman gave them cards. "Special Agent Kris Rodrigues" was neatly printed on the front.

They moved single file inside, Wade leading. When they reached the doorway of the kitchen, he stopped so abruptly that the special agent bumped into him. "Oh my God," he said.

Wade hadn't known that Jasper painted over the egg-shell-colored walls. Now they were a light greyish green. The kale and chard on the counter seemed to further disgust him. What right did he have to judge this house? It was hers now. She started to get angry and caught herself. Not now.

Rodrigues pointed to Fiona's table. She and Wade sat next to each other, and Rodrigues faced them. In the back window Fiona saw fog greying over the hydrangea and wisteria in her garden. She imagined Myles handcuffed behind the mist, Myles terrified, Myles beaten and thinking he'd be killed.

Rodrigues stood and reached for the box of Kleenex on the counter. She gave a tissue to Fiona and sat back down. "You can cry as much as you want," she said. "Crying doesn't mean you aren't strong."

It was something only a woman would think of. Fiona thanked her with her eyes.

Jasper's organic tea steeped in a slanted teapot on the table, his handmade cups and triangular saucers beside it. Rodrigues poured for her and Wade and then for herself. The special agent sipped and winced. She set down the cup on Jasper's saucer and reached for the laptop inside her bag.

Wade ran through what had happened while Rodrigues typed: Vanhoven showing up at his condo, the two of them fruitlessly searching for Myles in Tijuana, then the call from the kidnappers and Wade's contact with the police. His summary was so organized, so step-by-step. He sounded as if he were talking about some other father with some other son. Only Wade could manage that after the night he'd had.

When he'd finished, Wade asked, "Do you have someone in Tijuana, someone who can talk to witnesses?"

Rodrigues looked up from her laptop. "I guess you didn't know. We have to go through the local authorities."

Fiona thought she must have heard wrong. "What?"

"We're restricted by law," Rodrigues said. "We can't go there to work the case."

Everyone knew the reputation of the Mexican police. "Are you kidding me?"

Rodrigues waited a beat as if to let the silence calm them. Wade set his hand on her arm. She didn't shrug it off.

"There are a lot of good cops in Tijuana," Rodrigues said. "And the Baja Kidnapping Unit is first rate."

"How about Myles' phone?" Wade asked. "Can't you zero in on where it is?"

Rodrigues nodded, but Fiona could tell she'd already discounted the question. "By now his phone is destroyed," she said. "They'll use throwaways and telephone cards going forward. Or they might use voice-over I.P. and bounce it through foreign servers. Their calls will be untraceable." She raised her tea, stared at the cup, and set it back down on the saucer. "Look, this is not a run-of-the-mill kidnapping."

"There's nothing run-of-the-mill when it's your son," Fiona said.

The special agent looked at her, woman to woman. "You're absolutely right."

"Thank you."

Rodrigues drummed her fingers on the table. She seemed to be considering what she had to say next, as if she were running through a template for how to deal with them.

"Let me tell you something about abductions," Rodrigues said. "The most common are called 'express kidnappings.' That's because they take place in just a few hours. If that was the case with Myles, the kidnappers would call and make you transfer money to Myles' account. Then they'd go from cash machine to cash machine in Mexico. They'd do max withdrawals and pull out a few thousand dollars from his account. But that's not what they did, is it? Instead, they told you to sell your assets and borrow money. That takes time. They also didn't mention a ransom amount. Which leads me to believe that the phone call was only to prove they have your son. Proof of life is a good thing. It's very professional."

Professional. Fiona hated that word. *Professional* meant they'd kill Myles when they learned his parents had no money.

The special agent handed her another Kleenex.

Rodrigues asked Wade about the phone call and typed his answers into her computer. Male or female voice? Accented, but how fluent? How agitated? Did he demonstrate knowledge about Myles or anyone else in the family? How long was the call? Was any ransom amount hinted at? What kinds of threats? Fiona found the special agent's thoroughness comforting. Yet there was something strange about her demeanor. Maybe it was the way she studied them as they answered each question. As if she suspected that they weren't telling her something. But that was probably how the FBI interviewed everyone.

Rodrigues looked from Fiona to Wade and back. "Is there any reason—in your lives or Myles'—why someone in Mexico would want to kidnap him?"

"Besides money?" Wade asked.

"Besides money." Rodrigues waited as if they both should understand the meaning of her question.

"What are you talking about?" Fiona said.

Rodrigues frowned. "Do you think it could have had something to do with drugs?"

After a year at Hidden Road? After three months of perfect grades and school attendance? "Absolutely not," Fiona said.

Rodrigues fixed her eyes on Wade. "Do you do any business in Mexico?"

"No," Wade said.

Rodrigues typed into her computer. She looked at Fiona. "And you?"

These questions were useless. They were wasting time while her son languished with monsters. But she had to answer. "I'm CEO of a charitable foundation called Comunidad de Niños."

Rodrigues didn't type, her face blank. Fiona knew she was trying to make a connection to Myles' kidnapping. "We have orphanages and shelters," Fiona said. "Our business is to *save* children."

"Any link between your charitable foundation and Wade's banking?" she asked.

"My bank has nothing to do with Fiona's foundation," Wade said. "And I have nothing to do with Mexico. Why don't we cut the irrelevant questions and talk about how you can help us? Like with negotiating the ransom?"

"By law, we can't negotiate in another country."

It was so stunning that Fiona couldn't gather the meaning. She ran the sentence over in her head and it only seemed more outrageous. "But we're U.S. citizens. Myles is a U.S. citizen."

"My hands are tied," Rodrigues said.

This bureaucrat had actually come here, typed into her computer . . . and then claimed she couldn't do anything. "What the hell use are you then, Special Agent Rodrigues?" Fiona said.

Rodrigues picked up her tea and set it down. She stared at the table.

"I'm sorry," Fiona said. But she wasn't. Not really. This was a disgrace.

Rodrigues gave her an understanding smile. "You're fine. You've been through a lot this morning."

She's patronizing me now?

"Tell us how you *can* help us," Wade said.

"In more ways than you think. You have no idea what we can learn by indirectly being involved. For instance, we can listen to the kidnappers' phone calls. Maybe something in the caller's voice will give him away. There might be clues from background noise, like what kind of traffic is on the street. We'll also coordinate with the State Department and the Mexican Anti-Kidnapping Unit in Baja. The FBI can't speak directly to the kidnappers, but we can sit with you while you talk with them. We'll give hints on what to say and not to say. And if you want someone else to do the negotiation, we can help you find a consultant."

Jasper's opera broke out in Wade's old office down the hall. Fiona flinched. It was the rousing prelude to Tristan and Isolde.

"Jesus," Wade said.

"Does someone else live here?" Rodrigues asked.

"My boyfriend," Fiona said. "Wade and I are getting a divorce."

The FBI agent tapped her fingers and nodded. "I need to meet him."

Fiona walked down the hallway to get Jasper from his studio. This morning he wore his painting clothes—camouflage pants, a spattered Hawaiian shirt, and a flapped Alpaca cap. His hands were blotched with red. He looked as if he'd wandered in off the street, but it was too late to ask him to change. When they returned together, Rodrigues took in Jasper and glanced at Wade. For the first time, Fiona spotted sympathy in those unblinking brown eyes. Wade's face tightened; he hated to be pitied.

Before Rodrigues asked him a question, Jasper said, "I had no idea he'd snuck down to Mexico."

Rodrigues typed that into her laptop. "Do you do any business yourself in Mexico?" she asked.

Jasper studied their faces as if to ask, *Is that question for real?* "I'm just a painter. I never get out of California."

"Any collectors of your work in Mexico?" she asked.

"Any collectors anywhere?" Wade asked.

Fiona shot him a glance. *Please, not now.*

"Collectors *do* buy my work," Jasper said. He met Wade's eyes.

"Thank you," Rodrigues said. "I just need to talk with Wade and Fiona now."

Jasper turned and headed back to his studio, his boots clomping on the wooden floor. He closed the door and started up more of Tristan and Isolde. Wade seemed to listen to the music coming from his old office, the muscles in his jaw pulsing. He resented that Jasper's studio was there, but it had been the only empty room in the house.

Rodrigues closed her laptop and packed it up. "I know this is hard," she said.

"Do you?" Wade asked.

"Believe it or not, I do. Please call me if you hear anything."

"So you can *help* us?" Wade asked.

Rodrigues gave him a tight smile. "You'll be surprised how much we can help."

Fiona and Wade walked Rodrigues to the front of the house and watched Rodrigues tramp back to her car. They returned to the kitchen. She needed coffee, but Jasper didn't drink caffeine. Fiona found an old bag of Costa Rican and the grinder in the back of a top cabinet and boiled water. She ground beans and dumped them into the French press.

"Was that FBI pencil-pusher as useless as she seemed?" she asked.

"I hope not," Wade said.

They both watched the burner heat the water. "It's like old times," Wade said. "Drinking coffee in our kitchen and worrying about Myles."

Old times when they'd fought about every decision. Should they put Myles on Ritalin? What were the right limits on his behavior?

Which circumstances required consequences? What consequences wouldn't stunt his independence? Why couldn't the word *no* be final with their child? Then they'd go on to which of them was most at fault for their boy's struggles. For days.

He took one of his long breaths. She recognized the yoga breathing, what he did now to settle himself. "I don't blame you for what happened with Myles in Tijuana," he said. "I really don't."

"I know you're trying not to," she said. "I appreciate it."

She pushed down the plunger in the French press and was about to pour coffee. Then she saw she was using Jasper's crooked cups. She put them in the sink and found two old mugs in the cabinet by the sink. The coffee was black and strong, the way they used to drink it. She sat opposite Wade. They both sipped.

"I would have believed Myles about the camping," he said.

It was a lie, but she was touched that he offered it. She reached across and clasped his hand.

"You never gave up on Myles," he said. "You were his rock."

He'd never said that before. She rose and skirted the table. Wade stood and she folded her arms around him. She rested her forehead against the familiar soft crown of his head. She noticed her hands were higher up his back. Jasper was much taller than Wade.

"Myles needs us to work together," she said.

"I know." His voice was soft.

"We'll sell the house. What's a house compared to our son?"

He drew back and looked down at the table. "We have two mortgages."

They'd have nothing left after they repaid the loans. "What about your bank?"

His face looked hopeless—Wade, who could always come up with a way to finance anything. "The only loans they give employees are mortgages. And we've already maxed out that collateral."

The thought rose up like a bolt of energy. Andre Ouellette had been kidnapped in Mexico. It happened two years before, just prior to her start at Comunidad de Niños. She heard that his wife had used all her contacts to get him back. Of course Andre would help. She ran his nonprofit.

CHAPTER NINE

F ive minutes after Wade left, Fiona called him. Andre arrived at her house ten minutes later. Andre was more than a boss, he was a friend. On the first day she'd met him she'd felt a kinship with Andre about saving children. Just the sight of his gold Mercedes smoothed out her ragged breaths. He limped up the walkway, his blond hair uncombed and one of the pearl buttons on his shirt undone. Andre was always perfectly groomed, but today he'd rushed over, his plump cheeks unshaven. All because she had an emergency. Andre would jump off a cliff to help her. She threw open the door.

"We will get Myles back," he said. Even with a French accent, Andre always sounded confident.

He came inside, one cockeyed step lurching into another. He knew her house and turned into the living room. He regarded the red art deco couch that had replaced the faded Oxford print, then stared at the red walls Jasper had painted. Jasper's music came on from down the hallway—the ominously dissonant orchestra of Peter Grimes. His eyes winced and his thick glasses amplified his reaction. He would never approve of Jasper.

Fiona sat in the matching twill chair in front of the couch he sat on. "What will they do to Myles?" she said.

"It is what every mother worries. But think of this like them. Myles is their money, their payday. They will treat him that way."

"What if they hurt him?"

He leaned forward on the couch. "They will not if you have the correct *négociateur*."

Andre seemed so sure of it. And what he said fit with what Rodrigues had mentioned about a special consultant to negotiate. "But I have no idea who."

He pulled out a blue handkerchief and rubbed the lenses of his spectacles. "I already made calls. The network is working while we talk. We will find someone who knows how to deal with these creatures."

She eased out a breath. He'd used the word "we." Andre knew all about her troubles with Myles. Of course he would help. But there was a more frightening issue. "We had to take a second mortgage on the house to pay for Myles' treatment. Wade says even his own bank won't give us a loan."

"That is *his* institution."

Her mouth dropped open. "What do you mean?"

He grimaced as if she'd insulted him. "When you run the place, there is always a way to make the loan."

Andre's bank would give them the money. Andre would save Myles. She jumped up from the chair and reached down to hug him. Tears covered her eyes. She couldn't speak.

Andre extracted himself. "It is the right thing."

"Thank you thank you thank you."

He clutched the arm of the couch and pushed shakily to his feet. "Fiona, there is something I must tell you. It is about my foot."

She'd never asked, assuming he'd not wanted her to know how he'd become crippled. What did it have to do with Myles?

"The people who kidnapped me, they did not like how slow was my family to pay. They cut off my big toe."

She grabbed the chair.

"I had the surgery in Mexico. But they made mistakes with the nerves. Now my foot does not work the same."

They cut off Andre's toe.

"This does not happen to Myles," he said. "We will negotiate fast."

Myles without a toe, Myles limping the rest of his life. She clutched her arms around herself.

"You and Wade. You come to my office today. You must be fast. The timing is everything with the kidnappings. I will get a man in Mexico on the phone."

He'd find someone. An expert who could stop the kidnappers from . . . But what about Wade? She'd convince him to see Andre. She had to. No one was going to cut up her child.

CHAPTER TEN

Fiona often remembered a day when Jasper had painted in the next room and she still resonated with his touch. Her own happiness had nurtured sympathy for Wade all alone in his condo. She texted him, "I hope you're doing okay." Then Wade's response. "I never would have hurt you this way."

No, not this way. A different way.

Each time she came to see Wade she felt accused. He lived on the fifteenth floor of a high-rise in Little Italy and had somehow squeezed a La-Z-Boy, a leather couch, and an enormous flat-screen TV into the tiny living room. He didn't even watch sports. Wine boxes, rather than cases of beer, sat piled beside the couch and the window. Fiona rarely visited him, but when she did, an unavoidable thought tortured her: *Look what you did.*

He still hadn't slept this morning, but he glistened from a shower and shave. He led her the few steps to the couch, picked up his guitar, and set it against the leather side. Before Myles, before marriage, Wade had played a kind of jazzy folk style. When he'd needed his banking career to rise faster, he couldn't afford the time. But now, after she'd kicked him out of the house, he'd taken up playing again. *Another accusation.*

Fiona sat on the couch and he on the La-Z-Boy across from her. She saw work papers and bills and a plate with the remains of some meal on the dining room table.

"I was going to clean up today," he said.

No he wasn't. She edged into what she wanted. "I think the FBI would be okay in this country, but not in Mexico."

He frowned the way he always did when he didn't trust her words but couldn't refute her logic. "And you know someone who's an expert on Mexico?" he said.

She could tell he suspected where she was going. She had to be careful. "Timing is supposed to be crucial in a kidnapping. We have to get on this."

"I'm not sure the man giving you your information knows better than the FBI."

There was no point hiding whom she'd talked to. "Andre knows all kinds of people in Mexico. Powerful people. And his wife, Carmela, has even more contacts."

"Are they reputable?"

"What does that mean?"

"You know exactly what it means."

Her rejected husband had always thought that Andre's incredible success was tainted. She leaned in closer, set her arms on her knees. "Right now, he's offering to help. I, for one, would do anything to save our son."

Wade looked out the window. The sky was so pale that the color seemed bleached out. She took in the rolled-up mat on the carpet, Wade's latest "betterment" project. He could even make yoga seem like an item on a To-Do list.

She had to snap out of that thinking. For Myles. "Go see Andre for me," she said.

He sighed.

"You're a good father," she said.

His head jerked, the motion as sharp as a word: *Liar.*

"I mean it, Wade. Right now, I think being a good father is more important than anything in the world to you." It was true. But the words "right now" hung between them.

"I'll do it for you," he said.

CHAPTER ELEVEN

FIONA

Unity Coast Bank was headquartered a few miles from the Mexican border in Chula Vista. Fiona liked its plain look, a concrete facade with narrow windows extending up its three stories. Two long palm trees rose like feather dusters above the flat roof. "Even the building says it's for the people," she said.

"It looks like a prison," Wade said. He was driving his BMW, Fiona on the seat next to him.

She squinted at him. "Please."

"I promised I'd listen," he said.

They parked in the strip mall in the back. It was nearly noon and the hot sun shimmered in waves off the cracked blacktop. Wade frowned at the neighboring businesses: a mobile phone sales office, a physical rehab center, a Chinese buffet, and what might have been the last laser tag on earth. She knew what he was thinking. No bank in this low-rent strip mall could expand as fast as Unity Coast had. But she knew why they'd grown. Andre was in charge.

They hurried to the entrance of the building. The long floor inside was furnished with matted carpet, cheaply upholstered chairs, and desks resurrected from the nineties. No overpriced trophy furnishings here. Just functional decor for functional business that funded a foundation that she ran to save children. The place was humming. Clients sat in front of every loan officer. Other clients awaited their turns in rings of chairs or lines in front of the tellers and ATM machines.

"Look at all these people," Fiona said. "At a noon on a Saturday, no less."

"You could be on a defibrillator and get a loan here," Wade said.

She stopped and caught his eyes. "Please."

He shrugged.

Andre stood outside his office in a powder-blue suit and big, blue-framed glasses. He dressed so well, and yet there was always a hint of spirituality about him. His tie beamed out a kaleidoscope of red, yellow, and blue circles that could have been mandalas. She remembered the time he'd talked with Wade at a fundraiser. Andre had lectured him that he should experience life with more than his frontal lobes. Wade had barely listened.

"I am so sorry I get this call from you this morning," Andre said. "Terrible."

They went inside his office. Fiona admired how Andre hadn't felt obligated to make it look like the rest of the bank. Here, he needed to project that he was an owner of a thriving business. The mahogany furniture always looked polished, not a single sheet of paper on his desk. Andre controlled his bank rather than letting his bank control him. Just the kind of man who could help save Myles.

He limped to the gleaming table and Wade and Fiona sat across from him. After Wade summarized what had happened, Andre retrieved a red handkerchief from his suit jacket and rubbed the lenses of his spectacles. He raised his glasses to inspect them and his gold and ruby ring sparked in the light from the window. Fiona knew better than to press him. For Andre, life was not to be hurried, even in an emergency.

At last, he spoke. "Let me tell you how kidnapping people work. The professional gangs are organized in *départements*—spotters, a research unit, a team for abduction, a group that guards the hostage, a team for the negotiation of the ransom, et cetera. And none of these groups knows the other. Only the man at the top knows everything."

Andre always found information that no one else knew. Already he'd told them more than Special Agent Rodrigues had.

"They research you," Andre said. "First is the car. Maybe these people have a friend at the DMV. That friend gives them an address. Or they learn this information from your son. They look up your house on Zillow for the value. Some gangs have lawyers and they research with Lexus Nexus and the other databases. Then there is the question of your profession, Wade. LinkedIn shows them where that you work. It gives the kinds of transactions that you make. You are a senior vice president, and that only means one thing to them. You have much money."

"It's all a mirage," Wade said. "Myles' treatment drained everything— the investment accounts, the IRAs, the college fund. Even our cars are leased."

Andre reached across and set his hand on the table between their wrists. "There are always ways to get the money. You just do not know about them yet." He pointed at the yin and yang tattoo on Fiona's wrist. "The Chinese know that the world is not a straight line. Something we don't understand brings Fiona to my foundation. And you to me, Wade. There is a meaning in this."

"Karma?" Wade asked.

Fiona grimaced. Wade didn't believe in karma. Apparently, Andre knew that too and studied Wade with a pained smile. "The money that you need . . . it comes later. What you get now is a response consultant. Someone who knows the kidnapping market. A man that can get to the boss that controls what happens to your son."

He rose and hobbled to the mahogany desk. He pulled open a drawer, retrieved a piece of paper, and placed it on the table in front of them. Unity Coast Bank's logo stood out on the top—white stars above clasped tan hands on a blue background. Below it was typed "Wilfredo Polanco, Rapid Response Security Consulting, Federal District," and a phone number. As usual, Andre was ahead of everyone.

"Wilfredo is the best *négociateur* in all of Mexico. He negotiated my release two years ago." Andre turned to Wade. "The people who kidnapped me, they did not like how slow was my family to pay." He sighed. "They cut off my big toe and sent it to my home."

Wade's eyes widened. He shifted in the chair. Fiona guessed what he was thinking. They were entrusting their son's life to a negotiator who considered the loss of a toe a success.

"Polanco has the contacts with all the kidnapping gangs across the country," Andre said. "It is a kind of network. The amount of the ransom depends on the family's wealth and how much that the family loves the victim. The first is estimated easily on the internet. The second they measure a different way. They terrify the family."

"By sending them a toe," Wade said.

Andre nodded. "Or an ear. Or an eye."

Myles with one ear, Myles with a glass eye. Fiona covered her mouth and wouldn't let herself gasp.

"We do not let this happen to Myles," Andre said. He pointed to the speakerphone on the middle of the table. "I talked this morning to Polanco. He awaits for our call."

Fiona was ready, but Wade hesitated. He leaned back in his chair and she saw him calculating, drawing up a list of pros and cons. The banker in him couldn't stop himself. But the FBI was hamstrung in Mexico. Even Rodrigues said they needed a negotiator.

"Wade, we can't dither," she said.

He flashed her a reproachful look.

Andre said, "When someone jumps on you, you do not have the time to make all the analysis of the reasons. You do not have the time to make a plan for all the steps that you use in the counterattack. Sometimes instinct is the best advisor."

Fiona squeezed Wade's arm and beseeched him with her eyes. Wade nodded. She didn't care if he was only doing this for her.

Andre pressed some buttons on the speakerphone. Polanco answered in Mexico City. He told them he'd negotiated more than fifty kidnappings. Fiona found his deep voice reassuring—even over a conference phone. She imagined him as a middle-aged, balding man.

After Wade told him what had happened, Polanco said, "Your son saved that girl he was with."

"You think that the kidnappers wanted Melissa too?" Wade asked.

"Of course they did."

The girl with the blue hair and the screw in her lip. Why couldn't she have gone to the garage with Roberto instead of Myles? But Fiona knew why. Her son had protected her.

"How do we keep Myles safe?" she asked.

"Look, if they negotiate with me, they will not hurt him," Polanco said. "I'm known in their network."

The network of men who bought and sold lives. "Maybe you're reassured by that," she said. "But he's not your son."

Andre and Wade stared at her. The conference phone line hissed through the men's silence.

Polanco said, "The important thing is to negotiate quickly. They know that your son is valuable. If it looks like the ransom will take too long, they will sell him to another gang. That gang will hold him for months and demand much more money."

Andre leaned into the phone. "We need to prepare Wade and Fiona for what the ransom might be."

"For this type of victim, between four hundred and five hundred thousand dollars."

Fiona's mouth gaped. She looked at Wade. He stared at the phone as if it were a flying saucer. Fiona turned to Andre. He limped to the credenza behind his desk and slipped off his glasses. He brushed his red ruby ring over a carved mandala. Why wouldn't he look at her?

"Andre?" she said.

"Fiona and Wade will get the cash," he said.

She exhaled. Wade swung his face to her and she saw the doubt clouding his eyes. No legitimate bank would make this loan. She didn't care.

"I need my fee in advance," Polanco said. "Ten thousand dollars."

Wade raised his arms. They were so poor they couldn't even get their hands on that much cash.

"We'll wire the ten thousand today," Andre said.

Fiona caught Andre's eye and mouthed, "Thank you."

Polanco said, "Right now you do nothing. If they call, you give them my name and number. Then you hang up. You must show that they do not have all the power."

He disconnected, as if to prove the point.

Next to her, Wade's face looked unmoored. "Stop trying to see the holes," Fiona said. "Now is the time when you have to trust someone."

Andre said, "Wade, this is a different world than what you know. We must deal with people who have the different laws than you and I have."

"You mean criminal gangs?" Wade asked.

"People, Wade," Andre said.

Wade squeezed his eyes shut.

"This is for Myles," she said.

Wade nodded.

"I will get busy now," Andre said. Wade lurched unsteadily to his feet beside her. She opened the office door. The lobby's chatter swelled into the room. Wade didn't say a word as he closed the door behind them.

CHAPTER TWELVE

The next day, Sunday, Fiona was so cold and tired she huddled in bed under the covers and clutched her cellphone. At eleven o'clock, she rose and forced herself to put on jeans. Jasper draped his arms around her. He'd come from his studio, and she breathed in his scents of paint and turpentine. His face crumbled when she told him that once again she needed to be alone. "I can't manage my own emotions, much less yours," she said.

She paced the house's kitchen and the living room. She opened drawers and closed them, wiped the counters, moved chairs, tried to work on the budget for Comunidad de Niños. One minute dragged after another.

That evening Jasper put on a clean shirt. His long hair was so black the kitchen lights seemed to tinge it blue. He'd cooked her favorite stir-fry and opened a bottle of the sauvignon blanc she loved. But she barely felt his presence across from her at the table. She kept thinking of Myles shackled in a dark room, Myles terrified of death. The hours ticked by. Jasper went to bed, and she watched late night TV to put herself to sleep. It didn't work.

On Monday, Jasper insisted that, for her own sanity, she go to work at Comunidad de Niños. When she got dressed, even her clothes seemed heavy. Leticia, her controller, was already at the office. When Fiona told her what had happened, they hugged as mothers. Fiona didn't last the morning.

She got home and the kitchen phone rang. The console didn't show the number. The man on the other end of the line said, "Fiona Bosworth?" He had an accent.

"Who is this?"

"I am the one who decides if Myles dies."

She held onto the wall.

"Are you there, Mrs. Bosworth?"

She had to stay upright. Had to clutch her thoughts and get out the words. "Is he safe?"

"For the minute, yes. But this depends on you, Mrs. Bosworth."

Jasper slipped into the kitchen. She staggered to the table, and he massaged the back of her neck.

"What . . . what do you want?" she said.

"Something that is very simple. I want all of your money. I hope that you are not poor, Mrs. Bosworth. That will be very bad for your son."

She squeezed the phone so hard her fingers hurt. "Let me talk to him."

He laughed. "Do you think that this is a lie what I tell you? Yes, I put your little baby on the phone."

She heard the scratch of static, then music in the background. It was jazz trumpet, languid and sad. She looked out the window and tried to draw strength from her garden.

"Mom." Myles' voice sounded broken.

She shrugged off Jasper and pushed her hand against the table. "Are you okay?"

"I'm . . ."

He couldn't speak. What had they done to him?

"Talk to me," she said.

He shivered in breaths.

"We're doing everything to get you free," she said.

"You have to hurry." His voice had pitched higher.

"Your father is working on it right now."

"Mom, they beat me. They . . . they showed me a . . . a bolt cutter."

A scream clawed at her throat. She clamped her hand over her mouth. More static on the line. More wailing trumpets.

"We start with his toes and then his fingers." It was the man with the accented voice. "Last we cut his balls. We do not want to do this, but we do it many times before."

She tried to let his words pass through her, tried to imagine he was speaking Spanish. She was hyperventilating.

"Get all your money. Borrow all the money. Be a good mother."

Polanco. What did Polanco say? "Hold on," she said.

She stumbled past Jasper to the kitchen counter and retrieved the piece of paper. Laid it on the table. Jasper held the page down flat so she could read it. The sun from the window lit up the name and number. She put the phone to her face with one hand and bunched her other fist against the table. She wanted anger. Needed it.

"Write this name down. Wilfredo Polanco. That's who you talk to now. You got that?"

Silence. Had he hung up? What had she done? "Tell me you understand."

"Yes."

"Do you want the number?"

"I do not need the number. We know him."

"Call him," she said and hung up.

Jasper held her. She sobbed and sobbed.

CHAPTER THIRTEEN

W hat could she do, call Wade and scream that he had to raise the money? Wade was struggling day and night to do just that. Fiona called Andre.

Twenty minutes later his gold Mercedes parked in front of the house. He hobbled up the walk and Fiona opened the door. "Myles will return," he said. "He grows from this."

She needed more than platitudes. "What do we do about the ransom?"

He offered her a face of commiseration. "There is always a way. Let us talk in your garden. The sun and flowers always bring a new way that we look at things."

She led him past Jasper's studio. The door was closed and a Debussy prelude swirled inside. Andre frowned and followed her to the kitchen. Fiona slid open the patio door and they clomped over the deck to her miniature patch of grass and flowers. He took in the purple blossoms of her neighbor's plumeria, then touched the pink hydrangea and purple wisteria vine. He jerkily bent to smell the lilies.

His nonchalance infuriated her. "Say something."

Andre staggered to his feet and grabbed her hand. In any other man this would have been inappropriate. But with Andre, touch was connection.

He said, "Why is it that they call the mother?"

The question made the answer obvious. "The mother is the weakest link."

"Almost always, Fiona. They want that you feel Myles' fear. Fear is profit for them."

Gooseflesh broke out on her arm.

"Your son needs that you be *calme*. He needs that you protect yourself from how they grow the fear in you."

"How the hell can you expect his mother to do that?"

He pressed her hand. Waited a few beats. "Exactly." He let go and stepped back. "This is why you have Polanco."

"I gave that bastard Polanco's name. Then I hung up."

"Good." He removed his glasses and folded the stems. His pale blue eyes seemed purer without the lenses. And yet more intense.

She said, "Suppose hanging up is an insult? Suppose they take that out on Myles?"

"Do they know who Wilfredo Polanco is?"

"They said they did."

Andre gave a knowing half-smile. "The kidnappers realize that they deal with a professional. This is easier for you now. In many ways, this is easier for the kidnappers too."

Andre always made her calmer. She pulled in a long breath and smelled the grass and jasmine. A bird trilled a few feet away in the neighbor's yard.

"We need the money soon," she said.

He slipped on his eyeglasses and pulled an envelope from the pocket of his suit. Inside was some kind of legal document. The thick first page said that she owed Comunidad de Niños five hundred thousand dollars.

"I thought we were borrowing from the bank," she said.

"The credit officer and a committee must approve the loan there. This takes weeks. What happens if Polanco makes the deal fast?"

"But I'm the CEO of the foundation."

He shrugged as if it were nothing. "I have all the discretion there. I can make the loan today if you need it. Eventually, when the bank makes the loan, you take their money and you repay Comunidad de Niños."

It was a crime.

"Fiona, this is just timing," he said. "You will give back the money."

How could a legal detail be more important than her son's life? "If you think it's okay," she said.

"I knew that you would understand. Wade I am not as sure about. Maybe it is easier if you do not tell him."

Her face flushed. Sometimes Andre shocked her. "I couldn't possibly keep that from Wade."

His eyes seemed to swim behind the lenses. "Okay, you tell him. If Wade does not agree, you wait for the bank. But you must know something. If Polanco makes a deal and there is a delay, the kidnappers suspect something bad. They will do something that makes it faster."

She glanced down at Andre's shined loafers.

"In a few weeks my people will approve the loan," he said.

Principle always trumped bureaucracy for Andre. If she ended up needing to borrow from Comunidad de Niños, it would mean that Polanco had made a deal fast. Getting the money from the foundation would spare Myles from more suffering.

She glanced at the blooms of lilies below her, then the wisteria, jasmine, and hydrangea. This was her garden, no one else's. Only she made decisions here. Fiona signed.

He gave her a nod. "You tell Wade if you want. Or you do not tell him. It is up to you. But today you did what a good mother does to save her son."

Why poison her interactions with Wade? When Myles was home safe, she'd reveal what she'd done and withstand Wade's fury. Besides, Andre was also taking a risk. He'd expose his foundation and his reputation with this illegal loan. All to help a boy he didn't know. For her.

"I can't believe you're doing this," she said.

He stooped down and snapped a lily's flower from its stem. He pushed himself up and smelled the blossom. "Good karma is always a good investment."

CHAPTER FOURTEEN

WADE

Tuesday morning Wade stayed in his condo and waited for news. He tried to calm himself by strumming moody jazz progressions on his guitar. "Brother Can You Spare a Dime" and "Stairway to Heaven" and "Crazy." He remembered when Myles was five years old and sat on his lap strumming this same Martin guitar. Wade had formed the chord on the neck. When Myles drew his fingers across the strings, his whole body lit up. But Wade had never taught him more. He'd never had time.

He couldn't stop thinking about Andre's sketchy reputation. Andre's bank had too much cash business, questionable clients, and shadowy owners. Even his history was hard to believe. It was like a TV miniseries. The story was that he'd grown up poor in Montreal, hitchhiked across Canada and the U.S. and into Mexico, and married Carmela. Then he'd gotten rich in auto parts and exporting and importing. As if that weren't enough, Andre left it all and started over in San Diego by resurrecting a failing bank. A bank that was now one of the fastest growing financial institutions in California. Fiona thought Andre was a kind of business shaman. To Wade, the whole myth sounded make-believe.

But did it matter? Not if Andre got Myles home.

At two thirty Wade's phone launched into swing guitar and fiddle. The caller ID beamed out Unity Coast Bank. When he answered, Andre's secretary said, "You need to come here right away."

"Is it good news?"

"I'm just supposed to tell you to come to the bank."

Only a deal could happen that fast. It had to be.

Wade sped at eighty miles an hour through the traffic south to Chula Vista. He found a parking space between the Chinese buffet and laser tag and ran across the steaming blacktop to Unity Coast. The same receptionist hurried him through the crowded lobby.

Inside his office, Andre wore a fuchsia-colored suit and stood over the speakerphone on his table. No one else was there. "Where's Fiona?" Wade asked.

"It is better that just the two men are here," Andre said.

The speakerphone seemed to waver on the table. "It's . . . it's bad, isn't it?" Wade said.

On the speaker, Polanco said, "We have a deal."

Wade's mouth dropped open.

"As of an hour ago, we have an agreement," Polanco said.

Wade wouldn't let himself celebrate. "Is Myles okay?"

"Of course he is," Polanco said. "Otherwise, they do not get the ransom." He gave a deep laugh. "They thought they'd get millions. But they soon knew that would not happen with me. I got the price down to four hundred thousand."

So fast and less money than what he'd estimated. Polanco was a miracle.

"No one expects that such service comes from a bank, do they?" Andre said. "This is what makes us the best."

Maybe Fiona was right and Andre was some kind of shaman.

Polanco said, "I had to give them a concession in exchange for the lower amount. You have to pay it tonight in cash. In Tijuana."

"Tonight?" Wade said. "But that's impossible. No one can get that much cash the same day."

"We ordered the cash before," Andre said. "The delivery came one hour ago."

Wade collapsed into a chair in front of the table. "The amount . . . how did you know?"

Andre's teeth glinted white in the afternoon light from the window. "We requested five hundred thousand. But we do not forecast how well Wilfredo negotiated."

"I like to under-promise and over-deliver," Polanco said.

Wade couldn't get his head around it. "I . . . I don't know what to say."

"Wade, you deliver the money to Tijuana by yourself," Polanco said. "No one else."

He hadn't considered anyone else coming with him. Maybe he should have. "Suppose they take the money and still keep Myles? Or someone robs me?"

Andre said, "Good questions. They also maybe kidnap you. Then they have two people that they keep for a ransom."

"They will honor the agreement," Polanco said.

It was a kidnapping, not a city contract. Wade leaned into the speakerphone. "How can you possibly be sure of that?"

"If they do not do what they say, they will spoil the market for the gangs and the government officials they work with. I have others who enforce contracts."

Polanco was swimming in the same stream as the kidnappers. That was why the negotiation had gone so fast. What was he getting himself into? "I need to get the FBI involved," Wade said.

Polanco's sigh drifted through the speakerphone. "The last operation the FBI helped on . . . they gave the father marked bills. He got his daughter back in pieces."

Wade dropped his head in his hands. The FBI had told him they couldn't do anything in Mexico. This was the only hope he had.

Andre limped to his desk and retrieved a new disposable phone. "The kidnappers say that you do not bring your cellphone. It can be traced."

He and Polanco had anticipated everything.

Polanco read out an address in Tijuana where Wade was to go at eleven o'clock that night. He'd given the kidnappers Wade's license plate and the new cellphone number. After verifying that Wade wasn't followed, the kidnappers would give him further directions.

"A couple of things," Polanco said. "No matter what, be courteous. These men, when they are offended, are vicious. At the same time, you must show strength. They respect strength. But always remember, you have the money that they want. Call me after the delivery."

Polanco disconnected.

Andre said, "What is the most important thing in business, Wade? Reputation. Polanco has the best."

He needed more than reputation. "I want some assurance that he has the power to get this done," Wade said

Andre rose and retrieved a folder from his desk. He hobbled back to Wade at the table. Inside the folder was a loan application.

"You didn't answer my question," Wade said.

A new intensity shone in Andre's blue eyes. "He has the power, Wade. But these men respect something more than power. Do you know what that is?"

"Fear," Wade said.

Andre smiled. "Sometimes fear is more important than integrity."

The receptionist accompanied him to a conference room and Wade filled out the loan application. All the wording was familiar, yet the Unity Coast version required much less information than at his own institution. His had a rigid loan approval procedure that would often take an excruciating month. Here, the loan was already approved, and Wade could send in the tax statements and supporting documents later. Everything about this bank seemed off kilter.

Who cares, as long as they got Myles home.

A half hour later, Wade knocked on Andre's office door. Two stacks of Ben Franklin notes—the value of Myles' life—sat on his mahogany table. Wade sat and counted four thousand bills. The two piles couldn't have weighed more than ten or fifteen pounds. The receptionist helped him wrap the bundles in plastic. Andre slipped the package into a Nordstrom bag and handed Wade a promissory note. Wade started to read it and stopped himself.

Just get Myles home.

He signed.

"Listen to me," Andre said. "At the Mexican border, you do not declare the cash. The Mexican customs *inspecteurs* will not search a BMW for the buried money."

Not declaring this much currency had to break a law. But Mexican border inspectors could be corrupt. Announcing he was carrying four hundred thousand dollars would be an invitation to rob him.

"Maybe now you believe in what I do," Andre said.

"Fiona has always believed in it."

"I am talking about you, Wade."

Wade was quiet.

"Everyone in the world is connected. This connection is more powerful than language or *logique*."

"Karma," Wade said. After this, he might even believe in it.

"You get your son. That is the only important thing now. After, when Myles is safe, you do something for me."

Wade stiffened. "What?"

"You come work here. You start my commercial real estate division. You make us a player."

At this little rabbit hole?

"To do this deal I had to make agreement with some very hard people."

It was what Wade had always feared about Andre. "Criminals?"

"Businessmen. And all businessmen expect a return on investment."

There was no avoiding it. "Are you saying my part of the transaction is I come work for you?"

Andre sighed. "We sacrifice everything for our children."

This was only the tip of what he'd have to do. "Later I have to give these businessmen something they want. Is that the deal?"

"Nothing illegal," Andre said.

Absolutely illegal. Just when Wade had started to like this man.

"You will love it here. It is your chance to be more than a banker. You will be an *entrepreneur.*"

Just get Myles home.

CHAPTER FIFTEEN

Wade stood at the door to the house and wondered when Fiona's eyes had become so distant. It was gradual, like blinds slowly shutting. Today she wore her funky clothes: a tie-dyed tunic and brown boots with blue, orange, and yellow coils and swirls. Even the way she dressed separated her from him.

"Is everything all right?" she asked.

He held on to the concern in her voice before he spoke. "It's Polanco and Andre," he said.

She put her hand on his shoulder. Her palm was warm. "You can trust Andre," she said.

Maybe he should just blurt it out. Tell her that he suspected Andre, the man she idolized, worked with criminals in Mexico. And if the bank was dirty, the foundation had to be dirty too.

Flute and a soprano from some opera sounded from his old office. Jasper was working there. "Let's go for a walk," he said.

"Of course." Her smile looked worried.

He set the Nordstrom bag of money on the floor under Jasper's painting: an emaciated man on a rock spreading his arms to the desert. No, he didn't want the money there. He moved the bag to the red couch and they made their way outside.

As they walked, Fiona rubbed her palms, one drifting over the other. He'd watched her worry her hands that way as long as he'd known her. Only now there was no wedding ring on her finger.

An old wood-shingled house sat beside a corner garden. The fading light made the flowers and pine trees around it glow. They sat on an ancient wooden bench. Wade looked at the scraggly pine and said, "There's a catch to what Andre is doing for us. It's something you should know about. He and Polanco had to make some kind of arrangement with shadowy people in Mexico."

She didn't draw back. She didn't seem surprised. "Who else could they deal with? Those are the kinds of people who kidnapped our son."

Maybe that was how Andre had sold it to her. "Let me tell you what he asked for in return. I have to come work with him."

Her eyes widened, then narrowed. "I didn't know that."

"There are other people involved who want favors. I'm worried about what they might ask for. Not only from me, but from you."

She held his arm. "Oh, Wade."

"It's the deal for saving our son."

She reached across the bench. She hugged him long and hard. When she drew back he saw the outline of the yin and yang tattoo on her wrist that matched the one on his bicep. Inside the circle, two tadpole figures interlocked: one black with a blue eye, and one blue with a black eye. They'd gotten them before Myles was conceived, and the tattoos had outlasted their marriage. He drew in his breath. He didn't know what he was going to face in Tijuana and there was something else he wanted to—no, had to—say. If he couldn't muster the words now, when could he?

"Do you ever wonder what we could have done so we didn't have to send Myles to Utah?"

She flinched. He'd said it wrong. He was supposed to ask what *he* could have done.

"Every damn day I think about how I should have brought up Myles," she said. "I was always rescuing him, always trying to make him happy. Maybe that's why I ignored how much pot he was smoking."

The dying light illuminated the ache in her eyes. "I know how hard you tried," he said. "I was the one who was never home."

"His childhood happened, Wade. You can't redo those years."

The bench's old wood dug into his palm. "I was certainly part of the problem," he said.

"*Part* of the problem?"

He was trying to say he was sorry and she only blamed him. "It wasn't just me, you know. Sometimes you treated him like glass. Like the slightest blow would break him."

Her chest expanded and she sat taller on the bench. "Children are fragile. Myles was my first priority."

As if Myles wasn't *his* first priority.

She said, "I'm sorry, but I can't forget, no matter how hard I try. You just weren't there."

He couldn't get angry. He might never get another chance. "I apologize for that. There's nothing I regret more."

She wouldn't look at him. For a time she just stared at the cars on the street. She turned. "You know what I did during all those hours you spent at the bank? I was the one who had to leave work early and go home and fight with our son. Just so he'd do his homework. I had to make him go to a school he hated and ask for favors from his teachers. And when he repeated first grade, you know what he asked me? 'Will I ever be smart?' Have you considered how sad that question is? I did. Every day he was at Hidden Road."

"Fiona, I'm trying to say I'm sorry."

"I know you're sorry. But it's too late."

They were trapped inside a machine that looped the same recordings. They both knew, but neither of them could stop the gears from grinding.

"Okay, I was the bastard who worked too much. Was that why our kid became a drug user? Was that why he hid all those pills above his closet? I'm also the awful father who made him go to a treatment center where he could get better. And you know what? Hidden Road gave him a chance. But instead of getting better, he came home and lied to us. Is that my fault too? Is it my fault he took off to Mexico?"

"Maybe I should go back home," she said.

She wouldn't listen. She never would listen. He looked up and drew in a great breath of sky. He could do this. He had to. "Look, we both messed up, especially me. That's what I'm trying to say. But at some point, this stops being our fault and becomes Myles' responsibility."

"You're blaming him for getting kidnapped?"

"He wasn't down there eating tacos."

She squinted at him. Her sad, condemning look. Wade lurched to his feet and stalked away. He glared at the houses, bigger and more expensive with each block, the day darkening around him. Salt from the ocean pinched at his nose, then curry from a restaurant on Pearl Street.

It would serve her right if the kidnappers took his money and he and Myles never returned. She'd sure as hell forgive him then.

* * *

That night when he was driving on the highway to the border, his cell rang. "Wade, I'm sorry," Fiona said.

He was so surprised he almost dropped the phone.

"I know you've always done what you thought best for our son," she said.

Maybe she had listened. "Thank you."

"You're in danger. You think you might never come back and you wanted me to know . . . to know that you felt badly about your fathering."

She'd understood what lay behind his awkward words. "I'll always be sorry for that," he said.

"You were a better father than I give you credit for. And let me tell you something else. You don't think I forgive you, but I do."

He breathed in the car's cooled air to clear the tears from his eyes. The words came out by themselves and he knew they were true. "You were always the one who protected Myles. No matter how I criticized you, I always knew that."

She was so quiet he thought she'd disconnected.

"That means a lot to me," she said.

He saw the fortune teller's sign on the highway outside, the neon-red palm with green life lines and one all-seeing eye. There was something ominous about that hand, as if it was telling him to stop. But stop what?

"No matter what happens, be careful with Andre," he said. "He's the kind of man who can mean well and still be dangerous."

The only sound was the car tires clicking over the highway underneath him. Headlights blazed like warnings ahead and behind.

She said, "Please be careful. Myles and I both need you." She disconnected before either of them could ruin her words.

He couldn't die. Not now. He was going to bring Myles home.

CHAPTER SIXTEEN

Wade was sure this area of Tijuana couldn't be right. Electric signs lit up this block like Las Vegas. Women in all shapes and ages stood in the doorways while white taxis full of men jammed the wide boulevard. But Andre had written down the address. This had to be it.

He looked through his car windows and tried to pick out who in that crowd was his contact. The tourists were all men. They wore running shoes and backpacks, and their attention roamed over the women as if they were window shopping. Not them. The prostitutes only looked up from their cellphones to lock eyes with possible customers on the sidewalk or in cars. Then there were the taco vendors, ice-cream sellers, and shoe shine boys. But they all had their backs to him. That left the buildings. At the bar and strip club entrances, greeters in black shirts and orange and red ties were luring men through the roped entrances. Pharmacies, sexual aids stores, T-shirt boutiques, coiffure salons—even sushi bars—lined the street. Anyone could be watching him from behind those windows.

His new cellphone rang from the seat beside him. When Wade answered, a baritone voice said, "*Meester* Bosworth, continue driving."

A sniper could be targeting him through the telescopic sight of a high-powered rifle. They could shoot him in his car, break the window, and grab the Nordstrom bag in the back seat.

"I want to . . . to speak with my son."

The phone brushed against something. "Dad?"

His shoulders relaxed a little. "Are you okay?" he asked.

"I'm . . . o-kay."

Even with two words, Myles' voice had cracked. He sounded hoarse. Wade's hand squeezed the phone. "It won't be much longer," he said.

"Dad, they don't want to—"

Smack. The phone line scratched and thumped. Shouts in Spanish.

"Myles!" Wade shouted.

"I'm sorry!" Myles' voice came from somewhere far away. Plaintive, petrified.

Smack.

"Myles!" Wade kicked the underside of the dashboard. He shoved his left hand into the steering wheel.

"*Meester* Bosworth."

"Don't hurt him. I have the money."

A thud. A cry.

His stomach jumped into his chest. "Stop it! Please stop!"

"*Meester* Bosworth."

Wade was silent, afraid that if he said the wrong word, they'd hit Myles again.

"Do you see the street that is around you? Do you like it? If we do not get our money, we send Myles to a special place near there. People pay very much for a handsome white *puto*."

Polanco had warned that the kidnappers would try to scare him. He had to be courteous, no matter what.

"I'm trying to be an honorable businessman," Wade said. "Please stop threatening me."

The man laughed. "You think this is a threat? It is algebra, *Meester* Bosworth. Algebra is the god of my world. If the math says four hundred thousand dollars, then your son goes free. If it does not, then I get my money with another equation. Do you understand?"

Wade didn't answer.

"Do you understand?"

Wade's heart was thudding. "Yes."

"Be careful, *Meester* Bosworth. Or I do something to Myles in order that you pay attention. This is your onetime ticket. Keep driving."

The man directed Wade away from the downtown district. The only lights glowed from all-night pharmacies and currency exchanges. Metal accordion shutters were drawn over the display windows of little stores next to houses. He didn't like the look of the surroundings.

"Let's make the exchange now," Wade said.

"Do you think that you say where you pay your money? Keep going."

He merged onto Via Rápida and headed east, then curved up a hilltop lit with *maquiladoras* the size of ships: Medtronic, Maxwell, Sony. Maybe this man wanted him to pay the ransom outside an American factory. It would be a mockery of the life he and Myles had come from. No, that wasn't it. Lookouts had to be studying him for any sign of tail cars or a helicopter overhead.

Polanco had urged him to show strength. It would make them respect him. At a stoplight Wade said, "Polanco told me you'd be professional. Why are we wasting time?"

"That son of a bitch? He lives in the City of Mexico and he thinks that he controls Tijuana."

Polanco had humiliated them when he pressed the kidnappers to lower the ransom. This man might hate Polanco, but he also feared him. Wade had to use that leverage. "Wilfredo Polanco says you have a good reputation. If you hurt my son he will be very angry."

The man didn't shout or laugh. Just silence.

Wade made more turns and circles and entered a squatter's settlement. The car ground slowly over a dirt road. On either side, dimly lit houses were cobbled together with sheets of scrap wood, garage doors, and crumbling brick. A rickety scaffold seemed to hold up the unfinished second floor of a building. Wade smelled sweat drenching his shirt. This was the kind of barrio where police and undercover officers couldn't go. Men could shoot him here and take the money and the car. Or drag him out and kill Myles in front of his father.

As if he could read his mind, the man on the phone said, "If you turn around, we make that Myles is not so pretty. We cut him on his cheek. You decide which side."

He couldn't panic. Fear enabled them to outthink him.

Outside the car, people flitted through the dusty film of his headlight beams. In front of him, telephone poles stood like dead trees, their electrical wires stretching to some shacks but not to others. One hovel perched on a dirt hill that was buttressed by a retaining wall of buried tires. On its porch, an opened door backlit a man on a rocker.

The man on the phone said, "Do you like the tour of the Tijuana you never see? This is where I grew up. You are safer here than in the *Zona Rosa*. All my friends watch you. You are the *bolillo* that entertains them tonight."

Wade opened his window for air. An otherworldly sound floated in: the lilting notes of a distant trumpet. Miles Davis' *Kind of Blue* moaned through the night, the piano and bass thrumming underneath the mournful trumpet phrases.

More turns. Wade's hands ached from clenching the wheel. In this part of the barrio, no electrical wires stretched to metal and tarp roofs. No lights flickered inside the shacks. It was as if he'd been led to the darkest part of a jagged world.

His car lights picked up the shadow of a dog nosing through a smoldering mound of garbage. Rancid odors seemed to sway in his dusty beams and drift into the car. He heard ranchera trumpets bellowing somewhere above the beat of a bass. The tenor's voice turned into another voice riffing Spanish rap. As if shed from the music, dust particles flew through the window and adhered to his cheeks and mouth.

"Stop," the voice on his cell said. "Turn off the engine."

Wade did as he was told.

"Put the hands on the board dash," a voice outside said.

Wade jumped.

A flashlight burst on. Wade squinted through the open window and made out what might have been a black balaclava mask. He slowly set his palms on the dashboard.

"Where is the money?" the man outside said. He sounded young. Like a teenager. A teenager could do anything.

"Señor Polanco says I need to confirm that you're the right contact." Wade nodded toward the phone on the seat. The flashlight moved to illuminate it.

"Fastly," the figure outside said.

The man on the phone spoke as soon as Wade put it to his ear. Words rattled out in Spanish. Wade understood the last "*hijo de la chingada.*"

"Is this him?" Wade asked.

"Who else it is?"

The shadow behind the flashlight was short and rotund. Even if he had a weapon, Wade could slam the door into his body before he had a chance to pull the trigger.

And never see Myles again.

Wade spoke into the phone. "Wilfredo Polanco will punish you if you don't release my son."

"Shut up and give the money to Flaco,"

Wade turned to the broad shadow. "The money is in the bag on the back floor."

One arm of Flaco's leather jacket extended toward the back passenger door. The button clanked.

"The door!" Flaco raised a pistol.

"Sorry." Wade said. "Sorry." He jabbed the "unlock" button. Flaco opened the door and bent to kneel on the floor. The car shifted with his weight. Wade heard his hand feel around the carpet, his heavy breathing. The sweet odor of his cologne melted into the funk from the outside. The Nordstrom bag crinkled and the car shifted up. The door softly closed.

If they shot him, it would happen now through the car window. He squeezed his eyes shut. He'd done everything he could. He'd sacrificed everything for his son. What more could a father do?

Nothing happened.

Wade exhaled. "He has the money," he said into the phone.

"Very good, *Meester* Bosworth. It is so easier to follow the directions, no? Now we make sure that no one follows you. If all the money is there, we release Myles. If not, you will receive a message you do not like."

Wade pitched forward in the seat. "I've done everything you asked."

"You see Myles in a few hours. Myles is the same as before."

Myles would never be the same. "I want my son. Right now! Where is he?"

The man on the phone disconnected.

Wade looked out the window. The darkness had absorbed Flaco's broad shadow. Somewhere in the night a trumpet softly wailed.

CHAPTER SEVENTEEN

WADE

W ade found his way out of the dark thicket of squatter shacks to the entrance of the Vía Rápida highway and stopped. He listened to the traffic speeding into the night and inhaled the exhaust-clogged air.

His own cellphone was in the glove compartment. He fished it out and called Fiona. She answered on the first ring. "Are you okay?" she said.

There was no point delaying what she needed to know. "Myles . . . he hasn't been released yet."

He could hear her trying not to cry. She had to have the same worry he did. Now that the kidnappers had the money, would they really let Myles go? If not, they could demand more money or do something worse.

"All I want is for both of you to come home safely."

"I know."

"Andre will make sure Myles is okay."

His whole life had converged to Andre.

Wade said goodbye and disconnected. After a few long yoga breaths, he called Polanco. Polanco told him to check into a hotel and wait. "He'll be home in the next twelve hours," he said. "I know these people. I guarantee it."

Wade ended the call and stared at the phone hanging from his hand. What kind of man could guarantee what a kidnapper would do?

It was midnight. Instead of driving to a hotel, Wade wound his way back to the block of bars where Myles had been abducted and parked in the outside lot. He found his way to El Alacrán. Death metal snarled and screamed from inside. The birthday banner was gone from the dark ceiling beams and about twenty people downed shots and beers. The bar seemed even more like a cave with its crammed-together tables and dim lights.

The music stopped, as if the band's fury had blown a fuse. Alejandro the owner motioned to the quieter corner where Vanhoven, Melissa, and Wade had hunched together. He brought two mugs of beer to the table and sat opposite. Light from the bulb on the wall flickered off the piercings in his lips, eyebrows, and ears.

Wade told him about Polanco and the money he'd just paid to a shadow in a run-down barrio. "Do you think they'll honor the bargain?" Wade asked.

Alejandro brushed his silver nails over his buzz-cut, then over the silver ball embedded below his lower lip. He pulled on the cone in the bottom of his earlobe. "Much depends on your negotiator," he said. "He must have the connections that make the men afraid. Then they release your son."

This was where Myles had brought him. An old suspicion scraped at Wade's thoughts. He leaned in so Alejandro would get a close-up: the face of the scared and desperate father. "Did Myles go to that garage to buy drugs?"

Alejandro reached into the pocket of his yellow shirt. He pulled out a rolled joint and a silver lighter embossed with a black skull. "Do you mind?"

The joint seemed like a test of Wade's tolerance. "Pot is the least of my worries," he said.

Alejandro lit the blunt and took a drag.

Wade said, "It'll take years to pay off the money I borrowed for the ransom. I need to know what the hell my son was doing here."

Alejandro blew out musky smoke.

Maybe the bars in the complex paid protection. Or the cartel lords owned these little businesses and used them to launder cash. Wade tried something more desperate. "Are you a father?"

The rings in Alejandro's eyebrows dipped. He frowned.

"Already or soon?" Wade asked.

"In two months."

"In two months, you'll understand something better than you do now. A father has to protect his child no matter what. It's built into us."

Drunken laughter burst from the middle of the bar. Glasses clinked. The smell of beer oozed from the walls and floor and into Wade's head. Wade leaned in and kept his voice low and friendly. "This is a secret between fathers."

Alejandro exhaled a cone of smoke. Wade waited.

"Your son goes with the man in the leather jacket. They go to the garage to pay the money and to get the product."

Wade had expected it, but the words still slithered inside him. After all he and Fiona had done to help Myles—all the money, the time, the worry, the fighting. The end of their marriage.

"Forget these men," Alejandro said. "Think about that you get your son back. The money is just the money. It is already disappeared. Your family, that is the important."

They had nothing in common, yet Alejandro had risked telling him about drug dealing in his bar. He did it because they were both fathers. "You're going to make a great dad," Wade said.

"I hope I fight for my child like you fight," Alejandro said.

The music revved. A guitar shrieked while the bass drum jack-hammered against the walls. The explosion of sound made Wade sit back against the wall. He remembered another detonation—Myles' birth. The surgeons had to do an emergency C-section that scarred Fiona's uterus. Wade had always wondered how another brother or sister would have tempered their son. But Myles had made that impossible.

His son had hated naps, hated to go to sleep at night, hated diapers. Wade remembered him starting to walk and exploring every piece of furniture and prying the protective covers off electrical outlets. When they punished him, he'd sit on his time-out chair, his feet just beyond the boundary of the doorway to his room. In those early years, he and Fiona had marveled at his curiosity and drive. This was a boy who would grab hold of the world.

And maybe he would have with a better father. A good father would have gotten down on his knees with his son and shot monsters in video games. Or taken Myles to Boy Scouts, or made model robots, or coached him on a soccer or baseball team. A good father would have known that Myles and Melissa were dating. He would have suspected his son was dealing. He would have held his son close so he couldn't fall.

A good father would never give up on his son.

CHAPTER EIGHTEEN

MYLES

For three days Myles had been shut inside a wooden shack with boarded-up windows. He knew he was in the desert somewhere, but couldn't discern any location. He had a dirty mattress, a jug of water, and a stinking piss bucket. All day long he paced over the dusty cement floor from one side of the little room to the other. Five steps to the wall. Turn. Reverse. Repeat. There was a rhythm to the walking. Like when he'd had to put on the orange jumpsuit to do compost duty at Hidden Road. He remembered how he'd counted shovelful after shovelful to transfer one pile to another. Twelve hours with only breaks for food and water. All because he'd stolen a phone and called his mom. "They're abusing me," he'd yelled. She'd flown out the same day. His mom, the one person who always believed in him. And now, because they'd spent everything on Hidden Road, she and his dad didn't have the money to pay the ransom. "Next time you're in trouble, you're on your own," his dad had said.

On Saturday and Sunday they'd fed him rice and beans and tortillas. He'd listened for shouts and laughs from families and children outside the shack. He only heard men's voices. Occasional cars ground over dirt and gravel while their radios pumped out *rancheras*, American pop, and Mexican rap. No one was coming to rescue him.

On Monday morning, men came with a chair and duct-taped him to it. Someone brought in a sound system and blasted out extreme metal. Myles recognized it. Brujería's singers did a version of Macarena with the words "Eh, marijuana." The men started on him then. While he screamed, the singers shouted, guitars screeched, and bass drums pounded. Myles told them everything. Then they called his mom.

The next night he was asleep on the mattress when a flashlight snapped on. Three men rushed into the room and stuck a burlap sack over his head. They bound his hands with tape. Heavy shoes clomped across the cement floor. Myles looked down through a gap in the bottom of the sack and saw polished black cowboy boots with pointed toes. Blue wings and a red cross were stitched into the leather. Perhaps these boots would be the last thing he saw when this stranger killed him.

The man said, "You made a terrible mistake." He had a nasal baritone voice with barely any accent.

"I know," Myles said. "I really do."

"It's time."

But his dad had come to Tijuana to search for him. His mom said they were working to get the money. "My parents will pay," Myles said.

"That time has passed," the man said. He slid something in Myles' pocket. "Your passport and wallet. So people will know who you are."

"Please," Myles said. "They just need a little more time."

"Shhh," the man said. "This is when you show you are brave."

He was going to die. These men would bury him in a hole in Tijuana. He'd never see his mom and dad again. He'd never be with a girl again.

The other men pulled him forward and his feet and ankles screamed. His testicles ached and burned from what they'd done.

Outside, car lights shone faintly through the sack covering his head. He wasn't going to beg or cry. He was going to be strong.

The van door slid open. They pushed him inside and he lay on the riveted metal floor. The door scraped closed and the engine started. He still had a few more minutes. He still could breathe a little more of the dusty air. The wheels bounced and slid over dirt roads, then hummed on the highway.

At least he'd saved Melissa from getting kidnapped. At least his parents loved him and he loved them.

They stopped. The men pulled him out. He heard the whir of traffic as they walked him over a dirt path. Then over lumpy ground and through scraping thickets. They made him kneel. Rocks dug into his shins and knees. He shuddered. *Be brave. Brave brave brave.*

The man with the nasal voice stood behind him. He said, "Your life and your death are your own fault."

Myles imagined the pistol in the man's hand. He waited for the click of the trigger. Would he hear the explosion? "I'm sorry, Mom," he whispered. "I'm sorry, Dad." The trilling of the crickets pierced the bag and filled his head.

Someone cut the tape binding his hands. Myles fell to his side. He took in great gulps of air. Behind him the van door slid shut. The engine roared away. Myles listened for them to return.

After a minute he pulled off the bag. He heard the crickets singing. He looked up and breathed in the stars.

CHAPTER NINETEEN

Swing guitar and violin jolted Wade awake. It was Django Reinhardt and Stéphane Grappelli, the ringtone of his phone. A mug of coffee sat in front of him on the bar's gnarled table.

Myles.

He grabbed his cell. "Is this Mr. Wade Bosworth?"

"Who is this?"

"You are the father of Myles Bosworth?"

It could be some kind of ruse. A demand for more money. "What do you want?"

"Myles is here." It was a woman's voice. Accented.

"Where? Who is this?"

"The office of the police."

Alejandro was standing at the front counter with a push broom. No one else was in the bar. Alejandro pointed his thumb up and his pierced eyebrows rose. When Wade nodded "yes," he raised his fist and whooped and shouted.

"Is Myles okay?" Wade said.

"We find him by the highway."

"But is he okay?"

"He is alive, Mr. Bosworth." She gave him the address and, before Wade could ask another question, hung up.

Myles could be ill, dehydrated, beaten up.

The bolt cutter.

Wade saw hints of daylight through the front of the bar. It was early morning. He started to call Fiona and thought better of it. First, he had to know if Myles was seriously injured.

Outside, the sun was burning the haze pink. He ran to his BMW and drove into the center of a belching gridlock of cars. His GPS guided him to the same white and grey police station he'd visited before. The same van disgorged more drunken arrestees. As he hurried to the office, a middle-aged couple stumbled out. They were weeping so hard they could barely stay upright. Wade pulled open the door.

Inside, a line of people shifted and spoke quietly. The two police-women he'd seen before scowled from the black counter. In front of the opposite wall, someone was slumped on a bench, his face shadowed by grime. He was thin and gangly, his hair so dirty it looked like a cheap wig. As Wade peered at him, the figure's streaked mouth lifted into a crooked smile.

Myles.

They threw arms around each other. People clapped and cheered. Policemen ambled in from the back and shook their hands. In their broken English, they told Wade that so many abductions ended in tragedy. He should thank God that he had the money to pay. Then they wagged their fingers at Myles and said he owed his life to his father. Myles nodded as if struck mute.

He was limping. "What's wrong with your leg?" Wade said.

Myles put his hand on Wade's shoulder as if he were the comforting father. "It's my feet. Nothing I can't get over."

The trembling started in the car, first in Myles' hands, then traveling through his arms to his grimy face and rippling through the rest of his body. Wade hugged him close and listened to his son's quiet weeping.

Myles wiped his hollow eyes with the flats of his hands. The tears had formed pale rivulets down his muddy cheeks. "God, I stink. I so want a shower."

"As soon as we get home," Wade said.

"Home," Myles said, as if recollecting a memory.

Wade gave him his phone. Even in the noise from the grinding traffic, Wade heard Fiona gulping air between sobs.

Myles' lips quivered. "I'm okay," he said.

But he wasn't okay. Wade had no idea what part of him those men had taken.

Wade drove. Beside him, the leather seat groaned as Myles fidgeted. He slipped off his filthy hoody and Wade saw the teenage shallows between his neck and shoulders. His son was still a boy, despite the loose T-shirt emblazoned with a picture of Jesus toting a machine gun. He seemed to see Wade stare at the picture and thrust himself back into his filthy sweatshirt.

The kidnappers had given him back his passport and wallet. It seemed so strange, and yet so professional. They got to the Customs line. It was morning rush hour to San Diego and it took seventy minutes to get through. Myles kept silent the whole time, as if he didn't want to talk about his ordeal until they were safely across the border. The Customs agent barely asked a question.

Back in San Isidro, Wade said, "What did they do to you?"

"I'm okay." Myles glanced down and then away.

Maybe he'd been walking all night and torn up his feet. There was plenty of time to worry about that when they got home.

They headed north to San Diego. Wade looked out the windows at the two lanes of traffic, then at the mishmash of cement apartment buildings, houses, and car dealerships that bordered the highway. It hit him then, like a seismic shift.

Myles tried to buy drugs in that garage.

Drug dealer. The words wrenched him so hard Wade could barely see the road. Myles was eighteen. Was his next stop arrest, then prison? His son would spend the rest of his life banished to the hardest edges of the world.

Drug dealer. The words curled back into him. He had to hear it from his son. Right now.

He pulled off the highway and stopped on the service road by Chula Vista. Farther down the road, the lights of the Psychic Reader sign blazed as if it were still night. Wade fixed on the neon-red palm and its effervescent green lifelines. A single black-edged eye in the center looked back at him.

"Did you go to Tijuana to buy drugs?" he said.

Myles was sound asleep against the door, an exhausted and muddy boy.

He was pulling back on the highway when his cell rang. Not the throwaway but his own. It had to be Fiona. He reached over to the seat and answered.

"Your son is safe," Andre said.

Andre knew that he'd taken his own phone with him. But Myles was home; it didn't matter.

"He's in the car with me," Wade said.

"That is wonderful. You remember our deal, Wade?"

Wade couldn't work for his bank. Andre was doing business with criminals and maybe cartels. "I've been thinking about that. I can help you more where I am now. Funnel you deals and give you participations in the loans we put together. It will be a whole pipeline."

"We made a deal." It was the first time Wade had heard anger in his voice.

"But this is better."

"Listen, Wade. These men do not charge you a fine when you break a contract. You do not write a check to make a remedy of this."

Wade squeezed the phone. He was breathing hard and could barely see the road. The police couldn't protect him when he had no proof of any real threat. But he could delay. Wait a few days and then back out of the deal.

"I just want to get Myles home right now," Wade said. He disconnected.

Myles was staring at him.

CHAPTER TWENTY

Fiona watched Wade's BMW slide down the street and park in the driveway. When Myles pushed himself out, she flung open the front door and ran to him. Her arms swallowed him up and she didn't want to let go.

Myles gently pushed her away. "Mom, please."

She released him and stepped back. He was covered in dirt, as if he'd thrashed his way through a swamp. He smelled like the earth.

"We have to talk," he said.

Wade was scowling. What was going on? "We'll talk inside," Wade said.

Myles limped to the house, his face wincing with pain. "What happened?" she asked.

"Mom, I'm good." He sounded fine. Maybe he'd walked all night. But that couldn't be the reason for Wade's bleakness. What had Myles done?

Jasper stood at the kitchen table. Freshly brewed tea steeped on one of his slanted pots. Myles looked at him and said, "I need to just talk with my mom and dad."

"Of course," Jasper said. He must have sensed the strain snuffing out the joy they should be feeling. Fiona thought of the girlfriend who'd gone with Myles to Tijuana. Was Melissa pregnant?

Jasper shut the door behind him. Wade frowned at the greyish-green walls. He dropped the teapot into the sink basin and returned to the table. They sat, Fiona and Wade across from Myles. The silence trembled through her hands.

"Why were you in Tijuana?" Wade said.

Myles' face tipped down. His dirty index finger scraped the birch table. "I'm going to be honest," he said. "For real."

His words echoed his excuses before they'd sent him to Utah. She wasn't sure she wanted to hear what he was going to say. "If you're not ready, we can wait another day," she said.

"Christ," Wade said. "What the hell."

She whirled to face him. "You will not bully us. Not today."

Myles reached across the table and touched her arm. "You have to stop letting me off the hook."

Fiona sank back in her chair.

"Are you really going to be honest this time?" Wade said.

"I tell the truth more than you think," Myles said. He met Fiona's gaze. "Melissa and I were partying. But we were also buying drugs."

She felt as if he'd slapped her. She stared at Myles. *Tell me I've misunderstood.*

"We went to a kind of mall. Inside is this metalhead bar. It's hidden. Not the usual zero-chill tourist place."

After all they'd been through, after all the talks she'd had with him . . . She pushed her hands against her thighs. "You went to a bar in Mexico to buy drugs?"

Myles compressed his mouth. "I'm sorry. I let you down."

"I fought for you," she said. "Trusted you."

Myles swallowed. "I . . . I screwed up. I always screw up."

"You have no control of yourself?" Wade said. "Your body just tells you to screw up?"

She wheeled on him. "Stop it! We're the parents here."

Wade's lips drew apart and clamped shut. He shot her a dark look, and she saw him marshaling his words, drawing back his whip. But he stayed silent. She turned back to Myles and nailed him with her eyes. His self-pity used to suck out her sympathy. Not today. "Why?"

"I was trying to do Melissa a solid."

Melissa with her tight T-shirts, the lip piercing, and neon hair, the secret girlfriend she'd condoned.

"You always get involved with girls who bring trouble, don't you?" Wade said.

"Will you please let him speak before you start punishing him?" Fiona said.

A long sigh deflated Myles. "You're right, Dad. I always hang with the wrong girls."

Fiona said, "Did she rope you into going there and . . . ?"

Myles shook his head. "I was part of it."

The air was so still. No sounds of Jasper's opera. No birds calling outside the kitchen window.

Wade said, "I see something else you learned at Hidden Road. How to pretend to take responsibility."

"Stop it!" she yelled. "For God's sake, stop it!"

Wade pressed his forearms into the table.

"I should have done better," Myles said. "When I left Hidden Road, I really wanted to."

Myles had progressed through so many levels at Hidden Road she'd barely heard the warnings from the staff. Girls and friends, they'd said. Lies that could flame up into old patterns. Drugs. She'd been such an idiot.

"Just tell us what happened." Her voice was so calm it disconcerted her, as if a part of herself had vanished.

"This dude named Roberto said we both had to go to the parking lot and pay him. It didn't seem right. But Melissa was going whether I did or not. I decided it would be better if I kept her out of it."

"You wanted to protect her, didn't you?" Fiona said.

His mouth grew pained. He shrugged. "This van was in an underground garage. I knew it was totally whack. I should have skurted."

"But you didn't, did you?" Wade said.

"Let him talk," Fiona said.

Wade's stare burned into her.

"These men jumped out. They punched me and stuck a bag over my head and threw me in the van. Mom, I tried to shout but I couldn't. I couldn't breathe."

Her lungs strained for air. Her arms inched toward him.

"A couple days later they duct-taped me to a chair and this guy in a cowboy hat came in. Between the four of them, he said they'd murdered like fifty people—men, women, and children. They were gonna take my body to a pig roaster."

She imagined the inside of a giant oven. Her hands clung to both sides of the table.

"They wanted to know all about our house and where you and Dad worked. But I was on to them. I said our house was the biggest wreck in the neighborhood. Dad didn't earn much and, Mom, you were like a volunteer at a charity. I did everything right. I withdrew my emotion, didn't rush my words. Calmly assertive. I was like totally on point."

He'd used all he'd learned at Hidden Road.

"What happened?" Wade said.

"They beat my feet with an iron bar."

Her mouth opened. A sob, like a trapped breath, was caught inside her.

"They had a car battery. They attached electrodes to . . . to my balls. It hurt so much. One of them said, 'We torture you and your children.' They were laughing." Myles' jaw and arms trembled. His whole face curled into a squint.

Fiona didn't realize she'd gotten out of the chair. She didn't feel her shoes against the floor, only her arms melting around her son. Wade's arms encircled both of them. She breathed in the child she used to hold. It didn't matter what he did to get here. It didn't matter how they'd tried and failed. She looked at Wade beside her. Tears streamed down his cheeks.

"I told them everything. I'm . . . I'm sorry."

She held him tighter.

Myles pushed himself away and wiped his face. They sat back in the chairs. Their inhales and exhales seemed to come from the walls, as if the room were breathing. She was drained, couldn't absorb more. But she had to. Myles slipped off his shoes and socks and showed them his feet. The bruises looked like giant squashed grapes.

"When they stopped, the cowboy lifted up something with these wooden handles. It was a frigging bolt cutter. They were going to cut off my fingers." Myles peered at Fiona. "I didn't know what to do. I hurt so bad. That's when they called you."

"Oh my God," Wade said. He was breathing hard beside her. His face was gutted with pain.

"I thought you might leave me there," Myles said. "I deserved it."

How could he believe they'd abandon him? Even think it? "Never," she said. "Never never never."

She saw what her son was thinking in his wounded eyes. *You already banished me once.*

"Last night they took me outside with a sack on my head. I thought they'd shoot me. I think they wanted me to believe that. Then they left me in the dirt and bushes on the side of the road."

Would her boy ever come back to himself after this?

Fiona ran her hand in the air to encompass the kitchen. "We would have sold everything to stop what they did to you."

Wade said, "I would have given . . . my life to get you out of there."

Fiona believed him.

CHAPTER TWENTY-ONE

FIONA

The day after Myles came home, Fiona decided to go to work. She had to get some distance to think clearly about her son. In the three months since he'd returned from Utah, she'd grown to trust Myles. And now . . . ? As her BMW stuttered through traffic, she looked out the window at Sorrento Valley's long streets of strip malls and office hatcheries. All the grass and young trees seemed as fake as a film set. As fake as her son's rehabilitation at Hidden Road.

She remembered the other mirages, the other false hopes in Myles' life. When he was in fourth grade, his teachers had confirmed his talent and put him in advanced math. He was reading books—whole books—and those books were on the sixth-grade level. Fiona actually laughed at the child-teacher meetings. The years of struggling with him over homework, the special tutors, and learning specialists . . . it had all paid off. Yet she hadn't felt vindicated. It was as if she and Myles had been pinned beneath an avalanche and, without knowing which direction was up, she'd somehow dug a way out. She hadn't foreseen the two meteors that hurled into them.

The first one was girls. Initially, she didn't think it a bad thing that Myles talked and texted for hours on his phone. Then she consulted his history on their home computer and found an interest in porn and all its excesses. Hormones, she thought. There was an easy solution for that. Each morning she locked the router in the trunk of her car when she went to work. But Myles' grades crashed. "What do you expect from a kid who flunked first grade?" he said. She smelled the second meteor during that conversation—marijuana.

Sometimes Fiona wondered if her marriage would have survived if Myles had been a compliant and conscientious child. Their son always came between them. She and Wade argued and fought and fumed about him for most of Myles' life. Then he was gone to Utah and Wade moved out of the house. She hated their forced lunches and dinners in restaurants, meals where they sipped wine while everyone around them was full of words. Without Myles' disasters, they had nothing to talk about. She was at bottom when she started to work for Andre. It was like a resurrection. At Comunidad de Niños, no matter how corrupted her own life, she was saving children.

Fiona parked in her building's half-filled lot and climbed the stairs to the engineering company that shared space with Andre's foundation. Her assistant, Leticia, had taken the day off. Fiona turned on the lights to reveal her pots of red-leafed crotons and the white-flowered peace lilies. Walls of pictures showed smiling Hispanic children with new clothes and new desks. Between the photos she'd mounted the kids' crayon renditions of their orphanages and shelters and their thank-you notes with big letters in Spanish. These walls usually rekindled her faith in her work. But this morning nothing could inspire her to optimism. Her eye was drawn to one smiling child with a long nose and a gap between his teeth. It was an early picture when Mateo had first come to live at the orphanage. After three years he'd run away to join a street gang.

Wade always found reassurance in his numbers. Maybe financial reports would ease her mind. She pulled out binders from the file cabinet and flipped through the pages for the seven Latin American installations. The donations were as predictable as the tides. Most of the funding came from Andre and his friends. Even Egberto Martinez, the man whom she and Leticia called the Mexican Rottweiler, gave five hundred thousand the year before. There were also other big benefactors from Mexico, a country not known for private gifts. She knew she was fortunate she didn't have to scramble for money each month. But part of her had always thought that strange. Most charities had to struggle for money.

Something else bothered her. Uncle Sam was the biggest donor in the country, but not at Comunidad de Niños. Andre said he wanted their funding to come from people, not some bureaucracy. Government grants required the expense and drudgery of an audit and there was still no guarantee of winning one. How could Fiona disagree with him when they never had a budget shortfall? Even the donation boxes in Unity Coast's three branches attracted piles of cash. But another reason occurred to her for not wanting an audit. An audit verified the sources and uses of the money.

An audit would also expose the loan she'd taken.

She wrote down figures from the reports. There were pages and pages of expenses, but no receipts. Leticia, the accountant, reconciled all the details of the budget. That was her job. Fiona was too busy with the hundreds of tasks she could never get done—managing the board, strategic planning, overseeing teachers, analyzing the curriculum, arranging psychological counseling for the kids, purchasing supplies . . . and on and on. But as she went through the numbers, the expenses seemed bloated, as if extra cash had been funneled to the other locations. She knew what Wade would suspect—money laundering.

Fiona sank her head onto her desk and the computer keyboard jammed into her forehead. Andre was one of the men she admired most. He'd saved Myles' life. She owed it to him to file away any doubts and concentrate on saving children.

She didn't hear the door swing open.

"Are you all right?"

Her head jerked up. "It's personal," she said.

Andre's face creased. "Jasper?"

Her mind swirled over what to say. She nodded.

"All things they end sometime," he said.

Her mouth opened. She snapped it shut. "It's just a fight."

He seemed to take in the financial ledgers on her desk. "That is Leticia's job, no?"

She shrugged. "I should understand them. What if Leticia moves on?"

"Leticia is quitting?"

"All things end sometime."

He squinted behind the thick lenses. His gaze drifted over her desk. "How is Myles?"

"Recovering."

"That is good. Myles grows from this."

She noticed he wore spotless running shoes, pressed jeans, and a casual designer shirt. These weren't the clothes of Andre the CEO.

"I think that it is time that we are inspired," he said. "Get your passport."

*   *   *

Fiona thought this part of Tijuana seemed to breathe in the dusty air. The street was nothing but dirt and gravel and chunks of concrete. The houses were made of mismatched windows and painted scraps of wood. But not the orphanage's new buildings. Its brick walls were covered with pink and purple bougainvillea.

She walked through the gate and smelled the jacaranda tree. Kids rocketed down a yellow slide and soared up on red swings attached to a jungle gym with a crow's nest. Little boys constructed bridges and buildings with Legos and drove plastic Go cars. These were the toys she'd seen on purchase requisitions. Here was the proof that the money had gone where it was supposed to.

She and Andre walked to the first cottage, its framed windows painted red, yellow, and green. In a classroom, the teacher wrote on a new whiteboard that was flanked by shelves of books with shining spines. Colored drawings of zoo animals hung from the walls. The room was full of kids. Only weeks before, some of them had scratched out lives on the streets. Now they sat at desks with laptops in front of them.

"A child can be a child here," Andre said.

Yet something about this innocence stabbed at her. She remembered the rooms at Hidden Road Academy and how they'd seemed warm and nurturing. Myles had considered those same rooms a prison.

They toured different groups of children and made their way to the dining hall cottage. Smells of cooking meat drifted through the open door to the kitchen. She and Andre sat on miniature chairs. Her knees rose above her waist and she felt like a young girl again.

A plump woman in a wide skirt brought them cups of coffee on saucers. Andre stirred in sugar and tapped the spoon on the side of the cup. "Do you remember your work before this?

"Pharma sales were never the right fit." *Hell, actually.*

"You needed Comunidad de Niños and we needed you," he said.

He was too discreet to mention how low she became after her son's banishment and the collapse of her marriage. "This job has meant a lot to me," she said.

"But you helped us more than we helped you. And it is only right that Comunidad de Niños helps *you* now."

The giggles and shouts outside faded. "What do you mean?"

All the lightness had vanished from his face. He slipped off his spectacles and his blue eyes caught hers. "Unity Coast could not do the loan."

Her hand flinched. Her coffee spilled onto the saucer and the red plastic tablecloth. She held her voice steady and said, "The loan from Comunidad de Niños was temporary. The bank loan was supposed to replace it."

"Our credit officer says 'no.' The auditors will make this a major deviation from the credit policy."

She squeezed the coffee cup.

Andre laid his hand on her shoulder. "It is not so bad, Fiona. Now Wade comes to work with us and he earns a very good salary. You will pay it back quickly."

"I could—no, we could—go to jail."

He laughed. "Comunidad de Niños is my foundation. I make the rules. We all do what we have to do so that Myles is saved."

She stared at the dirty yellow light slanting through the windows. The room had grown smaller and hotter around the little chairs and tables.

CHAPTER TWENTY-TWO

FIONA

Andre had promised that she'd repay Comunidad de Niños in a few weeks. He should have known that his bank wouldn't approve the loan. Fiona had the feeling he'd always intended that she borrow from the foundation.

When Andre dropped her off, she was too crestfallen to stay at work. She drove home. Once inside the house, she heard someone talking in the living room. "It's as if O'Keefe moved on to a new phase." The voice was high and fluty. She wondered if Jasper had brought some woman to see his paintings. Some younger woman.

"She was a great influence," Jasper said.

Jasper hated comparisons to Georgia O'Keefe. He was trying to impress this person. Fiona headed to the living room. When she saw who Jasper was speaking with, she stopped in the doorway.

The voice came from a man. He was well over six feet tall with the bull neck and swollen torso of a weightlifter. The hand-painted red and yellow tie seemed too small for his purple shirt. Yellow pants? The stranger pointed at the painting of a naked man with a dream catcher. The sun from the bay window lit up the blue and brown feathers and made the beige rocks glow. The man turned and his buzz cut seemed to emphasize his lopsided grin. He approached and his hand swallowed hers.

"You must be Fiona. I'm Harold Wainscott." He reached into his shirt pocket and produced a thick card with gold lettering. It displayed an email and a phone number. No business name or profession. Not even an address.

"Are you an art collector?" Fiona asked.

"I think of myself more as an art investor," Wainscott said.

Jasper said, "Harold caught my work online and wanted to look at it in person."

Jasper was trying to keep his voice relaxed, trying to be the artist who was above caring about buyers. But anyone could see that he was about to leap out of his freshly polished boots.

"I made my money in biotech," Wainscott said. He pointed to Jasper's painting. "Now I get to pursue my passions."

Fiona said, "Someday Jasper's work is going to be famous." At least that was the fantasy.

"Harold has connections with galleries all over the U.S.," Jasper said.

Wainscott seemed to focus more on her than Jasper. Some men couldn't help honing in on the only woman in a room. "Assuming I don't snap these up myself," he said. He laughed and his voice pitched even higher. "I love, absolutely love, discovering new talent."

Jasper had put on his prized green and yellow shirt and fixed his hair back with his best wood and leather barrette. She wanted to tell him to take a breath. Give Goliath some space to pull himself into the paintings. Still, it was nice to see Jasper so happy.

"I understand you run a charity that helps kids," Wainscott said.

"A private foundation, actually."

"Helping children is my other passion. That's what my own foundation contributes to."

Foundation. Ex-biotech. Her donor sensors kicked in and the words came out before she considered them. "Our foundation has orphanages and shelters in seven countries. We try to get kids off the street and give them an education. Keep them out of gangs and prostitution."

Wainscott seemed to tilt a little toward her. "My wife's from Brazil. Any operations in Latin America?"

"All of them."

The enormous head drew back. "Now that's very interesting." He turned to Jasper. "I'd say this is a two-fer. Your work and the kind of foundation I'm interested in."

A two-fer? Really? Donors never got this excited over an elevator pitch.

"Do you happen to have a card?" he asked.

She dug one out of her canteen purse. The card looked miniature and fragile in his hand. "I hope I can be in touch with both of you," he said.

She and Jasper accompanied him down the hallway to the front door. Why did she have the feeling that Wainscott had been waiting for her to arrive? She wondered what Wade would think.

Jasper shut the door and waved. Jasper never waved through windows. He draped his arm around her and she sloughed it off. Her instincts were pinging. "Did he seem strange to you?"

"The guy thought my paintings were great, so there must be something wrong with him?"

"I didn't mean it that way."

"Well, he loved my work—no matter what you say. He wants to see a full portfolio."

She went to her kitchen and sat down at the birch table. Its sleek shininess seemed to reflect Harold Wainscott. He'd been too perfect, all his interests aligned with theirs. He was more interested in Comunidad de Niños than Jasper's paintings. There was something wrong with this man. Just look at the clothes he wore.

CHAPTER TWENTY-THREE

WADE

The next day Wade drove to work. He wanted to get back to the normal world and try to forget—if only for a day—Myles' drug buying and kidnapping. And the promise he'd made to Andre.

His office was on the 29th floor of the tallest building downtown, one floor below senior management and two below the penthouse restaurant. Exactly where Wade wanted to be in his bank. He arrived at seven thirty to the chatter from early-morning arrivals standing over cubicles. Wade breathed in the smell of fresh coffee. His shoulders loosened, then his chest and thighs and calves.

First one, then two, then five people popped out from behind the half-walls. Someone started to applaud and they all joined in. Evidently the regional president had beamed out the news about Myles' safe return. Wade shook hands. The women—and some of the men—embraced him and he realized how much he cherished this place.

Wade had one of the three offices on the floor. He shut the door and let the room settle him into the life he'd had only a week before. He took in the family and work pictures, then the credenza crammed with plexiglass-covered awards and models of buildings he'd financed. He nudged the smooth globe on the walnut stand. His fingers stopped on Mexico. He remembered the teetering houses glowing in the beams of his headlights, the dust floating through the window and sticking to his face, then Flaco's rotund shadow holding a gun in his shaking hand.

He just had to work. That would make the memory dissipate and fade. Wade made phone calls and replied to emails. Two hours later his phone rang from the reception desk on the ground level. To his surprise, the caller was Myles. "I figured it was about time I saw your office," his son said.

Wade and Fiona had let Myles stay home from school for another day to recover. Instead of watching TV or playing video games, Myles had chosen to visit him. Wade was touched. But he was also wary. As he waited for Myles to make his way to the 29th floor, he thought about how remorseful his son had been after his return. The kidnapping had shaken and maybe changed him. But Wade had been hopeful too many times before.

Wade went to the security door and let him in. It felt odd to hug Myles at the bank. When Myles stepped back, Wade saw that he'd combed his hair and wore slacks and a long-sleeved shirt. Instead of his usual sneakers, he'd put on dress shoes that looked as if they'd never been shined. Was that the sweet smell of cologne? He wondered why his son was trying so hard.

Myles limped slowly beside him through his staff's half-cubicles. Alan Jericho, his most aggressive marketer, stepped forward to shake Myles' hand. "Glad you made it home safe," he said.

"My dad came through extra this time," Myles said.

"He comes through for everybody," Alan said. Alan, the marketer, always knew the flattering thing to say.

"Everybody here," Myles said.

Myles' sarcasm was still there. Alan didn't seem to know how to react and pulled up a vacuous smile.

"It was terrible what those bastards did to him," Wade said. "I'm proud of how he withstood it." He put his hand on his son's shoulder and Myles looked at the floor.

"I'm glad to be home," Myles said.

Wade led him across the floor and into his office. Myles stared at the bookcase of awards and pictures, then a large model.

"It's the Creighton building," Wade said. "At the time it was the biggest commercial real estate deal our bank ever did in San Diego. We worked for months. Seven days a week. A total ball-buster."

Myles touched the windows of the twenty-story building, then the fake lawn and miniature plastic figures and model cars. "I remember. It was why you missed my fourth-grade pageant."

Wade winced. Even when his son didn't mean to, his words could burn the air inside him.

"It was no big deal," Myles said. "Only trophy wives came."

He hobbled to Wade's desk and looked down at the manila folders. "People still use these things?" He took in the picture of the three of them at the resort in the Dominican Republic. "God, that is so old. I'm like twelve."

Snorkeling, fishing, piña coladas. Their last good vacation.

"Super duper grouper," Myles said.

A waiter's words had turned into their slogan. Why hadn't they taken more trips? Because Myles changed and hated family vacations. Because a deal had always sucked away Wade's time.

Wade pointed to the yoga mat rolled up in the corner. "I'm the only senior VP who openly displays one in his office."

Myles grinned. "That slays."

"Is that good?"

"Yeah, Dad. It means you're a real rebel."

It was nice to hear a bit of snark after all Myles had gone through. Wade retrieved bottles of Perrier from the mini-fridge and he and

Myles sat at the round table. "What's it like being home?" Wade asked.

"I feel like the world gave me another chance."

He sounded sincere. "That's a good way of looking at it," Wade said.

"Melissa left a message she isn't at school. She's sick."

Anything to do with Melissa raised Wade's heart rate. He drank from the Perrier bottle. It pricked his throat like needles. "Will you call her back?"

"A week ago, I would've like cut class to talk to her."

"And?"

"Why touch poison?"

It was exactly what Wade wanted to hear. And Myles knew it.

"You know me and girls," Myles said. "I forget how easy it is to slide into destructive friendships."

Myles sipped Perrier and let the Hidden Road terminology resonate between them. Wade remembered the warnings from the staff at Hidden Road. Kids would hug their counselors and spout the principles they'd learned to get them off their backs. They'd do the same at home when they angled for something. Fiona had already erased the dating restriction. Did he want a relaxation of the curfew, less required courses at school, more car time?

"Mom told me you were going to work for Andre. It was like part of the deal. The deal for getting my ransom money."

Wade nodded.

"But you're like the king here." His face trembled. "I'm sorry. Really, really sorry."

Myles had come to apologize. Wade felt small. He set his hand on his son's arm. "You're worth it."

A knock on the door. Alan Jericho came inside and Wade stiffened. He pushed the emotion off his face.

"A package just arrived," Alan said and handed Wade a FedEx envelope. "It didn't take long for the world to know you're back."

He left and Myles stared at the envelope. "Shouldn't you see what it is?"

Wade opened it only because Myles wanted him to. It was a photo. Wade stifled a gasp. In the picture, Myles stood in front of the house in La Jolla. Something was written in magic marker over it. "A deal is a deal."

Wade shoved it back into the envelope. He pressed his arms against the hard, cold table. He couldn't start shaking. Not now.

"What is it?" Myles asked.

"Nothing. Just a photo of a building we financed."

He got up, walked to his desk, and looked at his computer terminal. His arms prickled under his shirt. The picture told him what was at stake. Nothing else mattered—not his career, not his marriage.

"What's wrong, Dad?"

"I was just thinking about what a nice change it will be to work with Andre," he said.

"You don't look like it will be nice."

"Sure it will."

Myles cocked his head at him. "Were you talking to Andre in the car?"

"When?"

"On the way back from Tijuana."

Wade shook his head. "That was your mom."

Myles stared into his eyes. His son knew he was lying.

CHAPTER TWENTY-FOUR

After Myles left, Wade stared out the window of the twenty-ninth floor and tried to think of a strategy. If he went to the police, all he had was a picture of Myles with some vague words on it. What could the police do?

He needed to get his mind away from Andre and analyzed some deals. A few hours later his phone rang and the caller ID said it was Chad Fisher. Chad had worked with him at another bank ten years before. "Is it true?" Chad asked. "Are you really joining Andre's bank?"

"How did you hear?" Wade said.

"I work for him."

It didn't seem possible that Chad could be at a sketchy bank like this. He'd been the toughest credit manager at Wade's old institution. Every detail had to be right.

"Did you call to congratulate me?" Wade asked.

"Something like that." There was no enthusiasm in his voice. "We have to talk," Chad said.

"Sure. Just say where."

"We'll meet at the little bar in the hotel where we talked about your son. Three o'clock today." He hung up.

They would meet at the U.S. Grant Hotel, the same place Wade had met him a year and a half before. It was the day after Fiona discovered the OxyContin in Myles' closet. Chad's own daughter had had drug and cutting problems, and he'd saved her by sending her to a special school. Wade wanted his advice.

That day the expansiveness of the hotel's lobby—elaborately carved furniture, great Persian rugs, huge gilded mirrors, and glowing chandeliers—had given them a kind of privacy. Wade had always viewed Chad as a credit officer, a job in which a lack of sympathy was a basic requirement—his nickname was Chad the Impaler. But when Wade related what Fiona and he had endured, Chad's eyes got blurry. He'd always had a tremor and his tumbler of scotch shook in his hand. Their unmanageable children connected them more than their profession ever would.

"It's like juggling hand grenades," Chad had said. "You get to a point where you want something good to happen for your kid. You want it so bad . . . you'll even make it up." His smile was so pained it seemed naked. "No one understands until it's your child who might never reach twenty." Chad pushed a card for Hidden Road Academy across the black, lacquered table. "Sometimes a parent has to do things he doesn't think himself capable of."

Wade was sure that Hidden Road had saved his son's life. Now Chad had called him and not mentioned the treatment center. He hadn't said a word about his daughter or Myles. That was odd.

The little bar was tucked in just beyond the lobby beside a marble-floored atrium. Not even piped-in music disturbed its quiet. Chad sat in a corner close to the French doors. Wade lowered himself opposite. The chandelier lights and the table's candle sparked through a martini Chad had already ordered for him.

Chad scooted forward on the banquette. His sun-bleached face looked puffy and his arm tremor was worse than Wade remembered. He'd grown stout. "Why didn't you talk to me before you picked up a grenade?" he said.

Wade drew back. "What?"

Chad sucked on his scotch and stared at the oriental wood sketches on the wall. A pack of Marlboros sat on the table. He was a smoker again. "This place is a shit explosion waiting to happen. The fuse is already lit."

"You're going to have to be a little less poetic," Wade said.

"Up to now, I knew I was walking along the side of a cliff, but I didn't look down. Now I'm starting to see past the cobwebs and into the dark corners. This could be bombs going off and craters smoking."

"What the hell are you talking about?"

Chad leaned closer and squeezed the edges of the table. "You can't work for Andre."

His breath rippled off him in rancid waves. Wade couldn't remember Chad ever being this rattled before.

"Tell your old management you came to your senses. They'll forgive anything to get their rainmaker back."

But what about the people who'd sent that picture? Wade shifted on the chair and the upholstered fabric scraped against him. "Andre saved my son's life. I owe him big."

"You know what he'll do to you for that? He'll ride you like a horse that's late for the glue factory."

Wade rewound the words and sort of understood them. "Why are you still there?" he asked.

"You know what it looks like when you're downsized. If you only stay a few months at the next place, no one wants to hire you. I need a year with Andre. Then I'm gone."

Wade sipped his martini. It was so bitter it puckered his mouth.

"I get it—you owe him for your son. So pay him back some other way." Chad seemed to press into the fleeced back of the banquette. He stared at the wall and the white squares and rectangles of the floor-to-ceiling paneling. "Have you looked where Andre's capital came from?"

"From all those businesses he owned in Mexico."

Chad shook his head. "It's from his wife's family."

That was a surprise. Fiona had always said that Andre was a self-made millionaire.

"No one talks about how Carmela's family made their money," Chad said.

Wade remembered meeting her at a Comunidad de Niños event. Every part of her face looked surgically tightened, her perfume a thick cloud around her. "It covers up what a dragon smells like," Fiona had said.

Two men walked through the French doors and sat down at the bar's marble counter at the far end of the little room. They ordered and the black-vested bartender pulled an amber bottle from glass shelves.

"I don't like the look of those two," Chad whispered. He raised his glass and they clinked. "To a renewed partnership." His voice could have projected to the back of an auditorium.

"To tons of real estate deals," Wade said. He saw that the men at the bar had their backs to them, but the mirror in front reflected their table. More mirrors hung between the brass sconces on the paneled walls.

Chad squeezed the crystal candle funnel as if he were trying to grasp the flame. He tilted toward Wade. "Then there's the cash from Mexico. It's all legal as shit, but it still doesn't seem right."

"Cash from Mexico?"

"People use Uncle Sam's bills there all the time. Consolidators rake them up from hotels and restaurants and mom-and-pop currency exchanges. They wrap them in plastic bales and ship them here in armored cars. All declared at the border."

"So what's the problem?"

The tumbler of scotch trembled in Chad's hand. He stilled it with his other hand and took a sip. "Who knows where that cash really comes from? There're currency exchanges on every corner in Tijuana. Too many for just the tourists. Sometimes the bags get delivered to our building late at night in unmarked vans."

"You think it's . . ." Wade glanced around. The men at the bar weren't looking at them in the mirrors. "Do you think it's drug money?"

Chad's tumbler was wet. He raised his eyebrows. "Let me give you a warning. Stay away from Egberto Martinez."

Wade recognized the name. He was on Fiona's board. She called him the Mexican Rottweiler and said he brought indigestion to any meeting.

"Martinez is the bank's major shareholder," Chad said.

How was he supposed to stay away from the bank's owner?

Chad gulped from his scotch. He contorted his mouth as if it were gasoline. "We've got five major shareholders, all directors on the board. Two are Andre and Martinez, and the other three I've never met. I don't know where or when the board meetings are."

Board members always insisted on talking with the chief credit officer. The wrong credit man, or the wrong policies, would quickly crash a bank so oriented to growth.

He couldn't possibly take this job. He had to talk to the police and get out of this sinkhole.

"Who lent you the ransom money?" Chad asked.

"What?"

"The ransom money. Who lent it to you?"

The martini scalded Wade's stomach. "You did."

Chad stared at him. "I didn't book any loan for you."

Andre's bank was too small for the chief credit officer not to know about a four-hundred-thousand-dollar loan. "But I signed a promissory note. I got the money."

Chad leaned back. He sipped his scotch and the ice rattled. "Shit."

It hit Wade then. Hit him like everything else about Fiona. "Andre had the foundation make the loan, didn't he?"

Chad didn't answer. The silence stretched out.

"But the promissory note I signed was made out to Unity Coast," Wade said.

"I never saw it."

Fiona had taken the money from her own foundation. This was embezzlement. This was prison time. The table quivered under Wade's arm.

Chad raised his tumbler. "Here's to walking together in tall cotton."

Wade took a quick swig of the martini. It burned down his throat.

Chad whispered, "Be very careful. You've got a son and wife to protect."

CHAPTER TWENTY-FIVE

WADE

It was dark out, and the light from inside the house spotlighted the worry on Fiona's face. He was supposed to call before he showed up. Wade didn't care. This was not going to be a cordial conversation.

"What's wrong?" she said.

"We need to talk." He didn't wait for her to invite him in. He pushed past her.

The changes in the house made him even more angry. The living room was so red it looked as if skin had been torn off the walls. Then there were Jasper's horrible paintings. Desiccated men and women stared out, their lined faces matching the harsh fissures in the surrounding rocks.

"I guess every house needs a little Darwin," he said.

Fiona frowned. "You're angry at me."

He sat on the red sofa. She sat on the matching upholstered wingback chair so her coffee table stood between them. Down the hallway, an opera rose from his old office. The soprano's voice shimmied above the other voices to something just short of a scream.

"At least I'd tell you if I did something illegal," he said.

She looked down. Her hands tangled themselves on her lap the way they always did when she'd done something behind his back. "It was supposed to be a loan for just a few days," she said. "Until Andre's bank came through."

"You knew it was against the law. That's why you didn't tell me."

"Come on, what was I supposed to do? You couldn't get the money we needed."

He lifted a leopard-spotted pillow and stared at it. His jaw was pulsing. "I guess you were going to get around to cluing me in *someday*."

"I didn't want to make you part of it."

He laughed. "Right. Oh, it's just my wife. She was the one who"— he put his fingers in quotes— "*borrowed* money from the foundation she ran. She thought it was only for a few days. She's the one in jail, not me. I had no idea."

Her face seemed to curl in on itself. He knew she hated his sarcasm more than his anger. "You know there are more important things than your pristine reputation," she said. "Like your son."

He pushed his back into the couch and crossed his legs. Fiona always struck back with guilt. But she wasn't going to escape so easily. "What else haven't you told me? Maybe you did another deal with Andre. You know, get us the money for the ransom and Wade will come work for you. I suppose you wanted to protect me when you didn't tell me that too."

She clenched the twill sides of the chair and stood. She was shaking. "You have to leave." The orchestra from Jasper's opera seemed to swell around her.

But he wasn't finished. Not even close. He slapped the pillow onto the couch beside him. "So who risked his life to save *our*—not *your*—son? Who's taking a job he doesn't want because that was the deal for saving Myles' life? Do you even think about the husband you kicked out of his own house?"

"You mean the man who loved his damn job more than his wife and child?"

He shook his head. "Just because you say it a thousand times doesn't make it true."

Fiona's hand rose to her face and she swatted away tears.

Wade saw someone at the entrance to the living room. He hadn't heard Myles open the front door. How long had he been standing there?

"Mom. Dad. Please stop fighting."

"It seems that I'm the only one with the problem," Wade said. "Your mother has you and Jasper and the house."

"You know, sarcasm is nothing but a shield," Myles said.

Words from Hidden Road. Words that were as hard as a punch. "Do you think you're the parent now?"

"Stop it!" Fiona yelled.

Myles' whole body seemed to flinch. "One thing Hidden Road taught me. I can't keep you guys together."

He turned from the living room and stomped up the stairs, two at a time. In a few seconds, an electric guitar screeched from Myles' room. Then a death growl. Pounding drums grew louder and louder until they seemed to pummel Jasper's opera.

Wade told himself he had a right to be furious. He hadn't done this; she had. She was the one who'd broken the law.

Fiona sat in the wingback chair. She looked up, pain in her eyes. "Do you remember what Myles' psychologist told us? He said that you and I had to stay together to help our son. That was why Myles acted out. He was stopping us from splitting apart."

Wade's head dropped. He slowly collapsed into the couch. For a time he heard the heavy metal guitars and drums. The volume faded and he didn't hear the opera. Only the silence between them. "Why do we keep hurting one another?" he said.

"Because we don't want to blame ourselves."

She was right. He couldn't deny it. More heavy metal drums beat through the ceiling. They both looked up. It was as if Myles were pounding against the house.

"So how do we get out of this?" Wade asked.

"We should both quit working for Andre at the same time," she said. "Then I could run to the regulators and make a confession. At least your career would be saved."

How could she hate him so much one moment, and be willing to sacrifice her life for him the next? It made no sense. And yet, he would do the same for her. All their years of arguing and yelling and crying, clawing and scratching... They could still forgive each other.

He knew who to talk to then. The FBI would know options for how to get out of this.

CHAPTER TWENTY-SIX

WADE

That night FBI Special Agent Rodrigues sat in Wade's little kitchen. This time she had no laptop and wore jeans. As she sipped Wade's reheated, burnt coffee, he saw her eyeballing the chipped mug, the dented and cracked oak table, and the dusty light fixture. Her gaze wandered to the sink full of dishes.

"I usually clean up in the morning," he said.

She looked down at the envelope he had on the table. "You wanted to talk."

"You know Andre loaned us the money for the ransom."

She nodded.

"Let me tell you what I had to do in exchange. Commit to work at his bank."

He didn't see any surprise in her eyes. She picked up the mug and sipped the coffee.

"I don't like what the bank is involved in," he said. "Apparently they have some criminal clients. They also might be involved in money laundering."

That should have produced a reaction. If not surprise, at least concern. She ticked her short nails on the table, first one hand, then the other. "Are you still going to work with them?"

Wade opened the envelope and pulled out the picture he'd received of Myles outside the house. "I tried to back out of the deal. Then someone sent me this."

Rodrigues lifted the picture toward the light fixture and read the inscription: *A deal is a deal.* She gave it back. Wade waited. She picked up her mug and set it back down as if aiming for a spot on the table.

She said, "You suspect something, but I don't think you have any idea what kind of people these are." She waited a few seconds for him to take that in. "Let me tell you what they're involved in. Drugs, prostitution, arms, human trafficking, and money laundering. They lock up thirteen-year-old girls in bordellos and hang their enemies' families from bridges."

The fear he'd been pushing away burbled in his stomach. "How in hell did they manage to buy a bank?"

"It was 2009, the year after the economic crash, and financial institutions were failing everywhere. The Treasury Department was selling them to anyone with cash."

"I'll bet his wife gave Andre the capital, didn't she?" he said.

Rodrigues nodded. "The Saezes."

It was the first he'd heard that name. Just the sound of it made him uneasy. "How do I get out of this?"

"Maybe you don't get out of it."

"What?"

She pushed her coffee mug toward him on the table. She leaned forward. "A violent drug cartel owns a chartered bank in this country. Doesn't that offend you?"

He knew where she was taking him. "You want me to help bring down Andre's bank."

"Ask yourself . . . what would be the right thing to do?"

"But Andre saved my son's life."

She leaned back in the seat. Her shoe beat against the tiled floor. "He also arranged to loan you four hundred thousand dollars for the ransom. But it wasn't for free, was it?"

He realized it then. Special Agent Rodrigues had her own agenda. She always had. "This is why you met with us so fast, isn't it? Not because Myles was kidnapped, but because Fiona worked for Andre."

"We also wanted to help you get your son back."

Bullshit. The FBI wanted to use them.

Rodrigues rose and went to the fridge. She found the pitcher of water and a glass in the cabinet. Sitting back down, she poured for him. "Drink. You need to keep hydrated with more than coffee."

He refused to touch the glass. "Why do the Saezes want me to work with them so badly?"

"Good question. And the answer is simple. They love real estate but have hardly ventured into the U.S. There's too much risk. Someone might learn who they are and the courts would grab their assets. But if they had the cover of a legitimate financial institution and a star banker . . ."

Unity Coast Bank could conceal who was really buying the buildings. And his reputation would give them credibility in the market.

"What do you think they'll do if you refuse to work with them?" she said.

"I don't know." But he did know. The picture of Myles in front of the house told everything.

"Here's something else to consider," she said. "We won't be able to protect you unless you work with us."

"But you're a government agency. Your job is to protect people like us."

She shook her head. "When you jump into the water with sharks it's not up to the FBI to pull you out."

Her nails synchronized with the ticks of his father's clock on the wall.

"Will you stop the tapping?"

Her fingers froze in mid-flight. She shifted on the chair and clasped the mug with both hands. "I'm going to highlight another fact you already know. A bank usually only has twenty or thirty thousand in cash on hand. It takes at least three business days to get four hundred thousand delivered."

Wade saw expectation in her eyes. She was waiting for her words to land. When they did, they hit him like a fist. "Andre ordered the currency before he talked to Polanco," he said. "Before Myles was kidnapped."

"Maybe Melissa's friend told Andre that your son was coming to Tijuana."

Roberto, the drug dealer. "But why would Andre kidnap Myles?"

She started to tap her nails on the table and stopped. "Suppose Andre needed a way to make you beholden. You're a loyal guy—even I see it. It's your greatest weakness. So Andre gets you the money for the ransom and saves your son. In return you're supposed to come on board at his bank. But Andre needed one more thing to sew up your loyalty. That was Fiona. He tricked her to illegally take money from the foundation."

She knew. She knew everything.

"All it takes is one word to the right people and Fiona could go to prison, Wade."

He squeezed the cold glass of water. He wanted to break it in his hand.

"Let me clue you in on something else," she said. "If you help us, we don't care that Fiona took that money. We don't even care about the little drug deal your son was doing with that girl in Mexico."

As if that isn't a threat.

He couldn't sit any longer. He walked to the living room. His chest was heaving. He stared out the big window beyond the lights of the sloops and Navy ships in the harbor. He imagined himself in the dark, swirling water. Sharks were pulling him under. All because of the man Fiona thought was a perfect banker, a man Wade had always known was a fake. But Andre was worse than that.

Wade balled up his fists. *It's time to stop being a cuckold.*

When he returned to the kitchen he couldn't sit down, he was so angry.

"Are you ready to do the right thing?" Rodrigues said.

He didn't care about doing the right thing. "How do we destroy them?"

She leaned back in the chair. She looked so relaxed now, so in control. "Go work there. Play along."

Could he talk to Andre and keep the hate out of his voice? Could he keep the rage out of his eyes?

"Just fit in," she said. "We'll protect you."

Rodrigues rose. Like all good salespeople, she knew when to make an exit. He walked her to the door. "This is a heroic thing you're doing," she said.

Heroism had nothing to do with it.

When she'd left he went back to the big window to stare at the lights from the buildings and the ships in the harbor. Beyond them was nothing but black. He thought of how his father had labored seven days a week at his bank. Wade was sixteen when he'd opened the house's front door to police. They said his father had died inside his Lincoln Mark VI in the bank's parking lot. A massive heart attack. Maybe he would also die alone in a bank's parking lot.

From bullets.

CHAPTER TWENTY-SEVEN

On Monday, Wade told his boss he was leaving for Andre's bank. "I assume you know their reputation," Beverly said. She ordered him to clear out immediately. He didn't fare better with his colleagues. They shook his hand and stared at him as if he'd been arrested. A man from Security carried his box of personal possessions to the lobby. As Wade looked a last time at the elevators to the twenty-ninth floor, the guard said, "I'm sorry you got fired."

On Tuesday morning Wade lugged pictures, expensive pens, a walnut clock, and his desk ornaments to Unity Coast Bank. He pretended he was excited to be at his new office on the very top of the building—the third floor. Andre limped over carpet that smelled new. He pointed out the redwood desk, the large redwood table, and the matching bookshelves and credenza. He seemed proud of the spindly bamboo palm and a white-leafed peace lily. "We only have real plants," he said.

The odor from the peace lily was overwhelming. Wade tried not to inhale and thought about how nice it would be to put this fake of a CEO in prison.

"Let me show you the *pièce de résistance*," Andre said. He rested his hand on an antique globe of the world that was more finely crafted than the one Wade had left behind. "We want that your clients think that you changed to a better *banque.*"

A kingly office in a shitty building in a shitty location for a bush-league organization. His colleagues and competitors would think he'd had a stroke.

Andre motioned him to the table. His eyes gleamed behind the thick walls of his glasses. He set down a single sheet of bank stationary with a heading that said *Executive Vice President, Commercial Real Estate.* "You will not be disappointed with the pay," he said.

Wade set his hands on the cold wooden table and studied the page. The first number of the employment letter was an eye-popper. A thirty percent increase in salary plus bonus plus options on ownership shares. Each month he worked for Andre would reduce the loan he owed, the entire four hundred thousand dollars expunged in two years.

If he was still alive.

"Now you are happy you join my bank," Andre said.

"And I've kept up my side of the deal."

"You are a man of the words you promise." Andre gave him a warm smile. "We are so happy you are here."

Andre had a charm that was hard to hate, Wade thought. But he'd manage. After Andre left, he walked to the window to take in his new view. He saw a busy street in front of Macy's, JC Penney, and the mall's upscale restaurant—Red Lobster. His other window looked out on the mobile phone sales office and its steady line of immigrant customers. Maybe coffee would help. He made a cup of dark roast from the Keurig machine. It tasted too bitter, but at least the smell blotted out the odor of the peace lily. Somehow, he was going to kill that plant.

An hour later Andre returned with a thin, tall man with a hatchet face. The stranger's black hair was swept with grey, and he wore a silk shirt with blue paisley patterns. His bolo tie was crested with a silver and gold ram's-head clasp. He didn't wear cowboy boots, but his belt buckle was as big as Texas.

"This is Egberto Martinez," Andre said.

The major shareholder Chad had warned him to stay away from, the Mexican Rottweiler who was on Fiona's board. Martinez shook his hand so lightly it felt threatening. When he let go, his brown eyes bore into Wade's. "I've heard about you." His baritone voice had an irritating nasal tone. No Spanish accent.

"I'm delighted to be part of the team," Wade said.

"Are you?" Martinez gave the antique globe a slow twirl. He watched the world spin for a few seconds and made his way to Wade's desk. He picked up the picture of Fiona and Myles. "You're not divorced?"

"He's separated," Andre said.

"Separated but not divorced," Martinez said. "Hope is the last thing a man lets go of."

There was a lethal edge to that sentence. Color heated Wade's cheeks.

"He does yoga to win his wife back," Andre said.

Martinez studied Wade's stomach. "Really?"

"Let me inform you why I do yoga," Wade said. "Because I enjoy it."

Martinez gave him a thin smile and sat at the redwood table, the largest piece of furniture in Wade's new office. He stretched his long legs. Wade sat opposite. Andre extracted bottles of water from Wade's new mini fridge and placed himself beside Martinez.

"We want to know how fast you grow our business," Andre said. "Mr. Martinez likes numbers."

In a meeting like this, Wade always started with the landscape. He gave a discourse on determining the right asset class, geographic targets, ranges of loan-to-value, and minimum borrower capital requirements. As he talked, Andre pursed his mouth and rubbed his ring. He looked bored so Wade jumped to Return on Equity. For bosses, nothing was so arousing as discussing profit numbers. Wade only got through a few sentences before Andre interrupted him.

"We want something very simple," Andre said. "That we are the leaders in commercial real estate lending in San Diego. In five years."

It was a marketing plan from Mars. Wade didn't know where to start. He pivoted to the major shareholder. "I'm not sure what your role is here, Mr. Martinez. What do you oversee?"

For what seemed like ten seconds, Martinez rolled an expensive blue and platinum Montblanc between his fingers. "Personnel," he said.

Andre guffawed. "You will find that Mr. Martinez never smiles when he makes the jokes."

Martinez picked up the water bottle and turned it in his hand. His nails looked professionally manicured. "I'm giving you your first deal," he said and set down the bottle. His briefcase was black and elongated like a doctor's bag. He opened it and pulled out a neatly rubber-banded folder. Most of Wade's loan packages arrived as electronically transmitted computer files. This was old school.

"I am just passing on the paperwork for this deal from people I know," Martinez said. "I have nothing to do with it. You won't have to worry about lending to an owner."

Be worried about lending to a bank owner. People went to prison for making those loans.

Wade opened the folder. As he read, Martinez tapped his pen on the table. Wade felt like a horse being spurred. The borrower was a group of partners in an LLC who had to be cutouts for Mexican cartels. They were buying Felton Tower, a twenty-story building with views of the harbor and top tenants. It was a San Diego jewel. That's why the price was $280 million.

Wade put on his sad-but-firm, loan-denial face. "We're too small for a transaction this size."

Andre slipped off his spectacles. He smiled as if he relished Wade's obscured image. "Think large, Wade. *Plus grande.* Why not a syndication?"

It was mind-bendingly bold. Unity Coast had never financed a major commercial real estate transaction. These men not only wanted to source a gigantic deal, they wanted Wade to convince other lenders to fund most of the loan. His credibility in the market would evaporate in this one bad transaction.

"The lead financial institution is supposed to finance at least as much as every other participant," Wade said. "But if you can only take ten million you'll never persuade other banks to take twenty-five or more."

"You act as if there's a law against it," Martinez said.

"Not *written* law."

"Everyone in San Diego wants to be part of your deals," Andre said.

Only a very high-profile real estate financier could sell a transaction like this to other lenders. That was why Andre had recruited him.

Martinez set a sample term sheet in front of him. The interest rate, the down payment, and the maturity were more lender-friendly than anything he'd seen in years. This was actually possible.

Martinez pointed his Montblanc at him. "When will you get it done?"

Wade had to slow this down. He needed time to talk with Rodrigues. "I'll need to sit with the borrowers."

"They are very wealthy people," Andre said. "I have the background that you will put into the files. You do not need to meet them."

Know-Your-Client rules required him to meet with the LLC's members and thoroughly understand their businesses. Wade looked inside the folder Martinez had given him and didn't recognize any of the names. This was impossible. The other participating banks weren't going to accept unknown borrowers.

Martinez rose. "I have to see Chad Fisher," he said.

Chad was the chief credit officer. He'd always been a fundamentalist about the procedures that regulators required. How could he go along with this?

"Come with me," Martinez said.

It wasn't a request.

CHAPTER TWENTY-EIGHT

WADE

Wade wasn't surprised to find Chad's office wedged into the middle of the second floor of Unity Coast Bank—most credit departments were located in the windowless bowels of a building. When Chad saw Wade and Martinez, he stood up from his desk. Grateful Dead played softly on his radio.

Martinez sniffed at the cigarette odor. He pointed his briefcase at the paper piles on the floor and on the credenza.

"It's all organized," Chad said. His hand pushed against a stack of pages on his desk as if he were steadying the tremor in his arm.

"I suppose that makes you feel indispensable." Martinez opened his doctor's-bag briefcase and lifted out a rubber-banded folder. "Send these to the usual bank in India."

Chad's shaking hands carefully pulled out heavy paper that looked like official documents. "This has nothing to do with real estate," Martinez said to Wade. "Let's go."

Wade was the only one who said goodbye when they left. Outside Chad's office, men with holstered pistols lugged canvas bags across the floor. They shouted in Spanish to a woman, and she opened a door to a large room. Two copier-like machines sucked up and wrapped U.S. currency in plastic. This had to be the cash from Mexico that Chad thought was dirty.

He followed Martinez down the stairs to the main lobby. Martinez stopped and his gaze swung from right to left as if absorbing data from the crowd of people in front of the tellers and loan officers. After a few moments he opened his briefcase and snaked his hand inside. "I have something for you."

Another deal from "friends"? Paper crinkled, and Martinez pulled out a brown bag, the kind that grocery stores used. "Welcome to our business."

Wade opened the top of the bag. It was half full of brown, sticky dates. His first thought was that they were poisonous.

"From Tunisia," Martinez said. "Some of the best in the world." Without another word, he walked out the back door to the parking lot and climbed into a Mustang from the seventies. It was in the Handicap spot. As he drove away, Wade wondered what the documents were that he'd given Chad. He returned to Chad's office and sat in front of his desk.

"Those were interesting papers Mr. Martinez gave you."

Chad gazed—longingly?—at the pack of Marlboros beside his laptop. "He uses us to process shipping documents for international trade deals." He put his fingers to his lips and pointed to the walls and ceiling as if his office was bugged. Chad leaned in and the smells of tobacco and sweat swept across the desk. "He ships gold all over the world," he whispered. "A lot comes from Colombia and goes to India. Some from South Africa to China. The gold never even touches down on U.S. soil. Just the shipping documents. Which go through us."

Wade kept his voice low. "What's wrong with that?"

"Nothing." But his raised eyebrows indicated "everything." "He also exports muscle cars from the sixties and seventies. They go to some interesting places. Panama, Paraguay, Macau, the Turks and

Caicos, the Philippines." All popular destinations for concealing dark money.

Chad shifted back in his chair and scowled at a stack of loan documents. "I'd better get busy. I've got another time bomb to approve."

Wade drew back. "You're letting a bad credit through?"

"I've been told my standards are too strict."

Chad used to be meticulous. Wade glanced at the Marlboros on Chad's desk, then the new paunch around his stomach. What had happened to him? Wade rose and walked around the piles of papers on the floor toward the door. As he passed the credenza, he saw a picture of Chad's daughter with a green ribbon around it. He should have asked about her earlier. "How is Haley doing?"

Chad's head drew back. "You don't know?"

"Know what?"

"Our girl took her life almost a year ago."

The air thickened. Words lumped in Wade's throat.

"Haley had a sickness . . . something we couldn't cure." His face was frozen but his eyes blinked. "She jumped off a building."

Wade stared down at his shoes, then the bottom of the credenza. Had he been so busy the last year he couldn't have called Chad?

"I needed a life raft," Chad said. "That's why I came here."

Where he'd barricaded himself inside this windowless office, shut the door, and smoked behind walls of paper.

In the hallway he thought about Myles. What if Andre and Martinez hurt him and the only thing left was a picture of a happy moment in Myles' life? Would his own life be like Chad's?

CHAPTER TWENTY-NINE

MYLES

The afternoon traffic made the Lyft ride from La Jolla take much longer than Myles had thought. He put on his earphones and listened to music while they rode. Archspire's drummer blasted out gravity beats while the vocalist snarled his incomprehensible phrases and the guitar riffed around them. He loved their pure technicality.

He looked up when they hit Chula Vista. It was nothing but car repair places, cheap motels, and every fast-food franchise known to man. When he saw Unity Coast Bank, he couldn't believe it. Just a cement box with miniature windows and a couple of emaciated palm trees. The car took him to the lumpy parking lot in the back. Was that actually laser tag? Myles hadn't seen one of those places since he was twelve. Next to it was a Chinese buffet. *Gag.* Myles turned off his music. Dropping in on his dad on his first day of work was supposed to be a happy surprise. But this place was fucking depressing.

And it was because of him.

His feet were recovering and he hardly limped as he made his way to the entrance. Inside, lines of people jabbered in all kinds of languages. Some woman rattled out Spanish and he told her who he was. Her eyes got all big and she switched to English. "You're

Wade's son. We're so thankful Andre got you back safe. Andre is amazing."

"My dad delivered the ransom," Myles said. "He could have been killed."

"Wade is amazing too."

The woman led him to a creaky elevator and pressed the faded third-floor button. "You will love his office," she said.

"His old office in the tower was *amazing*," Myles said.

She gave him one of those tight-ass smiles. "Someday Andre will give us our own building like that."

With a Chinese buffet and mini-golf.

The office was actually pretty glowed up compared to the rest of the place. The carpet looked barely stepped on. Nice wood furniture. A globe on a wooden stand that looked vintage. But no pictures and trophies of his deals. No rolled-up yoga mat.

His dad jumped up from the desk. "Aren't you supposed to be at school?"

"I wanted to check out your new place," Myles said. "I thought you'd be glad to see me."

"I am," his dad said.

His smile looked crooked. Maybe this would make him happier. "Melissa called me from her new school. She's in Massachusetts now."

"Good," his dad said. Was that all? His face should have lit up.

Someone knocked on the door. A round, blond man in a light blue suit. "You must be the *jeune homme* I saved," he said.

So this was Andre, the French guy his mom worked for. The dude walked with a hitch like he'd also gotten his feet beaten up. The big blue frames of his glasses looked like something from a Disney cartoon.

"We were very worried about you," Andre said. "But the world, it turns out okay."

Myles looked at his dad. "Thanks to him."

Andre said, "Now your father and your mother, we all work together at the bank and Comunidad de Niños. We change the world."

Hidden Road had been right about one thing. Don't trust a guy who promises to change your world. "How?" Myles asked.

"One customer at a time," Andre said.

His dad shifted on his polished shoes. He'd been a king where he worked before.

Andre pulled out his pocket handkerchief—dark blue like the frames of his glasses. "You know what my wife, Carmela, tells me this morning? She asks why Wade never visits. I ask the same question. You must have lunch with us on Saturday."

His dad's face looked like he was straining to lift something. He usually jumped at stuff like this.

Andre turned to Myles and his grin seemed to broaden into his bottle lenses. "You must come too. At one. A civilized time for the young man. Carmela wants so much that she meets you."

"Myles has schoolwork," his dad said.

Andre didn't seem to hear him. "When you visit you will taste my cabernet and zinfandel. My house in Tijuana has a wine cellar."

Tijuana. Just the name made Myles' insides go angsty. His dad must have known and that was why he'd put out the fake excuse about homework. He was trying to do him a solid.

"In life you must accept the shadows," Andre said. "The *bêtes noires,* the dark parts of who you are and what happens to you. This is the only way that you grow above the *horreur.* Myles, you will see that Tijuana is a jewel."

His dad needed this. It was the least he could do after ruining his job at the tower. Myles breathed through his fear as Hidden Road had taught him. "It's . . . it's fine."

CHAPTER THIRTY

WADE

The next night Wade picked up Myles at the house. The hall-way smelled of garlic and onions. Wade inhaled through his teeth so he wouldn't smell Jasper's cooking. As he waited with Fiona in the hallway, his son made his way down the stairs. Myles looked remorseful as he put his arm around Fiona. What had he done?

"Go ahead and tell him," Fiona said.

He wasn't going to get upset, despite the way his head had started to throb.

"I've decided to live with you, Dad," Myles said.

Wade's mouth opened.

"Mom and I both think it will be better."

Fiona stared at the floor. She had to be taking Myles' decision as a rebuke. It was like she'd been fired as a mother. "Are you sure?" Wade said, not certain whom he was asking.

"I need structure and boundaries. Mom and I are too enmeshed, too codependent. And this house has too many triggers."

All those Hidden Road terms made Wade wonder if Myles had written his speech beforehand. His son stamped up the stairs and was soon out of sight.

Wade imagined how much effort Fiona's smile took. His throat constricted. Sometimes he was so unfair to her. "It will only be for a few days," he said. "Then he'll want to come back."

"I think it's great that Myles and you will spend more time together," Fiona said. Despite all the fighting between them, Fiona always did what she thought best for her son.

Jasper emerged from the kitchen and brought another plume of garlic. Wade pretended he was happy to see him. Soon Myles clumped down the stairs with his suitcase. He kissed Fiona goodbye, gave Jasper a fist bump, and they were out the door. Once inside the Beamer, Myles grew absorbed in programming the car's Bluetooth. Double bass drums and a guitar whacked and screeched against the leather interior. A voice screamed like a devil.

"She has a great death growl," Myles said.

"It's a she?"

"Pretty dope, huh?"

She sounded like she was hawking up phlegm. But his son was playing his music for him. Wade didn't care what it sounded like.

"Can we eat beef tonight?" Myles said. "Or pork? OMG— sausage! Sausage would be awesome."

"Of course," Wade said. Tonight was about eating anything Myles' teenage body yearned for, even if it took his father a week to digest.

Twenty minutes later, they stood inside Wade's condo. Wade had forgotten to take out the garbage and it stank. But Myles didn't seem to notice. A teenage boy never smelled bad odors.

Myles walked to the dining room table and lifted up the rent notice. "You haven't paid?"

He was short this month, but the new salary would make up for it. "Just an oversight," Wade said.

"An oversight on a bill? You?"

It was embarrassing. Even his son knew he couldn't afford this high-rent condo. Wade looked down at the wine boxes on the floor. In the house in La Jolla, Myles had his own bed instead of a pullout couch.

Myles set down his suitcase and picked up Wade's guitar. He ran his fingers across the empty strings and the open chord was out of tune. "How come you never played when you lived with Mom and me?"

"No time," Wade said.

"I guess you had time after I moved away."

Wade wasn't sure what that meant. "I wanted to take up things beyond work."

Myles' eyes brightened as if he didn't believe what Wade had said. "Do you miss the house?" he asked.

He sure as hell wasn't going to let his son feel sorry for him. "I'm doing fine here." He had an idea then. Something better than just sausage. "How about a T-bone?"

"Really?" Myles' voice rose. "Can we afford it?"

"Of course we can afford it. I bet you don't get much steak around Jasper and Fiona."

"Jasper thinks cannibals got their starts at Burger King."

Wade laughed. Then he sighed. "It couldn't have been easy coming back from Hidden Road to Jasper."

Myles' mouth tightened. "I would have put up with anything to come home."

Would Hidden Road always stand between them? Wade didn't want to think about that tonight. Tonight, they'd bond with a blood-fest of beef. What was another hundred dollars added to the unpayable balance on his credit card? It would be a father-son meal before they had to go to Tijuana.

As he drove, Wade remembered his own special restaurant dinner when he was sixteen. Pictures of actors hung from the walls, and a man in a tux played movie music on a piano. Male waiters with white shirts and black vests stood beside burgundy-colored banquettes. He and his dad sat at a table for two facing each other over the dim light of a candle. His father's attention seemed to wrap around him and, for once, no brother or sister diffused the spotlight. The steaks were huge and the baked potato was drenched in butter and topped with chives and dollops of sour cream. "The broccoli is just for decoration," his father said. "Don't tell your mom." After they'd gotten halfway through the meal, his father asked, "What do you want to do in life?"

Wade didn't have to think about it. "I want to be in finance. Be part of the engine that makes the economy run."

His father didn't point out that Wade was appropriating his words. Instead he nodded sagely and sipped his martini. "Now that is a very noble ambition," he said.

Wade thought again of that meal as he and Myles sat down at Riordan's. His father would have liked the white tablecloths, lampshade candles, and dark wood paneling. He would have appreciated that the maître d' recognized Wade and said how nice it was to meet his son. But the maître d' never would have led his father to the back near the kitchen. Each time the door swung open, clouds of hickory, garlic, and basil drifted out.

A waiter in a white shirt soon hovered over them. "Real steak eaters always start with a martini or mixed drink," Wade said.

"I guess I'll have a martini?" Myles said

The waiter smiled. "Would you like a Coke or ginger ale?"

After the man withdrew, piped-in jazz folded over them. Wade saw Myles trying not to stare at the people leaning over their dates in the candlelit tables. He hoped that Myles would imagine himself here to close a deal, or on a Saturday night with a girl. Maybe the kidnapping had made him think about the rest of his life.

The drinks arrived. Wade said, "My dad took me to a place like this when I was in high school. It was the first time we talked about what I wanted to be in life. What are you thinking of doing?"

He waited, hoping that Myles wouldn't give a sarcastic smirk. But tonight his son sipped his Coke and seemed to consider the question. When Myles put down his drink, the candle flame flickered across his glass. "I want to start a business. One that makes a product that the whole world buys. Maybe with computers, but maybe something else. The kind of company everyone wants to work for."

For the first time Wade saw job passion igniting his eyes. "That's a noble ambition," he said.

"Noble?"

"I mean it's worthy of your talents."

Someone stood over them. It was Alan Jericho, the business developer who'd reported to Wade at his old bank. Alan reached down to shake their hands and said, "Don't get up."

Wade hadn't intended to.

"The department's not the same," Alan said.

Wade was supposed to offer encouragement about how well Alan would do without him. But Alan's face didn't look dejected.

Alan said, "Beverly hired a new senior VP from the East Coast. She's thirty-five."

Wade's eyebrows rose. "I haven't even been gone a week."

"You know Beverly. She probably had her eye on her for years."

In other words, Beverly had always been ready to replace him.

Alan itched his neck and glanced around the restaurant. Even now he scanned for prospects and clients. "Our new boss has done deals all over the U.S. She's really going to shake up the place. But in a good way. That's not to say we don't miss you."

Wade's hand tightened around the cold martini glass. An idea occurred to him. Maybe Alan deserved to finance something being purchased by a Mexican cartel. "I could have a participation for you in a couple of weeks."

Alan's face pinched.

"It's a big deal."

His former protégé heaved out a sigh so big and dramatic it was insulting. "After you left, we got a white paper on reputational risk. We only work with big, squeaky-clean institutions now."

Wade stared at him, the anger in his eyes beaming out more than words. But Alan never took back the comment. "Awfully nice of you to stop over to tell me how much I'm missed," Wade said.

"I'll leave you to your meal." Alan turned to Myles and said, "There's nothing like a steak at Riordan's."

Alan retreated to his date at the front of the restaurant.

Myles said, "Did he just double burn you?"

Wade couldn't manage the words to deny it. He looked down at the white tablecloth and the shimmering crystal water glass. The door to his old life was sealed as tight as a coffin.

"You know what I'd really like tonight?" Myles said. "City Tacos. They're like the gourmet of tacos." He ran his finger around Riordan's. "This place is a nursing home."

"I'd love tacos," Wade said.

Wade left too much money on the table and they walked outside to the Gaslamp and its noisy bars and eateries. The chill revived Wade. This night could still turn out well. His son was sharing the food that he loved.

"North Park is way more cool than around here," Myles said. "They have places to eat that actually opened this century."

Myles drove and Wade guided them with his phone. City Tacos was little more than a storefront with a few tables on the sidewalk and more tables and aqua-colored chairs inside. The blue walls were painted with flowers, and the lighting hung from the ceiling. They

sat down, and Wade breathed in the smells of fresh tortillas and cilantro. Behind the faded wooden bar, a blackboard listed the day's
specials. They ordered lamb, sausage, and chicken tacos with Oaxaca
cheese and garnished with pineapple, raisins, and almonds. Then
the special of scallops, leeks, bacon, and pepper-cream sauce. While
they ate, salsa trumpets sang from the speakers.

"All these tastes," Wade said. "It's glorious."

"Nothing like this in Utah," Myles said.

The words seemed spiteful, but his son was grinning. Wade
grinned back.

Myles pointed to Wade's shirt. "I like it better with the green
sauce on it."

Wade looked down at the stain. "Brooks Brothers will never be
the same." He took a spoonful of red sauce and dumped it next to
the green blotch. "It needed another color."

Myles started to giggle. "The dots look good," he said and flicked
some red sauce on his own shirt.

Wade didn't want their laughter to stop. But it did. Myles blinked
and his eyes brightened with tears. "I'm going to make you proud of
me, Dad."

Something crashed over Wade. He wanted to reach over and hug
his son. He pressed his hands into the restaurant's old wooden table
and said, "I'm already proud of you."

Myles shook his head. "I'm going to make up for it."

"You didn't kidnap yourself. It wasn't your fault, do you hear me?"

Myles was silent. Wade drank his Dos Equis. The taste of the
Mexican lime in the glass made him think about heading back to
Tijuana on Saturday. Nothing could happen in an afternoon. It was
just a couple of hours.

CHAPTER THIRTY-ONE

The house was so quiet for a Thursday morning. No shrieking guitar from Myles' room. No banging plates and bare feet stomping down the stairs or heavy thuds of a backpack. The sun was so warm it felt like skin around her.

She turned to look at Jasper asleep beside her. He never found it necessary to get up early. Should she shake him awake and confess the trouble that she and Wade were in? No, that would make it worse. He'd insist on an earnest talk with both of them and Wade would resent every minute and disagree with whatever Jasper said. But if she told Jasper she didn't want his help, he'd be miffed and hurt. She knew there was another reason that stopped her from confessing. As soon as she admitted to Jasper that she'd embezzled money, her life would leave the fantasy she shared with him.

Jasper stirred and raised his head. He looked so young when his hair covered half his face. It seemed to glisten with the scent of his shampoo. "What's wrong?" he said.

"Nothing."

He rose to sit up in the bed. "It's about Myles, isn't it? You know you can't keep shutting me out."

She was too exhausted to fight. She took what he offered. "I hope Myles will be all right."

"He just needs to be around his dad for a while. It doesn't mean you're not a good mom."

"Did you hear what he said? I don't give him structure or bound-aries. We're codependent."

"Since when have you believed everything that a teenager tells you?"

She didn't like Jasper's bemused smile. Like he knew all about raising an eighteen-year-old.

"Boundaries and rules and contracts . . . that's Wade, not you. So Myles needs his dad's inflexibility for a while. He'll come back."

Said the man who had no responsibility for anything but painting masterpieces . . . that no one bought. *Okay, how do you feel about this question then?* "I've been wondering something. What do you get out of our relationship?"

"Besides your perfect ass?"

"Don't avoid the question."

He drew back. His face was fully awake now. He studied her and she saw how he was evaluating what lay hidden underneath the un-comfortable question.

"You're someone who understands me," he said.

"What is it that I understand?"

"You know what it's like to long for a dream. You don't doubt me."

He'd told her before how his parents didn't believe in him: first his art major in college, then his refusal to get a master's in some-thing "useful" or to work anywhere but art galleries and bars. Here in her house, lying in her bed, Jasper's words seemed slight.

He lay back, his hair splayed black against the white pillow. His face had clouded. "You don't really want to talk about this now, do you?" he said.

She wondered if he would always remain a mystery to himself. "No."

Fiona rose and took her clothes to the bathroom. She remembered a year earlier and how big and empty the house was. One night she forced herself out and went to an exhibition. The theme was the union of art and science. The first big salon barely contained a giant model of DNA. Another was filled with a huge spinal cord of lights and bangles. A painting in the hallway rendered a desert of rocks and dirt and a dusty solar panel. The title was "In A Thousand Years Will Anyone Know What It Is?"

"Will they?" she asked the artist.

They'd talked about the world over shots at a bar down the street. She'd felt so awake, as if night had transformed itself to day. He came home with her. It was impulsive, but for once she didn't settle for the restraint that Wade and the world expected. And she didn't regret it. In the following days, Jasper's touches and lingering eyes made a wish she'd forgotten bloom—the yearning to be desired.

And now she didn't know what she felt.

By the time she'd dressed he was in the kitchen and had made her tea and toast. The toast was stiff and the tea was dreadfully organic. She took one bite, one small sip. This morning, the greyish-green walls seemed lifeless.

She retreated to the living room and sat on the art deco couch. She stared at his paintings. They were what he was and what he would be without her. In the piece in front of her, a naked man stood on a jagged beige rock and peered through a feathered dream catcher. Some day that man would fly through the circle into the eagle wheeling away.

All affairs eventually lost their poetry. Then she would be alone again in this house.

She went to work to get herself away from that thought. Leticia was running numbers. How could Leticia not have investigated why they had no receipts for the expenses? Fiona looked at the pictures on the wall of all the kids they'd helped. The only one she could focus on was Mateo, the smiling boy who they couldn't save. That didn't help.

She got on her laptop and approved new blackboards and desks and computers and toys, then a four-wheel-drive jeep for Colombia. She lingered on pictures of children joyfully playing with what she'd approved the month before. Yes, Andre had bent a law to help her. Maybe he also laundered some money. But the rest of the time he saved children.

By late afternoon she felt better. She sang with the radio on the way home and thought about dinner and a glass of wine with Jasper. Then she'd feel his arms around her.

But he'd shut himself up inside his studio. Harp and violins sounded a faint melody inside. Fiona recognized the last movement of Peter Grimes. A soprano and tenor wailed about a boat sinking far out at sea. Grimes had drowned himself because two children in his care had died. The chorus and full orchestra joined and the song rose to its heartbreaking crescendo. The lament faded into the sea.

She needed a walk. An alone-walk to figure out why she wasn't happy.

* * *

At Pacific Beach, the sinking sun cast a yellow column over the scudding waves. A distant kite surfer skated below clouds mottled with purple. Fiona made her way through piles of seaweed on the sand. She breathed in the salty air and felt it seep into her lungs.

A high voice said, "Jasper told me I'd find you here."

She whirled. It was the potential donor who'd shown up at the house to view Jasper's paintings. "Sorry to startle you," Harold Wainscott said.

His shoulders looked even bigger than before. She glanced around. On one side, booming waves blotted out sound. On the other, Wainscott. Farther down the beach a man with a surfboard was slipping off the top of his wetsuit. A jogger pumped toward her. She wasn't completely alone.

"I . . . I didn't expect to see you here," she said.

The dwindling light gave his face an orange glow. His head was the size of a pumpkin. "Comunidad de Niños is just so damn intriguing. I really want to explore if it's the right place for our money."

Bullshit. He could have just waited an hour or called. She glanced at the stairs that led to the boardwalk. They were about forty yards away, and the sky was getting darker. At least the jogger was getting close. She started toward the stairs.

"I don't have much time," he said. "That's why I had to barge into your walk." He'd changed out of his yellow pants into a pedestrian suit. Trudging beside her, his huge shoes slipped and slid in the sand.

The jogger passed by. It was darkening by the minute and the surf would overwhelm any sound she made. But she wasn't far from the stairs. She'd be close to houses and lights and people walking in La Jolla.

"What projects have you done?" she said.

"All kinds. We funnel money through one charity in a country. Then they dole it out to others in the area."

No donor she knew worked like that.

"I'd love to get some more information so we can move funds offshore through you," he said.

This sounded like money laundering. She stopped and his shoes skidded beside her. Fiona crouched and set her hand against the gritty sand. Small shells surrounded her foot like bits of bone. She untied and re-tied her sneaker. What should she say? Wade would tell her not to utter a word. Not until she knew who he was.

She rose. Even in the dusk she saw his smile harden. She continued walking. They reached the stairs. The overhead light flashed on and made his shadow loom over the sand.

"Does your board at Comunidad de Niños know about the money you took?" he said.

She forced herself to keep breathing.

"I didn't think so," he said.

"Who the hell are you?"

"I'd hate to see a good person like you go to prison."

"Damnit, tell me who you are."

He looked around. "I protected you by showing up as a donor. It's also why I'm meeting you on the beach where no one can hear us. You want to be very careful, Fiona."

"Careful of what?"

His eyebrows rose as if she were helplessly naive. "Who you talk to and what you say and what you do. You've got big risks from both sides." He paused as if to let her think about what he'd just said. "You need the kind of help the DEA provides."

She jabbed her foot into the sand to keep her balance. Comunidad de Niños was moving drug money.

"I'm going to give you my real name, but you can't ever call me that. Harold Cartuso. You've got my card. Call me when you're ready to talk."

The DEA was building a case against her. *The DEA.*

He clambered up the stairs to the walkway. He disappeared and the night air swooshed a chill over her shoulders. She hugged herself and stood still on the sand. The DEA wouldn't just target the foundation. They'd go after Unity Coast Bank. Where Wade was.

But Cartuso had never showed any identification. What if he was a fake, a test set up by Andre and Martinez?

CHAPTER THIRTY-TWO

At noon on Saturday, Wade parked in a lot beside the outlets and franchises that lined the U.S. side of the Mexican border. He and Myles walked across the visitor bridge to Tijuana. Myles stared at the Spanish billboards and the haggard palm trees and roaring cars and trucks.

"Are you okay?" Wade asked.

Myles kept walking.

Andre's driver waved from a black SUV. It was parked next to an exposed pharmacy advertising party packs of Viagra. "I don't think you need that at your age," Wade said. Myles didn't laugh.

They got in the vehicle, its air cooled to just the right temperature. The SUV soon meandered past car lots selling BMWs and Mercedes. Then gated communities, boutiques with French and Italian names, and valets in front of restaurants. Wade thought this route was Andre's doing—the scenic tour of rich Tijuana. But in the distance Wade saw a barrio shimmering on a dry hillside.

They reached a bluff of contemporary mansions—one as big as a football field—behind high cement walls. Guards sat in cars on the empty street of sun-scorched trees. Andre's house was one of the smaller ones. Two enormous iron mandalas stuck to each side of his thick steel door. Windows as small as castle slits peeked out of beige stucco.

"Is he worried about being attacked?" Myles asked.

"Apparently everyone in this neighborhood is."

Today Myles looked like a kid on a college tour: clean jeans and a button-down shirt. No images of burning babies or devil horns. Why couldn't his son have dressed like this before?

The driver pulled onto the Uni Stone driveway and they stepped out into the afternoon sun. The heavy brown lacquered door of the house opened and Andre stepped out in polished topsiders and a hand-painted shirt. Just seeing him made Wade seethe. Insisting that he and Myles come to Tijuana was pure cruelty.

Just a couple of hours.

Carmela called out a greeting beside Andre. The last time Wade had talked with her, Carmela's hair was dark brown. Today blond streaks highlighted it. Wade had forgotten how small she was—as petite as a gymnast. She wore an expensive-looking red and gold blouse and jeans with designer streaks and tears.

"She waves like a queen," Myles said.

"That's just the way you should treat her," Wade said.

He and Myles walked to the house. Above the door a video camera rotated as if it were body-scanning them.

"We are so happy that you and the *jeune homme* have come," Andre said.

"You look okay to me," Carmela said to Myles. "Are you going to make it?"

"Yes," Myles said. Next to her, he was a skinny boy giant.

"Buck up," she said.

Buck up? After what they'd done to him?

Andre boomed out a laugh. "Carmela always wanted to be a sergeant. But the Mexican Army does not accept her."

"I was too manly for them," Carmela said. There were no lines around her eye sockets, almost no lines on her face. The plastic surgery made her brown eyes reach out like pincers.

"I'll bet you're a very good businesswoman," Wade said.

"You have no idea," she said.

Andre limped into the house and Wade, Myles, and Carmela followed. The interior was nothing like the stark stucco of the outside. The open first floor was all wood and sisal rugs next to a wall of windows on the side opposite the street. In the corner, a Buddha looked over a live tree, and a waterfall dropped into a pond of water lilies. Light poured in through a gabled glass ceiling that stretched into the sky. It was as ethereal as a Buddhist temple. Even the rice-paper shades of the lamps seemed lit by the spirit of the house. It scared Wade. Andre's home was a mask that covered over something vile.

Myles strode to the windows and stared out at Tijuana. They were high on the arid hillside and houses and buildings stretched out over the desert below. "I feel like a god," he said.

Carmela snorted. "The gods *wish* they could afford this neighborhood."

Wade saw Myles' eyebrows rise. *Good.* He didn't want his son to feel at ease here. "I'm just glad to be invited," Wade said.

Carmela gave him a smirk full of edges. Her gaze caught on something behind them. Wade turned. A Japanese *shoji* room divider separated the sitting area from the rest of the house. A girl stood beside it. Wade had forgotten about Andre and Carmela's teenage daughter. She was small and delicate like her mother—before surgery—her long brown hair pluming out in curls.

"I'm Sofia," she said.

"How nice that you can spare five minutes from your busy agenda," Carmela said, lengthening the words "busy" and "agenda."

Sofia's mouth flinched. She turned to Myles. "Papá told me about what happened. It's terrible." Not even a hint of an accent.

"He is stronger for it," Carmela said.

Myles' eyes seemed to draw in Sofia. "I'll get over it," he said. *Why couldn't she be homely?*

Wade and Myles sat on a silk couch in the middle of Andre's airy living room. The couch was so low they practically touched the bamboo floor. Andre, Carmela, and Sofia faced them on matching chairs. Above them, wooden ceiling fans slowly paddled the cool air.

Andre pointed to the table between them. A bonsai tree stood next to a stone sculpture that looked like a smaller donut dribbling into a larger one. "It is a torus," he said. "The sacred geometry that is found in the atoms and all of life. Even the stars and the galaxies. Some think that the human soul is the shape of the torus."

Carmela snorted. "I think the decorator made that thing in her backyard."

"Just because you don't want to understand it." Sofia met her mother's eyes, then stared down at her cellphone on her lap.

Wade agreed with Carmela.

Andre smiled at his daughter. "Wade, you and I are only given the one child. But all the universe we see in each of them."

"The universe in a single person," Myles said. "I'm trying to take that in."

Sofia looked up from her phone. "Early dementia helps."

Andre guffawed. Carmela turned to Myles, and her eyes looked sharpened. They were going to have to be careful with her.

Andre rose. "Come."

Wade and the others followed Andre's lopsided gait through the airy room. They reached a six-foot, wooden carving beside the Buddha and the fountain, then a Chinese ink drawing. Myles glanced at Sofia and pointed to one of the symbols. "Yin."

He was showing off. Wade's stomach tightened.

"Yin and yang," Andre said. "Day and night. Birth and death, happiness and *la misère*. Life is the battle of opposites."

Wade considered his own yin-yang tattoo that matched Fiona's. In this house the symbol was profane.

Sofia spoke Spanish and Andre responded in French. She switched to that language, her voice rising. Carmela broke in with hissed words in Spanish. So much for the happy Buddhist family, Wade thought.

Andre chuckled. "My daughter says that I force my ideas to my guests."

"Not at all," Myles said.

Carmela leaned into Wade. "Your son is very smooth."

Wade wasn't sure if that was admiration or reproach. Her engineered face could hide anything. He said, "This is certainly not the kind of talk I hear around work."

"But it is also part of banking," Andre said. He pointed at the wooden carving. It had no legs—only a split torso that rose in two pieces to an elliptical head with bulging eyes. "Is it God or the devil?"

What puffery. But Wade had to at least pretend to answer the question. The sculpture was divided into two pieces and Andre had been talking about yin and yang. Wade made a guess. "Both."

Andre's sagging face looked surprised. "Very good. If you understand that, you understand many things."

Carmela gave Wade a compressed smile. It seemed to say, *You too are capable of the devil.* Yes, he was. That was why he was here.

They returned to the Zen furniture. Wade sat next to Myles on the couch and the others positioned themselves on the low chairs on the other side of the table. Wade looked again at the horrible sculpture. The stunted tree next to it resembled something in a sci-fi movie. At least the daughter looked normal. Flat shoes, cleanly pressed jeans, and a blouse that wasn't revealing or too tight. Not Myles' type.

"Have you applied to college yet?" Wade asked.

"I got early admission," Sofia said. "Stanford likes students with an unusual upbringing."

What an influence she could be on Myles. If only she weren't Andre and Carmela's daughter.

"What's unusual?" Myles asked.

"I'm born in the U.S. to a Canadian father and a Mexican mother. I'm like a commercial for NAFTA." She shrugged. "It's not as if I had anything to do with it."

"Sofia," Carmela said. "Self-effacement is very ugly." She looked at Myles. "How about you? Are you afraid to take credit for your victories?"

Myles shifted forward on the couch next to Wade. "That would be hiding out from people," he said.

Not Hidden Road. Not here.

Carmela turned to face her daughter. "I think Myles will have some very interesting things to say to you."

He never should have let Andre wheedle him into bringing his son.

Sofia aimed a perfect copy of her mother's tight smirk at Myles. "You don't want to talk about college, do you?"

"It would make me jealous."

Wade had to draw the discussion away from Myles. "After you finish Stanford maybe you can grow Unity Coast into a global business."

"I want to be a doctor. I want to help people."

As opposed to banking? Carmela's eyes slitted, but Andre grinned. It was obvious that Andre's weakness was his daughter. That was something the FBI could use.

The maid arrived and served them glasses of sparkling water with wedges of lime. Andre launched into a monologue about how Western culture should incorporate the Chinese concept of synchronicity. Wade wondered how a man so evil could be so boring. He saw Carmela studying the bubbles in her glass. Sofia fidgeted. Two years before, Myles would have mocked Andre's New Age blathering. Today he sat so still he seemed to hang on every morsel. If he was faking fascination, he was scarily good. And if he wasn't faking it? Scarier still.

Carmela reached out from her chair and put a hand on Andre's arm. She said, "Why don't you put a sock in it now? After a while it makes people fall asleep."

Andre's eyes expanded behind the thick lenses of his spectacles. There it was—anger. He wasn't impervious. Not when it came to his wife.

Andre found a handkerchief in his pocket and rubbed his lenses. He slipped his glasses back on and tapped his legs with his fingers as if he were playing a keyboard. He stood. "Wade, let us enjoy the *jardin*."

At last. A chance to probe for a way to destroy this asshole.

CHAPTER THIRTY-THREE

Wade followed Andre past the fountain and through a side door by the windows of Andre's house. Once in the garden, they stretched out on wicker chairs. The bird trills and scents from the flowers lulled Wade into relaxing. He squeezed his legs together to bring himself back into focus.

"Tell me about your family," Andre said. "Where you grew up."

Wade had no siblings close by, no crimes or mistresses that could put him at risk. Nothing in his past could make him more vulnerable than he already was. He related his early San Diego years in a boring monotone. Then the business courses at Northwestern and University of Chicago. He didn't mention his father's heart attack. Nor how his mother died in agony from cancer. Andre was too discreet to ask how he'd met his estranged wife or to bring up Comunidad de Niños. But no matter how dryly Wade catalogued his history, Andre seemed fascinated. His voice rose in exclamation, or he grew quiet and leaned in. Wade found it hard not to fall into his sway. He had to fight to keep his resentment stoked.

"Tell me about your vision for our business," Wade said.

Andre looked up at the cloudless sky.

"You've got a niche with Mexico. How are you developing that?"

Andre slipped off his glasses. His eyes seemed to latch more intently on Wade. "Do you know what you search to find in your life?"

No business colleague asked a question like that. "Probably not," Wade said.

Andre stared beyond the wall of his garden. Tijuana's buildings shimmered below. The afternoon traffic hummed on a distant highway over the arid land of a separate world. "You want that people think you are the stuffed banker," Andre said. "But you really want to be much more than this."

"Being a stuffed banker isn't so bad."

"You practice the yoga. You play the guitar. Why do you do these things?"

"They relax me."

Andre pointed to Wade's arm. "And the tattoo of the Tao?"

His long-sleeved shirt hid the tattoo.

"Don't worry, I do not spy on you. Fiona told me."

Maybe he *did* spy on him.

"What do you think when you say 'Namaste' in the yoga?" Andre asked.

He didn't say "namaste." It seemed fake. "Fiona doesn't know what she's looking for either," he said.

Andre put on his glasses. He smiled. "Of course, she knows."

A six-foot-four artist who recaptures the youth she lost. The anti-Wade. Andre was playing with him.

"How about where *you* grew up?" Wade asked. "Tell me about Montreal and what you're searching for."

Andre looked at his watch, a Bulgari that looked less expensive than it was. He rose. "Another time we must do that. Now is lunch."

Something secret and disreputable hid in Montreal. This was the tumor Wade had to find.

Back in the Zen house, Myles was drawing his hand through the air and talking in an avalanche of words, two of which Wade made out: "mosh pit." Myles mimed bodies jumping and slamming together at a concert. Across from him, Sofia's eyes had widened, and Carmela's mouth had compressed into a tight frown. Wade smiled. Maybe Carmela would seat her daughter at the opposite end of the lunch table from Myles.

"We were jumping into each other," Myles said. "I was covered in sweat . . . and none of it was mine."

The giggle started small. Then Carmela and Sofia were laughing so hard that Carmela leaned into her daughter. She dabbed her eyes with a Kleenex.

Andre said, "Your son has a talent with the women."

Wade's stomach was mashing itself. He had to get Myles out of there. But they still had to sit through lunch.

Andre's ruby ring glinted blood red in the light from the window. He pointed to the table behind the shoji divider. It was Japanese style, almost on the floor with a pit for their feet. "Let us eat," he said.

Sofia and Carmela were still giggling as they scooted into the far end of the table, opposite Myles. Wade sat next to his son and across from Andre.

"I saw the teacher's password written on a slip of paper," Myles said.

That prank had almost gotten Myles expelled. It was the kind of story unlikely to impress a high performing student and her pushy mother. Wade looked forward to their reaction.

"Everyone in algebra class hated it," Myles said. "So I hacked into the teacher's account and changed their grades on the quiz. They each got an 'x' or 'y.'"

More raucous laughter. *Shit.*

The cook served plates of beef with a Bordelaise sauce. The pungent scents of the meat seemed to fill the whole house. Andre might live like a Buddhist monk, but underneath he was a French carnivore. Andre opened two bottles of Mexican cabernet. The wine was superb, and Wade had to restrain himself with judicious sips. He felt relaxed for the first time since they'd arrived. Which could be dangerous.

"How is Fiona doing?" Carmela asked.

Wade started. "What?"

"Fiona. Is she still your wife?"

Wade's cheeks burned. "Fiona lives with her boyfriend in my house."

The table went silent. Carmela's stiff smile didn't shift. "And you let her?"

"How could you be so rude?" Sofia said.

"I want to know what the new executive vice president thinks about it," Carmela said.

Maybe this was a test. He met her eyes and said, "I don't think that's any of your business."

More silence. Myles looked horrified.

"I didn't mean to bring up something you do not feel comfortable talking about," Carmela said.

"Of course not," Wade said.

He glanced at his Shinola. It was after three o'clock. Maybe he could get Myles out of here in the next half hour.

Andre started gabbing as if to cover over his wife's discourtesy. First about wines, then Jungian archetypes. Meanwhile Sofia and Myles chatted in a quiet world Wade couldn't reach. The salad came, followed by the Mexican cheese that Andre assured Wade was just as good as unpasteurized French. Wade was too upset to tell. Finally, a dessert of churros and chocolate sauce that Andre didn't touch.

"He hates churros," Sofia said. "They remind him of Quebec."

"They're called beaver tails there," Carmela said. "Sounds delicious, don't you think? It was what Andre and his girlfriend used to eat at their little cafés."

Andre gave her a thin smile.

The maid served thimbles of port and cigars. At last they rose and said their goodbyes. As the others headed toward the door, Wade saw a fork Andre had used on the table. Wade slipped it into his pocket and followed. At least he'd gotten one thing useful out of this tortuous meal. Now Rodrigues would have DNA.

Andre staggered back a step and firmly gripped Wade's shoulder. Had Andre seen him take the fork?

"I am sorry that Carmela brings up Fiona and that *maricón artiste.*"

"It was nothing," Wade said.

"I am still sorry."

No wonder Fiona believed in him. The man was a master at faking sincerity.

They were at the doorway now. He and Myles were almost out of this haunted house. "I hope that you do better than the other commercial real estate lender," Carmela said. "He was unsatisfactory."

Wade stopped walking. "What other lender?"

"The man before you. Bill Langley."

Should he ask? He had to. "What happened to him?"

"He and his family died in a car accident," Sofia said. "Their car went over a cliff in Colorado."

"Such a pity," Andre said.

Carmela's cold eyes gazed past them to the street. "Such a pity for his family," she said.

He barely breathed until he and Myles climbed into the SUV. When Wade looked back, the three Ouellettes stood in the doorway smiling. As the car pulled away, they waved.

A car accident? The whole family dead? Carmela hadn't mentioned it innocently. She'd brought it up as a goodbye threat. But not just to him. Myles too.

"Sofia was cool," Myles said. "She helped me face my fear about Tijuana."

The visit had even poisoned the mantras from Hidden Road. "You should always be afraid of Tijuana," Wade said.

"Sofia asked me to come back."

Somehow Wade stayed quiet, his body perfectly still. He stared out the side window as the car floated like a boat over a calm lake. When he turned back, Myles' face had crinkled with boyish disappointment.

"What's wrong?" Myles said. "She's the kind of friend you always wanted me to have."

CHAPTER THIRTY-FOUR

What Fiona really wanted was a burger. She longed for rare meat that dripped grease down her chin, then bites of salty French fries dipped in ketchup. The craving had hit her three hours after Myles left to live with his father. It was six o'clock on a Saturday, and she was trying not to look disappointed with the onions, broccoli, and celery she saw on Jasper's cutting board. The whole kitchen reeked of the soybean paste sizzling in his wok.

Jasper stepped back from the stove and put his arm around her. "A Saturday night with just the two of us." When she was silent, he said, "Myles just needs to be with his dad for a while."

She wasn't worried about Myles. She was worried about the DEA. Should she tell him? But what could Jasper do to help?

"If you find the candles, we can set up a table on the deck," he said.

Candlelight beside her garden, as if romance would make her feel better. All she wanted was to go upstairs and get away from the smells of frying vegetables.

The doorbell rang. "I'll answer," Jasper said. "You pour yourself a glass of wine."

He gave her a sympathetic nod that said she deserved it. His flip-flops thwacked down the hallway. The front door opened and he said something. A nasal baritone responded. The voice sounded familiar. "I'll get her," Jasper said.

Who would show up without warning on a Saturday night? She rose and went to the hallway. Jasper was walking toward her from the door. Behind him, a man had stepped inside. She stopped. Her stomach clinched. It was Egberto Martinez.

"Is Andre all right?" she said.

"Yes, yes," Egberto Martinez said. "Andre is still in good health."

"Why didn't you call first?"

"I'm sorry."

There was no sign of remorse on his face. No expression of any emotion.

"I have good news," he said.

He was carrying something in an oblong paper bag that looked like a bottle of wine. It was all Fiona could do not to groan. Drinking wine with him could take hours. She led him to the living room and he sat on one of the twill chairs. She sat on the edge of the sofa, the birch table between them.

"Your walls are the color of blood," Martinez said.

"It's bright and festive," she said. "Like a piñata."

"Ah yes, a piñata. After it has burst open."

He pointed to a painting that depicted a desiccated man and woman staring out at a sun-drenched, faint blue sky. "What is it that is curling around the cactus?"

"A snake," she said.

"I like snakes."

Her hand latched onto the arm of the sofa. The rough upholstery dug into her palm. "His work is supposed to be archetypal," she said. "Like the myths that have been passed down through the ages."

Martinez nodded. "Do you approve of what Jasper did to Wade's office? Or the way he repainted your kitchen?"

How did he know? Martinez had never been in her house. She folded her arms around herself. "Tell me why you showed up here tonight."

His smile burned into her. "Very simple. We are doubling the budget of Comunidad de Niños."

She blinked. This was good news, wasn't it? "I'm . . . I'm pleased." But how could so much funding come in without her knowing about it? "Who is giving us the money?"

"New partners in Africa."

If Andre was laundering money, doubling the funding of the foundation doubled her exposure. But she couldn't think about Cartuso, couldn't look unsettled. "I'm just so touched you showed up at my house on a Saturday night to tell me." Did that sound sarcastic?

He studied her. "It is such good news I did not want to inform you over the phone. I wanted that you should celebrate." He opened the bag at his feet.

Yes, it was a bottle of white wine. Yes, he wanted to have a glass together. But she knew how to cut that short. She tried to rouse some excitement in her face. "Let me get Jasper and he can celebrate with us."

He rose. Martinez was not a man who tolerated hippy artists. "I cannot stay," he said.

"Jasper is cooking dinner. He could easily put more vegetables in the wok." She watched that sink in.

He handed her the bottle of white wine. It was a Louis Latour Grand Cru. Very expensive. And warm.

She stood. "This is wonderful news." She walked with him toward the front of the house and considered how careful she had to be. What if Cartuso wasn't really a DEA agent? This could be some kind of ruse to ambush her.

At the front door he turned and caught her eyes. "I told Andre that he shouldn't have doubts. You are the right person for this new funding. We don't need anyone with more experience." Another smile that wasn't quite a smile. "We both think it is time you got a nice salary increase. This way you can return the money you took sooner."

The Mexican Rottweiler couldn't deliver good news without wrapping it in a threat.

CHAPTER THIRTY-FIVE

A simple internet search revealed that Bill Langley and his family had plunged off a precipice at Monarch Pass in Colorado. The authorities called it an accident. But no one accidentally drove his family off a cliff.

Wade had to sever Myles' friendship with Sofia. A relationship with anyone in the Ouellette family was too dangerous. He decided it would be best if his son steamed off some energy before he hit him with his demand. The day after their trip to Tijuana, he persuaded Myles to hike with him at Torrey Pines State Park.

The park's sand and pebble path began atop a bluff of dry scrub and bedraggled pine trees. From there, it sloped down and was bordered by low-slung sagebrush, cacti, and trees. As their tennis shoes crunched over the sandy and rocky dirt, Wade pointed to the giant sandstone escarpments. "They're like gnarled brown fingers that reach out to the sea," he said.

"Uh-huh," Myles said.

"Look at those trees on top of the bluffs. Centuries of wind have bent them back. Do you smell the pines and the salt water?"

Myles stopped and looked at him. "Is this like some kind of bonding thing we're doing?"

"Would that be so bad?"

"Hiking reminds me of Utah."

Wade hadn't thought of that. He kept silent as they descended stone stairs through a cut in the cliffs to the beach. They headed north, walls of stratified sandstone on the right and the sea on the left. A cruise ship slid up the coast. Couples and families had spread out on the shore, their voices rising in snatches above the roar and hiss of the ocean. Wade smelled the seaweed and remembered Myles pulling up clumps of it as a child. He and Fiona had helped him build sand parapets and moats. So long ago.

He found a hollow in the cliff face and they drank water and munched on nuts and raisins. Behind them, beetles scuttled across the stone walls. In front, lines of waves billowed and uncoiled like an ancient clock.

"We could be any father and son in the last thousand years in here," Wade said.

Myles stiffly shifted beside him. "I think you want to talk about something."

It was pointless putting off what he had to ask. "You know, if you hang around with my boss's daughter, it really puts me in an awkward position."

Myles' eyes were already resentful.

Wade marched on. "I can't have you getting close to her right now. Not until I've worked for her father for a while."

When Myles expanded his chest, it used to foretell an eruption. This time his voice was calm. "We have this really cool dinner, then a weird trip to a place that gives me the shakes—which I only do for you. I make like the best impression possible on your boss's family. And what do you do? You ruin it by ordering me not to be friends with Sofia."

Had Hidden Road taught him to argue like a lawyer?

"Just until I'm sure the job will work out," Wade said. "Later you can be friends." It was such a feeble excuse.

"Let me tell you something, *Dad*. Something I learned in Utah. I shouldn't be empathetic to people motivated by fear."

More damn words from Hidden Road. Wade didn't know how to argue with him anymore. If he revealed the crimes of Carmela's family, Myles would demand to know why he stayed at Andre's bank. He'd have to tell him he was a confidential informant for the FBI. Why? Because Andre had helped kidnap Myles in Mexico. How could Wade expect an enraged teenager to keep that secret?

"I want you to stay away from Sofia," Wade said. "It's more than a request."

Myles let out an ostentatious sigh. "Isn't it enough that you sent me to the gulag?"

This was already veering sideways. Wade had to bring it back into focus. He pushed his hand against the gritty sand. "I'm not talking about Hidden Road."

"But it's the same thing. You couldn't get me to do what you wanted, so you forced me to go there."

"You didn't give us any damn choice."

"*Us*? Did you say 'us'? You were the one who made Mom do it."

Wade wanted to shout. He wanted to bang his hand on the rock. A year of outrageously expensive treatment and Myles still fought even the smallest requests. But this wasn't a curfew or pot smoking. The Saezes killed whole families.

"You banished me," Myles said.

There it was. He couldn't gloss over it. "You had OxyContin."

"I was just holding it for someone." Myles pushed his face closer. All the sound outside the hollow vanished. "You know the for-real reason I wanted to live with you instead of Mom?"

The blow was coming. Wade braced his hand against the rock.

"You saved my life when I was kidnapped. I had to, at least, *try* to forgive you. I had to *try* to love you as much as Mom."

He should stand up. He should leave Myles here. Let him find his own way home.

"You have no idea what it was like at Hidden Road, do you?" Myles said. "Forced labor. Mind control. Character assassination."

Wade pushed his back against the sandstone wall. He took a long yoga breath. "Tell me about it."

Myles shook his head. "You don't want to know."

His son's angry face showed how the words were bursting to get out. "I don't want this to be a cancer that grows between us," Wade said.

Myles scowled at the gouged and battered roof of the hollow. He dug his hand into the sand. "You know what I kept going back to when I was kidnapped? Those two thugs who came to our house and took me to Utah. I knew the first day that Hidden Road was hell."

Wade steadied his breathing. He could take these punches. "How?"

Myles nodded: *You wanted this.* "The first weeks were a prison-silence thing. I could only talk to staff. Not a word to other kids."

"They were worried you'd coalition and reinforce negative attitudes."

Myles groaned. "You know how many times a day they told me that? There were like hundreds of rules. No clocks. No watches. No books except the approved ones. No radio or TV. And the music? All this upbeat, cornball, next-level-cringe stuff. It was Christian camp without Jesus."

"They took away your control."

Myles gave a derisive chuckle. "You actually believe that propaganda? Mom sure doesn't."

Wade looked down. He felt his leg trembling.

"Everything was so extra. They woke us up at like six in the morning. Make the bed. Fold the clothes. Clean the house. All without talking and everything in a hurry. I had like five minutes to take a shit. Otherwise, I had to get back in line."

Myles studied him as if gauging how his words had landed. "Go on," Wade said.

"After four months I still had to ask permission to have a conversation. But I did get something on my birthday. A digital watch and sweatpants. I also got to go bowling and to a rodeo. Wasn't that nice of them?"

When he was hurt, Myles always fought back with sarcasm. But Wade wouldn't let it provoke him. Not today. "They had to break you down so you'd engage. It was like the Army."

"Oh, please. Even the Army had better food than that slop. At least in the Army I'd have a gun to end it."

Wade's eyes widened. "What does that mean?"

"Nothing."

"Then why did you say it?"

He shrugged.

Hidden Road had told them that, at some point, most of the students comforted themselves with thoughts of suicide. The staff would make sure that no one had the means to follow through. But Wade couldn't ignore the comment now. "So you wanted to end your life?"

Myles took a long drink from his water bottle. He seemed to listen to the waves breaking beyond them. Wade knew he was gauging what to say.

"Every night I asked myself if I could last another day," Myles said. "How many months till my sentence was over?"

"You didn't answer my question. Did you want to end your life?"

Myles ran his fingers over the edged layers of the sandstone, then looked back. "I knew I could survive. I didn't need to be happy."

He could have lied about an urge to kill himself. He could have made his father squirm and panic. But he didn't. Instead, Myles had used a different weapon. "So being happy was smoking all the pot you wanted and skipping school?"

Myles sneered at the ceiling of the enclosure as if his father were hopeless. But he'd been so ebullient on their later visits to Hidden Road. He'd even said that he loved what he'd become. By the end of his treatment, Myles had enthused about the kids he'd helped and all the program levels he'd achieved. Even Fiona had said how much he'd grown.

"You loved how well you did at Hidden Road," Wade said. "We were very proud."

"Nothing like writing those big checks to make you a believer."

More sarcasm. But this time to push his father away from what Myles didn't want to admit. Wade kept his voice low. "You can't tell me you didn't learn something about yourself."

"You mean the therapy? It was like being dissected without anesthesia. They went all the way back to when I flunked first grade. I even had to tell them what the neighbor kid said. You remember Bobby Linstumburg? He told me if I kept repeating, I'd be the only first grader to drive his teacher to school."

When Fiona had told him what Bobby had said, Wade had wanted to telephone the boy's parents. But he'd decided Myles needed to toughen up and didn't call anyone. What kind of father wouldn't defend his son from that?

"Then there was how you and Mom pretended you were so proud of me—the son who flunked grade school. I felt like a freak in my own family."

"Hidden Road wanted to understand how that affected you."

"Yeah, right. You know what they said when I told them about it? I was convincing myself that I was powerless. 'What do you get out of playing the victim?' That's what they understood."

A Hidden Road seminar had counseled all the parents to resist their children's self-pity. It was nothing but manipulation. Wade had thought they were right. And now? He wasn't sure of anything.

"It was all shade, Dad. When I said the right thing, my body language showed I didn't mean it. When I didn't rag the other kids, I was hiding out, afraid they'd reject me. The staff even found a way to take away my humor. My jokes were how I avoided dealing with problems. And you know what I got to do after they ripped me apart? I got to thank them for their insights."

But the results had been astounding. When Myles got home, he'd excelled in school. He organized himself and engaged in normal conversation. He was respectful. He thought about the future.

Myles grabbed a rock and threw it to thud into the sand outside the hollow. "It was such a hell for so long. I was afraid, literally, all the time. I had pains in my chest."

"I never picked that up in the conference calls," Wade said. "What I heard was a boy trying to better himself. A boy trying to heal his relationships with his family."

Myles peered at him. "You really didn't suss what was going on, did you? The minute I got negative, my therapist would cut off the phone call. So I had to shut up and listen to your endless complaints about me. Then I had to say the right thing. But it was the only chance I had to speak with you, the only thing—other than your visits—I looked forward to." He wiped his eyes. He glared at his water bottle and the bag of trail mix.

Wade felt something building in his chest. But instead of anger, it was sadness. Why had it taken him so long to listen to the anguish that scorched his child's memories? "I . . . I don't think I could have gotten through Hidden Road," he said.

Myles gave out a laugh, a short, derisive huff. "It was like being in a cult. I gave up my mind while I was inside. Let me tell you just how upside down it was. Me and one of the counselors were on good terms. One day he showed me pictures of him and his fiancée in Mexico. You know, all casual and sharing. He's flipping through his phone, and out pops this one of her on a beach . . . topless. It was an accident. He didn't mean anything. You know what I did? I reported him. I'd turned into such a bitch I thought it was my duty. My frigging duty. They put him on suspension and he had to apologize to me." Myles grimaced and shook his head. "I so wronged him."

"Part of you must have been glad for that power reversal," Wade said. "I would have been."

Myles gave another bitter snort. "You see power games in everything."

Wade's mouth opened. He snapped it shut.

Myles shook his head as if his father would never have the capacity to fathom him. He got up and left the cave. Wade followed fifteen feet behind, the rumbles and crashes of the ocean beside him. A military helicopter throbbed in the burnt sky.

They reached the stairs that led to the path back to the parking lot. Myles stopped and turned. "I know you did what you thought was best for me."

Wade was struck still. Even after a fight Myles was strong enough to bare himself to that truth. "Thank you," he said.

Myles turned. As he made his way up the stairs, Wade remembered his son's words. *You banished me.* Myles was never going to forgive him. But he would estrange his son forever if it saved his life. The Saezes killed people.

He broke into a trot to catch up. "I really appreciate you talking about this with me," he said. "I think I understand better what you went through."

"Do you?"

"Part of it."

Myles looked straight ahead.

"But there's something I don't want you to forget. I mean it about Sofia. You can't be friends with her right now."

CHAPTER THIRTY-SIX

At seven thirty on Monday morning, Fiona parked and walked two blocks to meet Wade on San Joaquin Street. She'd picked a place deep in the hills of Pacific Beach where they'd see anyone who was watching them. Wade was already there. He didn't look like a banker this morning. Instead of his usual suit he wore jeans and a short-sleeved polo shirt. For the first time in more than a year she spotted the yin and yang tattoo on his bicep. Today he hadn't covered it up. She looked down at her wrist at the image that matched his. Maybe this was a sign that this was the right time to tell him.

They trudged together uphill and, with each step, she felt more sweat in her hair. They stopped at the top of Pacifica. Below them the marine layer billowed over the shoreline and marshes beside Mission Bay. The water glinted like blue- and grey-tinted ice. She turned to the house across the street. Its green lawn looked as false as the man she had to talk about.

"Please tell me what's going on," he said.

She didn't know where to start.

"Just tell me."

She took in the air's salty smell and began. After a few sentences, the story opened up like the bay below them—Andre's deception, the money laundering through the foundation, giant Harold Cartuso, Martinez showing up at her house. When she'd finished, she pushed her shoes firmly on the street and braced herself for Wade's disapproval. But he looked more sad than angry.

"Why didn't I see what Andre was doing?" she said.

"You were desperate to save your son. I was too."

There was so much understanding in those two sentences. She saw from the worry on his face that he had more to say.

"I'm working for the FBI," he said.

Her head recoiled. She took a step back. "What?"

"Rodrigues recruited me. I'm a confidential informant at Andre's bank."

"Why the hell would you do that?"

He gave out a great sigh, the kind of frustrated and disappointed exhalation that usually led to a fight. But this time he only looked weary. "Carmela is part of the Saez drug family. They own Andre's bank and are running money through it."

Heat rose from her neck to her cheeks. "You knew a drug cartel was inside Andre's bank and you didn't tell me?"

"The less you knew, the safer you'd be."

She couldn't blame him for trying to keep her safe. But there had to be more. She knew what it was, and it made her cringe. "Rodrigues threatened to expose the money I got from the foundation, didn't she?"

"Yes."

"Did she know about Myles trying to buy drugs in Tijuana?"

He stared down at the street and the dead leaves along the curb. "Yes."

Wade was holding back, weighing how much something would hurt her. "What else?"

He made her sit with him on a curb, their feet on the ribbon of concrete between the sidewalk and the blacktopped street. He squinted up at the sky. A plane lanced a grey cloud like a needle.

"Andre had to order the cash for the ransom," Wade said. "That takes three business days."

Myles was kidnapped on Saturday and they'd paid the ransom on Tuesday. One business day.

Andre knew Myles would be kidnapped!

Her chest fisted. She didn't know if she would scream or cry. She gripped the rough edges of the curb. "Why?"

"Because he wanted me under his thumb. So I'd work at his bank."

The goal was so small it made the act even worse.

"The Saez family owns him," Wade said. "They want to buy up real estate, lots of it. That's where I come in. Having a well-known banker front their deals will kick-start their strategy."

"They kidnapped Myles so you'd help buy buildings? That's the reason?"

"They only care about their own people, Fiona. You know what Andre made me do? On Saturday I had to bring Myles to their house in Tijuana."

"You didn't!"

"We only went because Rodrigues promised to protect us. But here's the worst part. Myles impressed them. And they have a daughter."

She felt a scream wedged in her throat.

"There's something else I learned. Three years ago, another lender named Bill Langley worked for Unity Coast Bank. Carmela said his work was unsatisfactory."

Fiona wrapped her arms around herself. "No."

Wade nodded sadly, painfully. "Langley and his family were in a car on a mountain in Colorado. The car went over a cliff."

Fiona closed her eyes. She was breathing hard, imagining a gun, a knife, a club. "I want to kill these monsters," she said.

He hugged her. It was so unexpected she didn't resist. His arms pressed into her back and she reached around him and squeezed.

*   *   *

Jasper's studio door was closed. Fiona inhaled a long breath to fortify herself. She knocked and went inside. The room reeked of Jasper's paints, the floor tarp covered with drips and slashes of color. Jasper wore his Hawaiian painter's smock. Blue and orange and yellow paint streaked his hands. But it was the canvas on the easel that made her breath stop. An infant lay on cracked and dried desert ground. The boy's incandescent green eyes stared out at her, his face sun-lined and ancient. Vultures flew over the sun-scorched sky and a snake looped around the borders of the canvas. It was as if Jasper had absorbed the cruelty and enmity around her house.

"This is the wrong place for you," she said.

He pulled himself upright as if physically drawing back to her and the room. "I don't understand."

She circled her hand to encompass the study. Canvases, none of them finished, rested against the walls and moldings. They were supposed to evoke universal symbols, connections to a collective mind that was greater than conscious thought. She didn't feel a part of any of them. "These don't belong in my house," she said.

He stared at her.

"I have to save my family."

He didn't look surprised. Some part of him must have expected this. He looked down at the paintbrush in his hand. When he raised his head his eyes looked both forlorn and resigned. "When do you want me to leave?"

"As soon as possible."

He walked across the tarp and hugged her. She smelled the nutty odors of the oil paint on his hands, then his sweat. The bristles of his beard pressed down on her head. For a time, his music and his paintings and his body had made her so happy. But that happiness seemed distant now.

She knew what would happen. She'd go to work. By the time she got home, the house would be silent. All that remained of him would be the raw red walls in her living room and the vanishing scents of his body and his paints.

CHAPTER THIRTY-SEVEN

Peter Vanhoven, the executive whose daughter had persuaded Myles to go to Tijuana, sat next to Wade in Wade's car. Vanhoven was the FBI's idea. They thought a senior vice president from an investment bank that had nothing to do with Unity Coast would add to Wade's credibility. Wade wasn't so sure. As Wade drove, Vanhoven touched his gold and diamond cufflinks and unkinked his neck. Every few minutes he rearranged the pants of his Armani suit.

Wade hoped conversation would lighten him up. Nervous people made terrible salesmen. "How did Agent Rodrigues rope you into this?" he asked. "Did she tell you she didn't care about your daughter's drug deal?"

"I'll bet she told you the same thing about your son, didn't she?" Vanhoven said.

"She made it sound like it wasn't a threat."

Vanhoven locked eyes. "I think you want something else. I think you want to destroy the men who kidnapped Myles."

Rodrigues must have told him. Wade turned his focus to the highway.

"I'd want to kill them too," Vanhoven said.

"I don't want to kill anyone," Wade said. Even his tone of voice sounded like a lie.

He took the Barrio Logan exit and headed into its mix of houses and industrial buildings.

"Let's talk strategy," Vanhoven said. "The key to Egberto Martinez is he's just a hood, a hood who does international trade and is trying to finance a building. I've given presentations to big swinging dicks much tougher than this guy."

He hadn't met Martinez. "I'll run the meeting," Wade said.

Vanhoven shrugged.

Martinez's warehouse stood near the pylons of the bridge to Coronado Island and across the street from a Christian school and a boat-storage company. The building was covered with fading aluminum siding. Wade didn't see any business name. Only an address in small numbers next to a steel entrance door with its paint peeling. He parked in front of the warehouse.

Vanhoven shot his cufflinks and patted down his hair. "I'm ready," he said.

They got out. Cars huffed over the bridge above them as they trudged to the door. Wade rang the bell and the door burped open. It occurred to him that no one would hear anything that went on in this warehouse. He stepped inside.

The interior looked like a showroom for muscle cars and vintage automobiles. Maybe fifty Mustangs, GTOs, Torinos, Shelbies, Ferraris—even beach jalopies. Martinez appeared from the left side of the building. In jeans and a brown snap shirt, he stared at them without a word.

Vanhoven said, "I have a good friend you might know—Harry Murdoch. He owns Murdoch Industries and also invests in muscle cars. Really great guy. Been in this business—"

"I don't know him." Martinez turned and walked ahead.

Wade thought that would deter Vanhoven from making friendly. But it didn't. Vanhoven speeded up and after a few rows of cars he caught Martinez. He handed him a card and pointed to a red, two-door coupe. "Datsun 240Z. Eight cylinders and before fuel injection, right?"

Martinez squinted at him. "Do you always ask questions you know the answers to, Mr. Vanhoven?"

Vanhoven's mouth clamped shut.

Martinez opened a door in the corner of the warehouse. Inside was an administrative office where four men hunched into computers. Another door opened beside reflecting glass. When they entered the second door, Wade saw that the wall was actually a one-way mirror that gave a view of the employees outside. The overhead light in the room dimly illuminated a small, dusty desk with two cheap, mismatched chairs in front. No windows to the street. It looked like the basement cave of a failing accountant.

Martinez walked to a gleaming machine in the corner and steamed out espressos into demitasse cups. Wade and Vanhoven sat on the chairs, and Martinez set the cups in front of them on his desk—no saucers. He scooped out dates from a paper bag and placed them on a plate beside the cups. "Did you know that people in Arabia were eating dates seven thousand years ago?" Martinez asked.

Was he actually going to pontificate about dates? Wade thought back to his first meeting with Martinez. Perhaps he always said or did something to throw everyone off balance.

"How many varieties of dates do you think there are now?" Martinez asked.

"Hundreds," Vanhoven said.

Martinez shook his head. "Bankers are such limited thinkers."

"I have a feeling you're going to open our minds," Wade said.

"Thousands. They're produced in the Middle East, of course. But also North Africa, Spain, Turkey—even Mexico. As for America, some smart Spaniard imported date palm trees in the 1700s. He planted them in California and Arizona."

Wade picked up a date. When he bit down, the fruit hit his mouth in an explosion of sweetness.

"Deglet Noors," Martinez said. "They change from amber to golden brown as they ripen." He held up one to the overhead fluorescent light. The center looked light brown. "A very complex taste. Sweet but not too sweet. The tongue picks up the nuttiness—even hints of brown sugar."

"Obviously dates are one of the commodities that you trade," Vanhoven said.

"No."

Everything Vanhoven said was wrong. Next time Wade would talk with Martinez by himself.

Martinez picked up a Montblanc pen from his desk and pointed it at Vanhoven. "I looked you up on LinkedIn. You're a mergers-and-acquisition banker, not a real estate lender."

"I did some commercial real estate in the past," Vanhoven said. "I'm taking charge so my people do this deal right."

Martinez chuckled. "You want a referral commission, don't you?"

Vanhoven smiled painfully, as if Martinez had guessed correctly.

At least he did that right. Wade passed the term sheet to Martinez. It had almost the same conditions as Martinez had shown him at Unity Coast Bank. Martinez scanned the two pages and set them on his desk. He speared a date with his pen and chewed.

"Mr. Bosworth, you know as well as I do that you can do better." He leaned back in his chair and retrieved a crumpled tissue from the pocket of his jeans. He cleaned the date sap from his pen and pointed it at Vanhoven. "Maybe you should lead this deal."

Did he really think he could set them against each other?

"Wade's term sheet is very competitive," Vanhoven said.

Martinez sipped his espresso. "Arizona and California produce Medjool dates. Medjools are supposed to be the best in the world. But they're too big, their skin and meat too soft. Do they remind you of a few bankers?"

"No," Wade said.

Martinez picked up another date and leaned back in his chair. He chewed. Licked his fingers. He slowly drummed the pen on the blotter. "Tell me about your family, Mr. Vanhoven."

Vanhoven stared down at the demitasse cup. He touched his sleeve, then the expensive cufflink.

"How about *your* family, *Egberto?*" Wade asked.

"Answer my question, Mr. Vanhoven," Martinez said, his pen thumping the blotter.

"I'm divorced. One daughter."

"How old is the daughter?" Martinez asked.

Vanhoven fiddled with his tiepin. "Seventeen."

"Does your son know her, Mr. Bosworth?"

The only way to deter a bully was to shove back. "Neither of our children will be involved in this deal," Wade said. "Will yours, *Egberto?*"

Martinez sipped espresso. He lowered his cup to the blotter. "I want you to understand something. You do not want me disappointed with an uncompetitive term sheet."

The man was full of tricks to knock them off balance. Did he lick his fingers just to rattle them? The same fingers opened his desk drawer and withdrew a large envelope. He handed it to Wade.

"When you get back, give it to the trembler," Martinez said.

"You mean Chad?" Wade asked.

"I think you know who I mean, Mr. Bosworth."

Wade took the envelope. "I'll be glad to do you that favor, Egberto."

Martinez rose. They were dismissed.

Wade and Vanhoven filed out and Martinez closed his office door without saying goodbye. They silently trudged out of the warehouse and got in Wade's car. Wade pulled out and they stayed silent.

When they got on the highway, Vanhoven said, "Is that bastard as off as he seems?"

"That's certainly what he wants us to think."

They passed the grain elevators and port facilities.

"I don't get it," Vanhoven said. "Martinez seemed to threaten our kids. But we're not supposed to know he has any connection to drug cartels."

"He figures we'll eventually learn what he's up to," Wade said. "When that happens, he wants us to think twice about ever going to the police."

Vanhoven scratched his neck. Then his side.

They reached the exit to downtown San Diego. Just as Wade pulled onto E Street, Vanhoven broke into a grin.

"What's so funny?" Wade said.

"His cars are just a front."

Wade pulled over and parked. He turned in his seat.

Vanhoven said, "Someone who knows that much about dates should know everything about his collection of cars."

"The Datsun sports coupe," Wade said.

"My family had a 240Z when I was a kid. It has six cylinders, not eight. And fuel injection. A man like Martinez would correct me just to show how stupid I was. But he didn't. You know why? Because he didn't know."

Maybe he needed Vanhoven, after all.

* * *

They had to decompress. Wade took Vanhoven to McDonald's. As they ordered, the service staff stared at Vanhoven's gold and diamond tiepin and cufflinks. So much for being inconspicuous. Wade looked around. The whole room was brightened by wall-to-wall windows. But at one thirty, only older people and a few homeless slurped from drinks. Wade found a spot in the middle of the restaurant, far away from the other patrons. Only quiet voices and piped-in, happy jazz surrounded them.

Vanhoven tutted and pointed at Wade's sandwich. "You know Big Macs are the gateway drug to French fries."

Wade pointed a fry at Vanhoven's meal. "Grilled chicken with no fries is what they give you in the hospital. It helps you adjust to the thought of dying."

It felt good to laugh. Like releasing a breath held in too long.

A mother and her three boys sat down at the beige table beside them. The oldest was maybe eight and the youngest about three. While two of the brothers argued, the youngest boy dropped to the floor. Wade didn't see any danger from this family. He slid a plastic knife under the flap of the large manila envelope to open it.

The thick pages documented a buy and sell of gold. One invoice detailed Martinez's purchase from South Africa for three million dollars. Another invoice showed the sale of the same gold to an Indian company for five million.

"What have you found?" Vanhoven said.

"Think back to your trade finance training."

"I was too bored to remember anything in that class."

"Then I'll refresh you. It's a gold deal." He held up the bill of lading. "This is what the buyer in India needs when the ship arrives from South Africa. It allows him to claim the gold."

"A title document," Vanhoven said.

"Martinez has Unity Coast Bank send the bill of lading to a bank in India. But they only give it to the buyer when the buyer pays what he owes on the invoice. When he does, the bank gives him the bill of lading so he can take the gold from the shipping company. Then the Indian bank transfers the five million to Martinez here in San Diego. He bought it for three, so he has a profit of two million."

Vanhoven ran his fingers through his hair and gazed up at the ceiling lights. "I'm in the wrong business."

Wade surveilled the room and saw no one but the noisy kids close by. "No legitimate commodity trader has this big of a margin," he said. "It's layering."

"As in money laundering?"

Wade put his finger to his lips. "He probably does hundreds of deals with people he knows to move money around the world. After ten of these, no one can guess where the funds originated."

"Why bother?"

"Compliance departments."

Vanhoven sucked air through his teeth. "The bane of a business developer's existence. I had a client who transferred in a million from Switzerland. Compliance pestered him for two months. 'How did you earn the money?' 'Where?' 'Show me the invoices,' I lost the relationship because of them."

"If you paper your inflow as a trade transaction, no one will dig deeper."

Vanhoven considered that. "Why couldn't he just counterfeit the bill of lading and do the same thing?"

"He probably does that too."

Wade took a bite of his Big Mac. The juicy meat and sauce were just what he needed after Martinez's inquisition. At the table beside them, the two older brothers were giggling. The younger one crawled on the floor somewhere while the mother, her face drooping with exhaustion, chewed on her burger. Vanhoven started on his sandwich and crinkled his nose. He slapped it down on the tray.

"Why would you choose the health food at McDonald's?" Wade said.

Vanhoven made a sheepish frown. Wade noticed that he'd pillaged half his fries. Wade scavenged a handful and stuffed a few into his mouth.

"We need to get more detail about these deals," Vanhoven said. "Who's the guy at your office who gets the bills of lading?"

"Chad Fisher. Chad warned me to stay away from his bank."

"And you still came to work for them after what happened to Bill Langley?"

Wade shook his head. "I didn't know about Langley, and Chad never mentioned him."

Vanhoven chewed on the last fry. "Fisher must have known what happened to him."

"Look, I've known Chad for a long time. He's a good guy."

"You need to worry—we need to worry—about everyone. Even Chad."

No way was Chad involved in money laundering. Wade would talk to Rodrigues about him. Chad was not only familiar with Martinez's international trading, but other crimes hidden inside Unity Coast Bank. He would make a perfect confidential informant.

Something rubbed against Wade's knee. He jumped and his vinyl stool almost tipped over. A small face poked up beside his leg. "Chad Chad Chad," the youngest brother shouted.

The other two boys were throwing fries and giggling at their table. Vanhoven stood. "Damn kids," he said.

CHAPTER THIRTY-EIGHT

Monday afternoon Myles recognized the short, curly-haired girl in the high school courtyard. Her backpack was spotless, like she'd bought it that morning. Just looking at her he knew his dad was all wrong. You didn't avoid things just because you were afraid of them. Fear gave them power.

Sofia was watching the cheerleaders do their tricks in their little red and white and black uniforms. Two girls did headstands on the shoulders of the others. Myles leaned down and whispered, "Did you always want to be a cheerleader?"

She broke into a grin. "So you really do go to school here."

"I'm not in your accelerated Stanford classes," he said.

She made a give-me-a-break grimace.

She turned back to the cheerleaders. "I can't believe the ones on top are upside down."

Myles gave her his sage look. "More blood to the head. It helps them do math."

She burst out with a laugh and covered her mouth.

That was a good start. His humor was still working. "I want to offer you the chance to do something you've never done before."

She cocked her head doubtfully. "And that is . . ."

"Cut class."

They decided on the Pannikin Café. As they walked there, he saw some Hispanics repairing a roof on a house. "Why are Mexicans so good at construction?" he asked.

She frowned at him like he was being stupid. "Because it's work you can be good at without speaking English."

Shit. He'd sounded like some racist rich kid.

She said, "Most people around here think that we're all gardeners and nannies. Or kitchen help and construction. They think we don't make any other music but mariachi. The best thing we ever invented was fish tacos."

Myles stopped. "Wow."

She squeezed up her eyes. "I'm sorry. I tend to go off on that rant. As you can guess, I've said it a few times."

"But it's true," Myles said.

They continued to the café. The last time he'd been there was with his mom. It hadn't changed. Brazil-type music on the sound system. Men in suits next to surfers, housewives, and old artists. A few middle school kids. It was so extra it made him feel like he was twelve again.

Sofia ordered a double espresso. He'd never had a double and decided to match her. They sat in the chairs across from each other with the chessboard table between them.

"My dad and I come here sometimes," she said.

"I guess it's not totally zero chill then."

Her face crumpled a little.

"I'm sorry," he said. "It wasn't a burn. Really."

"If you say so."

Her eyes were so brown. She seemed to look right inside his head.

"What are your plans after you graduate?" she said.

What could he say? She was going to Stanford and he was headed for some junior college. Instead of answering he sipped his espresso.

It was so frigging strong. But if he went to the counter and asked for milk, he'd look like a total amateur. He spooned in sugar.

"I'm going to study to be a doctor," Sofia said.

"Are you thinking of psychology? I can be your patient."

She was supposed to laugh. She didn't. *Damn.*

"Mamá wants me to take over Unity Coast or become a real estate investor." She screwed up her mouth.

Anyone getting into Stanford would have to have a pushy mother. Carmela had seemed like such a bulldozer he couldn't resist. "Your mom was so nice." She'd been a total bitch.

Sofia groaned. "Wait five minutes. Then she turns into a harpy."

He couldn't remember what that was so he gave her something from Hidden Road. "You know, complaining is nothing but avoidance. You complain so you don't have to deal with things."

Her face stiffened. "Aren't you the all-knowing shrink."

"Sorry," he said. "I had to put up with thirteen months of that shit."

She considered what he'd said. "Was it really bad?"

He squeezed his coffee cup. Just thinking about Hidden Road made him do that. "My parents had these two thugs kidnap me to get me there. It was like a prison. I don't think I'll ever forgive them."

She shook her head and blew out air. Just the reaction he'd hoped for. "If my parents sent me to a place like that, I don't know what I'd do."

"You want to know the really strange thing? When they trekked all the way out to Utah . . . for the parenting seminars . . . I never felt closer to them."

She took that in, sipped her espresso. "You're lucky you can still feel like that with both of them," she said.

Myles could tell she loved her dad. But could anyone stand that mother? "I've got something else to deal with," he said. "I made my parents split up."

Her eyes went wide. "You really believe that?"

"My therapist said my acting out made them talk to each other. They only separated after they sent me away. But I think I was always pushing them apart."

She reached across the table. She looked like she wanted to touch his hand. "It's not your fault."

His throat felt lumpy. All this shrink talk was too much like Hidden Road. "Let's switch topics."

She folded the napkin. Her hands were so tiny. "I've been wondering about something. What were you and Melissa doing in Tijuana?"

"What do you think we were doing?"

She stared into him, waiting. He didn't want to lie to her. Not when they were being so up front. *Fuck it.* "I was helping her buy Oxy."

Sofia's face got the same salty look his mom's did. *Shit shit shit.* Why did he have to tell her that? She got up and went to the bathroom. She was going to come out, pick up her backpack, and skurt. But if he bought her something to eat, she'd have to stay, wouldn't she? He went to the counter and got a big chocolate chip cookie and more napkins.

When she returned, she sat and broke off an impossibly small piece of the cookie. "I'm sorry to get upset," she said. "In La Jolla drugs are just how high school kids have fun. It's different in Mexico. Drugs mean torture and murder."

Her words weren't preachy. She seemed to be saying only the tip of what she meant. "Do you know people who that happened to?"

"Yes."

Now he felt like an idiot. "Look, Melissa and I were doing some bad stuff. But those days are over."

Sofia munched on the piece of the cookie. Myles wondered if she thought about everything before she spoke.

"Being kidnapped changes you," she said. "And you've had it done twice."

"Yeah." Why was his voice so soft?

"But in Tijuana they tortured you," she said.

He shifted in his chair. Did she know how he'd screamed and wept and pissed his pants?

"Kids around here have no idea what you went through," she said.

He swallowed. "But you do."

"My dad was kidnapped."

He'd never known. "In Mexico?"

Her face fell and she examined the table. She took a shuddering breath. "The kidnappers screamed at us on the phone. Sometimes three times in the same day. Then nothing for weeks. After a couple of months, they sent us something."

Myles didn't want to ask but knew she wanted him to. "What . . . what was it?"

"His big toe. I opened the package."

He gasped. "Fuck. I can't fucking—" His voice cracked.

She'd squeezed her eyes shut. She was trembling. Myles wanted to reach over and push back her curls. He wanted to cradle her neck in his hand. He wanted to kiss her.

CHAPTER THIRTY-NINE

Wade took pictures of Martinez's shipping documents and emailed them to a secret FBI site. He waited the rest of the afternoon. At six thirty, when most employees had left, he went to Chad's office. Without commenting on the loose flap, Chad glanced inside the envelope of documents and set it on a pile of tax returns.

"Tell me about Martinez's international trading," Wade said.

Chad sat back in his chair. He seemed to stare at the piles of papers that stood like blockades on the floor. "I'm not sure that's the best thing for you."

He knew something. Had to. "What does that mean?"

Chad scratched down an address and "7:30" on a yellow stickie. He put his finger to his lips as if his office was bugged.

Wade pretended to work. At seven twenty, he drove to The Full Moon Saloon on El Cajon Boulevard. An old florescent sign out front looked as if it was last plugged in sometime in the nineties. Inside, most of the light came from beer signs that splotched yellow and red over Wade's suit. Piñatas hung from the ceiling. Wade took in the three middle-aged men nursing drinks at a bar in front of a dark TV. No pool or foosball. No signs for Happy Hour or food. No music. Wade had a feeling that Chad had come here before. It was where a man would go if his child committed suicide.

Chad sat at a booth in the darkest corner, his tumbler of scotch half empty, his head in full tremor. A martini for Wade stood on the table before an empty chair. Wade sat in front of him and they both drank. Chad leaned in and Wade smelled alcohol and cigarette breath.

"Why did you sign up with these rattlesnakes?" Chad said. "Did your son do something so Andre can hold a hatchet over your head?"

For the first time, Wade wondered if Chad had been sucked into Andre's schemes. "What's worrying you?"

"You answer my question and I'll answer yours."

Maybe Vanhoven was right not to trust anyone yet. "I came here because Andre saved Myles' life."

"There are other ways to pay him back."

"I also needed the money. Private school, all the shrinks . . . not to mention the fortune we had to pay for that treatment center. Then there are the mortgages and the rent for the condo and the new loan I owe for the ransom. I'm about as close to bankruptcy as a financial expert can get."

Wade saw in his eyes that Chad wanted to tell him something. "You can't just keep this to yourself," he said. "What's bothering you?"

Chad took in the three men staring at their drinks at the bar, then the entrance door.

"Do you think Martinez's shipments are hiding something?" Wade asked. "Something like money laundering?"

"It's the whole damn bank."

There it was. The words hovered in the air between them. Wade took a slug of martini. "Everything Unity Coast does?"

"Of course not. But there's a lot of shit hidden in the corners."

And if the bank was dirty . . . "Do you think Comunidad de Niños is laundering too?"

"How could they not be?"

Just as Fiona and the DEA suspected. Fiona was in as much danger as he was.

Chad's head and hands were in full quiver. "This is only going to get worse for you and your wife. That's why I'm going to file a Suspicious Transaction Report with FinCen."

"FinCen?"

"The Financial Crimes Enforcement Network."

Filing a SAR with them would ruin the whole case the FBI and DEA were developing. It would put Fiona and him in even more jeopardy and could be a death sentence for Chad.

"Won't Martinez and Andre find out?" Wade said.

"I'm doing it anyway."

He had to slow it down. Get Chad to pull back. "Do you know what happened to Bill Langley?"

"Yes."

"That could happen to you, you know."

"You think I'm not aware of that?"

Wade took in Chad's blotched, tired face and shaking hands. Maybe Chad loved his daughter by standing on his own cliff ledge. Maybe he was ready to do something suicidally heroic.

"Come on, Wade. This is our industry. It's about time someone stood up for what's right."

He seemed as if he'd already written the SAR, as if he was about to transmit it. "Let's give this some thought first," Wade said.

"Why?"

"I'll tell you later."

Chad drew back and squinted at Wade. "Are you working with the Feds?"

Wade shook his head too fast and too hard. He had to get to his car and talk with Rodrigues about Chad.

"I'll give you a few days," Chad said. "Then I'm going to file the SAR."

CHAPTER FORTY

WADE

By eight o'clock that night Rodrigues still hadn't called back, so Wade texted her. "Patience," she replied. But he couldn't be patient. He told Myles that he was going to the pharmacy and went to his car in the underground garage. As soon as he pulled into the street, he got her on Bluetooth. He told her about Chad and said, "He's a perfect informant."

"Wade, you have to be careful who you trust," she said.

"Are you saying what I think you are?"

"Some people lose their compass after their kid dies. Especially when they're under pressure."

"Not Chad."

"Look, it's easy to keep his SAR under the radar. There are about three thousand of them filed in San Diego each month. His will be hidden among many."

Wade's fist slammed against the dashboard. He swerved into the other lane on the highway and swerved back. An SUV behind him honked and flashed its high beams. The driver passed him and gave him the finger.

"What's going on?" she said.

"Don't you see? The problem isn't what happens at FinCen, it's what happens at the bank. Chad's office is bugged. And if they bug his office they must monitor everything else he does. The minute he sends a SAR, Andre and Martinez will know."

"I can't make someone a confidential source because you told me to. We have to check him out."

It was always a waste of time to keep pummeling a wall. But now he wondered if any of the evidence he'd provided was being used. "What happened with the fork I gave your agent in my garage?"

"We got some good DNA, but no hits on anything."

"How about what Andre did in Montreal?"

"Of course he ran away from something. But it was years ago. It was Canada."

Wade squeezed the steering wheel so hard his hands hurt. "And the shipping documents?"

"The shipments actually took place. We can't charge someone for making too much profit. Not based on one deal."

"So, in other words, I've been risking my life—and Fiona's life—for nothing. Thanks."

"No one's in danger."

"That's not what Harold Cartuso said to Fiona."

Silence.

"Did you hear me, Special Agent Rodrigues?"

"Was he talking about Comunidad de Niños or Unity Coast Bank?"

"Don't act like you don't know."

"Special Agent Cartuso never told us."

Wade sucked in a long breath so he wouldn't erupt. These were the people who were going to keep his family alive. *Savasana. Inhale, longer exhale.* But it did no good.

"You mean to tell me you don't know what the DEA is doing with your own case?" Wade asked.

"We're independent agencies. Separate files and investigations."

"He's been harassing Fiona, scaring her to death. You didn't know that?"

"No."

"I suppose you also don't know anything about Bill Langley and his family."

More silence.

"Was he a confidential informant?" When she didn't answer, he said, "Come on, it isn't a hard question."

"We were talking."

"And then he happened to drive his family off a cliff. I suppose you're going to say it was an accident."

"That's what the police report said."

He was so angry he didn't want to talk more and disconnected. She'd hidden Langley from him. How could she not know about Cartuso?

Instead of going home, Wade drove. He got on Highway 5 and was heading toward Chula Vista and the bank before he realized it. He had an idea. Chad had said that bags of cash arrived every night. Wade could get pictures. Maybe the pictures would prod Rodrigues to stop slow walking the investigation.

For two hours he circled the blocks around the bank. Then he saw it, a panel van parked in the alley beside the building. Next to it, a man in a hoody pulled out two canvas bags. This was not a cleaning crew.

He made his way to the parking lot of the mall next to the Red Lobster. In front of him, Unity Coast stood a hundred yards away beyond the edge of the lot and on the other side of the street. Wade's hands trembled as he snapped photos with his phone.

An hour later, the van pulled out and he followed. They passed a mishmash of fast-food restaurants, offices, and used-car lots, then bounced over trolley tracks and turned north on the highway. The

van was in no hurry. Matching its slow speed made him conspicu-
ous, but Wade had no choice. Soon the palmistry sign glowed beside
them, then National City with its huge apartment buildings and the
turnoff for the bridge to Coronado. Wade knew where they were
going.

After a few minutes, they exited the highway. The van slowed beside the boat storage depot and Christian school. It pulled into the
loading bay's door of Martinez's warehouse on the other side of the
street. Wade circled and parked a block away.

He walked back and reached the intersection in front of the
building. On the other side of the street, the warehouse loading bay
door was shut. A light glowed through the window ten feet beyond
the door. At this time of night no one was around to see him loiter-
ing in front. He could look through the glass and the light from
inside would block out his face to the men in the warehouse.

He hurried across the empty street and along the aluminum siding to the window. Inside the warehouse, pieces of a green Mustang
lay on the cement floor: door panels, front and back seats, parts of
the dashboard and the spare tire. Drugs must have been hidden inside them. But he didn't see them. A tall, thin figure with black hair
stepped forward with a shotgun. Martinez. Wade stepped to the
side of the window. He leaned against the aluminum siding and
pressed his back into the hard metal.

When his breathing had settled, Wade peeked through the window again. Two men bent over a seat on the cement floor. One
looked as if he'd been chugging steroids. The other was potbellied
and had greying hair. Some bundles glinted beside them. Wade saw
green under the clear plastic wrapping. Not drugs. Cash.

About eight or ten other stacks stood beside parts of the car. An
old fact drifted into Wade's head. A million dollars of hundred-dollar
bills would form a column a bit less than four feet tall. Maybe four

or five million dollars was on that floor. The men were fitting bundles into the Mustang's seat. It didn't make sense that cash would be in cars that Martinez exported. Launderers were supposed to bring money *to* the bank. Wade raised his phone and snapped pictures.

Martinez yelled something and pointed toward Wade's window.

Wade sprinted across the street. He folded himself into the shadows of the darkened Christian school. He slipped along the edge of its walls. Massive shadows crisscrossed the sidewalk in front of another building. Cement planters. Wade dropped behind the first planter. He curled up and pushed himself into the gritty sidewalk.

The warehouse door creaked open and slammed shut. Someone with a nasal voice spoke in Spanish. Martinez. The other two men answered in deferential tones. They were receiving orders. Orders to start searching the street?

Wade looked around the base of the planter. Martinez clutched the shotgun as if he were poised to raise it and shoot. The other two men swiveled their heads to take in every part of the block. If he leapt up and ran, Martinez would blast him in the back. No one was around to hear the shot. No one would see them drag his body into the warehouse. Wade made himself smaller behind the planter.

The voices continued and their tone downshifted to something lighter. Wade smelled smoke from their cigarettes. The door slammed shut. Above him, cars whizzed over the bridge to Coronado. He waited until he could no longer smell the odor of the tobacco and peeked around the planter. No one.

He rose and the streetlights cast his silhouette onto the sidewalk. He pushed himself into the shadows of the buildings and made his way farther down the block away from the warehouse. When he turned out of sight, he gulped in a breath.

He realized what they were doing. Martinez didn't need to know anything about cars. Not for this operation. Yes, his men secretly delivered bags of cash to the bank. But not to deposit the money. Unity Coast was sorting, counting, and bundling bills. Then the panel van transported the plastic-wrapped money to Martinez's warehouse. They planted the bundles inside the cars he shipped abroad. U.S. dollars were king in developing countries, and Martinez was supplying the currency.

All Rodrigues and the FBI had to do was look at the pictures and get a warrant to search the cars. They'd have everything they needed to arrest Martinez.

Why hadn't those men scoured every hiding place on the street? Maybe they decided they'd only imagined someone spying on them through the window. But there was another possibility. Perhaps Martinez had recognized him and put off dealing with his banker. Perhaps he wanted to have time to enjoy what he would do to him?

CHAPTER FORTY-ONE

FIONA

Fiona was alone in her house. She sat on the red chair in the red living room, the afternoon light dimming around her. The door out front opened and she jumped. She heard rubber soles stamp against the hallway's wooden floor. Myles' tread was unmistakable. Two years before she'd worried her hands each time he came home. Would he be high? Had he skipped school? Now she felt joy as he came into the living room and dropped his bag of books. He gave her a hug. She was lucky that her eighteen-year-old would still wrap his arms around her.

"Sorry I'm late," he said. "I had a school project."

It was a lie, but the glow on his face made her happy. He must have found a girl and was keeping it a secret. She tried not to smile as they walked to the kitchen, the place where they talked.

In the doorway, his eyes widened. "Hamburger?" The meat sat on the cutting board next to sliced onion, hunks of cheese, and thick buns. "Are you sure?" he asked.

"I've been dreaming about hamburger for months," she said.

He grinned. "Do I smell French fries?"

"I confess. But you have to wait twenty minutes."

They sat across from each other. She looked down at the shiny wood and missed the old table with its scratches and dents and solid pedestal. But Wade had seemed to so need that table, and she wasn't sorry she'd let him have it. She poured coffee from the French press and she and Myles clicked the old ceramic mugs.

He breathed in the scent and said, "Real java. I feel like I traveled back in time."

She smiled. "But no shouting now."

His eyes shifted downward

"Sorry, we won't talk about those days. We were both different then."

She could tell he was contemplating how to tell her something. She sipped and waited.

"You know, if you want to get back with Jasper, I'm okay with it," he said.

Myles wanted her to be happy. She loved him all over again for that. "I know how hard it was for you having Jasper here," she said.

He shrugged. "It wasn't that bad. He was a good guy."

Hidden Road had insisted on brutal honesty, but her boy would still lie to make her feel better. It was something good the treatment center hadn't taken away. "The only one I want in this house is you," she said.

He rubbed his shoulder through the rugby shirt. "Dad needs me right now."

Her heart fell a little, but she understood. Wade had to work with Andre and guard what he did every second at that bank. He needed the balance his son would provide. Besides, Myles wouldn't be any safer with her than with Wade. She considered telling him about the FBI and DEA. Myles deserved to know. But how could she ask a teenager to keep such a dangerous secret? He was less at risk not knowing.

"Tell me about how you and Dad met," he said.

She raised her eyebrows. Myles never asked about their courtship. He had to have his eye on a girl. He wanted to talk with her about love.

"I was twenty-one and at Northwestern," she said. She half smiled. Twenty-one would no longer seem like a distant age to him. "I was out with my two best girlfriends at a new jazz club on Morena Boulevard."

"And Dad was there?"

She nodded. "He and these two other guys. All of them in their junior executive suits."

"Why did you talk to him?"

She raised her hands. Wasn't it obvious? "I wanted a free glass of chardonnay."

"You were working it."

"Come on, don't tell me that concept is foreign to you."

Myles gave her a mischievous grin. "Hidden Road changed me."

She rolled her eyes. "We asked the three of them if they got the wrong location. Maybe they thought it was a sports bar or a place where some band played eighties cover songs. They laughed, and your dad pulled his chair up beside me. He told me he was a banker."

"Was he ever not a banker?"

She chuckled. "I think you're going to be surprised. I told him I was a student and asked him if he was also a jazz musician. Maybe he did night gigs to come down from the excitement of his day job."

"You were slinging the burn."

"You know what he said? 'I'm a jazz guitarist in my dreams.' Jesus, who wouldn't get sarcastic when someone said that? But before I could come up with an insult, he asked me a question. What was the last book I'd read? If you ever want to give a girl a line she's never heard before, try that one." She rubbed the finger where her ring used to be. "I thought of a book related to finance, but something he'd never look at."

"I can't believe you read a book about finance."

"It was Mohamed Yunus' *Banker to the Poor*. He invented micro lending, loans to the destitute. But here's the shocker. Your dad knew about it."

"*Banker to the Poor*? Dad?"

"Well, he knew enough to talk about the three chapters I'd read."

Myles was laughing. She knew he could see *her* acting this way. But not Dad.

"Wade asked me what I planned to do after I stopped going to jazz bars. Maybe it was the wine, but I didn't hold back. I said I was studying biology and wanted to become a doctor. Someday I'd help indigenous children in Latin America and Africa."

She'd never told him that part. His face grew pained. "You wanted to travel the world?"

"I was also testing the buttoned-up banker. If he'd said one condescending or sarcastic thing, you wouldn't be here."

Myles thought that over. "I guess I'm lucky to be around."

She laughed. "You know what else he said? That he'd always wanted to travel to Latin America or Asia or Africa and meet the real inhabitants of the world. But student debt got in the way."

"Really? Third World countries?"

"Swear to God. I didn't believe him. I thought he was playing me just to . . . you know."

"I know, Mom."

"He was different then." She pointed to the yin and yang tattoo on her wrist. "We got the tats two weeks after we met. I came up with it and Mr. Plan Everything agreed in less than five seconds."

Myles scratched his head and stared at the table. He looked up, and his eyes were so genuine she worried what he would ask. "So when did you know he was the one?"

She'd spent so long resenting Wade it was hard to answer that question. But her son was being so open and curious, and this was a conversation both of them would cherish. "It started when I stood up that night. You should have seen his face. He hadn't realized I was two inches taller than he was. You know what he said? 'Next time wear heels.'"

They both giggled. It was so un-Wade. "That one-liner told you he was the one?" Myles asked.

"It was everything, even the way he heard the music. He made these slight nods with the beat of the jazz. And in between songs he explained how the bass underpinned everything—the melody, the rhythm, and even the chords. I went home with him that night."

Myles' eyes swelled. "Mom!"

She shrugged. "I was in love."

She looked out the kitchen window and the memory floated in the air over her garden and the fading light. The two of them drinking coffee at her little table the next morning, his hand lingering on the doorway when he had to leave. "I keep saying your name," he'd said. The gentleness of his voice was like another kiss.

Myles said something. She jerked back. "What?"

"What changed him?"

"Life."

"You mean what he did for a living?"

"Sure. But not just that."

She wouldn't say, but Myles knew. Sadness filled his face. "You never got to go to Latin America."

She reached out and held his arm. "You were worth it."

He leaned in, his face earnest. "It was an accident, and you were like twenty-two or twenty-three. You never wanted to get an abortion?"

She ran her hand through his hair. "Best decision I ever made."

He thought about that. Then pointed to the yin and yang tattoo on her wrist. "The male yang is supposed to be the positive, bright opposite of the female yin," he said. "Did you know that?"

"I used to."

"But with you and Dad, I think you're that symbol."

Her face flushed. She had to blink away the tears. She didn't know what to say.

He rose. "I've got to get something in my room."

Myles went down the hall, and she listened to him pound up the stairs. Even as a child his footsteps had been loud and insistent. His door slammed shut on the second floor. He'd always slammed doors. He'd always exerted his will on things and people. She remembered the baths when he was a toddler, and Wade was at the bank working. Myles had screamed and stamped when she washed his head. After, she'd wrapped him up in a towel and buried her nose in the sweet, clean smell of his silky hair. He squeezed her tight. Then she'd put him to bed and he made her lie down with him. Sometimes she fell asleep with his arms around her. During those years she'd physically felt something about Myles that Wade had missed with all his hours of work. Myles was a child who could barely contain his need to hold someone close.

For a moment she would let contentment warm the room she loved.

For a moment she didn't have to think about anything else.

CHAPTER FORTY-TWO

FIONA

The next day, just being at the office made Fiona obsess about the danger her family was in. She felt so dejected she left work early and drove to La Jolla High. Having coffee with Myles after his classes would make her feel better.

Fiona had always thought that the school looked like a spa with its stucco Spanish architecture, outdoor pool, and vine-covered fences. Some of these teenagers had brand-new cars. She searched for Myles in the stream of kids coming through the side door. They all looked alike, backpacks hanging from their shoulders, thumbs tapping phones.

One boy by the door had his back to Fiona and talked intensely to a petite girl with brown curly hair. His bony arms caught her eye. The boy slowly bent to touch the girl's lips. His tender kiss had nothing of a teenager's rampaging hormones.

It was Myles.

Fiona sighed. Hidden Road's rule about not dating for a year was ludicrous. For a teenage boy, dating was an immutable law of nature. The girl wore a buttoned-up blouse. She had nice jeans—no slits across the knees or worn, stringy patches at mid-thigh. No purple hair or visible piercings. She looked so wholesome. That should have been a relief but was a tad disappointing, as if Myles had sold out and moved to the suburbs. Still, something about the gentleness of that kiss made her proud.

Myles and the girl walked to the street. Myles draped his arm around her and they headed toward Fiona, laughing and chatting. They were so caught up in each other they didn't see her in the car. There was something familiar about this girl.

Another teen yelled, "Sofia," and burst out in Spanish.

Sofia Ouellette, Andre's daughter. Fiona pushed her hand against her mouth. She had to stop this. Now.

Myles and Sofia strolled down Fay Avenue. Andre's condo was close by. Oh God, they were going to visit him. But Andre was working, and Carmela rarely left their house in Tijuana. That meant Myles and Sofia were on their way to an empty home. Fiona pressed her hands together, fingers sliding into one another and out. Now that soft kiss seemed as threatening as a gun.

After Myles and Sofia had drifted a block ahead of her, she pulled out behind some cars. The two teens took a leisurely right turn at the street that led to the elementary school. That was the wrong direction for the condo. Fiona's heart slowed a little. At least they weren't aiming for a place where they could be alone together.

She drove to Pearl Street, then backtracked. At the corner she pulled into a blacktop lot of small storefront businesses. Myles and Sofia meandered toward her from the opposite direction, barely sensing anything but each other. They passed the used bookstore and climbed the steps to the deck of Pannikin Café. She and Myles had talked over coffee at this same place. There was no reason Fiona wouldn't go there today for a cup.

She found a parking spot on the side street and walked to the coffeehouse. She made her way inside and straight to the ancient wooden serving bar. Crosby, Stills, Nash, and Young were harmonizing above the hissing espresso machine. Fiona ordered and tried to appear as if she were searching for a place to sit. She took in the antique armoire and the folding auditorium chairs by the window, then the walls of local art and photography. Myles and Sofia were snuggling on a banquette at the back wall while they bent over a picture on the table.

"Myles!" she called.

His head shot up and his eyes widened. "Mom?"

He didn't look overjoyed to see her. He set the picture beside him on the banquette and put his arm back around Sofia's shoulders. Her son had no guilt or embarrassment about the forbidden girl-friend. For an instant her pride in him overcame her fear.

Fiona carried her mug of coffee to their table in the corner. Sofia pushed off Myles' arm and stood to shake Fiona's hand. Myles stood up slowly, as if each part of his body were a separate piece.

"Mrs. Bosworth, it is so nice to see you. Please join us." Sofia frowned a nod at Myles, as if to chide him for not inviting his mother to sit. He stepped away to retrieve another chair. Already this girl had more power over her son than she did.

Fiona sat in front of them. She watched her son sip his espresso, his pinkie extended. He held the coffee in his mouth as if to more fully absorb the taste. She'd never noticed Myles had learned to drink like an Italian.

"You're having coffee every day," Myles said to her.

"Now that Jasper has left, I've gone back to it."

Myles laughed. "When I lived with you, I'd sneak it into my room."

Hidden Road forbade any kind of stimulant, including coffee. Here was another rule Myles had broken since coming home. But also another honest admission. She couldn't get her mind around all these contradictions.

"I could really use a brownie right now," Myles said.

"Go for it," Fiona said.

He rose and walked to the serving counter. He stood behind a man in a tailored suit, who stood behind a forever-surfer with grey pigtails. She'd have a couple of minutes alone with Sofia. Like her mother, Sofia was as delicate as a fairy and made Fiona feel like a giant.

"So, are you two dating?" Fiona made her voice light and friendly.

"I guess we are," Sofia said. "It's been very fast."

She was straightforward, no prevaricating or New Age aphorisms. Not like her father. "Does Andre know?"

Sofia's eyes lit up. "He thinks Myles is wonderful."

Fiona took a gulp of coffee. She remembered Carmela, her face as sharp as a hatchet, and set down the mug too hard. "Then your mother knows too?"

Sofia's face contracted. "It's not Mamá's choice who I date."

Evidently the dragon mother had higher aspirations for her Stanford girl.

Myles set down a plate with two brownies, a knife, and three forks. With Sofia, he'd rediscovered his manners. Sitting close to her, he said, "I think we're a bit beyond Hidden Road's rules, don't you, Mom? I'm getting straight A's."

Sofia nodded at him. "And I'm going to make sure that continues."

She must have known all about Hidden Road. Some girls would be drawn to a boy so dangerous he was sent away. Especially girls who'd studied their whole lives.

This was insane. She and Wade were destroying a cartel bank run by this girl's father.

She thought of an angle. "Wade is a stickler for contracts. And you're living with him now." *No dating for a year.*

"Sofia and I are friends," he said. "The home contract doesn't prohibit friends."

"Friends" didn't encompass that kiss.

"Sofia is going to Stanford," Myles said.

He knew how to make a girl appeal to his mother. "I heard," Fiona said.

Sofia cut the brownie in pieces, and they drank their coffee, the chatter in the room bouncing into the spaces between them. Fiona remembered the picture Myles had set beside him. She said, "What were you two so engrossed in?"

Myles put it on the table—a framed ink drawing of a scaly snake with two frog's legs. Its body looped around in a circle until the snake's unhinged mouth was about to swallow its own tail. It looked like some kind of black magic.

"Alchemists made it like five or six hundred years ago," Myles said. "It's called an ouroboros. I think it's totally cool."

"It's my dad's," Sofia said. "He should have been born in the Middle Ages. He would have been a wizard."

Myles had only just met Andre, and Andre gave him this? Fiona pushed her fingers into the sticky table.

"The alchemists really had things figured out," Myles said. "The ouroboros is like the cycle of life. It consumes and is eaten—life, death, and rebirth. It's everything at the same time."

The way his face glowed made her shiver. It was as if Andre had slithered inside him.

Sofia grabbed the drawing and put it in her backpack. She must have seen how much this dark art had unsettled her boyfriend's mother. "I'm sorry, I have an essay to finish," she said.

An essay to *finish*, not *start*. A month before, Fiona would have been overjoyed that Myles was dating her. She and Wade were going to have to work together to suppress this budding crush.

But that kiss . . . It was so sad.

They left the café. Outside, Sofia walked toward her condo, and she and Myles trudged to Fiona's car. As Fiona unlocked the doors, a man in a blue suit and a buzz cut passed by on the sidewalk. He was built like a weightlifter. Harold Cartuso met her eyes and looked away.

CHAPTER FORTY-THREE

WADE

Three days had passed since Wade fled from Martinez's warehouse, and he hadn't seen Martinez since. Rodrigues thought that the reflected light in the warehouse window had masked his image, and he had nothing to worry about. But Wade wasn't at all sure. It was Halloween and the street was full of drunken people in costumes. Wade couldn't help thinking that someone in a mask was following him.

Myles wasn't at the condo when he got home from the bank, and he was free to pace between the kitchen and the living room. How long could he hide the pressure inside him? This might go on for months, and Myles' and Fiona's lives were also in his hands. He looked at his watch. It was too late for a yoga class, so he sat at the kitchen table and opened a good Bordeaux. It was the only tranquilizer he had.

His cellphone rang. Wade stared at it on the table. If he didn't pick up, the caller would just telephone him again. His arm was shaking as he answered.

"*Des bonnes nouvelles*," Andre said. "You pitch the Felton building to investors tomorrow."

Wade blew out a relieved breath. An investor presentation meant all the partners were coming to the bank. Andre would never offer that if he thought Wade was a spy. "Great news," he said.

"Yes. This is a big step toward our goal."

The FBI could get pictures and identify each participant. This was even better than he could have predicted. Wade gripped the sides of his kitchen table. He had to keep his voice neutral. "I'll get to work on the presentation," he said.

"It will be at my house in Tijuana."

Wade knocked over his glass of wine.

"Just you, not Vanhoven. My driver picks you up in the same place at eleven." Andre hung up.

Andre knows. Martinez knows.

"Dad, everything all right?" Myles stood in the entranceway to the little kitchen. When had he come home? Myles stared at the wine dripping into a deep red pool on the tiled floor.

"I have to go out," Wade said.

"Where you going?" Myles asked.

"A drink with a friend."

"On Halloween? Won't the bars be jammed?"

"I know a quiet place."

Myles raised his eyebrows. *A drink with a woman besides Mom?*

"It's with a guy I used to work with," Wade said.

He left while Myles mopped the floor with paper towels. As he trudged down the fifteenth floor's hallway, he remembered how he'd punished Myles his whole life for lying. He took the elevator to the underground garage. By the time he got inside his car he was shaking.

Rodrigues set up an emergency meeting. Wade drove to a CVS and examined shampoos while Rodrigues' colleagues checked for tail cars and scanned his BMW for a tracking device. Some young men walked by him dressed as tigers and skeletons. A woman wore a Mona Lisa mask with a single eye. The eye stared at Wade.

Rodrigues didn't call, which meant he was clear to drive to the Marriott, one of many hotels crammed along Highway 8. Once there, Wade went to the reception desk and said he was Mr. Butler. The key card was for a room on the eighth floor. When he got there, Rodrigues opened the door and ushered him past a king bed to a chair beside a table and drawn curtains. The air reeked of furniture polish.

She sat opposite at the table. Her pocked grin didn't make him feel any better. "Wade, this is a really great development."

"You seem to have forgotten that Martinez saw me spying at his warehouse."

She beat her nails on the table as if considering the truth of what he'd said. "His men would have chased you down."

"Maybe they prefer that entertainment in Mexico."

"You're going to Mexico because that's where people way up on their org chart meet. People who can't risk arrest by coming to San Diego."

Or because getting rid of someone in Tijuana was much easier than arranging a car crash in Colorado. "I'm not going."

She frowned and tapped her nails.

"Stop that. You sound like a fucking clock."

She flattened her hand. "Look, I understand how you're worried. But the DEA will be watching the whole time you're there. They'll swoop in if anything looks dangerous."

"In Mexico?"

"They have more cross-border freedom than we do."

But they wouldn't be inside Andre's house. He shook his head.

Someone knocked on the door and opened it. A man with huge shoulders and a buzz cut stepped inside. He wore a ring as large as a brass knuckle. "Harold Cartuso," he announced in a high voice. He had to be the DEA special agent who'd harassed Fiona. Wade rose and Cartuso's hand enveloped his. When Cartuso sat on the bed it looked more like a queen than a king.

"Wade is worried about going to Tijuana," Rodrigues said. "Because of what happened at Martinez's warehouse."

"We had no idea you were going there," Cartuso said. "It's pretty hard to protect you if you don't tell us what you're doing."

"The question is, what will happen in Tijuana?" Wade said.

"Before you decide to go or not, let me show you the tech we'll give you," Rodrigues said. She opened her briefcase and placed a tie pin and a black pen on the table in front of him. "This stuff is amazing."

It was the latest FBI version of a wire. The diamond in the gold tie pin was actually glass—a lens of a miniaturized video camera. The sleek pen was a microphone.

"No way any cartel technician can discover this," Rodrigues said. "These only record, so no one can pick up a transmission signal. It's military grade."

"But you won't hear anything in real time," Wade said. Like his screams.

Cartuso itched his big cheeks. "Think about Andre, Wade. Do you really think he'd soil himself by doing wet work at his house?"

Each sentence this man's tiny voice uttered was more frightening. "But you've already got plenty of evidence to nail Martinez and Andre."

"And we thank you for that," Cartuso said. "But they're just operations men. We want the CEOs who'll be at your meeting. The kingpins."

The only place where the DEA wouldn't be following him was inside Andre's house. But Andre wouldn't kill or torture anyone inside his temple. Wade took a deep yoga breath. The furniture polish was so overpowering he coughed.

"I knew you were braver than that," Rodrigues said.

"You were giving it the normal banker's caution," Cartuso said.

False compliments to nudge him forward. Wade knew the game.

They instructed him how to use the micro-electronics and he went home. His little kitchen smelled like curry. Myles had nuked some frozen Indian food in the microwave before he went out. Wade thought about Fiona. They were committed to sharing everything. Should he call and tell her he was going back to Tijuana? She'd try to persuade him not to, and he didn't want that argument.

He put on music in the living room, then bent over in a yoga rag doll pose. His spine and shoulders loosened while Joe Pass improvised with Oscar Peterson. Then the cellist from Oregon played a melody inspired by Icarus. What if this was the last time he got to hear them? No, he couldn't think that way. He turned off the music and went to the bedroom. He lay down on his bed and stared at the dark ceiling.

CHAPTER FORTY-FOUR

November 1 was Day of the Dead in Mexico. Not a good time to make a presentation to killers, Wade thought. He felt both run-down and jumpy, but Chad looked as if he were dissolving. His hair was greasy, his cheeks streaked and flaccid. His black suit must have been twenty years old. This was the first time Wade had seen him in almost a week. They were in a parking lot in San Isidro and about to cross the border together. Chad would go to conduct Know-Your-Client meetings while Wade made his presentation.

As they walked, Wade asked, "Everything okay at the bank?"

"No comment."

Wade stopped on the blacktop between rows of cars. "Chad, you look exhausted. What's going on?"

"I didn't sleep well." His voice was hoarse. "A nightmare scared the shit out of me."

"What was it?"

Chad fumbled in his suit coat and pulled out cigarettes. He frowned and slipped the pack back. "You really want to know?"

"Why not? We don't have to be anywhere yet."

He stared at Wade as if gauging his sincerity, then said, "This giant black crow swoops down from a huge building and carries away a child. I chase after it and start flying through the air. But I can't catch the thing. When I wake up, I'm not breathing." Chad's face quivered. He pointed to his ancient black Samsonite briefcase. A green cord was tied around the handle. "Haley liked green. She passed a year ago this week."

Wade didn't know what to say. The dream was ominous. They continued in silence into the building entrance to Mexico, then through a Customs passageway above the lanes of border traffic below. At the Mexican inspection counter, the official pointed at the dents and scratches that gouged Chad's hard-shelled briefcase. "You should buy a new one in Tijuana," he said.

"I like this one," Chad said. "It's as old and beat up as I am."

Wade laughed. Chad didn't. They walked to a staircase that led to the same sputtering and honking traffic that he and Myles had faced the prior weekend. Andre's driver waited in the side street. Wade surveyed the area around the Mercedes. No burly goons waiting in front of the exposed pharmacy. No SUVs with opaque windows. He only saw an old man and a few tourists. Maybe they were the DEA agents.

The inside of the Mercedes was as quiet as a library. The car wound through traffic as if it were floating on air. When they stopped at a light, Chad stared at a mother and child in black veils on the sidewalk. They had matching white-painted faces and black lines drawn around their lips and eyes. Their hair was festooned with crepe flowers.

"I hate the costumes people wear on Day of the Dead," Chad said. A weariness seemed to weigh him down.

Why did the presentation have to be today?

Soon the car slid up the hill past the water-starved trees and stopped at Andre's house. Three Mercedes, a Lamborghini, a Ferrari, and a Bugatti had parked on the street. Each had its own black-suited driver and black-suited bodyguard. Wade relaxed a little. These rich people wouldn't want to be around if anyone planned to hurt him. He wasn't in any danger.

Wade turned to Chad. "Eventually the days will get better."

Chad shot him a scowl. "Bullshit just makes it worse." His breath smelled as if the air was curdling inside him.

Wade got out and the car drove away. Wade walked to the front door and the camera above it turned to stare at him. The sun beat down on his head for several seconds before the door opened. He took a breath. Time to go where no one from the DEA could see anything.

Andre and Carmela had transformed their house from a Buddhist sanctuary to a high-priced conference center. They'd switched out the silk furniture, glass table, and bonsai tree with sleek chrome and leather chairs. The *shoji* divider had disappeared and the Japanese table was raised up for a banquet spread: sushi, endive hors d'oeuvres, Wagyu beef sliders, and—for old-schoolers—filet and cilantro tacos. Oysters in the half shell were stacked on a waterfall of ice. The sheer volume drained Wade's appetite.

About twenty men and women mingled over the sisal rugs and polished floors. Wade didn't recognize anyone but Andre and Carmela. No Day of the Dead costumes in this group. The men were dressed in tailored slacks and open-necked shirts. The women wore wraps and pencil skirts that looked hand-painted. Wade's tie clip was the cheapest accessory in the room. He shifted his torso so the miniature camera would get shots of all of them. He looked out the full-length windows and saw black-suited guards roaming the land beyond Andre's walls.

A spicy citrus perfume wafted over him. Carmela was scented and dressed for battle. Her black dress had flourishes of gold and a big "V"—Versace?—on the torso. The thick bracelet and earrings were encrusted with diamonds. She looked like something out of a display case.

"Well?" she said. No hug or kiss on the cheek today.

"I feel like I'm doing a presentation on Halloween."

"Halloween? That's a children's holiday. Day of the Dead is much more important than Halloween." She straightened, and her pride broke through her stiff face. "In Mexico we honor the dead like the Aztecs. Families go to the cemetery with food and blankets and marigolds are everywhere. You know who we talk to? The souls of the people we loved."

After the crowd here listened to him, they'd get ready to go commune with the dead. Wade shifted his shoes on the bamboo floor.

"What's the key issue for these people?" Wade said.

"Why in the hell do you ask me this now?"

"Andre only told me about the presentation last night. I barely had time to put the slides together."

She glowered at him for a few interminable seconds. "You tell them that you will help them discreetly acquire assets. This is just the first of many deals."

Discreetly, as in using cutouts to buy the buildings. The real owners would stay in the shadows with their machine guns and chain saws.

"Don't disappoint me," she said.

He blurted out the words before he could stop himself. "I didn't realize I work for you."

"Now you know. Never forget it."

She turned and walked over to plant a kiss on another woman's cheek. Wade lifted his chest. He was determined to look confident, no matter what. A maid in a black dress handed him a glass of sparkling water. A slice of lime floated in it like a dead fish. The ceiling fan paddled whiffs of perfume over him.

A stubby bald man approached. They were the only two people in suits.

"It's great that you're working with Andre," the man said.

His deep, slightly accented voice sounded familiar.

"Wilfredo Polanco," the man said.

"The kidnap negotiator?"

"None other."

Of course the negotiator had to be part of this. Wade shook his hand and made sure the tie clip got a good shot. "Unity Coast is going to be fun."

"Fun?" Polanco squinted.

Wrong word. Wade segued. "You're an investor too?"

"Andre invited me as a favor. After his own kidnapping, he was grateful."

Grateful for a negotiation that had dragged on for months and cost Andre his big toe.

Polanco put a hand on Wade's arm and gave a gentle squeeze. "A word about your presentation. Don't say that what you do is fun. These are very serious investors." Polanco smiled and grimaced at the same time. "I'm sure you will be fantastic. Drink your Perrier. Otherwise, you look nervous."

Wade sipped. The water was prickly and sour.

Andre limped over. His face was so relaxed it looked sleepy. Not a single wrinkle blemished his purple shirt and grey blazer, whereas Wade's suit had rumpled up in the car. Wade smelled a cologne that was like cedar wood but sickeningly more earthy.

Andre said, "These people expect something better than the boring banker. You must give them the wow."

"The wow?"

"I know you can do it. It is why I hired you."

There was nothing "wow" about numbers and ratios and technical expertise.

Andre guided him to a group of men standing as they ate from plates. After he made introductions in English, Andre walked away. Wade shifted his torso so his tie clip captured their faces. He took another sip and managed a smile.

"You're Andre's new finance man?" one of them asked.

"We're going to do great things together," Wade said.

"I hope you're better than the last one he brought here," the man next to him said.

He had to be referring to Bill Langley. "What happened to him?" Wade asked.

"He was terminated," the first man said.

"You mean fired," the other man said.

Both men excused themselves and wandered on. Wade slipped over to the waterfall and pretended to admire the tree and water lilies. The Buddha statue appeared amused, as if he knew the answers if Wade knew the questions. But Wade had no idea what to ask.

Andre rang a bell. The room quieted and people sat in the chrome and leather chairs. "Thank you for coming," Andre said. "Today I introduce you to Wade Bosworth. He tells you about the best investment in Southern California. Then we celebrate the Day of the Dead."

CHAPTER FORTY-FIVE

Servants pulled down cloth blinds over the windows at Andre's house. The first PowerPoint slide materialized on a blank wall and the room grew quiet. Below a purple sky, the Felton building cast a yellow, white, and rose shadow onto the dark waters of the Pacific Ocean. The shot was so good that people nodded to each other.

"This is the first of many excellent investments we'll help you discreetly acquire," Wade said. He paused to let them take in the photo for a few more seconds, then launched into the numbers. The slides flashed assumptions, then rents, occupancy, expenses, cash flow, and debt coverage. The Return on Investment was good for San Diego's high-end commercial real estate market.

But something was wrong. The whole group began to chatter in Spanish and the woman next to Carmela shriveled up her face. Wade realized why, but it was too late to change the presentation. This return couldn't compare with yields from drugs.

"The numbers don't include another advantage," Wade said. "The depreciation is a big tax deduction. Not just on the building."

An old man rubbed hair so thick and brown it had to be a weave. "We pay taxes in Mexico," he said.

"If you do, you're the only one," someone shouted.

The eruption of laughter hit like a siren. Wade pushed his shoes into the wooden floor to steady himself. He waited for the mirth to die, then explained that their California limited liability company would own the building. Maybe they didn't pay taxes in Mexico, but the LLC would owe them in the U.S.

The frowns and eye-rolling moved from row to row. Wade heard the ceiling fans beating the air above him.

Andre hobbled forward. "It's a long-term *stratégie*. In five years, the building has value fifty percent more."

Wade tried to look as if fifty percent were a conservative estimate rather than sheer delusion. He said, "None of San Diego's other skyscrapers has this architecture and view." At best, a gross exaggeration.

No acknowledgment. Not even a head nod.

Wade soldiered on with the details of the financing plan. The investors would need to put down twenty percent of the value of the purchase. A consortium of financial institutions would lend the rest. At least that produced a few shrugs.

Carmela stood up in the front corner and turned. She glared from one side of the room to the other and spoke in Spanish. Wade heard the word *familia* over and over again. He knew then how he should have framed the proposal. Buying the Felton building wasn't about Return on Investment. It was about getting their families out of the drug business and into clean U.S. assets. Unity Coast gave them the legitimacy they needed for the first step in the transition: a perfectly legal purchase of the best real estate in San Diego.

And then it was over. The investors didn't shake his hand or approach him. He smelled citrus perfume behind him and knew what was coming. Carmela handed him a gin and tonic.

"You are the one who is supposed to sell the deal, not me," Carmela said.

"The market is overvalued. If it was up to me, I wouldn't have bought this building."

She lifted her face and watched the ceiling fan slice the air. "I'm not happy with your performance today. Maybe Peter Vanhoven should do the presentation next time." She walked away. After three steps she yelled something in Spanish. A man in a striped shirt and emerald cufflinks laughed with the deep roar of a lion.

Had she told Bill Langley that she wasn't happy with his performance?

Andre limped over and the cedar wood scent of his cologne blocked out Carmela's perfume. "We have liftoff," he said. "Think of our *banque* in five years. We are the leading commercial real estate lender in Southern California. Every other bank is jealous. The headhunters all call you and your money worries are over. Myles' college is paid. And . . ." His sly grin seemed to lean in and embrace Wade. "Fiona kicks away that *artiste maricón.*"

Wade decided not to tell him that Jasper was already gone. "Did you have to say we'd be the number-one real estate lender?"

Andre clucked his tongue and squinted through the thick lenses at Wade. "Do not let what is in front of you be a limitation. Imagine about the new life you will lead. The *sueños,* the *rêves,* they are your guide." He put his hand on Wade's shoulder. "Come."

As they walked, the enormous airy room seemed as off-kilter as Andre's limping steps. He led Wade to the tree beside the Buddha. The waterfall murmured softly beside them as Andre's face sank into concern. "Do not become like Chad. His terrible shadow covers him."

Wade remembered how beaten down Chad had looked this morning. "Losing a daughter will do that to you."

Andre sighed. He gripped Wade's shoulder. "Maybe you can help him. You are a good friend."

Wade caught an undercurrent. He tightened his mind into focus. "Help him with what?"

"I thought that he comes to my bank and he feels better. But now he is in a terrible tunnel. His work suffers. I feel something very bad inside him."

"Like what?"

"Like he might try to hurt himself."

CHAPTER FORTY-SIX

The doorbell rang. Fiona walked to the front. "Who is it?" she called through the door.

"I want to take another look at the paintings," a high voice said.

She let in Cartuso. Today he wore an ugly blue suit that fit with his clodhopper shoes. He lumbered into the living room and ran his finger in the air to encompass the red furniture and red walls. "This room looks like it needs a tourniquet."

His sarcasm didn't bother her; she wasn't afraid of him anymore. Not since she learned he was a DEA agent and not some spy hired by Andre. "Jasper has moved out. But I think you know that."

Cartuso sat, and the wingback chair looked small around him. He expanded his chest and looked down at the coffee table. "Can't say I'm going to miss his tea. God, even the smell . . ." He winced and shook his head.

"What do you want?"

He stared at her. She waited him out.

"Agent Rodrigues and I fitted out Wade with some state-of-the-art electronics last night."

"He's recording his conversations at the bank?"

He studied her for a few seconds. "Let me give you a bit of information you don't know. Right now Wade is at Andre's house in Tijuana. He's pitching to some higher-ups in the drug business."

Her breath caught in her throat. Wade in Tijuana? Wade with Andre and Carmela and their killers? She made her way to the couch and held on to one of its arms. She knew why Wade hadn't told her. Because it was dangerous and he didn't want her to worry. Which only made it more frightening.

"What do you want?" She heard the edge in her voice.

"Just some information."

"What information?"

"Simple stuff. Where the money in the foundation goes. Amounts, purposes, destinations. Donor names and addresses."

"Do you think no one will notice if I start copying files?"

He pulled something out of the pocket of his suit. The bracelet looked small in his hand. "This takes pictures," he said.

She took the bracelet from him. It was a silver band with a single ugly, clear stone. At least it didn't look like a camera.

"You press the clasp to take a shot," he said.

Shot. The word made her wince.

"You know these people are corrupting the nonprofit world just like they're corrupting Wade's industry. What they do for kids is all pretend, all just a front. They're hiding money, Fiona. Money they get from addicting teenagers like Myles. Doesn't that offend you?"

"Don't patronize me about morality."

"Because you've got that covered?"

She was silent.

"Look, it's not just me and all the big government agencies. Wade is also with us. He wants to stop them. That's why he's putting his life on the line by going to Mexico."

He's protecting his family, that's what he's doing.

As if he could read her thoughts, he said, "Do you think your family will ever be safe while these killers are walking around?"

She detested this man, but they had no other allies. They'd be defenseless without Rodrigues and Cartuso and their resources. What were a few pictures compared to what Wade was doing in Tijuana?

"Just documents?" she asked.

"It's a good place to start." His smile seemed forced. "Don't worry, we'll look out for you and Wade and Myles."

Should she believe that hard face? *No.*

He took out his phone from his suit pocket and glanced at it. He rose while he read the message. The floor creaked. "We'll talk soon," he said.

She didn't walk him out. He thumped down the hall. The front door whined open and clicked shut. The bracelet lay on the coffee table. She picked it up and ran it through her hand. The metal was warm and the stone smooth. It didn't look threatening, but she knew it was.

CHAPTER FORTY-SEVEN

WADE

In the frigid back seat of the Mercedes, Wade closed his eyes and inhaled and exhaled to dispel the tension. He needed a trip to the yoga studio. He needed to stretch and twist and bake out the stress. But first he had to protect Chad, both from himself and from Andre and Martinez. Andre's warnings were on the recording Wade carried with him. Rodrigues and Cartuso had to arrange something now.

An announcement blared in Spanish. Wade looked out the window and saw speakers on the back of a flatbed truck. Cars were jammed on each side of the street, a yellow median of thin palms between them. On his right, a line of women in tight pants and short skirts stood along a green wall beside a barbershop pole.

Wade pushed forward on the seat. "Why are we here?"

"You finish late so I pick up your friend on the trip. I do not have time to return later."

"In the red-light district?"

"He is a man, no?"

This was a trap. They wanted Wade to look for Chad inside a bordello so they could take pictures. *Your wife will never come back if she sees these.* He had to stay in the car.

Groups of three or four prostitutes, some in Day of the Dead costumes, sashayed down the sidewalks. Suppose one of these women—or two—tried to clamber into the car? He'd block the door. If another entered through the other door, he'd push himself outside and run to a taxi. There were at least ten on this block.

The Mercedes slid by a taco stand, a shoeshine boy, and a sushi bar. Then a hair salon and a perfume shop. The car stopped. A singer belted out a ballad in English on a loudspeaker somewhere. A woman in an orange dress and pointed hat walked beside them. Her gloves were painted to look like skeleton hands, and she carried a skeleton doll swaddled in orange cloth. Wade turned to his left. A huge hotel and bar stood on the other side of the yellow street divide. Strings of Christmas bulbs twinkled green, red, and white around the hotel's palm trees.

A white stucco church was next to the hotel. "Is he in the church?" Wade asked.

The driver pointed to someone in a green tux and a Donald Trump mask. The greeter ushered men past green ropes and through a black door. Above the entrance, a rippling purple and white banner of light poured out a single word: "Delicias."

Chad would never come here.

"I order you to go on," Wade said. "You must come back for him."

Bang!

Something had hit a cleared space on the sidewalk in front of the bar. A few men and the greeter moved back. A briefcase had burst open. It was an old black and silver model. Papers sailed and dove; pages slid along the cement sidewalk. The greeter slid off his mask and slowly approached the exploded case. He looked up the six stories of the hotel. The other men on the sidewalk looked up.

Something large flew beside the building, its black arms flapping. Chad thudded against the cement.

Wade threw open the car door and sprinted across the median. Chad lay facedown, his arms and legs splayed out on the sidewalk in front of the Delicias building. The greeter, his Trump mask hanging from his neck, drew himself down to Chad's black suit. He touched him as if Chad might break into pieces.

Wade kneeled and put his hand on the back of Chad's suit coat. It was wet. Wade felt for breathing. Nothing. He laid his head down next to him and whispered, "Chad."

Chad's face was a mash of red.

Wade caressed the back of his head. "I'm here with you," he said. "You're not alone." He smelled blood, then frying beef and tortillas. Voices spoke in Spanish and somewhere someone was weeping. A radio announcer was selling something. A siren wailed.

A hand touched Wade's shoulder. "There is nothing that you can do for poor Chad," Andre said.

"I won't leave him here," Wade said.

"The police say that you must leave. They must take care of him now."

"No."

"If you do not leave, they arrest you. How does that help Chad?"

Andre and the tuxedoed greeter pulled him to his feet. In the crowd in front of him, a skeleton crossed his arms. A woman with her face painted white held a red parasol and squinted as if she were crying. Her eyes were rimmed with dabs of aqua.

Andre led him past the green ropes and through the black door. Inside, red and blue lights blinked and wavered around an upraised stage and a metal pole. Two long counter bars stood on either side. The room looked as if it should burst with noise, but it was quiet and empty.

Wade collapsed into a leather chair at a table bordering the stage and Andre sat beside him. The greeter cleared away painted toy skulls and orange candles. Another man scooped up half-filled beer bottles and glasses and set down a double shot of mezcal and a chaser. Wade took in the red of the tomato juice. His stomach pitched and he looked away. A skeleton mannequin lay on its back at the closest bar. The skeleton chugged from a huge bottle of tequila it held with its hands and legs.

A soft-faced policeman sat in front of them. The front door opened behind the man and the white light cast his head in a halo. In English, he said, "It is terrible."

"What happened?" Wade said.

The policeman pulled out a small notebook and pen and spoke in Spanish.

Andre said, "Detective Garcia wants to know what you saw first."

Wade told them what he'd seen from the Mercedes. After he'd finished, Andre and the policeman conferred in Spanish. Wade's eyes drifted to the other bar without the skeleton. Mounted TVs soundlessly churned out soccer and UFC fights.

"Detective Garcia says he talked with the people here," Andre said. "Chad went with one of the women. They spent time together in a room on the highest floor. Then Chad runs to the roof. He was there perhaps twenty minutes and he throws his *maletín*. Then he throws himself."

The story seemed as false as Bill Langley driving his family off a cliff.

Andre released a long, sorrowful sigh. "I am sorry, Wade. His daughter, she also suicided herself. She also jumped from a building."

Wade remembered Chad in his office surrounded by walls of paper, Chad sucking down alcohol and tobacco. He wouldn't end his agony in a leap from a building. Chad forced himself to go on feeling the pain each day. It was how he kept on loving his daughter.

Andre rose and led him to the front entrance. The black door opened, and the bright day hit him like a flame. Chad still lay crumpled on the sidewalk, his black suit in a pool of red. A young woman with a face painted gold stared down at him. Sticks like rays of sun stuck out from the flowers in her hair. Next to her stood a girl in a school uniform of a pleated tartan skirt and knee socks.

"Go home," Andre said. "I will take care of this."

No matter what happened, Andre would always know how to clean it up. Wade loathed him for that. "I'm staying," he said.

An ambulance appeared down the block. It slowly passed a street band of men holding tubas, trumpets, and drums, then nosed through the crowd around Chad. Men in red sweatshirts got out. They moved him into a black bag as if Chad's body might fall apart. They lifted the bag onto the stretcher.

"These men do not let you come into the ambulance or go to the morgue," Andre said. "You must go home now."

Wade knew he was in shock, but he forced his mind to think. The briefcase. He looked for signs of it and the business papers that had flown out. There was nothing by the cement walls of the building. Nothing by the green ropes and the black door. He spotted the remains of the handle on the sidewalk. The green cord was still wrapped around it. He picked it up and put it in his pocket.

Andre led him across the street. Wade pushed himself into the Mercedes and Andre eased the door closed. "I am very sorry," the driver said.

The car muffled the outside sounds as if he were wearing earmuffs. Wade turned for a last look. A cook in the blue-canopied taco stand was struggling to keep up with his business, every stool taken. Wade shivered. The driver reached forward and turned down the air conditioner.

A Mexican policeman met him at the long line waiting to get through U.S. Customs. He took Wade to the front and another man in a suit ceded his place to him. Wade didn't mention murder to the U.S. Customs official.

Back in San Isidro, his feet sleepwalked through the parking lot. Once inside his car, he punched in Rodrigues' phone number. The call skipped to voicemail. He called again from the highway. More voicemail. "They murdered Chad Fisher," he said into the recording. "I don't care what risks I have to take. These people don't deserve to be alive."

On the right side of the road, the hand on the psychic reader's sign extended toward the car. The eye in the center of the palm glared at him. *Do you think this isn't your fault?*

CHAPTER FORTY-EIGHT

As soon as the door of his condo closed, the blackness didn't so much descend as congeal inside Wade. If he'd just been able to persuade the FBI to protect Chad . . . Wade wanted to go to his bedroom, turn off the lights, and lie down. But Myles was staring from the couch in the living room.

"Dad?"

"I thought you were supposed to be at school," Wade said.

"Got out early."

Myles' face looked as if he could see how crushed his father was. There was no point in trying to hide it. "I was in Tijuana today," Wade said.

"You were in Tijuana? Really?"

"On the way back to the border, I saw someone fall from the top of a building. I think he was pushed."

"Oh my God."

"It was Chad Fisher, the guy I work with at Unity Coast."

Myles' eyes expanded. "Dad, this is terrible. Do you want me to call Mom?"

His son wanted to comfort his father but didn't know how. How could he? Wade said, "I just need a half hour. Just a little time to gather myself."

"Do you want tea? Can I get you something to eat?"

Wade dredged up a weak smile. "Thanks. No."

He went into his bedroom and shut the door. He fished out the black handle of Chad's briefcase from his pocket and touched the green cord around it. He picked up his guitar from the bed. His quivering hands plucked sad minor seventh and minor ninth chords. Wade let himself sink into the music.

Myles knocked and opened the door. "I want to go to hot yoga," he said.

"Yoga? You hate yoga."

"I want to try it again."

Myles was only doing this for him. It was such a kind gesture that Wade couldn't refuse. He pushed himself to his feet. Myles checked his phone and there was a class in thirty minutes near La Jolla. They both slipped on gym shorts and T-shirts and grabbed towels, water bottles, and mats. For a few minutes Wade didn't think about Chad.

They arrived just as the instructor started. The studio's practice room was so hot it steamed the walls. Wade huffed and sweated and twisted through the *asanas* beside his son. Sometimes he saw Myles studying him in the mirror. Myles' worried face made him remember Chad's crumpled body on the sidewalk. He tried to breathe it out of his mind: inhales and long exhales. But he couldn't. They sank into runner's lunge and half-pigeon, then the release of *savasana*. None of it helped.

Myles suggested a walk by the ocean. They went to Pacific Beach and strolled along the boardwalk. Music roared from the bar terraces. Skateboarders and skaters rattled by beside homeless sitting on the walls. Someone played a guitar, and the musky odor of pot drifted in wisps over them. "Let's go to Crystal Pier," Myles said.

The sun was setting as they made their way there. They walked out and the beams of the pier swayed under their feet. At the far end, fishing lines, like the threads of spiderwebs, reached into the swells. Now the only sounds were the ocean's rumbles and sputters. The cold from the water blew over them, and Wade looped his arm around Myles' thin shoulders.

"You tried to help your friend," Myles said.

"No one should die alone like that," Wade said.

They looked out at the orange and yellow sun cutting the horizon. Wade heard a child shout and giggle somewhere.

"You want to find who pushed him from that building," Myles said.

It was pointless denying it. "I hope I'm doing the right thing," Wade said.

"Dad, you always try to do what's right. That's why you sent me to Hidden Road."

Wade blinked back tears. He tightened his arm around his son. "Sometimes what you think is right turns out to be wrong," he said.

They watched the waves rumble and whisper as the sun smoldered. The seagulls screeched around them. They turned and walked back to shore.

CHAPTER FORTY-NINE

FIONA

Fiona's kitchen was full of the smells and hisses from sautéed mushrooms and onions. She heard the front door slam. Did she remember to lock it? She was sure she did. Only Myles and Wade had keys.

Myles' tennis shoes smacked down the wooden floor of the hallway. When he reached the kitchen, the light fell on him. His face was so drawn she dropped the knife on the cutting board. "Are you all right?"

"Dad's in the car outside. He needs you to talk to him."

Her arms tightened. "What happened?"

"He was in Tijuana and—"

"Is he all right?"

Myles shook his head. "The guy he works with fell from the top of a building. Dad thinks he was pushed."

She threw the apron on the counter and rushed down the hallway. "Turn off the burner," she yelled. She yanked open the front door.

Wade's BMW was parked across the street. He was staring blankly through the windshield. She knocked on his window and he clicked open the lock on the passenger door. She slid into the seat, and the anguish on his face made something pitch inside her.

"They murdered Chad," he said.

Murdered. She reached across and hugged him. He slid his arms around her, and she listened to his shallow breaths. Smelled his sweat. Wade needed her. Needed her to help him think through this.

She extracted herself so he could see her face. "We have to end this now," she said. "The first thing to do is resign from Unity Coast and Comunidad de Niños."

He cocked his head. "You know what that will mean?"

"I don't care if we go bankrupt."

He studied her as if he wasn't sure she'd meant what she'd said.

She pointed across the street. "We're more important than that damn house."

"If we resign, Andre and Martinez will see through it. The FBI will stop protecting us."

She clamped her mouth shut. There had to be some way to extract themselves from this horror.

He slid his hand along the steering wheel. She knew that inward expression on his face. He was pulling his thoughts together and weighing the facts. She used to think his analytical mind was cold and calculating. Now she saw the concern that made him mull over what to do.

"There was only one reason the driver took me to that part of Tijuana," he said. "Martinez wanted to make sure I saw what he did to his enemies. That's why they threw Chad's briefcase from the building first. To get my attention."

She remembered Martinez coming to the house. He'd never been there before but knew what was inside the rooms. He'd smiled when he said it, as if he enjoyed her shock. It was a threat to terrorize her. Even the story about the doubled budget seemed a test to gauge how much she knew. What would he do to them if he learned that she and Wade were spies?

But weakening now would just create suspicion and more risk. Fiona reached for Wade's hand. His skin was hot, as if he had a fever. "We can do this." She heard the determination in her voice. He seemed to hear it too and straightened his back.

"What about Myles?" he said. "I think he already suspects something."

Myles was too smart not to pick up on the danger they were navigating. And there was something worse. "He's dating Andre's daughter," she said. "I saw him kissing her at school."

Wade swiveled in the seat. "Kissing?"

"They're in love."

His head dropped.

He was spent and wanted her strength. She loved him for it. She tightened her hand around his. "We're going to figure this out," she said.

CHAPTER FIFTY

FIONA

Fiona didn't want to travel to Tijuana, not after Chad Fisher's death. But there was a leak in one of the septic tanks at the orphanage. The contractor said they had to dig it up and replace the whole unit, an expense that the CEO had to verify and approve. Even on a Saturday.

She parked in San Isidro and walked across the border causeway. Andre's driver stood on the street beside the tinted windows of a black SUV. He opened the back door. Her foot stopped in mid-step. Egberto Martinez sat on the far side of the seat.

"I . . . I didn't expect you," she said.

"We're riding together."

Martinez was a board member and had a right to accompany her. If she refused to get in the car, he'd interpret it as a sign that she saw him as the killer he really was. Then what? Would men appear and force her inside?

She climbed onto the seat next to Martinez, and the SUV started forward through the thick traffic. The car was so smooth she barely felt the street underneath her. They were heading toward downtown Tijuana, not in the direction of the orphanage.

Martinez offered her a date from a plastic bag. She ignored it. She willed her voice to be strong. "I have an emergency at the orphanage."

He chewed on a date and said, "They can wait."

"That's for me to decide. I want you to turn this car around."

The car didn't slow. He said, "We're going to a part of Tijuana you've probably never seen. You'll find it very illuminating."

He knows about Cartuso. Fling open the door. Run.

Before she got ten yards, Martinez and the driver would catch her.

"You need to take this trip for your son's sake," he said.

Her fingers clawed into the seat. "What does that mean?"

"Don't worry. He's not in danger."

Be very worried.

They were heading into the tourist zone, not some barrio on the outskirts of Tijuana. She could jump out anywhere in this traffic. If the safety locks weren't engaged.

He pointed at the sidewalk displays. "Look at them. Think about what they tell you."

Under the brightly colored tarps she saw statues of Elvis lined up next to stuffed-animal donkeys and piñatas. There were T-shirts with images of Tupac and Frida Kahlo beside framed pictures of Jesus and embroidered children's dresses. Serapes and blue and red and green hats above leather purses and brown pottery bowls. "What am I supposed to see?"

"Skulls and little girls' folk dresses. Children and death mixed together."

She wrapped her arms around herself.

"Let me tell you about how I grew up," he said. "You will find it interesting."

He'd never revealed anything about his past. There had to be a reason for his openness, a reason that connected to Myles and where they were going.

"My mother was a whore, and I don't know who my father was." He paused and his unwavering stare took her in.

"You were like the children at the orphanage," she said.

"There was no orphanage for me. The streets of Tijuana were my parents. They were both lax and unforgiving. You know what the streets taught me was most important for a child?" He stared at her with his intense eyes. When she didn't answer, he said, "Survival."

It was only one word. But it was a word that could erase all the joy of childhood.

"The kind of people who you condemn took me in. Killers, Mrs. Bosworth. Killers gave me food and a place to sleep. They saw I had an engineer's mind and sent me to UCLA. Can you believe that *sicarios* did that?"

Should she shake her head "no" or nod "yes"? They both seemed wrong. She said, "They gave you a family."

"That is only from blood."

He caressed a date and the plastic bag crinkled. He gazed out the window at the patchwork of hotels, restaurants, and shops. The street was a blinding mix of reds and oranges and yellows.

"I have a wife and children," he said.

She'd always thought he was unmarried. "Where are they?"

"Somewhere else. They have a better life without me."

The man had lost his family. "I'm so sorry," she said.

He whirled. He crowded her with his face. "Do you think I don't know how to be a good father? Is that what you think? That is such a woman's way of seeing."

She drew her body into the window and turned her head away from him. They were stuck in a snarl of traffic. He wouldn't hurt her here. There were too many people. A deep voice from the speaker on the back of a truck seemed to tell her what to do. But she didn't understand the Spanish.

"Do you know the most important obligations for a parent, Mrs. Bosworth? Let me give you a hint. Love is overrated."

She said it reflexively, before she could stop herself. "That's so sad."

He glowered at her. "When you have a child, there are two commandments. The first is that he must survive. The second is that he must be better than you are. Everything else is *telenovela* mush."

The rest was all of life.

The SUV turned a corner to a street of women in short skirts and tight, butt-lifting pants. Men looked them over as they walked by. One prostitute held a man's hand and pulled him into a doorway. She saw their mouths moving but only heard a female singer's voice blare from speakers.

"Why are we here?" she said.

His gaze drifted to the window. "My mother was hit by a car when I was seven years old. The whorehouse where we lived kicked me out. Blocks like this were the mother that raised me."

Here was the wound that drove this man. It was the most vulnerable and dangerous part of him. "No child should have that happen to him," she said.

"Don't you dare pity me."

The SUV stopped beside a shoeshine stand and a kiosk selling perfumes. Fiona couldn't help but inhale. But there was no scent of anything inside the SUV. Martinez pointed to a tall hotel bar on the other side of the scraggly-treed median. The neon sign on the front said, "Delicias." Next to it was a white church. Some drunken men reeled out of a taxi and stumbled through the hotel bar's black door.

"This is where your husband's friend fell."

She put her hand to her mouth.

"He fell from his world to the sidewalk of mine. Right in front of the greeter with the orange bow tie. Look how well they cleaned it."

She was hyperventilating. He was going to make her walk to the spot where Chad had landed. Then to the roof. As soon as the door opened, she'd run. She'd shout and scream. If he caught her, she'd beat her fists against him.

The bag of dates rustled on his lap. He said, "What do you think Chad Fisher regretted most when he fell? Was it the loss of his own life or his child's?"

She couldn't let him see her fear. Fear was fuel to him. She pushed herself back against the seat and filled her lungs with air. She tried to breathe hardness into her face.

"Parents must be willing to do anything so their children survive," Martinez said. "That's what you did with Myles. Will you also follow the second commandment?"

Would she do anything to make him better than his parents? "Not anything," she said.

"Let me make it clearer. You are a mother. Carmela Saez de Ouellette is also a mother. Her daughter must be better than she is. That is why her daughter cannot be with your son."

His words closed around her throat. Her eyes sprang wide. She didn't care what he did to her. "My son is a good person. Carmela's daughter is lucky he loves her."

He popped another date in his mouth. He chomped it with his mouth open. "Myles will find someone else."

"How would you know?"

He looked at the prostitutes and men wandering over the sidewalk.

She and Carmela wanted the same thing—to break off the romance between their children. But Carmela would do anything to protect her daughter. She would destroy Myles.

Martinez said, "You and your husband also have commitments. If you fail, this street will judge you."

CHAPTER FIFTY-ONE

Sofia texted him at eight o'clock on Sunday morning. He'd pro-grammed a special ringtone for her and roused himself to check his phone. "Meet me by the lifeguard stand at La Jolla Beach," the message said. "Don't tell anyone."

Myles dressed and looked out the window of the condo. Grey clouds drizzled rain over the bay. If Sofia wanted to meet on a beach in this weather, it had to be an emergency. His dad was gone some-place so he could disappear without answering questions. He grabbed the broken umbrella in the closet. One of his dad's jackets was waterproof. He grabbed that too.

He had to go by bus and by foot. It took an hour to get there. In front of the lifeguard stand, Sofia sat on a bench in a blue raincoat and held a blue umbrella. When she saw him, she jumped up and clutched his arm.

"What's going on?" he said.

"Not here. Someone might be watching."

He glanced around, unsure who he should be looking for, or why anyone would be on the beach in the rain.

She hurried him down the wet cement walk. They cut over to green swaths of grass that led to a path to the sand. She found a se-cluded nook in the stone embankment that shielded them from sight and gave a view of the ocean. Not even surfers were out this Sunday morning. Myles and she sat close with her umbrella shielding them.

"You're scaring me," he said.

Her face shrank as if she would cry. "Mamá forbids me to see you."

"I thought she liked me."

Sofia was silent, the only sound the roar of the ocean.

"She can't fucking control us," he said.

"It's not that simple."

"Yes, it is that simple."

"Mamá's family is dangerous."

He glared at the pounding waves. No one could tell them not to love each other.

"Did you hear what I said? They're dangerous."

It took a few seconds to register. "Like criminals?"

"Yes."

"Like Mexican cartel dangerous?"

Her face pinched. "I'm not supposed to talk to anyone about it."

Mexican cartel. Drug trafficking. Killers. His dad's friend pushed off a roof. He reached out and held her hand. "You can tell me anything. You know that, right?"

She stared at him, her lips clamped together and her eyes afraid. He knew she was holding back to protect him. "Tell me," he said.

"They call it *The Company*. I know Papá isn't part of it. But my aunts and uncles, my cousins, they're all in it. That's our family business. That's what I'll never escape."

He hugged her and the umbrella fell to the sand. Her arms locked around him and the rain beat down on them. He thought of Hidden Road. *You control your future.*

He pulled away. "Sofia, look at me. You're going to Stanford. You're becoming a doctor."

"What about us?" she said.

"Let me tell you about us." He kissed her. He caressed her wet hair. He no longer heard the ocean or felt the rainfall.

"I see how you obey your mother," a voice said.

A man stood in front of them, waves rolling and gushing white behind him. He wore jeans and a denim shirt with pockets and snap buttons. He was sopping wet but seemed impervious to the drizzle.

Sofia rose to her feet. "You're who she picks to follow me? You're her pet watchdog now?"

The man was tall with swept-back, black and grey hair that glistened with moisture. His eyes were like high beams. "I'm here to give you the message," he said. "So you understand the seriousness."

Myles wasn't going to cower. He stood and took two steps forward. He stuck out his hand.

The man didn't even look at it. "I know who you are." There was something sick in his nasal voice.

"This is Mr. Martinez," Sofia said.

Myles looked around. No one was on the beach.

"What did your mother tell you about being with him?" Martinez said.

Sofia's mom had sent this guy. Carmela, whose family was part of a drug cartel.

Face your fear.

"You have no right to follow us," Myles said.

"Do you know what your mother calls me? The Mexican Rottweiler."

His mom knew him. *His mom.* Myles forced his feet to stay still on the sand. "Sir, I think Sofia asked you to leave."

"Aren't you the young warrior?" he said.

He felt Sofia's hand on his shoulder through the jacket. Rivulets of water ran down her cheeks. Her hair stuck to the sides of her neck. "Mr. Martinez will give me a ride home. You stay here." Her eyes seemed to plead that he not be brave.

He couldn't leave Sofia with this man.

"I'm fine," Sofia said. "Really."

He should de-escalate now, ratchet down the anger. That's what Hidden Road had taught him.

Fuck that! "You have no right to treat her this way."

Martinez laughed. "Let's go."

Myles walked with them over the sand and up the rocks. They reached the grassy knoll beside the street. A vintage Mustang was parked there. Martinez opened the passenger door.

"Please just go home," Sofia said. She stepped inside the car, her face stiff and clenched.

Martinez turned. "If you hurry, you can catch the bus to your daddy's little condo."

He knows where I live.

"I hope we don't see each other again, Myles," Martinez said. "Remember, your life and your death are your own fault."

The words seemed familiar. Myles noticed Martinez's cowboy boots: polished black with pointed toes. The stitching was in the shape of two blue wings separated by a red cross. He knew where he'd seen them.

CHAPTER FIFTY-TWO

WADE

On Monday morning Rodrigues arranged a secret meeting in Kearney Mesa, a part of San Diego brimming with highways, strip malls, and big-box stores. The meeting was inside the office of a chiropractor whose son worked in the Bureau. The receptionist brought Wade to an examining room that smelled of eucalyptus oil and only had one chair. He laid his suit coat over the chair and sat on the adjustment table. Next to him were shelves of anatomy and physical therapy books and a full-sized model skeleton. The body contained so many bones that could break. Only an insect could fall six stories and not shatter.

Special Agent Rodrigues arrived and closed the door behind her. She settled in the chair with Wade's suit coat draped over it. For once, her face had lost its stony composure and her eyes looked pained. Her shoe tapped the beige carpet.

"The Mexican police say it was suicide," she said.

Wade shook his head.

"Our consulate talked to the prostitute. Chad paid her and it's on his credit card. The prostitute said they had sex and, afterward, Chad got despondent and left. She never suspected he took the stairs to the top of the building."

"The roof door just happened to be unlocked?"

"It's not San Diego. That can happen in Mexico."

She couldn't possibly believe this. "You know he was pushed, right?"

"There were no bruises on his arm or torn clothing. No kicked-off shoes or sign of struggle."

It was so obvious. "They drugged him."

She leaned back. The fingers of both hands drummed against the knees of her dark slacks. Wade reached into his pocket and pulled out what he'd found.

"This was the only part of his briefcase left on the sidewalk. You see this cord. It's wrapped around the handle in memory of his daughter. He'd never throw his tribute to her off the side of a building."

Her face was tense. Air softly hissed in and out of her nose. "He filed a SAR with FinCen."

Wade lurched forward so hard he almost fell off the table. "Why the hell are you telling me he committed suicide?"

Rodrigues frowned at the carpet. "I wanted the value of your opinion."

In a way, filing a SAR *was* suicide. Chad had been so despondent on the morning they'd gone to Tijuana. In his dream he'd tried to catch a child that a black bird was carrying away. Maybe he'd known that Andre and Martinez were going to kill him.

"They didn't murder him because he knew too much," Wade said. "They murdered him for reporting them."

She rose and walked to the life-size skeleton. Her back was to Wade. As she ran her hand over the plastic bones, Wade wondered if she was thinking about how she could have saved Chad. Perhaps she'd faced away from him because FBI agents weren't allowed to show remorse.

She turned and caught his eyes. "I can get you out now. You've done more than enough."

He shook his head. "I'm going to destroy these bastards."

CHAPTER FIFTY-THREE

MYLES

On Monday Myles decided he had to tell Sofia what he'd figured out. He couldn't do it in school—too many kids around. But Carmela was in Tijuana and Andre at the bank. They could be alone at the condo. Sofia walked there by herself, and Myles followed a half hour later. He didn't see anyone in the alley behind the building or by the entrance to the underground garage. Sofia opened the iron gate for him, and they hurried across the cement floor to the back entrance of the building. They were the only ones there.

Inside the condo, Sofia led Myles to a silk couch. He didn't know where to begin; Sofia worshipped her dad. Myles looked down at the coffee table. An African mask stared back at him with holes in its eyes.

She opened a wooden cabinet and retrieved a brown bottle of tequila and some small, tulip-shaped glasses. She poured and sat beside him. The liquor floated into his stomach like a warm cloud. After a few sips, he put their glasses on the table and cupped her hands in his.

"Tell me what's wrong," she said.

"Is Mr. Martinez connected to your dad's bank?"

"He owns part of it."

Myles swallowed. He had to keep going. "I've seen him before. In Mexico."

Her eyes grew distant and he could tell she was trying to remember when that could be.

"Did you see his boots yesterday?" Myles asked.

"His cowboy boots?"

"They have special stitching. Two blue wings separated by a red cross. The boss of the kidnappers wore those boots."

Her mouth opened. Then closed. She shook her head. "Many people must have boots like that."

Myles squeezed her hands. "The man ordering around the kidnappers had the same nasal voice. He spoke English without an accent. You know what he said when he let me go? 'Your life and your death are your own fault.' That's what Martinez said yesterday."

Sofia disengaged her hands and sat back. She crossed her arms. He saw from her frightened face that she was putting it together.

"He works for your mom's family, doesn't he?" Myles said.

He expected her to deny it, but she only looked down at the mask, then at the walls of the condo. "Why would he kidnap you?"

Now was the part where she could get salty and never want to speak to him again. But they couldn't hide from this. "Andre wanted my dad to work at his bank, and Dad turned him down like five times. But that was the deal for getting a loan to pay the ransom. My dad comes to work for him."

"Papá? Papá was involved?"

"He had to be."

She shook her head. "No frigging way."

"Do you think Andre wouldn't know what Martinez was doing?"

She reached for the glass of tequila and took a swig. "Mamá, I could believe. She and Martinez are close."

Myles moved his head nearer to her. "Then there was the guy who negotiated. He comes in all on point and does it in like two days. Polanco."

"Wilfredo Polanco?"

"Do you know him?"

She set down her tequila and put her head in her hands. Myles rubbed her back, then her neck. The only sounds were the wind chimes pinging through the window screen.

Sofia lifted her head out of her hands. "I . . . I heard Mamá talk with Martinez. She said that they'd found a way to convince your dad . . . you know, to work at Unity Coast. I thought she was talking about money."

"Sofia, they tortured me."

Tears dribbled down her cheeks.

"Then there's the guy my dad worked with. My dad doesn't think he jumped from that building."

"No no no." Her voice was so soft. She pushed her face into his shoulder and her sobs swelled against him. He hadn't expected her to break down crying.

Water. Water would help. He hurried to the kitchen. Myles got some from the refrigerator and rushed back to Sofia on the couch. He guided her fingers around the glass and coaxed her to drink.

"Not Papi," she said. "Never Papi."

It didn't seem possible that a man who'd been kidnapped could kidnap another person. "Maybe it's just your mom and Martinez," Myles said.

She drank. Her face slowly turned and her eyes reached into him. "What will your dad do when he finds out about Martinez?"

"He'll have to quit working at the bank. And my mom will quit the foundation. It's the only way to get clear of this."

"Martinez won't let them."

"How will he do that?"

She grimaced and bit her bottom lip. "There was a man before your dad. Bill Langley. He was with his family in Colorado and their car went off a cliff."

Carmela had mentioned that name when they'd left their house in Tijuana. "Oh fuck!"

"Martinez was telling Mamá about it and they didn't see me come into a room. They stopped talking in the middle of a sentence. But I heard something. He told her he had a man who could drive a truck."

"A truck pushed Langley's car over the cliff?"

She raised her hands. "What do you think?"

"But why?"

"Because he knew too much and wanted to quit."

Myles poured more tequila.

Sofia said, "Everyone really works for my aunt, Mamá's sister. They call her *La Jefa*. There's something wrong with her. Like she's missing a part of her brain. The story is that one of my uncles—my aunt's own brother—was an informant for the DEA. She . . . she told Martinez to murder him and his family."

They'd kill his mom, his dad. They'd kill him. They'd kill everyone. Myles' arm shook. He pushed it against his stomach.

Face your fear.

"We can figure a way out of this," Myles said.

She shook her head. "You have to stop seeing me."

"I can't. I won't."

"You have to for my sake too."

"Are you in danger?"

"Everyone is in danger."

It was so fucked up.

She drew him to her and he kissed her lips, then her hair. She lay back on the couch. The rest happened before he could think about it. He unbuttoned her blouse, then his shirt. He pulled down his pants. When he kissed her again, she grasped his cheeks and raised his face. He knew then.

"This is your first time, isn't it?" he said.

"I want this with you," she said.

The wind chimes pinged outside. Then he only heard the movements of their bodies.

*   *   *

They dressed and lay again on the couch, arms coiled around each other. He listened to her soft breaths. He smelled the orange and coconut of her shampoo. Outside, the wind chimes sounded like a faraway song. He wanted to stop time like in a movie.

A key turned the lock on the front door. Myles jumped up.

"It's Papá," Sofia whispered.

Myles pretended to study the aqua seahorse painting on the wall. Sofia picked at the buttons on her blouse as if worried she'd forgotten one.

Andre limped through the door. "The world is full of the surprises," he said. "Like you, Myles."

Andre had on his Buddha face: a half smile that showed nothing. The lenses of his glasses looked as thick as walls. Why didn't Sofia say something?

"We were reviewing some schoolwork," Myles said.

Andre hobbled to the wall by the door to the kitchen. He touched an ancient brass figure with a round body and a headdress that looked like the sun. "This is Viracocha, the chief god of the Incas," he said.

"Like Peru?" His voice seemed to squirt out of him.

"Viracocha is bigger than Peru," Andre said. "He holds a bolt of thunder in his hand. But he also has something really much different from the other gods."

"Not now, Papi." Sofia's voice was soft, like she was begging.

Andre said, "It is his tears. His tears are the sadness of what the life is. But the tears, they are also the water that makes the crops grow and the life continue. This is something you must think about, Myles."

"I don't understand," Myles said.

"Someday you are a father and you will."

How could Andre have told those men to torture him? His pale, soft eyes, his spiritual sayings, they all seemed to say that was impossible.

Myles had to think. He had to get out of here. He said goodbye and hurried outside and through the front gate. As he walked home, one thought thudded into each step. *I have to warn Dad.*

CHAPTER FIFTY-FOUR

When Wade arrived at his condo, it was dark and Myles wasn't there. No backpack. No odors of Myles' microwaved poisons. Wade called Myles' cell. Nothing. Fiona had told him about Martinez's threats. He telephoned her and she didn't pick up. All he could do was pace, his shoes digging into the carpet while his calves tightened.

A half hour later the front door opened. "Where the hell were you?" Wade said.

"I walked from La Jolla."

It was more than ten miles, two hours of trudging. In an aching instant Wade's anger morphed to apprehension. He led Myles to the kitchen, and they sat at the table. Pain filled Myles' eyes. Something had turned him upside down. Wade heard his father's cherrywood clock on the wall. His dad never had to deal with a son dating a girl from a family of killers.

"Tell me what's going on, and we'll figure this out," Wade said.

Myles sucked in a breath. Wade waited.

"I met Sofia on the beach in La Jolla yesterday." He raised his eyes as if to see how his dad reacted to the forbidden girlfriend. Wade didn't say anything. It was too late to chastise him for that. He and Sofia were so in love they'd met in a rainstorm.

"It was just us until this guy I'd never seen before showed up. He was like your age and wearing this whole denim cowboy outfit."

A new dread took up space in Wade's gut. He leaned forward and dug his elbows into the battered table. He focused on keeping his voice calm. "Was his name Egberto Martinez?"

Myles nodded. "Sofia was all sass and acted like she hated the guy. And you know what he said? He didn't come to talk with her. He'd come to give me a warning."

"What kind of warning?"

Myles' mouth curled into a trembling sneer. "Sofia's mom doesn't like Sofia and me dating. I'm not good enough for her."

Carmela was actually condemning his son. Carmela, whose family hung people from bridges and put little girls in bordellos. His heart was drumming. "Did you ever think that maybe Sofia isn't good enough for *you*?" he said.

"Yeah, right. I'm like top of my class at the treatment center."

"Your mom and I think you're pretty amazing."

"Stop it, Dad. You're just making it worse."

"I guess you'd rather be the victim."

Not feeling sorry for yourself was one of Hidden Road's commandments. But even that reference didn't dial him down. Myles' eyes were filled with the angry defiance he used to have before he went to Utah. His fingers clutched his thighs through his jeans. Was there anything more frightening than a teenager's lovestruck rage?

"I recognized the man's boots," Myles said.

"His cowboy boots?"

"The guy who was in charge of the kidnapping, the guy who all the other men took orders from . . . he wore the same boots."

Of course it was Martinez. Who else would Andre send to kidnap someone?

"You know what he told me?" Myles said. 'Your life and your death are your own fault.' That was the exact same thing the head kidnapper guy told me."

It was a message. Martinez wanted Myles and his family to know what he'd done. The bastard wanted them to know he could do it again.

Myles said, "He kidnapped me so you'd have to join up with the bank. That was the price for getting me back, wasn't it?"

Wade had to deflect this, or at least scale it down. "That's a pretty big jump."

"Come on, Dad, cut the bullshit. We both know it's why you didn't want me to hang with Sofia. You knew her family was in a drug cartel."

He had to say something, something that wouldn't hurt them if Myles let it slip to Sofia. "I won't be at the bank long. Just a few more weeks and I'm resigning."

"Sofia says they'll never let you quit. They'll kill you like they killed the other guy before you."

He even knew about Bill Langley. Wade reached over and put his hand on his arm. "He died in a car accident," he said. "That's what you have to believe."

His son shook his head. "Sofia said her mom and Martinez hired someone. The guy used a truck to push Langley's car off the cliff. All because he was going to quit."

Myles deserved to know everything. But Wade couldn't tell him when he was so close to Sofia. One unintended word could get them all killed.

"They murdered the guy you worked with, Dad. They pushed him off a building."

"I've taken precautions."

Myles' head drew back. His eyes widened. "What kind of precautions?"

"It's best you don't know anything else."

"Because if you tell me, I'll tell Sofia?" There was acid in his voice. He was so enraptured with this girl he could do anything.

"You have to do what Martinez told you. Just for a while."

Myles squinted down at the table.

"It's too dangerous," Wade said. "For you and us and even for Sofia."

"You want me to break it off with Sofia, don't you?" His voice sounded broken.

"Sometimes there are more important things than love. It's one of the saddest truths in life."

Myles raised his head. "That family will destroy Sofia. We have to save her."

CHAPTER FIFTY-FIVE

FIONA

It was eight o'clock on Tuesday morning when Fiona stepped inside Wade's condo. They'd scheduled this meeting when Myles was at school. She noticed that Wade had cleared the clutter from his dining room table. The wine boxes and yoga mat were out of the living room and a new dresser for Myles stood next to the pullout couch. He'd even cleaned up the kitchen. There were no fast-food boxes on the counter, no dishes in the sink. It was as if his son had inspired Wade to put his life back in stride. Fiona was a little jealous.

The special agents were already at the table. Today Rodrigues looked like a well-dressed dwarf sitting next to Cartuso. Wade poured Fiona a mug from the coffeemaker. The coffee bag said it was her favorite Indonesian Sulawesi, dark and earthy the way she liked it. She thanked him with her eyes.

"Are you okay?" Rodrigues asked her.

"You mean after Martinez threatened to throw me off a roof?"

"He was just scaring you," Cartuso said.

"Do you think Chad believed they were just scaring him?" Wade asked.

Cartuso's shrug seemed to take up half the table. "You never even went into the building."

She loathed everything about this man. "How would I know he wasn't about to take me there?"

Wade shoved the pot onto the burner of the coffeemaker. He sat with Fiona across from the agents. She was glad he was beside her.

Cartuso tapped an enormous ring like a gavel. "We have to talk about what happens after you finish the operation," he said.

"But you're arresting them," Fiona said. "I thought our lives were supposed to go back to normal."

"Unfortunately, that can't happen," Rodrigues said.

Fiona jerked forward in the seat. "Why the hell not?"

"Because the real power is someone you haven't met," Cartuso said. "She's a woman they call *La Jefa*. She'll stay in Mexico and hire a lot of people to track you down."

It hit Fiona then. Full force. It took all her strength to stop her face from crumbling. "Are you saying that, after all we've done, you can't keep us safe?"

"Come on, Fiona," Cartuso said. "Your lives were in danger as soon as you started working for Ouellette."

Rodrigues put up her hands. "Please, let's just back up a bit. First of all, both of you have helped us a lot. Secondly, we're going to keep your family safe. That's what Witness Protection is for."

Witness Protection? "But our lives are here." Fiona stole a glance at Wade, and he looked as appalled as she felt.

"It will be like one of you has taken a new job in another part of the country," Rodrigues said. "You'll have money and a house and jobs. And here's the most important thing of all. You won't have to worry about your security."

Wade shook his head and turned to Cartuso. "I think we'll stay here."

"La Jefa will kill you if you do that," Cartuso said.

Fiona had to stand. She carried her mug across the kitchen to the coffeemaker on the counter. She picked up the pot to pour and saw that her mug was still full. Her mind was spinning: Utah, Wyoming, Montana, the middle of some empty landscape.

When she turned, Rodrigues was studying her over the lip of her mug. "I gather Jasper isn't in the picture now," she said.

"No, he's not."

Fiona expected to see a spark in Wade's eyes. Instead, he looked as if he felt sorry for her. She sat beside him.

"I know this is hard," Rodrigues said.

"Cut the fake sympathy," Fiona said.

Wade touched her arm. She had to calm herself down.

"Where will we go?" Wade asked.

"It's up to the U.S. Marshals," Rodrigues said. "We don't know anything—aren't allowed to know anything—about the arrangements. We'll exfiltrate you to a safe place and they'll spend some time preparing you for wherever you'll end up. The marshals are really good. Not a single person has been hurt who followed their directions."

How could having your life ripped away not be classified as being *hurt*? "Our son won't want to go," she said.

"What?" Cartuso said.

"He won't go. He's in love."

Cartuso leaned forward and his body seemed to shadow the table. "Let's get real here. Myles was the one who got you into this mess. It's not that big of a sacrifice."

"He's never had a relationship this deep," Wade said.

"He's a teenager for chrissake," Cartuso said. "They fall in love every five minutes."

Fiona brought herself to her full height in the chair. She pushed her fingers into the table. "Special Agent Cartuso, are you telling us what our son feels? Maybe you're an expert on teenagers who are deeply in love. Maybe you can illuminate us with your vast knowledge."

Cartuso lifted his eyebrows. She glared back. Wade squeezed her wrist.

"Myles figured out what I'm doing," Wade said.

Panic climbed up her back. "Everything? Are you saying he knows everything?"

"I think he knows more about Sofia's family than we do," Wade said.

"Shit!" Cartuso said.

Fiona knew what her brave, impractical son would do. "He's going to try to rescue Sofia," she said.

All of them stared at their coffee mugs, but no one drank.

Cartuso spoke first. "They'll kill him if he tries anything. We'll have to force him to safety any way we have to."

Drag him. Handcuff him. Push him into a jail cell. It would be even worse than when they sent him to Utah.

But it would save his life.

Wade's cellphone rang. Everyone stared at him. He slipped it from his pocket. "It's Andre."

Cartuso extended his big palm for Wade to answer.

"Yes," Wade said into the phone.

The room itself seemed to hold its breath.

"But why can't we do it in San Diego?" Wade listened, then pressed the "Disconnect" button. He stared at the cellphone in his hand. "Vanhoven and I are making a presentation tomorrow. At Andre's house in Tijuana."

"I don't like it," Fiona said.

"He won't be in danger," Rodrigues said. "People will be watching and listening every second. We'll have his back."

"Like you had my back when Martinez threatened me?"

"He's already been there once," Cartuso said. "There was no indication they suspected anything then and there isn't now. Even if they wanted to do something, they'd wait until after they got the Felton building done." His eyes seemed to sear into Wade. "This is battle time. Time to strap in and fight."

Fiona slammed her palm on the table. "Making him go to Tijuana is too dangerous. And you know it."

Wade reached under the table and squeezed her hand. His palm was warm and his grip calm. Her eyes blurred with tears.

CHAPTER FIFTY-SIX

WADE

The next morning, Andre's black SUV idled across the street from the Mexican Customs exit in Tijuana. Vanhoven and Wade climbed into the back seat of the car. This time the driver took a different route. Wade leaned forward in the gap between the cargo seats and said, "We're supposed to go to Andre's house."

The driver shrugged.

"Where are we going?"

"The ranch."

Andre had never mentioned owning a ranch. "Whose ranch?"

"The ranch."

Wade looked at Vanhoven. He was excavating his gold and diamond cufflinks.

The driver understood some English, so they couldn't talk. Wade stared out the windows as the SUV skirted a poorer section of Tijuana and followed a toll road along the coast. He saw houses and buildings clutching the brown, rocky soil, then stretches of empty desert where someone could bury a body and no one would find it.

At Ensenada they turned east and wound upward to a valley of rocky hills with swaths of trees, dirt roads, and haphazard fences. They reached cultivated green fields, and Wade recognized rows of bushy grapevines. The ranch was in wine country. He knew they were close when he saw the eight-foot fences. Their metal signs displayed a yellow lightning bolt and a single word: *Electricidad*.

"Electric fences keep people out," Wade said.

"Or in," Vanhoven said. He fiddled with his tie clip and collar.

The SUV slowed. A guardhouse with tinted windows stood beside a heavy steel gate. Two armed men came out to meet them. The driver lowered the window and spoke in Spanish. One of the guards stuffed his assault rifle into the crook of his armpit. He ticked off something on his clipboard, and the steel gate slowly opened.

The paved road led through more rows of green vines, then steel storage towers and one-story white stucco cottages. Two men with rifles sped by on golf carts. The SUV turned to face a huge white two-story house with multiple ceramic-tiled roofs. The front yard had pink and red flowering trees and lush green grass. On one side of the house, horses loped in a corral next to a white stable. On the other side stood a large wooden building that could have been full of wine vats and barrels.

"A palace in the middle of nowhere," Vanhoven said.

Wade was looking at the back of the house. A small white jet parked on a long paved road that extended from it. "She's arrived," he said. He didn't have to say the name. *La Jefa.*

The SUV stopped under a portico supported by Greek columns. The driver and one of the guards opened the passenger doors. "*Bienvenido.*" The guard grinned like a bellboy when he said it.

They clambered out and Wade picked up whiffs of manure. Before he had time to think, the guard ran a metal detection wand over him and his briefcase. The device shrieked at his tie clip. "Please remove," the guard said.

Rodrigues had promised that the camera and recording devices were undetectable. "Is this really necessary?" Wade said. "For chrissakes, we're bankers."

The guard's mouth hardened. He held out his hand. Another guard with a shotgun appeared at the right side of the house.

"Do you want us to take off our shirts and pants too?" Vanhoven said. The guard's wand hadn't made a sound at his expensive accessories.

Wade looked around. *Run. Grab the keys from the driver. Hijack the car. Smash through the front gate.*

And die.

He fumbled with the clip and gave it to the guard. Even in the shade of the portico, the dry heat burned his cheeks.

The guard raised the tie clip to the sun and clucked his tongue.

"What's wrong?" Vanhoven said, his voice high.

"Diamond no is real," the guard said.

Wade exhaled. "Diamonds are expensive." He put his finger to his lips. "Shhh."

The guard chuckled. He gave Wade back his fake-diamond tiepin and his briefcase. He didn't ask for Wade's pen, just their cellphones. Wade combed back his damp hair.

The house's carved wooden door opened and they strode inside to cool marble tiles the color of sand. Beside them, freshly cut flowers overflowed a glass vase on an antique hutch. Marble-topped stairs rose beside a beige wall with lights in wooden sconces. The guard didn't lead them to the stairs but proceeded through another door on the first floor. Bronze sculptures of pre-Columbian figures stood on marble pedestals that lined the hallway. As Wade followed, he noticed the guard wasn't armed. They'd made it into the sanctum.

A third door opened. This time into a large, high-ceilinged meeting room of wooden floors and slowly revolving ceiling fans. On three walls, big arrangements of fresh flowers stood next to oil paintings of natives beside green vegetation and waterfalls. Wall-length

windows on the fourth side gave view to a swimming pool surrounded by warm brown tiles, empty lounge chairs, and furled um-
brellas. Another pool seemed to drop off the edge of the earth.

Thirty people could have met in the room, but only three sat behind the huge ebony table. Andre waved. Next to him, Polanco,
short and bald, called hello in his deep voice. Then Carmela, her
hair brown today. She wore a silk cowgirl blouse. Everyone but he
and Vanhoven were in designer jeans. Andre limped over. Wade
hadn't known that Dolce & Gabbana made a cowboy shirt.

"I am sorry," Andre said. "At the ranch we dress different. I should
have told you."

"I guess everyone knows who the hired help is," Vanhoven said.

Carmela's focus shifted to the door behind them. A small woman
swept in. Late forties and thin, dark hair pulled back, her face as
delicate as a porcelain doll. Wade turned so the pinhole camera got
good shots of her.

La Jefa drew up beside them. Age lines coursed the skin around
her eyes. This woman didn't need plastic surgery to project her
power. Wade had always believed that no one had blue irises in
Mexico. Hers were luminous.

Wade said, "My name is—"

"I know who you are," La Jefa said, her voice deep.

She wore no jewelry and dressed in plain off-the-rack slacks and
running shoes. Her shapeless blouse seemed to be muslin. Wade saw
a coffee stain.

She turned to Vanhoven. "And you are the backup banker." She
spoke English with barely an accent.

"Co-lead," Vanhoven said.

"Ah, co-lead. Does that mean co-responsible?"

Vanhoven swallowed and his Adam's apple plummeted. La Jefa
gave an amused smile.

Footsteps ran across the floor behind them. La Jefa's eyes softened. She reached out and hugged a boy of about four. A stream of warm Spanish flowed from her.

The boy took in the rest of them. "Hello," he said in English.

Even this child knew that he and Vanhoven were Americans. "Hi, I'm Wade." He stuck out his hand.

La Jefa held the child's arm as if Wade were contagious. She kissed the boy on the forehead and nudged him toward the door. When she turned back, her face had hardened. "Sit."

Without a word, everyone arranged themselves at the end of the carved ebony table closest to the wall-length windows. Vanhoven and Wade perched on one side and the others sat on the opposite, La Jefa directly in front of Wade. On either side of her, Carmela, Andre, and Polanco spoke softly in Spanish. La Jefa listened and said nothing. A servant raised a handheld vacuum and sucked up a fly.

La Jefa motioned to someone, and servants set down glasses of water and bowls of mixed nuts. Just to make them acknowledge them, Wade removed the pitch books from his briefcase and passed them out. No one said "thank you" or made eye contact. La Jefa seemed to have deadened the light and the colors of the room.

The door opened. Martinez walked over the wooden floor. Polanco nodded at him, but La Jefa looked away. Without a word, Martinez sat next to Vanhoven on their side of the table.

Wade wasn't going to be intimidated by these people. "It's good to see you, Egberto," he said.

"Is it?" Martinez said. He glared at the bowl of nuts in front of him and pushed it away.

La Jefa said something and the others leaned in. She turned to Wade. "Begin."

Wade wasn't going to be rushed. He slipped off his suit jacket and Vanhoven did the same. They moved to face the others from the front of the table, the wall of windows behind them. Wade started by describing their backgrounds, concentrating his attention on La Jefa so the tie clip could get more shots. While he talked, she leafed through the pitch book, as if she'd muted him. He'd just gotten to the Felton building's cash flow numbers when someone shouted outside.

Pop!

Wade held still. He must have imagined it.

Boom!

Wade's pitch book fell and slapped against the wooden floor. The windows exposed them to the pool. Wade looked for cover. He bent down. Vanhoven crouched beside him.

CHAPTER FIFTY-SEVEN

Myles met Sofia at a spot in the middle of the high school's athletic field bleachers. He didn't want to be overheard. She stared at him as he sat down. She knew something was wrong.

"My dad knows about your family," he said.

Her eyes widened. "How much does he know?"

"Everything, I think. He's like taking precautions to protect us."

"Precautions?"

"Yeah, he won't tell me what."

She sat back against the hard cement bleacher. "Oh my God."

"What?"

"He's working with the DEA."

His dad? The DEA?

"They recruit informants. That's what my uncle was."

Her aunt had killed her own brother! Myles forced himself to stay calm for both of them. Words from Hidden Road drifted back to him. *Put your mind in an open state.*

It couldn't be hopeless. There had to be a way out. "Your parents could make a deal with the DEA. You know, we all go into Witness Protection."

She shook her head. "Mamá would never do that."

"So they run and you stay here. You haven't done anything."

She let out a hard, sharp bark of a laugh. "You think my aunt cares if I'm innocent? I'm collateral. Just like you are."

Collateral. It was one of his dad's banker words. But so much worse with this family. He took deep breaths to ease the tension. "How about I get my dad to include you in his precautions?"

"You think the DEA will help me? The only way that happens is if my parents cooperate."

She looked so miserable. He couldn't let himself catch her shade. "Okay, so I run away with you and your parents."

Her eyes grew bright with tears. He couldn't bear it and wrapped her up in his arms. For a moment the world got smaller. He visualized their future, a place where no one could find them.

Myles pulled himself apart and clutched her hands in his. "We can buy new names. Start our lives over. You and me. Fuck the world."

She gave him a sad, hopeless smile. "But we don't have any money."

"You have a bank account, so you empty it and I hide the cash. I take a little each day from my mom and dad. We can save enough to give us a start."

"Where?"

"We go to someplace like Montana. Your aunt's men won't look for us there."

He saw her thinking, getting her mind around it. She just had to step into the possibility. "We can do this," he said. "Don't give into surrender."

"I could sell some jewelry," she said. "Some designer purses."

She wasn't shook now. She was with him. "Yes!"

"But how do we get there? We need IDs to buy plane tickets. People can trace us."

"That's why we get a stash of cash. So we can buy new IDs."

"That's possible?"

He laughed. She had parents in a drug cartel but sometimes he knew so much more about the world. "Of course we can. There are sites all over the internet that will sell them to you."

Sites that could be fake. But he couldn't think about that yet. He also had another idea for doubling their cash, an idea she wouldn't like. But she didn't have to find out.

He said, "We have to pretend we don't know shit about what our parents are doing."

CHAPTER FIFTY-EIGHT

Wade's heart boomed in his chest, his breathing fast and shallow. He and Vanhoven were kneeling on the floor of the meeting room in La Jefa's house, but the others still sat in their chairs at the table.

More shots outside.

La Jefa yelled something in Spanish. The door opened and a guard with an assault rifle said something. She hissed out a response and the guard shut the door.

La Jefa lifted her water and took a sip. "You can get up now. It is safe for you to show courage."

Wade and Vanhoven clambered to their feet. They sat beside Martinez and faced the others. Wade sipped water to settle himself.

"*Coyotes*," La Jefa said, pronouncing the word in Spanish. She stared at Wade and Vanhoven, the fingers of one hand stroking a page of the pitch book.

Beside her, Carmela said, "When the *coyotes* get hungry, they like the grapes." Her smile looked as if she were wincing.

Martinez said, "*Coyotes* hide everywhere these days. We shoot as many as we can."

Maybe they called DEA agents *coyotes*. Maybe they were torturing the man they'd found. In an hour La Jefa's men would learn why he and Vanhoven were really there.

Martinez tapped his blue and platinum Montblanc on the pitch book. La Jefa cast him a glance and the pen stopped in mid-air. She pointed at Vanhoven. "What does the co-lead add to this meeting?"

Vanhoven's face looked scalded. "We're . . . Our institution is taking the biggest . . . part of the deal."

"And this one knows all the other banks." Martinez pointed his pen at Wade.

La Jefa grimaced. "You lend us money that we do not need. How does that help me?"

She was an accountant, and accountants routinely minimized the value of banks. But it was also a test. When he didn't answer immediately, Carmela frowned. She rose from her chair.

Before she could speak, Wade said, "Excuse me, *señora*." He stood, and Carmela settled back in her chair. He walked to the front of the table. Wade slowly drummed the ebony with his fingers.

"We are waiting," La Jefa said

"The loan is insurance," Wade said. "You only risk the down payment."

La Jefa stared into her water glass and considered his statement. Maybe she'd never heard a financial advisor equate a loan with insurance.

Wade said, "What happens if someone seizes your building?"

"Like an agency of the U.S. government?" La Jefa asked.

If he admitted that, he and Vanhoven could no longer pretend to be innocent bankers. But continuing the pretense would make them look stupid. Or cause La Jefa to grow suspicious.

"Yes," Wade said.

She motioned with her hand for him to continue.

"Without us financing the deal, you'll pay cash for the whole building. If law enforcement seizes it, you lose everything you invested. That's too much of your capital. But that doesn't happen when banks loan you eighty percent of the purchase. If the building is seized, you stop paying the loan and the syndication of banks absorbs eighty percent of the loss. Your twenty percent down payment is like a deductible."

La Jefa took in the slowly twirling ceiling fan. Martinez's pen wagged in the air. Wade couldn't tell if his pitch had caught.

La Jefa spoke in Spanish to Carmela and Andre and their bodies relaxed. On the other side of her, Polanco nodded his agreement. The wooden floor felt more solid under Wade's shoes.

Vanhoven stood and cleared his throat. Why was he talking now? They had an agreement.

"Look what the Russians did in New York and London," Vanhoven said. "They bought buildings all over those cities. In ten years, their children will be the owners, and no one will care how the parents got their money."

"Stop selling," La Jefa said.

Vanhoven looked down at the pitch book on the table. He scratched at his neck and shirt collar.

"Unity Coast will make sure that everything goes right," Martinez said.

La Jefa aimed her blue eyes at him. "Do I have your guarantee?"

Martinez's face reddened. For the first time, Wade thought he saw fear eclipse his arrogance. Fiona and Myles would never be safe from La Jefa in San Diego.

"When can we close in Tijuana?" La Jefa said.

La Jefa controlled Tijuana. The FBI couldn't coordinate an arrest there. Beside him, Vanhoven said, "Our participants require closing in San Diego."

La Jefa's mouth tightened. She hissed something in Spanish to Andre.

"It's standard practice," Vanhoven said.

Wade tried to catch Vanhoven's eye. Had he forgotten those shots outside?

La Jefa rose and started toward the door.

Wade could see what would happen next. The guards would take Vanhoven and him to a hole already dug by the grapevines. They'd fertilize a special vintage.

"We'll figure out something," Wade said.

La Jefa stopped. Anger had stretched away the lines in her face. Wade and Vanhoven were both still standing, but she looked only at Wade. "I want financial advisors who are more clever than procedures." She shifted her gaze to Vanhoven. "Do you understand?"

"Yes," Vanhoven said. His perfectly arranged hair glistened.

La Jefa's eyes moved back to pin Wade. "We all know what is expected. Right?"

"Yes," Wade said.

As if they'd received a hidden signal, the servants appeared with bottles of champagne and more plates of mixed nuts. Wade looked through the window. Water fell over the wall of the second pool as if off a cliff.

A warm, damp hand touched his arm. "You did well," Polanco said. His bass voice sounded hoarse.

"Did I?" Wade said.

"She makes everyone afraid."

Martinez clomped over the wooden floor, and Wade saw his cowboy boots. He wanted to kill this bastard.

"Too much selling," Martinez said.

"Like you would know anything about that," Wade said.

Martinez huffed. He turned to Polanco. "Where is the report?"

Polanco's shoulders sank as if his body were swallowing itself. He stared at the wooden floor. "We're still investigating," he said.

"Let me tell you something, Mr. Bosworth," Martinez said. He nodded toward La Jefa. "She sees if a single penny is missing. So do I."

As if she'd heard them, La Jefa approached. Polanco retreated. La Jefa held a plate of nuts in one hand and a flute of champagne in the other. "You have nothing to fear," she said to Wade. "As long as you do what you promised."

Be afraid. Be very afraid.

She gave her plate to a servant and drew close to Wade. When she kissed him on the cheek, it was so sudden, so contrary to the meeting, it was all he could do not to jerk away. Her lips were cold. She smelled of lime and peanuts.

"We kiss our business partners here," she said.

La Jefa reached up toward Martinez. He slowly folded his body and she pecked him on the cheek. She stepped back. "You've done well for the son of a whore," she said.

She had to be making a joke, but Martinez didn't laugh. La Jefa didn't smile. She pointed at Wade's wrist. "I like your watch. It is expensive but doesn't try to show off."

His watch was hidden under the cuff of his shirt. Yet she knew it was the most expensive Shinola made.

La Jefa and Martinez walked away without another word, each to different parts of the floor. Wade took a flute of champagne and forced down sips. Then a lime-flavored peanut that made him want to gag. He inhaled to calm himself. The scent of the flowers was overpowering.

Fifteen minutes later, he and Vanhoven escaped into the SUV's cool leather back seat. The car silently slid forward. Wade wanted to call Fiona and reassure her that he was coming home. But not until he crossed the border.

At the corral, a jockey cantered a horse along the railings of the fence. They passed long fields of grapes and Wade smelled manure. His tight calves and hamstrings ached for release, but he couldn't relax. If he let down, his body would start to shake.

Vanhoven slumped on the other side of the seat, his long legs splayed out, his knees wide. He looked as if he'd almost drowned. "Those weren't coyotes," he whispered.

CHAPTER FIFTY-NINE

The next day Wade and Vanhoven met at a nondescript three-story building among the office complexes in the Sorrento Valley part of San Diego. They took the elevator to a basement hallway and a man motioned them to a door without a name or number. They stepped inside and followed him through another door to a large open room.

About fifteen people sat in front of their laptops at two long tables, folders and mugs of coffee beside them. All but Cartuso were dressed in jeans, Hawaiian shirts, and casual blouses. So this was the strike force, Wade thought. Tented placards showed each name and agency: FBI, DEA, IRS, Homeland Security, District Attorney's Office, San Diego Police, CIA. At the end of a table, Harold Cartuso moved one blue-suited shoulder, then the other, as if he were squeezing himself into a smaller air pocket. He didn't have a name tent.

Rodrigues gave Wade and Vanhoven bottles of water and motioned for them to sit in chairs facing the others. She took a chair in front of them at one of the tables. Today she sat straighter, her shoulders broader. Wade recognized that she was nervous in front of her peers. He didn't like this atmosphere. It wasn't a friendly review of what had gone down the day before at the ranch.

"Make yourselves comfortable," Rodrigues said.

They slipped off their jackets and ties. Vanhoven fumbled with his tie pin for what seemed a minute before he shoved it into his shirt pocket.

Cartuso tapped his heavy ring. All his colleagues turned to him. Wade wondered if he had to be the alpha at every meeting because of that voice.

"These two gentlemen have provided excellent evidence," Rodrigues said. "The warehouse photos go a long way to bringing charges under Title 31, USC Section 5332." She turned to Wade and Vanhoven. "That's illegal bulk cash smuggling. You've also obtained evidence of international money laundering." Pivoting back to face Cartuso, she said, "We have illegal processing at the bank and falsification of a loan application."

Cartuso tapped his ring on the table in what could only be mock applause. Rodrigues' grainy cheeks flushed.

Wade was tired of the posturing. "What were those gunshots?" he said.

Rodrigues got a nod from Cartuso. "The spy in the sky picked up a man hiding in the vineyards," she said. "We alerted our Mexican police contact."

Vanhoven stared at Rodrigues and Cartuso as if he couldn't believe what he'd heard. "Are you actually saying you warned the police? And then they warned her people at the ranch?"

Cartuso said, "If we ask for help to arrest La Jefa, we get nowhere. But if we want to save her life? That message gets through in five minutes."

Wade was stunned. "Someone wanted to kill La Jefa?"

"The man was from the Cartel Jalisco Nueva Generación," Rodrigues said. "The CJNG. They're at war with La Jefa and got wind of the meeting. He had a Stovepipe. That's an antitank weapon. He was hiding in the vineyard and was going to destroy the entire house."

"We saved your lives," Cartuso said.

The industrial grey carpet rippled under Wade. He looked at Vanhoven. His face was as white as milk.

"You said the meeting wouldn't be dangerous," Vanhoven said.

"We were on top of it," Cartuso said. "We kept you safe."

By warning their enemies so someone else wouldn't kill all of them. Wade couldn't get his mind around it.

"We're all on the same team," Rodrigues said.

This was insane. "We're done with this," Wade said.

Cartuso furrowed his eyes at him. He shook his head. "We need La Jefa to come to the U.S."

This would never end, each objective changing as soon as it was reached. Wade had to stop it. "Peter, tell them what happened when you suggested the closing be in San Diego."

"She almost shot us," Vanhoven said.

Cartuso pursed his mouth as if they smelled bad. "Are bankers really this uncreative?"

It hit Wade then, the whole play. Cartuso knew that La Jefa would never come to San Diego. He was aiming for another way to hurt her. "You want La Jefa to lose the entire two hundred eighty million," he said.

Cartuso tapped his ring on the table. As if given a signal, everyone else in the room nodded.

"Let me lay it out for you," Cartuso said. "La Jefa's investors factor in losing *some* money. But when we do a civil seizure of the two hundred eighty million . . . ? Now that's different."

With such a big loss, the investors would completely distrust her. Maybe a war would break out.

"Reducing their capital at risk was the whole reason we got them to listen in the first place," Vanhoven said. "Now you want us to propose a complete reversal?"

"Show me how creative bankers can be," Cartuso said.

An unavoidable truth hit Wade. Cartuso was just as dangerous as La Jefa. But he had an idea, an idea that made him more afraid than ever. Reaching into his pocket, he felt the handle from Chad's briefcase. He needed it to bolster his courage.

CHAPTER SIXTY

FIONA

Leticia had left the office early, and Fiona had a whole afternoon to photograph the financial reports, bank statements, and correspondence from the files. She pulled them from the cabinet a few at a time and used the camera bracelet the DEA had given her. As she worked, she couldn't help but glance up at the walls of children's photos and thank-you letters. So many days they'd inspired her. Now her eyes always landed on Mateo, the boy with the dimpled smile who'd run away and joined a gang.

At four o'clock she heard footsteps and a knock. The door swung open, and Andre stood outside. Something about him was different. He wore his typical light blue suit with a purple tie and a purple pocket handkerchief. That wasn't it. It was his posture—straighter and more formal. Andre limped stiffly inside and sat in front of her desk. "We need to go somewhere beautiful," he said. His smile looked forced.

She didn't like that he'd glanced at the donor folder on her desk. His cheerful words could be just to throw her off. "I . . . I have a lot of work to do."

"This won't take long."

"Where are we going?"

"To look at the sunset."

If she resisted, he'd see her fear. He'd know she was hiding something. "Just give me a minute. I have to go to the ladies' room."

"Of course," he said.

She walked through the engineering company offices to the restroom at the end of the floor. No one was inside. Once in the stall, she sat on the toilet and trembled. Andre must have noticed her scrutinizing the reports and knew about her work with law enforcement. He was taking her where other hard men were waiting.

She punched in Wade's number. The call went to voicemail and she spoke quickly. "Andre says I have to go with him and won't say where. I'll try to reach Cartuso." The next words came out before she could think about them. "I love you, Wade."

She disconnected and dialed Cartuso's number. *Please be there.*

"Hello." The voice was unmistakable.

"Andre showed up at my office. He wants me to go with him and won't say where."

Cartuso considered that. Then, "We'll track your phone and have someone physically on your tail in the next ten minutes. Keep your cell turned on inside your purse."

"Would he do something to me?"

Cartuso gave a high laugh. "Andre would never get his clothes dirty."

"What if he drives to Mexico?"

"If he gets close to the border, we'll stop his car."

Would Cartuso really sacrifice the whole operation to save her?

"The most important thing is to keep you safe," he said.

She slipped the phone into her purse and made sure it still showed Cartuso's number. Then she flushed the toilet and washed her hands. Her gut told her Andre wouldn't let anyone hurt her. But her intuition had been wrong before.

After five minutes, she couldn't delay any longer and returned to her office. Andre was waiting outside her door. "Are you all right?" he asked.

"Women take longer than men, you know."

No laugh or even a smile.

She wanted to give Cartuso a location through the phone. "Aren't you going to tell me where we're going? I have to let Leticia know."

He glanced back through the doorway at the empty office.

"She's coming in soon," Fiona said. But it was already the end of the workday. It was such an obvious lie.

"We won't be long," he said.

Outside, the daylight was fading. She got in Andre's Mercedes and he drove west on the highway. He was so quiet, as if he was planning something. They exited at Pacific Beach. At least they weren't headed to the border. They rode up Soledad Mountain past blocks lined with houses. She looked through the window at the outside mirror but couldn't make out anyone following. The day was getting dark.

They reached the top of the mountain, passed the cellphone towers, and turned into the public park. She expected to see people, but the first lot was empty. No cars in the second lot either. She looked at the veterans memorial monument. Its empty brick steps led to a white cross.

"Today we watch the sun disappear from our lives," Andre said. "Like men do for thousands of years."

What did that mean? She looked around. There had to be security cameras here. Andre must know that.

They parked in one of the empty spaces on the far side of the monument and got out. "Leave your purse in the car," Andre said. "I will lock it."

"I always take my purse in case someone needs to reach me," she said.

He put his hand on her shoulder. She flinched and his head drew back a little. "Fiona, nothing happens in the next half hour. I want that no phone interrupts our talk."

He could tell that she was nervous but didn't ask why. He had to know something. *Cartuso, please be here.*

She put her purse below the front seat and Andre locked the doors. They walked past the monument. The surrounding black walls were embedded with hundreds of names and photos of the war dead. Why did they have to look at the sunset here? They reached the grassy lip that overlooked La Jolla and Del Mar and the sea. A dirt path lined with tall sagebrush descended from the summit. No way was she going down there.

Andre found a concrete bench and she sat next to him. For a few minutes they watched the sun flare orange and red over the edge of the ocean. She smelled the sea. A light breeze made her arms shiver.

The park's lights flashed on behind them. She jumped.

"Don't worry, you are safe," Andre said.

She glanced behind her. No cars had pulled into the lot. Maybe the DEA had a drone overhead or somehow could see them from a satellite.

Andre reached into his suit coat pocket. Fiona bunched her fists.

He pulled out a long-stemmed white rose. He held it out so it crossed the burnt horizon and the darkening sea. "Have you ever thought about what a rose means?" he said.

He'd forced her to this park, made her feel petrified . . . for this? "Are you courting me now?" She heard the rancor in her voice.

"I guess I am, in a way." He brought the rose to his nose and drew in its scent. "Do you see the old paintings of Mother Mary? She usually holds a rose. In Christianity it symbolizes the union of man and God, *l'homme et le Dieu.* That tradition comes from the alchemists. For them, each color of the rose means something different. Red is the passion, white the purity, black is death."

He seemed relaxed. He always was when he delivered another round of his New Age piety. "And your rose is white for purity?" she asked.

"White also means innocence and unconditional love, like the love for a child. Or the first love between two teenagers."

Fiona's eyes widened. He was actually using her son's romance with Sofia to get to her. She turned to the sea so he wouldn't see the fury on her face.

"Our two children are very much in love," he said. "It is wonderful."

He sounded so genuine. Time to change the subject and delve into what he hid under his shaman act. "Did the alchemists use roses to turn lead into gold?"

He chuckled. "You make a joke, but you are more correct than you think. The *alchimie* is the perfection of the soul. To make the gold, the alchemist must also transform himself."

Lights twinkled like stars below them in La Jolla and Del Mar. The sea was transforming into dark emerald, the clouds into purple bruises. Soon it would be sunset, but the park lights would illuminate them for Cartuso's people.

"The *alchimie* exists in Europe for five thousand years. More than one hundred fifty thousand books are written about it. Aristotle, Thomas Aquinas, and Isaac Newton. They use the *alchimie* to study the man, the world . . . the universe."

Gravel and dirt rattled on the path below them. Two shadows climbed up through the sage. Fiona's heels pushed into the dirt. She tensed to run.

The two people passed by and were bickering about something. One of them was huge and turned to her. Harold Cartuso. Then he was gone, his boots clunking against the blacktop behind them. She couldn't let herself relax. Something about this conversation was still dangerous. Andre had brought her here for more than talk about alchemy

He set the rose down on the cement slab under the bench and picked up a small rock. He rolled it between his thumb and forefinger. When he turned to her, the illumination from the park lights made his face glow. The man was so duplicitous, and yet there was something guileless about his expression.

"Our families—they too change from the lead to gold." He tossed the rock and it bounced and rustled like an animal scurrying through the brush.

She saw the opening to pivot the conversation. "Do you think that Unity Coast and Comunidad de Niños will help our families evolve to a higher level?"

"*Oui oui oui. C'est ça. Exactement.*" French seemed to confer the deeper meaning that his English couldn't. He took off his glasses and his eyes reached into her.

Maybe what Andre was laundering wasn't really money, but his family. "The Kennedys changed," she said. "The father was a bootlegger, and the son became president."

He shook his head. "For what I did, I need more than the power of the politics."

He was atoning for his past. "Do you think a sin can change into something good?" *Like a charitable foundation?*

"If that is not true, there is no hope in this life."

He looked down toward the lights of the faraway houses and the endless dark of the sea. "There is something else I believe. The Chinese meaning of the random events, *les événements aléatoires.* Like the connections in the *I Ching.*"

"What connections?"

"You, Myles, Wade, and Sofia and me. We come together because Myles is kidnapped. It is a random event, but there is meaning. Together we make the transformations that rebirths our families."

She wouldn't let herself be pulled in. Andre had orchestrated Myles' abduction and torture. He'd tricked her into taking an illegal loan. He'd been part of Chad Fisher's murder. Nothing was random about those events.

She had to find his weakness. That meant teasing out its underbelly. She started with her own admission. "We've all done bad things. Especially me."

He looked up at the few stars that flickered through the clouds. "We must accept our shadows. The more that we push them away, the more powerful they are. The bad is also part of us."

It sounded like a rationalization, a self-forgiveness for the evil he'd done. "What are the shadows you've come to accept?" she said.

"They are more than the things I do. They are the parts of my character. I do not need to name them."

Andre put on his spectacles. The lenses were like a thick wall between them. This whole scary pilgrimage to a mountaintop was for nothing.

"Myles listens to me," he said. "I think that he is full of potential. He can be a great man."

She went rigid. The lights swirled below her.

"You know Tulum, the holy Mayan city on the ocean? It is where I saw my history and my potential. My true self. I want to take Myles there. I can teach him to listen to the wisdom of his ancestors."

Panic pounded in her head. What should she say? *What what what?*

"I'll think about it."

No fucking way.

CHAPTER SIXTY-ONE

During the next few days Wade and Vanhoven sneaked away to meetings with the strike team at the same basement room. They engaged companies with websites and public records to forge supporting environmental and engineering reports, title insurance, appraisals, and legal opinions. Wade emailed documents to banks that had agreed to cooperate. At night he paced behind the closed door of his bedroom to whisper the pitch and his responses to all the questions. He tried to ignore the danger underneath the stage set.

When he was ready, Wade called Martinez from his office at the bank. "We've got a problem," he said.

"I do not like problems," Martinez said. "*La Jefa* likes them even less."

"Can she come to San Diego so we can work this out?"

Martinez laughed. "Call me when you're serious." He hung up, just as Wade had predicted.

Wade didn't call him back. An hour later, Martinez telephoned. "The meeting is tomorrow."

"Vanhoven and I will be there," Wade said.

"Not Vanhoven. Just you. The driver will be outside the Tijuana Customs exit at ten in the morning."

Wade knew better than to ask where they were going.

He talked to Rodrigues while he drove his car home from the office. She assured him that the DEA would have men on the ground to follow him in Tijuana. But once he was at the ranch or in Andre's house he was on his own. She didn't pretend that an extraction would work. "We appreciate and admire what you're doing," she said.

Last words to a dying man? "This time no recording devices," he said.

"Why? There's no way they can detect them."

Wade didn't care. He had a bad feeling about this meeting. "You've already got plenty of evidence," he said. And if he was murdered, he didn't want it recorded.

All the way home he reassured himself that the DEA and FBI had helped engineer every detail. There wasn't a question he hadn't prepared for. No way anything could go wrong. Still, he didn't tell Fiona where he was going. He didn't want to argue with her.

The next morning, he walked over the causeway to Tijuana. A black SUV waited in front of the open-sided pharmacy. Wade crossed the street and a paunchy, goateed man with a ponytail climbed out of the back seat.

"Your cellphone, please," the goateed man said.

Wade handed him his phone and the man gave it to someone else. Now the DEA couldn't electronically track him.

Wade climbed into the back and the SUV started forward. Beside him, the goateed man slipped out a pistol and tapped his thigh as if keeping time with a song. Wade took long yoga breaths.

They reached streets of tourist shops. Wade recognized the area. At ten o'clock in the morning, the bars, restaurants, and boutiques were closed, but a few prostitutes wandered the sidewalks and stood in doorways. The driver did a U-turn. They drove back on the other side of the palm-lined median and stopped beside the Delicias Hotel bar.

"This is where Chad fell off the roof," Wade said.

The goateed man smiled. "Fell?"

Wade got out. He looked down at the briefcase in his hand, then up at the six-story façade of windows. Someone with a rifle stared from the roof.

It was a setup.

The ponytailed man beside him dangled his pistol from his hand. It would be suicide to run. There was no way but forward. The greeter out front pulled back the green rope and opened the black door. Then Wade was inside, and it was too late.

This morning the TVs were dark and the lights extinguished around the empty stage. A maid wiped down the stripper pole with a rag and a spray bottle. It was so quiet—no music, and the few people there spoke in whispers. Three women sat at the front table. In the back another woman displayed her bikini-clad rear to three men. Her smirk looked as if it were carved into her face.

Two women approached. The shapelier one displayed her breasts through the slit sides of her dress. The other took a big bite of an ice-cream sandwich and grinned. Before Wade knew what was happening, they draped their arms around him. A waiter held a cellphone and it flashed. Wade pushed them away, but it was too late. This was the cover story for his fall from the building. Fiona would never believe it; she'd know what happened.

He filled his chest with air. If these were his last minutes, he was going to fight.

"The meeting is in a room upstairs," the goateed man said.

Somewhere close to the roof.

They walked to the rear of the bar and through the opening in the wall, then past a two-tiered lounge with couches and deep chairs. At the hotel reception desk, a man with a Delicias emblem didn't look up. They boarded an elevator with faux marble walls and exited on the fifth floor. Wade imagined Chad on this same path, Chad sucking on a cigarette as he stepped inside a room.

The goateed man knocked on a door. They weren't going to the roof. Not yet.

The door slid open a crack, then all the way. Wade entered and took in the closed entry to the bathroom. Inside that room a Jacuzzi might be full of water. Would it be cold or hot when they pushed his head under?

Everything in the room was red—the walls, the covers over the bulging-heart bed, the reflections on the ceiling mirror. A red chair faced a table with two red chairs behind it. A woman in khaki pants fiddled with electronics on the table. No sign of car batteries. No restraints or blowtorches. Wade took a breath.

The goateed man motioned him where to stand. He took Wade's briefcase and gave it to a broad-shouldered man. The woman in khaki pants put on earphones and held a wand attached by wire to an electronic console. The wand glided over Wade. The broad-shouldered man held out the briefcase and she scanned it.

"I'm a banker," Wade said. "What can you possibly hope to find?"

The ponytailed man rubbed his goatee with his pistol hand. "It is the men in the suits that always threat the most."

The woman with the wand said something in Spanish. She picked up her equipment from the table and walked away. The door to the hallway opened. Martinez and La Jefa walked past her as she exited. Now Wade knew why Chad was pushed from this building. La Jefa owned Delicias.

The roof was two floors up.

CHAPTER SIXTY-TWO

La Jefa and Martinez sat behind the table facing Wade in the red chair. The window was open to the street below Delicias, and he heard cars and vendors. Anyone outside would hear him shout.

La Jefa poured two glasses of water and passed one to Martinez. They drank and stared at him. La Jefa's white business suit was spotless. She looked like an angel with frigid blue eyes. She said, "Señor Martinez says that you have a problem with our transaction. You told us that this would never happen." Her voice was soft and steady.

Wade said, "It would have occurred even if I wasn't involved." He motioned to the broad-shouldered guard carrying his briefcase. "May I?"

La Jefa nodded. The man opened the case, flipped through the papers inside, and inspected the felt interior. He handed it over. Wade pulled out a manila folder and extracted the consulting company's fake study.

Wade said, "All banks require an environmental report before they finance a building. There could be chemical spills in the soil, foundation problems, asbestos in the ceilings or walls, maybe electrical and plumbing issues, maybe—"

"Get to the point," Martinez said.

"The point is, the financial institutions have the deepest pockets, so they get sued for any of these problems. So banks reduce the risk by requiring an environmental study."

La Jefa said, "Why didn't you know about environmental problems before?"

"We did. The irregularities are really minor. But one of the participants just had two big real estate loans go bad. They wanted an excuse to back out of the deal."

La Jefa scowled at Martinez. "We wouldn't have this problem in Mexico."

"It's a different game in America," Martinez said.

She turned back to Wade, still frowning. "What are the problems?"

Wade didn't want to leap into the details. That would make him look weak and desperate. He raised his gaze as if recollecting the report. "Insufficient ramps for the disabled, ventilation problems in the restrooms." He paused. "The paint on some of the hallway walls and offices had too much lead. And there was a small soil contamination problem on one side of the building." He made an embarrassed face as if he were ashamed of how minor the issues were. "Normally the others would just increase their funding. That would make up for the one that dropped out. But the other banks are up against their own lending limits."

Martinez slipped out his Montblanc from his shirt pocket. He turned it in his fingers. La Jefa rotated the glass of water.

"You could sue the bank that changed its mind," Martinez said.

"We could do that," Wade said. "But that takes time."

"How unfortunate," La Jefa said.

Unfortunate might have been her last word to Chad. Wade glanced at the window.

"Continue," La Jefa said.

"Another buyer made a bid for the building. It's a lower price but without a financing contingency. Straight cash."

He reached into the folder for a copy of the offer. The buyer was a real company that had gone along with the scheme. The broad-shouldered guard handed over the pages to La Jefa. She read and passed them to Martinez. Martinez photographed the offer with his phone.

"The seller has loans coming due," Wade said. "He needs the money now."

Something pounded through the ceiling. A customer was busy in a bed in the room above them. The mirror on this room's ceiling shook. Wade saw himself: a man in a suit hunched in a chair, his reflection trembling.

He snapped his eyes back to La Jefa. "The seller has given us three days to come up with a financing commitment. Otherwise, he goes with the lower, all-cash buyer. That buyer, by the way, says he can close in two weeks."

La Jefa's mouth tightened. Her eyes seethed.

"There's always a way out of these predicaments," Wade said. "I've thought of some options."

"I hope that you have," La Jefa said.

Confidence. No hurry. Wade inhaled twice before he spoke. "You could just walk away from the deal if you decide it's too much risk."

"Option two," Martinez said.

"You could increase your offer, then transfer the down payment now as earnest money. It might be enough cash for the seller to fend off his creditors."

Martinez pointed his Montblanc at him. "Cut the suspense and get to option three."

They were either biting on the lure or sending him to the roof. "It's the most straightforward. You transfer the two hundred eighty million to Unity Coast now and buy the building. I'm a hundred percent positive we can find another bank and re-form the syndicate. Just not in three days. You'll get your money back in less than a month."

Wade had said it slowly, his voice strong but not too emphatic. He willed himself to believe his own bullshit.

"What happens if the syndicate isn't formed in thirty days?" La Jefa asked.

Wade shook his head. "That won't happen. I've already got three banks who want to replace the one dropping out. But they need more time."

La Jefa looked past him to the open window. Below on the street, men laughed as if they were drunk. Wade wondered if it was the DEA. If they stormed the building, he'd be dead by the time they got to the fifth floor.

"Why do you not suggest this before?" La Jefa said.

"I wanted the loan done in a single step. It's simpler. This takes two steps."

She drank small sips of water while she weighed what he'd said. She didn't look convinced.

"The financing will sail through," Wade said. "In five years no one will think anything about the owners of the Felton building. Your family's next generation will have a jewel in its U.S. holdings."

Martinez pointed his Montblanc at him. "Stop talking."

La Jefa's eyes caught his. Wade didn't discern any anger, just calculation. He stood, but she remained seated. He sat down.

"We secure our deals with something more important to a man than just his own life," Martinez said.

Wade had steeled himself for this threat, yet the words still left him mute.

"If anyone cheats me and gets away with it, everyone cheats me," La Jefa said. "That's why my business is a family business."

The goateed man and the broad-shouldered guard pulled him to his feet. They led him to the hallway and another door. Wade tensed his arms and legs. If he saw stairs he was going to kick and punch.

They pushed him into another room. It was dark with the night shades drawn. The guards shut the door. Wade slid his fingers over the wall and found the light switch. The ceiling fixture gave off a red-tinged glow. Someone lay covered with a red blanket in the bed. No movement. La Jefa had talked about families as collateral. *Fiona. Myles.*

He edged one step closer. Then another.

Wade pulled back the blanket. Underneath, a round face as pale as flour stared out. The chin had whiskers. It was Polanco.

Wade collapsed to the floor.

A half hour later, Martinez opened the door. "Option three," he said.

CHAPTER SIXTY-THREE

With the money Sofia had scavenged and the cash he'd pilfered from his parents, Myles had three thousand dollars. He'd found some sites on the web where he could buy birth certificates, social security cards, and drivers licenses with barcodes, holograms, and magnetic strips. They could get high school graduation diplomas from other states. All it took was Bitcoin.

They just needed more money to buy it.

His high school friend Alex had to vouch for him to establish the contact and set up the meeting. Myles found his passport in his dad's dresser. He cut school and took the battery out of his new phone to prevent tracking. A Lyft or Uber ride would leave a credit card trail, so he called a taxi and paid cash. In San Isidro, it was just a short walk across the tourist bridge to Tijuana. Another taxi took him to the same mall of bars where he'd been kidnapped.

Seeing those bars made his stomach hurt. He remembered the beating and the electric shock. But this time he was here for escape money. Just two deals, then he'd be done forever with this shit.

He walked along the mall's slate and cement walkways and passed El Alacrán with its scorpion sign out front. The little shrine of candles and pictures by the entrance looked cheesy in the daylight. He heard old-time metal from inside. One goth sat under the unlit chandelier. The dude looked like he was still dressed up in his Halloween costume.

The bar for the meeting appeared harmless enough. The entrance was a big open door framed by rivet-encrusted metal. On the sound system, a woman wailed in Spanish and was accompanied by a Mexican accordion and a thumping bass. Pictures of ranchera bands hung on the walls next to ceramic chiles and onions. It looked like a family place but for the two TVs showing cage fights.

A man in a fancy printed shirt stood up at the closest table. "Myles?" he said.

He looked only a few years older than he was. Next to the man sat a woman in a tight flowered blouse that showed off her curves. She was blinged out in gold and diamond earrings and seemed to be in her twenties. The scariest one was the old man in the cowboy hat. His angry eyes took him in like he was a mouse wriggling out of a hole.

Myles reached over the marble tabletop and shook their hands. The younger man said his name was Salvador and the others didn't tell him theirs. Myles set down his backpack and sat across from them on a stool. Salvador grinned in the same way Roberto the kid-napper had. No glowed-up smile was going to fool him this time.

The three of them were drinking mugs of dark beer. Myles signaled the waiter and ordered a Dos Equis. It would be for show. He didn't want alcohol to draw him off point.

"How is Melissa?" Salvador asked. His English was accented but good.

"She's at boarding school," Myles said. "It's just Alex and me now."

The waiter brought his mug of beer from the bar and set it down.

The salty old man in the cowboy hat leaned forward. "What products you want?"

It was just as well there was no small talk. Still, Myles hesitated. No matter how many times he told himself he was only doing two deals, this seemed like the first step in quicksand. He picked up the mug of beer and pretended to sip. He watched them watch him.

He put down the mug. "Oxy, Ex, PCP, and Molly."

"Aren't you the entrepreneur?" Salvador said. "No cocaine or meth or heroin?"

He would never deal meth or heroin. Those drugs killed people. Salvador's mouth twitched, and Myles realized that he was mocking him. They thought he was some kid wannabe.

"My investment group wants the first deal to be a sample," Myles said. "We see which of your products we like and then we'll make a big order." Like he had lots of money behind him.

The woman eyed him, first his Oxford shirt, then his just-washed jeans and backpack. She said, "How much you want this time?"

Myles sat back and folded his arms. He looked up at the red lamps that hung from the dusty ceiling. "Three thousand for the first order."

"That's it?" The designer-label woman looked at Salvador.

"If we like it, we go each month," Myles said. "There are a lot of high schools and colleges around San Diego."

Salvador spoke in Spanish. The old man took off his hat and scratched thin grey hair. His watch was full of diamonds. Even the band looked expensive.

"We start small," Myles said. "We're conservative like a bank."

The older man leaned forward and set his hands flat on the table. The look in his eyes was pure shade. Like he was trying to see the lies on Myles' face.

Salvador said, "We will give you a tryout." He took a napkin from the dispenser and wrote something on it. He slid over the napkin.

Myles had swiped one of his dad's gold pens. He slipped it out of his shirt pocket and ran through the numbers. They had to be high.

Everyone knew to negotiate in Mexico. He increased the volumes, lowered the prices by a third, and passed back the napkin.

All three of them laughed.

"You think that we are some stand on the street that sells sombreros and serapes?" Salvador said.

Myles took a sip of beer. When they only stared at him, he stood. It was a risk, but he could always come back. "Thank you for your time." He slipped on his backpack and reached for his wallet to pay for the beer.

"Where are you going, *guapo?*" the woman said.

Myles stayed standing.

Salvador crossed out Myles' figures on the napkin and wrote others.

Myles sat. He slowly turned his beer mug while he pretended to study the new numbers. He took a sip.

Designer-label woman tapped her aqua nails on the tabletop. "Have you got the money?"

Myles nodded. "Delivery of the product in National City."

Salvador shook his head. "This is a Tijuana price. We charge more for San Diego."

No way was he transporting drugs across the border. "National City," he said. "Just the way you did it last time for Alex."

Salvador conferred with the old man in Spanish. The man took off his hat and fingered the sides of it.

"We deliver it there in a week," Salvador said. "We notify Alex about the time and where that you pick up it."

Myles rotated his mug to make them wait. "Half the money now and half on delivery."

More laughter.

"You know, the way you do this, you look like the amateur," the woman said.

Her pursed mouth told him what she really thought. The amateur was out-negotiating them.

Salvador rose. "We'll go to the parking lot. We don't touch money in here."

Myles would never go to that parking lot. He reached down for his backpack.

Fury rose into the old man's eyes. He rose and pushed the tips of his fingers into the table.

Myles pulled out an iPhone box and slid it across the marble top to him. "It's not a phone," he said.

The old man stared down at the box. He chuckled, and they all caught his laugh. Mexican music started up on the sound system. Men belted out some kind of happy chorus and trumpets blew out riffs.

Myles lifted his mug and clinked it against theirs. "To a long friendship," he said.

Two weeks, two deals, and that was it. Drugs might have ruined the lives of Sofia's parents, but they would save hers. And they'd be together.

CHAPTER SIXTY-FOUR

WADE

A half bottle of cab hadn't pushed Polanco's lifeless face out of Wade's mind. Myles was with Fiona so he didn't have to pretend to be calm. He'd just made another circuit from the kitchen to the living room of his condo when he heard a soft knock on the door.

Rodrigues and Cartuso came in and sat on the couch. "You're upset," Rodrigues said.

"Where the fuck were you when they forced me into that whorehouse?" Wade said.

Cartuso pointed to the La-Z-Boy. "Sit down."

His body was too hyped to sit. Wade clutched the back of the big chair. "Polanco was my son's negotiator."

"We know," Rodrigues said.

Cartuso leaned over the side of the couch and picked up Wade's guitar. His thumb fit all the way around the neck to press against the bass E-string. He flicked out an out-of-tune seventh chord. "They weren't going to hurt you. They need you too much."

"As soon as they didn't believe me, I'd be as dead as Polanco."

Rodrigues nodded as if she understood. "I can see how you would think that," she said.

"Cut the bullshit," Wade said.

Cartuso strummed a flat-five chord. This man's indifference made Wade want to hit something. "Will you put down my guitar?"

Cartuso leaned the instrument against the couch. "Look, we're going to make these bastards pay. But we'll do it as coldly as arithmetic. Got it?"

Wade walked to the window. He looked at the blinking lights in the dark harbor and thought of yoga *asanas*. He took long breaths. Four beats in and eight beats out.

He turned back and stepped over to stand beside the La-Z-Boy. "Martinez was quizzing Polanco at the ranch. Something about missing funds."

"He was skimming," Cartuso said.

"What do you think La Jefa will do when I skim two hundred eighty million?"

Cartuso leaned over the side of the couch and plucked the strings high up the neck by the tuning keys. He said, "Look, your job is simple. Get them to transfer the funds. Then we whisk you and your family to Witness Protection."

Wade grabbed the guitar and set it down against the side of the La-Z-Boy.

"We have more news," Rodrigues said. "We sent Andre's DNA analysis to a friend in Canada. She dug up some cold cases. One was a body buried in a container yard for twenty years. I'll bet you know where."

"Montreal," Wade said.

Rodrigues nodded. "It's a good DNA match. Bits of Andre's hair and skin were on the corpse."

"Andre killed someone?"

"The Mounties think he beat him to death with a tire iron," Cartuso said.

Wade collapsed into the La-Z-Boy. He tried to picture Andre striking someone over and over.

Rodrigues said, "The dead man lived in the Hell's Angels' compound in Sherbrooke. That's just across the Saint Lawrence River from Montreal. Those people would have wanted revenge. That explains why Andre got out of Canada."

"Once he got to Mexico, Carmela's family protected him," Cartuso said. "I'd call that marrying up."

Wade scowled at him. "Is this a joke to you?"

"No," Cartuso said. "Of course not."

"My wife works with this man."

"We don't think he's killed since," Rodrigues said. "He doesn't appear violent now."

As if anyone who killed someone with a tire iron would stop being dangerous. Wade barely listened to what else they said. When they were done, he ushered the two special agents to the door. Returning to the living room, he stared at the TV's blank screen. Fiona needed to be warned.

He drove to the house. Inside, Myles' music thumped and screeched through the ceiling. It was so loud that he and Fiona decided to go outside. She grabbed a bottle of wine and two glasses, and they slipped into her garden. They sat on chairs in a corner where the neighbor's plumeria tree blocked out half the night sky.

Wade drew in the tree's scent. He told her about the body in Montreal. When he'd finished, she didn't seem shocked. She sipped her wine and shook her head. "No way is Andre violent—I'd feel it."

"We can't afford not to be paranoid now," he said. "This is the most dangerous part of the operation."

The music pulsed louder from the house. She leaned forward on the chair. "Wade, I really appreciate how you're trying to protect Myles and me."

"Fiona, I'll be devastated if something happens to you."

She stood and reached over to hug him. He wrapped his arms around her and closed his eyes. Myles' heavy metal grew softer, more melodic, and seeped into the trilling of the crickets.

She unraveled her arms. "You've drunk a lot, and it's late," she said. "Stay here tonight. There are clean sheets in the guest room."

Jasper was gone, and he'd be on the same floor as she was. It was a start.

CHAPTER SIXTY-FIVE

FIONA

Fiona arrived at the chiropractor's office in Kearny Mesa at 1:00 p.m. the next day. The receptionist led her to a treatment room with a bookcase, some spider plants, and a life-size skeleton model in the corner. The only places to sit were an adjustment table and one chair in front of a workbench with a computer on it. Fiona took the chair. She looked at the skeleton and tried to imagine Andre beating it with a tire iron. She couldn't.

Rodrigues slipped in and leaned against the adjustment table. She was all focus and efficiency today and didn't bother with pleasantries. "We have to talk about logistics," she said. "The international wire is supposed to arrive early tomorrow. You'll head into work from your place, as usual. Game time will be some time that morning."

Game time? Was that really what she called this?

"We'll pick you up at work and exfiltrate you. The marshals will handle relocation of you and Wade and Myles."

A year before, the idea of living under the same roof with Wade would have appalled her. She didn't know how she felt about it now. At least they'd be in an unfamiliar city without the old triggers. But she was more worried about her son.

"You know Myles will refuse to go without Sofia," she said.

Rodrigues nodded. "We've come up with a work-around for that. We'll arrest him on drug charges."

Fiona jerked straight in the chair. "What?"

"It's just for show. We'll do it at school. When he's safe, we'll tell him what's going on and work with him."

It was so extreme. So humiliating.

"At least he'll be out of danger," Rodrigues said.

Safe when the girl he loved was left behind. "What about Sofia?"

Rodrigues put her foot on the adjustment table's floor pedal. Its steel legs lowered the leather top closer to the floor. She sat and pushed her hands into the surface.

Fiona didn't like her silence. "Sofia will be in danger, won't she?"

"La Jefa won't forgive losing this much money. She'll want to send a message to everyone they work with."

Fiona's hand flew to her face. "Oh my God!"

"There's no mercy in her world, Fiona. Sofia's family knows the rules."

"But . . . but . . . they must have an escape plan."

"Maybe Sofia knows how to secretly make it across the border to Mexico. Then she'll link up with her mom."

La Jefa had enough resources to find them anywhere—especially in Mexico. This plan would never work. "Damnit, you can't just let them kill an innocent girl!"

Rodrigues stood. She walked past the bookcase and touched the potted spider plant while she looked at a drawing of a spine. Fiona closed her eyes. She felt the tears gather behind her eyelids. It was so merciless. So despicable. And what about Myles? If Sofia was killed, he'd carry that wound forever.

"There may be a way to help her," Rodrigues said.

Fiona's eyes flew open. Rodrigues had walked back to stand in front of the adjustment table. "What way?"

"If her father fully cooperates, we might be able to do something for both Sofia and her mother."

"I can't believe you would play them like this," Fiona said.

"I'm not playing them. I want to help Sofia."

"As long as Andre gives you what you want."

Rodrigues sat on the table and leaned forward. "Think about it, Fiona. I can't just offer protection because I want to. The FBI has its own strict rules."

"I guess you hold children as hostages too."

Rodrigues' eyes fired with anger. "We didn't do this to Sofia—her parents did."

"Let me just see if I've got this right. If Andre cooperates, he'll save his daughter. Otherwise, Sofia, the girl my son loves, will die. But you don't call that kidnapping, do you?"

CHAPTER SIXTY-SIX

Without a word, Sofia had gone missing from school. Just the way her mother would send her back to Mexico. Myles barely heard the teachers in class. At lunch he searched the hallways, the rooms, and the bleachers. When the school day ended, he hurried to Fay Avenue. He'd go to her condo and demand to know where she was.

Someone grabbed his arm. He wrenched it away and whirled.

"It's okay," Sofia said.

He blew out some air. "Where were you?"

"You need to talk with my dad."

He glanced at the street and saw the gold Mercedes. The door opened, and Andre climbed out in a light blue suit and red glasses. "Tell me what's going on," Myles said.

"Do you trust me?"

He reached across and kissed her. He didn't care if Andre saw them. He didn't care if Carmela's spies reported it. Let them all see how powerless they were to stop them from being together.

"Papi will help you," she said.

"How?"

"Just go. You will see."

Myles walked toward the Mercedes. What if Andre had told Sofia lies to lure him to his car? Myles could see through the windows. No one else was inside. He took a last glance at Sofia on the sidewalk and got in beside Andre.

From behind the wheel, Andre said, "I have a surprise for you. You will love it."

Myles suspected anything with the word "surprise" in it. "What is it?"

"If I tell you, it is not a surprise."

Andre headed out of La Jolla and squeezed into the traffic on Highway 5. They were heading south toward Mexico.

What if Andre knew about the drug deal? What if he knew that Sofia was running away with him? But it was too late. They were going seventy miles an hour.

Andre hit his sound system and Myles heard sitar, then guitar and synthesized voices. It was Pryapisme. Andre beamed out a smile so big it looked glued onto his face. "Is this your music?"

"Yes."

"I think it is cool."

Did he really say that? But even his dad liked Pryapisme, with its beat and repeated guitar themes and orchestration and synthesizers.

"I think we should do something men to men," Andre said.

"Like what?"

"Why are you so worried? I am a modern man. I know what the young people in La Jolla do together."

Myles stared at the floor mat. Didn't Mexicans get all crashy about sex with their daughters? But Andre was Canadian. And the French part had to be looser.

Andre said, "Now Carmela? She is the old school. She is very Mexican. Be careful of Carmela."

Like he didn't know that.

They got off the highway at Pacific Beach. The heavy traffic chilled Myles a bit. There were lots of lights, and it would be easy to jump out of the car. They passed strip malls and fast-food places, Home Depot and Target. Then little concrete buildings and apartments. Myles couldn't figure out where they were going.

Andre pulled into a drive with cars parked on it. The sign on the building said: "HOME ON THE RANGE." There were pickups, a Tesla, and a Prius with a bike on the back. Two people opened a trunk and unpacked carrying cases.

"Every young man must know how to shoot," Andre said.

Myles drew his head back. "We're going to shoot guns?"

"Only you," Andre said.

Did accidents happen at shooting ranges? No shit they did. But with all these witnesses?

Andre parked. They got out on the blacktop and Andre clapped him on the back. That was weird. Andre gripped, he touched, even rubbed people's necks and shoulders, but he didn't give man claps.

"This will be much fun," Andre said.

Myles looked around. No Hispanics with machine guns. No bikers with Harleys and beards down to humongous bellies. They were beside some kind of sales office. The people behind the windows could see them. The traffic cruising down Balboa Avenue could too.

Andre pressed a button on his key fob and the trunk rose. He fished out a small plastic case and they walked inside to the showroom. Rifles with huge magazines were fastened upright to the walls. Pistols—even a six-shooter—lay in a display case.

"Andre!" The old woman at the counter flashed a toothy grin.

"Susie," Andre said. "You are the prettiest redneck gun nut who I know."

She laughed. "Better not let Carmela hear you. Or you'll be out with the targets."

OMG, this place is hee-haw-ville with guns.

"I want to introduce you to Myles," Andre said. "It is his first time."

The woman eyed him and winked. "I'll bet it's not."

Andre and the woman started giggling. Myles hated it when parents made sex jokes.

She handed them both ear protectors, then plastic glasses for Myles. Andre pointed to his own thick, red-framed spectacles. "These are good enough."

Andre opened a steel door. They walked down a ten-foot tunnel to another steel door. On the other side was a room that seemed to be all concrete. Ten people stood behind counters and fired their weapons down lanes that were about thirty yards long. It was so loud.

They really were going to shoot. This was whacked. He and Andre put on their ear protectors and Myles his goggles. Andre fiddled with the computer terminal at an empty counter. He attached a target with a human outline to a cardboard backing, and the computer sent it out on a wire.

"We start at seven yards," Andre said. "Most of the time you do not shoot a pistol farther than this."

When you shoot people.

Andre opened the case and gave the pistol and magazine to Myles. "This is a Glock 19. Very common."

He showed Myles the pistol's trigger safety. He placed his hands over Myles' shoulders and positioned him so his torso wouldn't move the pistol. The right index finger was held outside the trigger guard and the left hand around the pistol grip.

"Only point it at what you want to destroy," Andre said.

Myles flinched. "Are . . . are you training me for combat?"

Andre didn't answer. He gazed out front at the target and the concrete wall behind it. "Make the aim at the torso, not the head."

Myles' arm had stopped shaking. He closed his non-dominant eye, relaxed his shoulders, and positioned the front site over the target. He squeezed the trigger.

The bang made him jump but the pistol barely recoiled. "It's so smooth," he said.

"That is because it is only nine millimeters," Andre said. "A Magnum handgun, that is like a big kick."

The man had shot a Magnum. All his shit about the ouroboros and archetypes, meanings deeper than language . . . and he'd shot a fucking Magnum.

Soon Myles was hitting the silhouette in the middle of the chest. Andre kept changing the targets and moving them farther and farther away. But it wasn't fun like at an amusement park. This was like he was about to get shipped off to Afghanistan.

After an hour, Myles had fired the last bullet. He slipped off the ear protectors, and they made their way back to the showroom and outside.

When Andre had opened the Mercedes' trunk, Myles asked, "Does Sofia know how to shoot?"

"Of course."

Sofia must have had a gun. Carmela sure as shit did. While his own mom and dad treated "gun control" like words from God.

Andre put the pistol case in his hands. "My gift to the man who is so close to my daughter."

This was wrecked. He could only think of one excuse. "I'm not registered or anything."

Andre's face got shady. "This pistol is not for the registration. You put it somewhere that no one knows, somewhere you can find it quickly."

It was a ticket into gangland, a world his parents knew nothing about—*couldn't* know anything about. Myles looked around the parking lot at people getting into cars. Would he always look around for someone now?

"You protect Sofia," Andre said. "You protect your mother."

Myles stared at the case. This was what Sofia had meant when she'd said that Andre would help him. He was teaching him how to kill people.

"Am I supposed to protect them from Martinez?" Myles said.

"It maybe is him. Or it maybe is a stranger."

A killer that Sofia's aunt would send. His throat felt like sandpaper.

Andre grabbed his arm. "Sofia guessed where you went yesterday. She came to me because this is very *stupide*. This is not the work for you or my daughter."

Myles looked down. An oil stain on the blacktop glinted back at him like a dark mirror. "I'm sorry," he said.

They got in the car. Once inside, Andre gripped Myles' shoulder. "Love does not follow a clock. When the one-in-the-million hits, it hits very hard. Is Sofia the one-in-the-million for you, Myles?"

Something about the warmth of his hand . . . the tone of his voice . . . it all lined up with what Andre was asking. "Yes," Myles said.

Andre released his shoulder and drew in long, noisy breaths. "This happened to me also once. Many years ago, I fell in love with a girl in Montreal."

"Not Carmela?" Myles asked.

Andre's mouth constricted. He shook his head. "She and I, we went to the cafés and we ate the beaver tails that are like churros. It is the kind of love that the universe only gives to two people the once."

His face was so sad. Like he'd loved this girl more than anyone. More than Carmela. "What happened?" Myles asked.

Andre watched an SUV pass by and pull into the traffic on Balboa.

"I shouldn't have asked," Myles said.

Andre shook his head. He sighed. "Her old boyfriend was part of the Hell's Angels. One day she disappeared and I could not find her. I am frantic. I cannot sleep. I cannot eat. My body shakes all the time. Then I learn what her old boyfriend did."

He looked like he was in a trance.

"He was jealous. He beat Nanette until she died."

Myles gasped.

"For the rest of my life I cannot forget that I did not defend her."

Andre's eyes had closed up. Like he was still seeing that girl.

"This man rode his motorcycle in the back roads of the Laurentian Mountains. Always by himself. I attached a wire across the road and to two trees."

Myles had seen it in movies. He imagined a big Harley going sixty, then hitting the wire and skidding along the road, sparks flying. Andre had killed him. *He killed him.*

Wouldn't I do the same thing if someone murdered Sofia?

"Revenge is a strange thing," Andre said. "When you get it, you see that you are someone else, someone who you thought you never were. For the rest of my life I live with what I did to that man."

And what he didn't do to save the girl he loved.

"I will help you," Andre said.

"How?"

"There is a solution. Always a solution. I just do not know it yet."

But somehow that solution involved a gun.

CHAPTER SIXTY-SEVEN

It was Friday. Battle time. Wade was waiting for the two hundred eighty million to be wired through SWIFT and the Clearing House for International Payments. Then a New York financial institution would transfer the money by Fedwire to Unity Coast. As soon as the funds were verified, the FBI would seize them. They'd raid the bank building and pandemonium would erupt.

Wade got to work at almost nine o'clock. Nothing looked untoward. The main floor already hummed with activity from loan officers and their clients. At the far end, Andre's office door was open. He stood calmly, talking on his phone.

He hurried upstairs and shut his office door. Slipping off his suit coat, he did some yoga rag doll poses to loosen his back. If he could get down on the floor, he'd do Child's Pose or Happy Baby, but suppose someone came in? He sat at his desk and pretended to look at emails while he waited for the world to blow up.

At nine fifteen, the money arrived. At nine thirty, he got a call on his cellphone from a blocked number. "Mr. Bosworth," the voice said. "I wanted to tell you that we perfected our collateral."

Wade flinched. It was Martinez. "What collateral?"

The phone scraped. "Dad, it's Myles. I'm with Mom and Sofia. We're—"

The phone scraped again.

"We picked up Myles and Sofia on the way to school. We found Fiona in the parking lot of Comunidad de Niños. You can never have too much collateral."

Wade grabbed the side of his chair. His mind was roiling, his thoughts landing on nothing.

"As long as our deal is fine, they are fine, Mr. Bosworth." Martinez disconnected.

Wade pressed the cellphone into his ear and gulped in air.

He called Rodrigues. "They've got Myles and Fiona," he said.

For a minute he heard her tapping a keyboard.

"I see signals and locations from both phones," she said. "But they aren't moving."

"What does that mean?"

"Martinez's men probably dumped their cellphones in trash cans so they couldn't be traced."

Wade knew where Martinez would take them. "They're in Tijuana, aren't they?"

"We have no reason to think that yet."

"You have every reason to think exactly that. Where the hell else would he take them?"

Silence.

"Say something, dammit!"

"Let's assume they're in Tijuana. It's a big city. We'd have to involve the local police and that takes time."

"Are you actually saying you're going to do nothing?"

"You have to stay calm, Wade."

"Don't tell me to calm down. It's my wife and son, dammit!"

"I understand."

He rose to his feet. He wanted to hit something, anything. The globe was close by, so he kicked it onto the carpet. He sat back in his chair and took some breaths.

"Listen, Wade, the best strategy is to go ahead with the operation. Then we negotiate from a position of strength. We'll have their bank and their money."

Wade pushed his head into his hand. "But you're not permitted to pay a ransom!"

"We can string out a negotiation. It gives us time to find them."

Wade couldn't take the bullshit. He disconnected. The papers on his new desk wavered between his hands.

When he looked up, Andre stood in front of him. He'd come through the office door and closed it without Wade hearing anything. Andre's pale eyes seemed to swell behind his glasses. "What have you done?" he said.

CHAPTER SIXTY-EIGHT

Andre stood over Wade's desk, his face soapy white. Wade decided it was past the time for secrets. "The FBI and Treasury are raiding the bank today," he said.

Andre drew back. "You are working for them."

"You were the one who put this in motion. You're the bastard who kidnapped my son."

Andre set down a plastic bag and slumped in the chair in front of Wade's desk. He stared at his lap. "Now is not the time for anger."

Wade wanted to leap over the desk and grab his neck.

Andre said, "Egberto Martinez called me also. But he does not know that the FBI and Treasury Department will seize us. Not yet. When he does . . ."

"Do you think they're in Tijuana?"

He looked at Wade as if he were being willfully stupid. "We must go there. Right now."

"Are you crazy? The city's huge. We have to get help."

"From who? La Jefa controls the police. The DEA? The minute they start looking in Tijuana, La Jefa and Martinez know it. Look, Wade, Martinez does not expect that you and I come there. We must find them before the bank is taken."

"And then what? Are we supposed to talk Martinez into letting them go?"

Andre reached into the bag he'd set on the carpet. He laid two pistols on Wade's desk. "We use these."

Wade stared at the weapons. "I have no idea how to shoot one."

Andre showed him the magazine of bullets and how to work the trigger safety. "Hold it with both hands," he said. "And most important—go close."

Two armed men against all Martinez's killers? It was insane. But the strike force was mobilizing this very moment. Myles, Fiona, and Sofia would be killed minutes after they seized the bank.

He started to call Rodrigues and stopped. As soon as she learned they were crossing the border, she'd order the police to stop them. Wade pulled his passport from his desk drawer. He slipped the pistols into the plastic bag and he and Andre hurried downstairs and out to the parking lot.

"Take your car," Andre said. "The FBI will track my car. They won't expect you to go to Mexico."

Maybe Andre was scheming. Maybe he was trying to escape and lure the informer to Mexico. But even if that were true, Wade couldn't stay here. Not when Martinez had Myles and Fiona.

They got in Wade's car and sped through Chula Vista's stoplights. They reached the highway and he accelerated to eighty. He looked up and saw the fortune teller's sign. The eye in the middle of the red palm glared at him.

"The drawing is the Hamsa from the Middle East," Andre said. "The Hand of God. A protection. It keeps away the evil eye."

Or God was making him suffer for all he'd done wrong. Wade yanked his focus back to the highway. "Where are we going?"

"I will give you direction."

His intuition screamed not to trust this man. But Andre wouldn't have given him the pistol if he planned to betray him. Wade pushed

down on the pedal. He wasn't going to let any part of himself recon-
sider. They passed bunches of cars and trucks.

"What happens if the police catch you for going too fast?" Andre
said.

Wade slowed to seventy-five.

"You think that I kidnapped Myles so that you must borrow the
money from me. Then you have to work at Unity Coast and make
the real estate syndications. It is all my big plot." Andre raised his
pale eyebrows in a question.

"We can blame each other later," Wade said. "Right now we need
a plan."

"Americans, they always need a plan. First A, then B, then C.
They follow their plan and miss the signs that the world gives them.
Life is more than the frontal lobes, Wade. It is synchronicity."

"Will you cut the bullshit? I can't stand it anymore."

Andre groaned. "Please, Wade, this is important. A man like you
must understand it before we are in Tijuana. A month ago I did not
know that Myles went there to buy the drugs. I did not know that
Myles was kidnapped that night. Fiona came to me the next morning, and I called my contacts. I know Polanco. Polanco knows the
kidnappers. You do not realize what this gang does. They take all the
money from the family and then they kill the victim. But La Jefa has
power. Egberto Martinez has power, and he has the cash for the
ransom. La Jefa and Martinez made it so the gang did not kill your
son, Wade. Where is my big plan?"

Even in English, Andre could spin smoke. Wade stared through
the windshield at the tunnel of highway.

"La Jefa and Martinez demanded something in exchange. They
demanded that you help with their real estate in the U.S. I know
that my operation is too small for you. But that was the deal that
they required. You agreed. For me your word is gold, but not for

them. They needed more leverage. That is why I made the loan from my foundation to Fiona. It is why Martinez sent that picture of your son."

Wade wasn't interested in any justification Andre made. "What do we do after we find them?" he asked.

"We find the connections and the meaning."

"No more fucking psychobabble!"

"There is no plan. Not until we find them. Then we open our sight to the possibilities."

Wade looked at his watch. They might not have long until a horde of government agents swarmed Unity Coast Bank. He set his mouth and passed more cars. To his right the salt marshes stretched out pale and empty toward Mexico.

They reached San Isidro and the lines of vehicles into Tijuana. Wade rolled his shoulders. He sucked in long breaths, but his heart wouldn't slow down.

"There is something else that is not logic or cause and effect," Andre said. "I did not predict that the man I helped, his son I saved, the man I gave the ransom . . . this man betrays me." Andre's long sigh echoed through the car. "Wade, you destroyed all that I built. But I forgive you."

Andre was forgiving *him?* Wade focused on the cars ahead.

They reached the entrance to the Mexican border. Blue-suited officers walked between cars. Andre filled out tourist cards. The officers took the cards and waved them through. They emerged on a busy street.

Wade's phone rang. The screen showed a number that had to be from Mexico. He hit the icon and the call came through.

"Has the wire transfer arrived yet?" Martinez demanded.

He didn't know where Wade was, or that he was with Andre. Wade responded as though he were in his office. "The money is here. There's no reason to hold them now."

He heard something in the background. "Is this the room where you brought Wade's friend?" It was Fiona's voice.

Martinez cut off the connection.

Wade knew where they were. He pulled the car off the street.

"What do you know?" Andre said.

Wade ignored him. He called Rodrigues. "I just got proof Martinez has Fiona and Myles in Tijuana. He has Sofia too. For God's sake, postpone the operation."

She was quiet. The traffic outside shook Wade's car.

"Well?" he said.

"Look, even if we postpone for a week, Martinez will hold onto them. It doesn't do any good."

They were determined to continue. Wade only had one more ploy. "They're in Delicias Hotel. You have to get the DEA to raid it."

She fell silent for a moment, and he knew she was considering what he'd said. Then, "I'll see what kind of DEA operation Cartuso can put together, maybe slow down the raid. Don't do anything until I call you back." She disconnected.

Wade smashed his fist on the dash. Rodrigues and Cartuso weren't going to put off seizing the bank.

Andre said, "Wade, this does not help our children."

"Are you the expert on violence now?"

Wade took some long breaths and settled himself. He was just about to pull back into the street when Andre clasped his arm. "What?" Wade said.

"I need you to promise. If Carmela and I do not survive, you will help Sofia. She cannot be with Carmela's family. They destroy everyone that they touch."

Why should he help anyone in Andre's family?

"You will do this because your son loves her. You will also do this because Sofia is innocent, and you are a good man."

Wade drew his arm away. "Let's just save our kids, okay?"

He pulled back onto the street. This morning the traffic wasn't as clogged up as he remembered. They reached the main blocks of the red-light district. Vendors were setting up their carts and stands. A few women chatted before they went to work in the stores and strip clubs or stationed themselves in their doorways. Wade didn't see anyone who looked suspicious. He passed Delicias. No greeter or guard stood outside the closed-up, black door. No sign of a shooter on the roof.

Andre said, "Martinez did not tell me that he planned to kill Chad. He only told Carmela."

Wade swiveled to face him. "Do you think that makes you less responsible?"

Andre pressed his mouth closed.

Wade made his way into the alley behind the buildings. When they got to the rear of Delicias, his cellphone vibrated with a text.

Operation at 11:20.

Wade scanned the back of the hotel. A beer truck was parked next to an open door to the kitchen. Now he knew where they'd enter the building.

Andre said, "You see why we do not make a plan?"

He parked farther down the alley. They got out and Wade took one of the pistols from the plastic bag and Andre took the other. Wade released the safety. His watch said 10:55. How could it be so late? But his Shinola kept perfect time.

CHAPTER SIXTY-NINE

Wade and Andre tucked the pistols into their suits and ran down the alley toward the back of the Delicias building. They slowed at the beer truck and walked into the back door of the kitchen. A man in jeans and an apron was ticking off boxes and bottles on a checklist. Two cooks did food prep on a stainless-steel counter. Andre announced something authoritatively in Spanish and the men looked away. Wade followed Andre through a swinging door into a passageway.

"What did you tell them?" Wade said.

"We have an appointment."

"Are you kidding me? What if they call someone?"

Andre stared at him as if that was preposterous.

"How do we find out which room?" Wade asked.

"I will pay a maid to tell us."

No maid would risk her life to do that. Wade had a better idea. "They must have a guard in front of the door to the room, right? We go to each floor until we spot him."

Andre broke into a crooked smile. "This is what happens when you have no plan. Your mind opens to ideas."

Will this man ever stop pontificating?

They headed down the passageway in the opposite direction from the kitchen and away from the hotel and the elevator. They passed the empty two-level lounge. On their left, Wade saw the entrance into the large bar with its stage and stripper pole. It was quiet this morning. A few women drank coffee, and a bartender stocked beer in a refrigerator. Wade and Andre moved on to an exit door and ran up cement stairs.

On the next floor, Wade peeked through the door to the hallway and saw no one. They hurried down the carpet and turned right at the elevator. There was no sign of anyone in the two perpendicular passageways.

Wade looked at his watch. Fifteen minutes until the strike force seized Unity Coast. They ran back to the stairs and climbed another flight. No guard on that floor either.

Another flight. This time someone was talking in the last corridor that extended from the elevator. He was about halfway down the hallway, his back to them. The man wore a holster with a pistol.

Wade and Andre crept toward the guard. He was thin, less than six feet tall. The man laughed into his phone, his back loose and swaying. His voice seemed tender, as if he were talking to his girlfriend.

They were twenty feet away. The guard lowered his voice and made a kiss into the phone.

Ten feet away.

The man put the phone in his pocket and turned. His eyes bulged and he reached for his pistol. Wade and Andre trained their weapons on him and the guard raised his hands. He was just a boy, his mustache barely a shadow. Andre snatched the pistol from his holster.

Andre spoke quietly to him in Spanish and the guard pointed to the room behind them that bordered the street. Andre nodded and stepped close to Wade's ear. "He says that they are there. Martinez is not in the room."

Wade checked his watch. Eight minutes left. If Fiona, Myles, and Sofia weren't there, they at best could check one more floor before the raid. "He might be lying," Wade whispered. "We should go in fast with the guard in front."

The boy opened the hotel room door with a key card. Wade shoved him ahead and pushed in behind. No Martinez. The bathroom was empty. Three figures stood in the front of the bed by a table and chairs—Fiona, Myles, and Sofia.

Wade and Andre threw their arms around them.

"Welcome to Delicias."

Wade turned. Martinez pointed a pistol at them. He stood in the open door.

CHAPTER SEVENTY

Fiona was amazed at how easily Egberto Martinez had ambushed her that morning. She'd been about to walk across the parking lot to the Comunidad de Niños building when his men pushed her into the SUV. Martinez had sat with her in the back seat as they drove to Tijuana. Mexican Customs took the tourist cards and didn't even look at the car. Then they'd arrived at that terrible hotel, and two guards held her arms as they walked inside. At the reception desk neither the employee nor the man checking out made eye contact with them. They boarded an elevator, and she realized that Martinez and his men were taking her to the roof. In a half hour I'll be dead, she thought. At least Myles and Wade were safe.

They exited on the fourth floor, and Martinez opened a door to a room. When she saw Myles and Sofia there, Fiona could barely breathe. They hugged each other. For two hours, the three of them made quiet, hopeless plans to escape. Then the door burst open and it was Wade and Andre.

Hope followed by Martinez.

He disarmed Wade and Andre and ordered all of them into the hotel's hallway. Their hands weren't bound and the guard looked younger than Myles. He was toothpick thin, his shoulders not yet grown in. Even if he carried a pistol, this child couldn't be a hard-ened killer, could he? Maybe there was hope.

Martinez avoided the elevator and walked down another hallway past a row of rooms to the end of the building. The boy opened a door that led to a dimly lit stairwell. It led up toward the roof.

Fiona's eyes cut left and right. All the doors to the rooms were closed up. Locked.

"La Jefa wants to talk," Martinez said. "There's better cell recep-tion on the top of the building."

The deceit was so obvious. Wade must have thought the same. He said, "The DEA will trade La Jefa's money for our lives." Fiona heard a quiver in his voice. It betrayed his lie.

"Anything is negotiable," Martinez said.

He was manipulating them to climb the stairs. If they refused, he'd shoot them in the hallway. Three flights would give her time to think.

The young guard led the way, followed by Sofia, Myles, and her. Then Wade and Andre. Martinez trailed a few paces behind, his pistol aimed at their backs. Fiona looked up and down the dusty, zigzagging steps. She imagined Wade and Andre rushing Martinez. He or the boy guard would shoot them before they could get close.

The taps of their shoes echoed from the cracked and pitted ce-ment. Fiona studied the teenager ahead of her. He wore a shiny black tie over a shirt with cheap cufflinks—a poor kid's attempt at chic. Something about him was familiar. She asked his name in one of the few Spanish phrases she knew. "¿Cómo te llamas?"

He sneered. How could such disdain register on that young face?

Martinez spoke from behind her. "Don't you remember Mateo?"

She recognized him then: the long nose, the gap between his teeth, the dimples, and what used to be a child's innocent smile. With each step up these stairs, all that her life stood for was collapsing.

Wade's hand touched her shoulder. The blaze in his eyes told her to keep fighting. They still had a few minutes to think of something.

She spoke to Sofia. "Tell Mateo I've seen other kids just like him who spent time at the orphanage. They've grown up to be good men with families."

"He doesn't want to speak to you," Martinez said.

Mateo's wispy-mustached face was expressionless—unreachable.

At the top of the stairs a door led to the tar and gravel roof. Fiona shielded her eyes against the sun outside. Car horns and voices rose from below the building. She smelled the exhaust from the traffic.

Martinez made them stand against the wall of the hutch that covered the stairs. Fiona stood on the far left beside Wade and Andre. Myles stood on Andre's right next to Sofia and Mateo. Sofia was fighting back sobs. Fiona told herself she had to stay strong. It was the only way to find an opening.

"A few minutes ago I had a phone call," Martinez said. "Do you know what it was about?" When no one answered, he said, "It seems that the FBI and the Treasury Department just forced their way into my bank." When no one responded, he said, "I had a feeling you wouldn't be surprised."

Sofia looked at Andre as if beseeching him. Her father's eyes looked glassy behind the lenses of his spectacles, as if he were already slipping out of his life. Fiona realized it would be up to Wade, Myles, and her.

"Sofia has nothing to do with anything," Myles said. "You can let her go."

My brave son. Fiona struck with the only thing she knew was important to Martinez. "The FBI can arrange protection for your family. New identities. You can be a father to your children. You can get back together with your wife."

Martinez gave a snort. "You always talk to me as if I'm a woman."

She looked up and searched for something she could bargain with, some inspiration. But there was no answer in that empty and scalded sky.

"You can spare Myles and Sofia," Wade said.

That was the only solution. "Just let us pay the price," she said.

"Yes," Andre said.

Martinez pulled out a plastic bag of dates. He pushed one in his mouth and chewed thoughtfully. "Carmela is with La Jefa right now."

Sofia whirled to face her father. She burst into French. Andre smiled at his daughter and spoke, his French sounding soft and consoling.

Fiona tried to catch Myles' eyes. She wanted him to know that she and Wade had chosen this trade off. He refused to look at her. His legs were jittering.

"I will present your offer to La Jefa," Martinez said.

La Jefa had to be a mother. A mother would spare children.

Martinez punched a number into his phone and spoke in Spanish. He disconnected and said, "La Jefa has accepted."

Fiona braced against the wall. There were worse deaths than being shot.

"Under one condition," Martinez said. "You must jump from this rooftop."

She had to leap from six stories. Smash into the pavement. She didn't know if she could do it.

Next to her, Wade said, "You want a spectacle, don't you? All of Tijuana will know you didn't just kill us. You made us jump."

"Jumped to save your children," Martinez said. "It shows that La Jefa is both hard and merciful."

Fiona gripped Wade's hand. She saw the tired surrender on his face. "I love you," she said. He gave her a mournful smile. He squeezed her hand.

Martinez put the phone on speaker, and Carmela's voice emerged. Fiona understood *mi amor* and *futuro* and *mi cariña*. Carmela's soft tones confirmed she was saying goodbye to her husband and daughter.

Sofia burst into sobs. She sank onto the hard gravel and gripped her face with her hands. Her father bent down and kissed her on the head.

Martinez shut off his phone and slipped it into his pocket.

"Stop this," Myles said. "Please . . . stop." There were tears in his eyes.

Her boy would wonder all his life how he could have saved them. "Myles, it's not your fault," she said. "You have to remember that I told you that."

She'd never see him become a man and a father. She'd never see a grandchild. She put her hand over her heart and watched Myles' mouth contort.

Wade started his goodbyes. She heard "proud" and "brave" and "loving man."

"It is time," Martinez said. The ledge stood behind him. Thirty feet away.

Fiona and Wade trudged next to Andre, step after slow step. Martinez walked a few paces to the left of Andre. He didn't train his pistol on them. He had no doubt that they'd jump for their children. At the edge, she looked down at the people snaking over the sidewalk six stories below.

Wade's arms closed around her and she shut her eyes. His lips brushed her hair and cheek and settled on her lips. His hands drew her in and she stroked the thin hair on the back of his head. Her hand moved down to the nape of his neck and the familiar shoulder blades. She remembered slipping her feet under his legs as he sat on the couch and she lay beside him. Wade in his late twenties at her door and not wanting to leave. The miniature apartment in Clairemont and snuggling together with the new baby. Then Myles' first steps and their child's fearless explorations. The worrying and shouting and making up—all part of the sacred tangle that was her family.

*   *   *

Andre said something. Fiona opened her eyes. They still stood in front of the ledge. The world moved on the street below. She felt the tar and gravel roof below her shoes, the sun warming her face.

"Did you go somewhere special to eat the dates your mother gave you?" Andre said. He stood beside Martinez.

Martinez stared at the empty air above the building. "A park," he said.

Fiona pictured a mother taking a little boy from the bordello to green grass. A child relishing a sugary treat.

"The car that hits her does not even slow up," Andre said. "You lost her when you were so young."

Martinez must have known that Andre was working him, but he didn't stop it. As if he was giving way to the loss that lived inside him.

"The street is a terrible mother," Andre said. "This is why you give money to Comunidad de Niños."

"Do you think I'll show mercy because you talk about my mother?" Martinez said.

"I am talking about your shadow. It is the hidden part of you that you cannot escape. It is the wound that never gets better."

Fiona was afraid to breathe.

Martinez pulled out a date from the bag. Fiona saw the sugar hit his mouth, an explosion of taste that must have both brought back, then pushed away, his childhood. He wiped away a drop of sweat from his forehead.

He swung the tip of the gun toward the emptiness beyond the ledge. "What I want is for all of you to jump. I want you to save your children."

Andre was six feet from Martinez. He reached out his shoe to touch the ledge. His face was so relaxed. "Some of the people on this street have the same shadow as yours. Mateo also will never find the father who abandons him. Or the mother's love that he loses."

The rest was so fast, so instinctive, that Fiona saw it in a kind of slow choreography. Myles jumped on Mateo. Sofia shrieked and pummeled the boy. Andre lunged. He wrapped his arms around Martinez. Martinez staggered and his back leaned over the side of the building. For a moment he and Andre hugged like lovers, one short and chubby, one tall and thin. Their four feet kicked up and they were gone.

Bang.

Mateo shoved himself away and ran for the door to the stairs. His footsteps pounded down the cement steps.

All that remained of Andre were his glasses. They lay broken on the roof.

"Sofia's been shot!" Myles yelled.

CHAPTER SEVENTY-ONE

WADE

Car horns bellowed. Men shouted. Screams from every direction.

Sofia sat on the tar and gravel, Myles hugging her close, the blood spreading on her blouse and his shirt. Wade had to get them off the roof. He had to get Sofia to a hospital or she would bleed to death. He picked up the pistol that Martinez had dropped. Fiona and Myles lifted Sofia and they rushed to the stairwell. Wade aimed the pistol through the doorway.

He saw no one. Heard no one.

They descended the stairs. After three flights a door banged open above them. Wade heard loud voices. Shoes pounded on the cement stairs. But the men were headed up, not down. The roof door slammed shut.

By the time they reached the ground level, an electric guitar and an amplified announcer's voice throbbed through the walls and echoed in the stairwell. The stripper show had started at the bar. Wade pushed through the door and the music roared and pounded over them.

On his right, the dark passageway opened to the bar but no one looked their way. Men sipped beer at dimly lit tables while prostitutes wandered among them. On the stage, lights flashed through a fake fog to spotlight a naked woman. She caressed a pole with her breasts. Farther down the hallway on the left was the two-level lounge. Beyond it, the kitchen door swung out and a rectangle of light bathed the floor. Waiters brought out food. Wade walked quickly to the swinging door.

The chefs and prep cooks gaped at the gun, then at Myles carrying Sofia. Fiona grabbed kitchen towels and pressed them against Sofia's wound. Wade hurried them past sizzling stoves and grills and stainless-steel counters. Everywhere the smell of garlic and frying food.

They scrambled out the back door. Wade's BMW stood fifty feet down the alley. He looked back at the building and saw men on the roof. They were pointing at him. Wade gave his key fob to Fiona. He turned back to the building while Fiona and Myles carried Sofia to the car. He looked down the barrel at the building. Someone stepped through the kitchen's back door and aimed a pistol. Wade fired two shots.

He ran to the car and yanked open the driver's door. He jumped in and started the engine. The BMW peeled down the chipped blacktop away from Delicias. Wade glanced at the mirror. In the back seat Myles and Fiona held Sofia as she squinted in pain. Her face had grown chalky.

Behind the car a man aimed a weapon. "Duck," Wade shouted.

A shot. Glass shattered. Fiona screamed.

They reached the end of the alley and screeched through a right turn onto another street. The traffic was thick and the BMW had to creep behind a line of cars and trucks. In the rearview mirror Wade saw two men running a block behind. He bounced the car over the curb onto the sidewalk and passed the cars ahead. Walkers yelled and jumped out of the way. Horns blared. At the next block, Wade ran the light and turned left. There was less traffic here. He floored the engine.

He drove a mile and parked at the curb. Breathing hard, he turned to the back seat. Myles and Fiona pushed the blood-soaked towels against Sofia's chest. She clenched her teeth. Her face was paler than before.

Wade yanked out his phone and called Rodrigues. "I'm in Tijuana. I've got Fiona and Myles and Sofia. Sofia's been shot."

Rodrigues didn't ask questions. "Stop the bleeding with any material you have, even your hands."

"We're doing that."

"You have to get to the U.S. The ambulance can't go to Mexico."

"What about the traffic at the border?" Wade said. "It could be backed up for miles."

"Get to the San Isidro pedestrian bridge and go on foot. We'll get an agent there."

In the back seat, Fiona pressed a towel into Sofia's wound. Myles held her, tears dribbling down his face. He was hyperventilating. Wade shoved his phone into Myles' hand.

"Google maps," Wade shouted. "The pedestrian bridge."

Myles pressed his bloody fingers into the phone.

Wade drove, Myles telling him where to turn. They ran lights and weaved through traffic. Sofia had quieted. Wade didn't dare ask about her.

They reached a long line of people beside closed-up buildings and walls of advertisements. The thirty feet of street between the traffic and the line was blocked off by yellow cement barriers. Wade drove beside the barriers toward the border as far as he could and stopped the car.

"I should take the pistol," Myles said. "I know how to shoot."

Wade gave it to him and they jumped out. Fiona helped Wade lift Sofia from the back of the car. The girl was so small she weighed almost nothing. Her breathing seemed shallow. Blood had pooled on the seat of the BMW.

They squeezed through a space between the barriers. A metal railing separated them from the line waiting to go through the border. Myles pointed his weapon at the crowd and they scattered and ducked down. Some held up rolling suitcases as shields.

A motorcycle roared behind Wade. Fiona yelled. Wade turned with Sofia cradled in his arms. He saw the driver raise his arm. Mateo pointed a pistol.

Bang.

Mateo's chest blotted red.

Bang.

More bright red on his chest. Mateo teetered and fell. Myles was still aiming the pistol.

A voice shouted in English. A man in sunglasses waved to them from an opening in the metal railing. He was in a suit and not a policeman's uniform. "DEA," he yelled.

Myles had dropped the pistol. He stared at the boy he'd shot.

"Carry Sofia!" Fiona shouted.

His son seemed to jerk himself awake. He took Sofia in his arms from Wade. They hurried through the opening in the railing. The man in sunglasses led them beside the line in a half-run. People crossed themselves and pressed back to give them space.

They passed through a corridor covered with chain-link fence. Three blue-suited guards stood under a white tent top. The guards opened a gate. More people shrank back. They rushed through the entryway and a metal detector screamed behind them. They ran into a building. Past steel booths of staring U.S. inspectors in bullet-proof vests. The grey wall said, "United States of America."

Two emergency techs stepped forward. They set Sofia on a stretcher and bent over her. When the techs saw Sofia's wound, their faces grew grim.

CHAPTER SEVENTY-TWO

MYLES

Myles took a step and his sneakers screeched against the room's tiled floor. He couldn't stand how his parents were treating him like a little kid. *"Drink some water." "Take a deep breath."* The whiteness and cold of the hospital's conference room made him want to pound a hole in the plaster. He looked at the wall clock. Sofia had been in surgery for two hours. She was so small and the wound so big.

Everything was so fucked up, and he was the one who'd started it.

A knock on the door. The person who came in wore a blue business jacket and carried a pistol on her belt. She caught his eyes and said, "I'm Special Agent Rodrigues."

The FBI agent.

"Sofia is stable. She's coming out of surgery now."

Myles took a huge, lung-filling inhale of air. He wanted to shout, but Rodrigues' glum expression told him it was still bad.

"We can't talk unless you sit down," she said to him.

He pulled out a chair between his mom and dad. The agent sat across from the three of them at the table. "Is the boy I shot dead?" Myles asked.

Rodrigues nodded.

He'd killed him. *Killed him.*

Myles sank his head. "I guess I'll be arrested."

"Of course not," his dad said. "It was self-defense."

"Mateo was going to shoot us," his mom said.

His parents would have jumped from that roof to save him. It felt so right to sit together with them.

"There won't be any charges in Mexico," Rodrigues said.

That was supposed to relieve him, but it didn't. The boy was dead. Sophia's parents were dead and . . . Sofia was in surgery.

His mom put her arm around him and leaned her face close to his. "We have to go into Witness Protection."

It took him a second to get what she meant. Witness Protection meant they'd all have to take new names. They'd have to live in some dipshit town far away from anything. A place like where he was in Utah. But there was something worse. "What about Sofia?"

"We'll contact her remaining family," Rodrigues said.

Did she really say that? This was beyond crazy.

His dad put up his hand. "La Jefa murdered her own brother and sister."

The special agent looked down at the table. Myles wanted to reach across and shake her. He forced himself to inhale. Slowly exhale. Just like his dad's yoga breaths.

Rodrigues said, "Sofia's not a U.S. citizen. She can apply for refugee status if her life is in danger."

If? *Did she really say* if?

"She has to go back to Mexico to do that, doesn't she?" his mom said.

Myles tried to mirror his dad's calm confidence. Talk businesslike. That was the way to get through to the special agent. "Her aunt will kill her before she even fills out the application," he said.

Rodrigues leaned toward him. "I know this is very hard for you."

Like hell she did. "Thank you, Ms. Rodrigues. But we have to think of a way to save her."

His mom wrung her hands. His dad stared at the tabletop.

"We can't just let her die," Myles said.

"How about if we adopt Sofia?" his mom said.

Yes.

"Absolutely," his dad said.

The agent shook her head. "She's eighteen. She's an adult. Adopting an adult doesn't confer citizenship."

Myles squeezed his eyes shut and forced his mind open like Hidden Road had taught him. He imagined himself relaxed at their kitchen table. The answer came. It was so clear.

"I'll marry her," Myles said. "We marry and she becomes a citizen."

His mom looked stunned. Then smiled.

"She gets to stay in the country while she gets her green card," his dad said.

"And she goes with us into Witness Protection," his mom said. "Obviously."

His parents were pinging glances back and forth to each other. They were so together on this. They were so with him.

"Assuming Sofia wants to get married," Rodrigues said.

Of course Sofia wanted to get married. Myles scooted forward in the chair. "It shouldn't be hard to find a judge."

Rodrigues drummed the table. "I don't know. That kind of approval is way above me."

"I'll get a lawyer if I need to," Myles said. "She's going to be my wife."

His dad clasped his arm. His dad's eyes seemed to take in Rodrigues as if he knew exactly how to manage her. "Let's just review the pros and cons here," he said. "You've got two hundred and eighty million. You've shut down a dirty financial institution. You've got La Jefa's investors screaming for their money and probably wanting to kill her. I'd say you and Cartuso and everyone on the strike team are up for commendations. Maybe bonuses. Against what? Protecting a girl who had nothing to do with her parents' business. And here's something else. If you don't do it, I have to seriously consider whether I testify."

His dad was awesome.

EPILOGUE

WADE

Six Weeks Later

Wade started to hyperventilate before he finished reading the article on his computer. He recognized the blond hair and thin face in the picture. He remembered Peter Vanhoven sweating with him under the portico of La Jefa's ranch. But in Sioux Falls, South Dakota, Vanhoven was known as John Masterson. John Masterson had been tortured and murdered.

He got up and paced his little office. The U.S. marshals had said that no one who followed their guidelines was ever killed. Maybe Vanhoven got careless. Maybe he let his picture get on the internet or left a message for a stranger who could analyze his voice signature. He could have contacted family or old associates.

Wade hadn't made any of those mistakes. His office didn't have a nameplate, and he wasn't on the building directory. He'd hired an actress to record the voicemail greeting. His new business invested in buildings, but no one would ever know that the capital came from the FBI reward money. He felt safe except for one thing. Teenagers. Myles and Sofia had to use the web for school. They said they avoided selfies and didn't confide in other teens, but what eighteen-year-old had meticulous self-control? Teenagers could put anyone in danger.

He dialed the witness inspector and left a message. Then slipped on his coat, galoshes, scarf, and fur hat. He turned off the office lights and looked out the window. Specks of snow blew through the haze of the street illumination. He didn't see anyone lingering on the icy sidewalks or beside the crusty snowdrifts. But who would be out in this weather? The attack would come from a van waiting for him to walk to his car. He stuffed the semiautomatic in his pocket and set the office alarm.

On the ground floor he saw a man with a black scarf covering his face. Wade clutched the pistol in his pocket before he recognized him. He was the lawyer, the ambulance chaser with the office between the insurance salesman and the shrink.

Wade pushed through the two doors, and the wind blasted the upper parts of his face that the scarf didn't cover. Cars slowly ground past his block of old brick buildings. He hunched into his coat and slogged over the sidewalk. Each breath burned his lungs and made him long for San Diego.

The Nissan was parked between two other snow-encrusted cars. He ran the engine while he cleared the windows. It was so cold he had to push down on the plastic scraper with both hands. Even in gloves his fingers were freezing. He thought of fingernails and then Vanhoven. Was that how they tortured him? Wade's whole body shivered.

He drove through snow-cleared streets, all the while glancing in his rearview and side mirrors, the heater whooshing. He stuck a hand into the compartment between the seats. He grasped Chad's briefcase handle with the green cord around it, his talisman. He and Fiona both had the same life goal: stay alive until Myles and Sofia could protect themselves.

He picked up the deep-dish pizza at Edwardo's. The smell of the cheese and crust usually made him hungry, but not tonight. As he headed home to Evanston, he wondered if they'd made a tragic mistake living there. He and Fiona had believed they could better disappear among millions of people rather than in the nether regions where they'd stand out. But as soon as La Jefa suspected he was in the Chicago area, she'd pull up a whole list of local contractors.

Wade parked in the driveway of their little house. He hunched into his coat and hurried inside. In the vestibule he stamped his feet on the rug and slipped off his galoshes. He hung his coat and hat and scarf on his hook next to the other coats and hats and scarves. Then opened the second door to the warmth inside.

He hated the living room. It looked like an IKEA display: cheaply upholstered chairs, a sleek couch, and a thin wooden table with weird, slanted legs. There were abstract paintings of mountains and wildflowers by people he'd never heard of. But the loss of their old furniture was the price of having to flee fast. Each of them had only been able to take some clothes and one or two personal possessions. This furniture made him feel like he was living inside someone else's memory. Only the two Martin guitars on stands made the room bearable. One guitar belonged to Myles.

Myles sat at the dining room table and tiny Sofia stood over him. "We don't have any choice," Myles said. "We've been through this." Tonight his voice was as soft and patient as a middle-aged man.

"I know," she said. "Damnit, I know."

She stalked out of the dining room and through the living room. She passed Wade and said, "Pizza? Again?" She muttered something in Spanish and stomped up the stairs to their bedroom.

Once again Wade told himself that Sofia had lost the most. Her family and the country where she'd grown up were someone else's past. She'd even had to abandon Stanford. A huge university in the Midwest would be a better hiding place from the army of investigators La Jefa had hired to find her.

Fiona approached Wade from the kitchen. She cast her eyes upstairs and frowned.

"Peter Vanhoven's been murdered," Wade said. "In Sioux Falls, South Dakota."

It took her a second to recollect the name. She drew back and seemed to realize what the news meant.

"The Witness Protection inspector hasn't called back yet," Wade said. "Maybe he's digging into what happened before he talks to us."

"Then it's pointless worrying about it, isn't it?" she said.

Nothing threw Fiona now. She'd crunched through the move and pulled the rest of them along with her. Fiona took the pizza box from his hand and he saw the Taoist yin and yang tattoo on her wrist. Which of them was yin and which of them was yang? He couldn't remember.

Wade followed her into the dining room. Myles was glaring at the table. He'd grown a beard as a disguise, but it was so thin it only drew attention to his face. The central heat came on and added to Myles' harsh, fast breathing.

"This is insanity," Myles said.

Fiona set the pizza down and headed to the kitchen. Wade sat across from Myles. "Sofia has a lot to deal with," he said.

Myles' laugh came out a single huff. "Don't I know it."

"You've got to be patient. Give her time to get over it."

"If she doesn't kill me first."

Fiona brought back plates and silverware. She cut a slice of the deep dish and set it on a plate with a knife and fork. "Take this to her," she said to Myles. "Give her a hug if she'll let you."

Myles glowered at the plate. "Why would I want to hug barbed wire?"

"Sometimes you have to hug barbed wire when you're married," Wade said. Maybe one day Myles would learn that a fight could be a gift.

Myles gave a long, weary sigh. "I guess I have to rise above her hurt."

"Hidden Road?" Fiona asked him.

"I don't remember anymore."

Wade watched Myles take a longing glance at the pizza box and breathe in the smell. His son didn't grab a piece for himself, as if he knew it was better to take one plate to Sofia and watch her eat. His boy had had to absorb so much so fast—a soldier's vigilance and a husband's sensitivity. Underneath it all was a heavy blanket of guilt for setting off this avalanche. And now Wade had to announce another person gone. There was no sense in putting it off. He related the news about Vanhoven.

Myles' shoulders sagged. "Is Melissa . . . ?"

They all knew that La Jefa wouldn't spare Vanhoven's family. "There's no mention about the daughter or the ex-wife," Wade said.

His son blew out air and shook his head. He grabbed the plate of pizza and clomped up the stairs.

Fiona rose. When she went to the kitchen, Wade ran his hand over the smooth, thin wood of someone else's idea of a table. He considered his two teenagers. This, their final year before college, was supposed to be a capstone that solidified their childhoods and the friends they grew up with. Instead, Myles and Sofia were in separate schools and had no friends but each other. They had to keep their marriage and their pasts a secret. It seemed both brave and tragic.

Fiona brought back glasses and a bottle of expensive California pinot. It was already opened. She sat next to him and set thick slices of pizza on plates.

"Let's not think about Peter Vanhoven tonight," she said.

He could get behind that agenda. To survive was to compartmentalize. "How's the office?" he asked.

"Good."

She was stuck in a cubicle at the YMCA downtown and never enthused about her work. She never complained either. He was amazed at her changes. She even dressed differently: conservative pants and plain-colored blouses, a winter coat that was an uninspired dark blue. Tonight he took in the new blond highlights in her hair. A cobweb of lines had started to form around her eyes. Something about her aging made her look stronger, more grounded than when she was with Jasper—wherever Jasper was.

They heard shouts upstairs.

"I can't imagine being married at eighteen," Wade said.

"Marriage is hard at any age," Fiona said. She took a long drink of wine.

"I hope she can forgive us for what happened," Wade said.

Fiona rubbed the stem of the wineglass. "Someday Sofia will get beyond this. She'll realize that's what her father wanted."

Wade thought of Andre limping and stumbling toward redemption. In the end, he'd died so his daughter could have a future.

"If they stay together, Myles will help her," Fiona said.

Wade avoided considering if his son's marriage would last. The important thing had been to save Sofia. He said, "Sometimes two people stay together so each of them won't fall apart. Then they grow to love each other. Maybe more than they thought possible."

Fiona smiled. "There are times when you truly surprise me."

"About what?"

"You never would have said that a year ago."

The upstairs had quieted. Sofia and Myles were probably making up. Wade heard melodic jazz guitar on Myles' sound system. Pat

Metheny was Myles' latest interest. Sometimes he even listened to Joe Pass.

Wade put his arm around Fiona and drew her into him. In a few months they'd get to see Chicago in bloom, then Lake Michigan in summer. If they didn't have to flee to another city. If they weren't dead.

He looked at the cherrywood clock on the wall, the one piece of furniture the marshals had allowed him to take. The clock had endured through both his father's marriage as well as his. But he and Fiona had survived only by changing. Then discovered that they cherished each other for the new people they'd become.

"In a way, it's nice we have new names," Fiona said. She clinked her glass against his and smiled. "Here's to you, Bill Thompson."

"Here's to you, Susan Thompson."

And to whatever they'd become in the days they had left, he thought.

ACKNOWLEDGMENTS

There are so many people who helped me improve *Saving Myles*. First is my writing group of Peggy Lang, Barbara Brown, Suzanne Delzio, Eleanor Bluestein, Linda Moore, Louise Julig, Karen Johnson, and James Jones. It took me years to write this novel and they helped at every step.

I got a great deal of help from another writing group led by Carolyn Wheat. Carolyn, along with Penne Horn, Matt Coyle, Becca Jenkins, and Ellen Holzman, gave great feedback. Carolyn also provided wonderful individual guidance. She helped me with structure, character, and the elimination of some bad habits. She had terrific suggestions about additional scenes that the book needed.

Not many people know how the FBI and DEA can assist authors. Betsy Glick and her colleagues at the FBI provided great background about kidnapping, confidential informants, money laundering, and Mexican cartels. Thanks also to J. Todd Scott and Ray Amador of the DEA for educating me on what their agency can do in Mexico and about money laundering. I'm sure I made some mistakes, but they were all mine.

Settings are never easy. I prefer to visit the places in my books and take notes. My friends at the YMCA in Mexico, Uriel Gonzalez and

Octavio Mendoza, were kind enough to shepherd me around Tijuana to find locations that would fit the events in the story. They also offered advice that greatly improved the story.

A separate and very big thanks to my agent, Michelle Richter, who believed in this novel enough to read it twice. She doggedly pursued publishers until we found the right one.

I'm grateful to Pat and Bob Gussin, Faith Matson, and Lee Randall at Oceanview for taking on *Saving Myles*, and for their helpful editing suggestions and promotion of the book.

A big thanks also to Lisa Daily for her help in marketing and promotion.

Lastly, a big thanks to my family. They've always rooted for me and my dream of being a writer.

BOOK CLUB
DISCUSSION QUESTIONS

1. How did you feel about the opening scene when Myles was forcibly removed and taken to a distant place? Did you consider this Wade's decision? Or a joint decision by Fiona and Wade?

2. If the only way to save your child's life was to do something to him that he would never forgive you for, would you do it? What would be your greatest concern?

3. How do the three different points of view distinguish each character? Include their varying interests and attitudes toward work.

4. How did the Tijuana scenes impact you? Did you feel this was a realistic depiction of this Mexican border town?

5. How were Wade and Fiona both good and bad parents?

6. As the story progresses, how would you describe the relationship between Myles and his father? Getting closer? Drifting farther apart? Reconcilable?

7. Do you think that Fiona's relationship with Jasper had an adverse effect on Myles' relationship with her? What about Myles' relationship with Wade?

8. Fiona and Wade both have the same Taoist tattoo of yin and yang on their wrists. How does this play into the ways they change and reunite?

9. Did Carmela's family change your perspective of Mexican cartel families? In what way?

10. What would you predict for the future of Myles and Sophia?

11. What is your prediction for the future integrity of the Bosworth family?